Love, off the Record

A Love, off the Record

SAMANTHA MARKUM

Margaret K. McElderry Books
New York   London   Toronto   Sydney   New Delhi

MARGARET K. McELDERRY BOOKS

An imprint of Simon & Schuster Children's Publishing Division

1230 Avenue of the Americas, New York, New York 10020

This book is a work of fiction. Any references to historical events, real people, or real places are used fictitiously. Other names, characters, places, and events are products of the author's imagination, and any resemblance to actual events or places or persons, living or dead, is entirely coincidental.

MARGARET K. McELDERRY BOOKS is a trademark of Simon & Schuster, LLC.

Simon & Schuster: Celebrating 100 Years of Publishing in 2024

For information about special discounts for bulk purchases, please contact Simon & Schuster Special Sales at 1-866-506-1949 or business@simonandschuster.com.

The Simon & Schuster Speakers Bureau can bring authors to your live event. For more information or to book an event, contact the Simon & Schuster Speakers Bureau at 1-866-248-3049 or visit our website at www.simonspeakers.com.

Interior design by Irene Metaxatos

The text for this book was set in Minion Pro.

Manufactured in the United States of America

First Edition

10 9 8 7 6 5 4 3 2 1

Library of Congress Cataloging-in-Publication Data

Names: Markum, Samantha, author.

Title: Love, off the record / Samantha Markum.

Description: First edition. | New York : Margaret K. McElderry Books, 2024. | Audience: Ages 14 up. | Audience: Grades 10–12. | Summary: Wyn and Three, vying for a reporter spot on the university newspaper, engage in a cutthroat game of sabotage, but when Wyn's pursuit of a perfect story on a dating app connects her with a mystery man, it forces Wyn and Three to confront their true feelings.

Identifiers: LCCN 2023041651 (print) | LCCN 2023041652 (ebook) | ISBN 9781665955720 (hardcover) | ISBN 9781665955744 (ebook)

Subjects: CYAC: Newspapers—Fiction. | Universities and colleges—Fiction. | Interpersonal relations—Fiction. | LCGFT: Novels.

Classification: LCC PZ7.1.M37243 Lo 2024 (print) | LCC PZ7.1.M37243 (ebook) | DDC [Fic]—dc23

LC record available at https://lccn.loc.gov/2023041651

LC ebook record available at https://lccn.loc.gov/2023041652

For anyone who has ever suffered from second lead syndrome—especially if you had it for Three. This one's for you.

And for Ashley, Sonya, and Whitney. Because of everything.

AUTHOR'S NOTE

This book contains references to fatphobia, both internal and external. I realized in writing this book that sometimes our journeys can take longer than others', and sometimes they can't end within the pages. Wyn acknowledges her love for her body, that it is beautiful *and* fat, but those thoughts aren't always perfect, and she grapples a lot with how she expects to be treated or viewed for being fat.

I hope that Wyn's moments of backsliding aren't too hard to read. I hope my fellow plus-size folks understand that our own internalized fatphobia doesn't make us villains, as we're fighting so hard against everything society has fed us (or tried to starve us of). I poured much of my own heart into Wyn, and a lot of my own insecurities, past and present. Books are, after all, another way we try to therapize ourselves. I hesitated for a long time to write fat characters for fear of getting it wrong. But the truth is, there is no wrong way to be fat.

ONE

"Grunts!"

At the sound of our collective title, my deskmate and I look up. The *Torch* managing editor, Christopher, is twisted around in his chair, staring at us.

"Did you get those cutlines to Angelica?"

I point at my deskmate at the same time he points at me.

"Oh, no-no-no," I say, jabbing my finger closer. "You said you'd do it."

He pushes his glasses up onto his forehead, his expression overly patient—something I've learned means he's truly exasperated. "You know, I love these imaginary little scenarios you like to invent—"

"It's not imaginary!" I swivel to face him in the small space beneath our desk. The arm of my chair bangs into his, narrowly missing his fingers, earning me a glare in response.

"You literally said yesterday that you'd take care of the cutlines! Is your memory really that bad?"

His expression cools. "I said I'd take care of formatting the *headlines*. Is your hearing really that bad?"

"Hey!" Christopher barks, waving an arm to get our attention. "I don't care if one of you said you'd be doing the cancan lines on a Mississippi steamboat—we need the cutlines *now*. Get it done."

Sometimes I wonder if Christopher thinks we're running the *Washington Post* or something.

My deskmate puts on his best politician voice. "You know what? It's okay. I'll handle the cutlines too." He shoots me a nauseating smile. "No problem."

Three Wellborn, everyone: suck-up of the highest order.

If I'd known accepting a grunt internship with the *Torch* would land me at a desk with the most obnoxious and devious person I've ever met, I might have given the decision a second thought. But my first and most important goal at college was to land a spot—*any* spot—on the school newspaper.

The university's journalism program is highly competitive and accessible only to existing students through an application process. Most of the other freshmen who'll apply in the spring will have their sights on broadcasting, spending fall semester on one of the dozens of school-centric podcasts or clawing their way into spots on campus video channels, like the *Torch*'s biggest rival, *Two Minute News*. They're a short-form video daily news update run by a revolving door of "reporters" who do little more than shuttle gossip around campus. Unfortunately, their viewership leaves the *Torch* in the dust.

But they're also oversaturated with content creators, which is why securing my place at the *Torch* is essential. Having writing credits as a freshman will boost my application beyond the competition. I'm sort of counting on it, because when you've got your long-term sights set on a job in the struggling print-media industry, failing to get into the journalism program at a state school is not an option.

Three must feel the same, because he hasn't quit yet, despite the hours we've spent bumping elbows and trading long, silent looks of disdain in the quiet newsroom. Our superiors have made it clear that as long as we get our work done, we're free to attempt to murder each other with our eyes as much as we wish. When we *don't* get our work done, we get publicly dragged for it in front of the rest of the staff, like today.

I try to remind myself that future Pulitzer Prize winners don't let flies like Three get under their skin. But if he thinks I'm going to let him take over the cutlines like he's picking up my slack, he's not as smart as he wants everyone to believe.

"Oh no, don't worry about it," I say sweetly. "I'm happy to take one for the team."

"But you'll have to stay late." Three reaches over and pats my hand lightly. "Really, I don't mind."

I can't fight my grimace as I pick up his hand with two fingers and drop it back on his side of the desk. "Ew."

Three grins, knowing he's won. Because that's the goal: whoever gets a rise out of the other first wins. It's a twisted little game we're playing every second we spend together.

He flicks his gaze toward Christopher. "I've got the cutlines. I'll have them to you before I leave tonight."

"I don't know how to convey to you how little I care," says Christopher. "I thought I did a good job of it earlier with that line about the cancan, but it seems your skulls are getting thicker by the second. Don't talk to me again until they're done. I don't care who does them. I'm not your babysitter."

Three turns to me, tapping his pen against his lower lip. There is a victorious fire in his eyes that makes me want to grab the nearest sharp object and gouge them out of their sockets. "I guess it's all me. I'm pretty sure you have a job to get to."

It kills me that he knows my schedule so well. Because I do, in fact, have a shift at the library in fifteen minutes. I'll already need to rush to get there on time.

"Fine." The word comes out bitten off as I stand, grabbing my bag.

I shove my chair in, bashing it a little harder than necessary against Three's seat. Even from behind, he looks smug. It fills me with rage, which makes it very difficult to put on a normal, well-adjusted voice as I call goodbye to the rest of the staff in the newsroom.

I shoulder my bag with enough force that it smacks Three in the back of the head.

"Whoops," I say lightly, glancing back. His glasses have gone askew, and his glare is deadly. I manage to choke out, "Sorry!" and rush for the exit, making it into the hall just as my laughter explodes out of me.

It's a small victory in our ongoing war.

The worst part about Three isn't that he's, arguably, the most unpleasant human being I've ever met. It isn't his sneer, or his perfectly timed jabs, or the way he pushes his reading glasses up onto his forehead like he's some kind of movie reporter.

It's the fact that everyone else thinks he's incredible. The rest of the *Torch* staff finds him charming. I've caught more than one person in our shared statistics class shooting him major heart eyes. He's well-spoken and, unfortunately, intelligent, so professors love him. No one would ever believe that under his nice hair and his kind smile and his good manners, there lies a plotting, poisonous snake.

The second-worst part about Three is that he's cute. He's got the kind of face you would inherently trust—or at least not be surprised to find in a Vineyard Vines ad. He's got the look of East Coast old money, though really he's just Midwest old money. It doesn't matter—it's all money either way. He even went to boarding school, where I imagine he earned such a boarding school nickname like Three. As though a normal nickname, when he is Nathaniel Wellborn III, would be too pleb.

It stings to acknowledge, but when I first saw him, my

brain did a deep dive into every campus romance webcomic I've ever read. We were very firmly *not* friends—Three was impossible to be friends with back then, no matter how hard I tried. But for five minutes at a time, when I arrived with a cup of coffee just for him, he was *charming*. I'd get a morsel of him for myself to stow away for giggling, feet-kicking fantasies as soon as I was alone. And at the grunt desk, we handled the work like partners, dutifully tackling the to-do list together.

It all fell apart a few weeks ago when Angelica, the Campus Life editor, found out she got an internship at the *Columbus Dispatch* starting next semester. Now that she's leaving the *Torch* and others in her section are moving up, there's going to be a spot for a new Campus Life reporter.

A spot that's going to be *mine*.

Landing a staff position on the *Torch* blows a little writing credit straight out of the water. It'll prove I have real value to the paper beyond a few articles they happened to like. (Not that I've gotten to write any articles yet.)

Three might think he needs to win for the same reason, but I've looked at the numbers—there is a disproportionate amount of female applicants over male applicants, but a fairly even number of male and female journalism students. He has nothing to worry about—or at least less to worry about than I do.

And yet, the day Angelica announced she would be leaving, Three waited until the noise in the room picked up again before turning to me and saying, casual as ever, "You know I'll destroy you before I let you win that spot, right?"

And just like that, every happy, flirty thought I'd ever had about him got flushed. We were at war.

There's a guy coming out of my dorm room when I arrive late that night. It's after midnight, the hall quiet and the lounge mostly empty except for one person studying.

"Um, hi?" I say when the guy nearly knocks into me.

"'Sup," he says, but it's not a question, because he's already walking away.

I catch the door before it swings shut and poke my head into the room, the rest of my body following, relieved, when I see my roommate, Ellie, sitting at her desk. She's wearing sweats that are baggy on her thin frame, her brown hair pulled up in a messy bun—her go-to when she hasn't washed it in a while. She has the overhead fluorescents turned off, the room lit by her color-changing lamp, which is currently blue. It makes her look extra pale.

Not that I have room to talk. The sight of my reflection in our vanity is staggering—shoulder-length brown hair in tangles from the windy walk home, dark eyes bloodshot from staring at my computer in the newsroom all afternoon, and skin sheet-white now that we've left summer far behind.

Even though we've been here for weeks, Ellie's side of the room is still pretty bare-bones. Other than the single poster for some obscure film I've never heard of, there is very little to be learned about Ellie from her decor.

Which I think is partly to blame for why she still feels a bit like a stranger, even though I know she brushes her teeth three times a day and listens to *Rumours* by Fleetwood Mac on repeat whenever she's in a bad mood. But anything more than what you learn simply from sleeping four feet away from someone for a few weeks? Maybe just one: Ellie is a vault.

"Hey." I shut the door behind me, jerking my thumb over my shoulder. "Who was that?"

She glances up from her computer for only a second. "We have a class together."

I want to ask more, but I can tell from her tone that I've been dismissed. Not meanly, but that she simply won't be saying anything else.

When I first got to school, I was excited for a room-mate. I thought we'd hang out in the lounge, share meals in the dining hall, walk to class together sometimes. When I arrived and saw the little astronauts our RA had posted on our door—*Elizabeth* and *Éowyn* written on them—I seriously got butterflies.

Ellie and I had texted a few times, and of course I looked her up as soon as I got my room assignment. But she isn't very active on social media, and her texts were pretty basic as we decided what we'd each bring for the room.

Even as my parents helped me unpack, Ellie was nice but distant. The second they left, she took one look at the hand-made Middle-earth blanket Mom had insisted I bring with me and said, "I was wondering about the name, but now . . ."

"My parents are big fans," I replied, pulling the blanket from my bed. I started folding it up, making it as small as possible so I could shove it into the top of my closet. "I go by Wyn."

My parents' love for *The Lord of the Rings* is boundless beyond sensibility. They didn't notice when I started moving the memorabilia from my room to other parts of the house, or that I stopped dressing up as characters for Halloween sometime around the age of thirteen. If you asked my parents if I was teased much for my name or their obsession, they'd probably say no.

They have no idea.

"Got it," Ellie said. "We'll have to let the RA know for when she makes her new little name tags." The eye roll was implied.

I liked the name tags on our door. I still do, actually: now we have *Ellie* and *Wyn* on hot-air balloons.

It became clear over the next couple of weeks that Ellie and I get along but have little in common. We don't hang out unless we both happen to be in our room at the same time. We don't share meals or walk to class together, though not for my lack of trying at first. But I got shot down too many times for my pride to handle. Ellie was always too busy for me, because as it turns out, she already has friends here. And if I didn't spot them in the dining hall or out on campus, I'd know anyway, because there is a constant revolving door of people in and out of our room.

Like tonight.

"Hey, is that Wyn?" A voice echoes through the shared bathroom that links our room and the one next door.

I shouldn't be surprised they heard me come home. The walls in this place are paper-thin. The other day I sneezed, and someone in the next room said, "Bless you."

A moment later, Dara pokes her head in. She's dressed for bed in a pumpkin-print pajama set and silk bonnet, dark skin shining with cocoa butter.

Of my three suitemates, Dara is the easiest to talk to. But like Ellie, she already has friends at school—Kayla and Yasmin, who drop by Dara's room all the time. Kayla is Dara's friend from back home, and Yasmin is a girl who lives on Kayla's floor. The three of them quickly became a unit, to the point where you'd never guess Yasmin hasn't known Dara and Kayla forever. It's what I wished for myself, coming to school. To find my people. And not the same people I've always known— the ones I've spotted on campus that crossed the stage with me back in Troy, who are familiar-faced strangers at best. I want *friends*. Kindred spirits. Something I've never had before.

Sure, I had friends in high school—people to hang out with on the weekends, or sit with at lunch, or talk to between classes. But I always felt like a hanger-on, and I learned later, that's basically what I was. Friendships forged in elementary school over crayons and lunch boxes and which cartoon fairy was our favorite soured as we got to middle school and rotted entirely when we reached high school. In the end, there was nothing left between us but thin, worn strings of obligation. Apparently playing investigator with me had been fun when we were kids—figuring out which teachers were secretly dating, or helping get the word out about a lost dog—but when I wrote in our school paper about football players stealing concessions money after games or a tradition of test-sharing among certain honors students, it was "embarrassing" and "over-the-top." I found myself being invited out less and less as the years wore on, until graduation rolled around and no one was calling at all.

"Can Madison borrow your cape?" Dara asks now, hanging on the doorframe.

From their room, Madison calls, "I don't need it, Wyn! It's really okay!"

"Yeah, no problem. What for?" I go to my closet, pushing aside my clothes to pull out the cape my parents slipped into my luggage. It's part of a replica of Éowyn's funeral gown, a graduation gift from my parents.

Madison appears in the doorway on the other side of the bathroom. From my closet, I have a view straight across to their room—or more specifically, Madison's closet, which is all pastels. I once overheard Ellie telling one of her friends that Madison is a priss, which is rude but also kind of accurate.

Madison tugs at her long ponytail, which is shampoo-commercial shiny. "Don't worry about it. I don't think—"

"At least try it." Dara takes the cape from me and crosses the bathroom to Madison. She glances back at me and shrugs. "It's for this new routine she's doing for glee club."

I follow them into their room, which is miles cozier than mine and Ellie's. It helps that they have a very similar style. Everything is feminine and floral, with flower-print sheets and a cohesive color palette. They planned it before they came to school—something I wish Ellie and I had done, even though Ellie clearly has no interest in decorating, and I could never afford to make my side of the room look like a Pottery Barn catalog. My decor options were whatever was cheapest at Target, and even that in limited quantity.

Which is fine. I don't need a flower-shaped desk lamp like Madison, or Dara's watercolor tapestry. Or their fluffy, flower-print area rug. Or the little butterfly lights hanging over their window. Or . . .

I should stop. Jealousy is like a pulled thread—it'll unravel me quickly.

Next to her bed, Madison holds my cape like it might bite her. When she sees I've followed, she flushes and quickly pulls it on.

I see the problem right away, and judging from her face, Madison knew it first. We might be close in height, but where I'm firmly plus-size, Madison is the only person I've ever met in real life who wears an extra-extra-small.

My cape dwarfs her.

"Sorry," she says, taking it off again.

"For what?" I ask.

Madison sucks in a breath, stops, then looks to Dara for help.

Dara shrugs, holding out a hand for the cape. "Sorry for . . . wasting your time?" She glances at Madison, who frowns.

"Sorry for . . . being thin?" I ask, forcing out a small laugh to show I'm joking.

Madison's light skin colors red. She splutters, but nothing coherent comes out.

"I'm kidding." I take the cape from Dara. Madison won't even come near me.

Sometimes I wonder if she thinks fat is catching. It's something I've dealt with many times. I had plenty of friends in high school who were uncomfortable at the mention of my weight. They were happy to lament their own—*I look so bloated* and *I had to wear my fat pants today* and *I'm not eating fast food until after prom*—but never wanted to admit, to me or to themselves, that the truth of those statements was that a body like mine was their nightmare. That I never lamented with them must have felt like a blessing, so they didn't have to acknowledge the way I looked at all. But for me, it wasn't about making them comfortable. It was because I've always taken my relationship with my body seriously, and wishing it were different—or worse, insulting it outright—felt like a betrayal.

I can be uncomfortable sometimes, and I can dislike how I look occasionally, but I can't go through life hating my body. It's the only one I get. I'd rather work to love the way it looks than work to change the way it looks, which is often fruitless effort anyway.

And I know that bothers people sometimes, that I refuse

to treat my body like a worst-case scenario. That I deign to care for it, and love it, even if I'm not always the most confident in it. Even if I have to sometimes be realistic about how others see me because of it.

"Well, good luck. I'm going to bed." I head back to my room, shutting the bathroom door behind me. Ellie is at our vanity sink now, brushing her teeth.

She glances over at me as I shove the cape back in my closet. Spitting into the sink, she says, "Did she drown in it?"

"Yep," I answer, heading for my dresser. I pull out my pajamas and start to change.

Ellie snorts. "Of course."

I'll give Ellie one thing—at least she doesn't shy away from the truth of a situation.

TWO

I knew Three for weeks before I got my spot at the *Torch*—or at least, I knew *of* him. It was hard not to notice him in my twice-a-week statistics class, where I split my time struggling to pay attention, struggling to understand the lecture, and struggling to ignore what felt like, based on the noise level, half the Tau Delta Pi pledge class.

Three is one of them, which is one more mark against him in my book. When I came to college, there was a single rule that reigned above all others: stay away from frat boys. It's one of the only rules Mom gave me as my parents prepared to send me off, but one I already knew on my own.

I thought it'd be my easiest rule to follow—until I got stuck at the grunt desk with the king of the pledges.

It's unnerving, I think as we leave the classroom and Three falls into the center of his group, how charming he can be. Even now he jokes with the other Tau Delt pledges, shoving each other and laughing. Yet under that smile, I know he's twisted and sadistic. Like one of those serial killers whose friends and coworkers all say, "We never could have guessed. He was so *nice*."

Three glances back, his smile dipping into a smirk like he can read my exact thoughts.

I stop, and someone bumps into me from behind, nearly knocking me to my knees. My bag slips from my shoulder, falling into the crook of my elbow.

"Whoa! Sorry!" A hand catches my arm, steadying me. "You stopped really fast."

"No, *I'm* sorry," I say quickly, shouldering my bag again. "I don't know what I . . ." I trail off when I see who bumped me. "Hey—you're Lincoln, right?"

He adjusts his backpack, peering down at me. "And you're . . . on Chloe's floor." He chuckles, looking sheepish. "Sorry, I don't remember your name. I'm still trying to learn everyone on my *own* floor."

I smile. "I'm Wyn."

"Wyn," he repeats, nodding. "Wyn. Wyn. Wyn. Got it."

We briefly met the other RAs in our building during move-in day. It was mostly in passing, but Lincoln is hard to forget. He's the type of tall and broad that's difficult to miss in a crowd—not like an athlete, but like he belongs on a farm. He's wearing a T-shirt even though it's chilly out, and his arms are still summer-tanned and thick with muscle. His brown hair is a little long, but not purposely so—more like he keeps forgetting to get it trimmed.

"You on your way to class?" Lincoln asks.

"I have work. Then newspaper. And then class, late. Thursdays are the worst."

"Newspaper? You work for the *Torch*?"

"Yeah, I work my ass off," I joke. "But only as a grunt. I don't get to do any real reporting yet."

"That's impressive, though. I don't know how it is now, with the *Two Minute News* takeover, but it used to seem really hard to get a spot there."

I give a flippant hand wave. "*Two Minute News* isn't exactly drawing in the serious reporters. The *Torch* is cut-throat. I think I'm the only one in the newsroom who wasn't editor-in-chief in high school."

It's a very sore subject, and an old one. When I lost editor-in-chief last year, it was to a friend—or someone I'd thought was one. I didn't even know she was running until the ballots came out with two names—Wyn and Clara. I was outvoted almost unanimously. Apparently the rest of the newspaper staff found me too intense. I was pushing for stories and design that might win us a Pacemaker Award. Everyone else was just happy to have the newspaper on their college applications.

The election was one of many moments throughout my senior year that stuck like tiny barbs. At the time, it was one bad thing—albeit a big bad thing that I cried over for a whole weekend. Yet by the end of the year, I found I'd been pricked all over by a thousand things just like it.

"Hey, don't let imposter syndrome sneak in." Lincoln has a kind, comforting smile; I can tell why they made him an RA. "It's like the first freshman-year souvenir you get, and it's brutal. Trust me, as someone who already did it and dealt with it."

His words manage to put my brain back on track, which is a relief. Dwelling on old hurts helps no one. Besides, I plan to become editor-in-chief of the *Torch* one day. If I land the Campus Life spot, I could be well on my way there. That would certainly numb the sting from high school.

And even though my goals have nothing to do with Three, I don't hate the idea of one day being able to hold that over him.

When I get to the newsroom that evening after work, there are only a few people inside. One of them is Three, hunched over at the grunt desk.

"Has anyone ever told you that you have the posture of a cooked shrimp?" I ask, dropping my bag on the floor.

Three straightens, then cracks his neck. He rolls his head in my direction. "It's really nice of you to worry about my spine health."

I grimace, making a small, grossed-out noise.

Three grins, pushing his glasses up onto his forehead as he looks me over. "You seem tired. You sure you don't want to just head home for the night?"

"And give up all our quality time together? Why would I ever want to do that?"

I pull out my chair to sit but stop when our editor-in-chief says, "Wyn, do you have a sec?"

When I first looked up the *Torch*, it didn't take me long to find my dream mentor. The best articles all had the same byline: *written by Sabina Noor*.

Reading her articles reminded me of those first fluttery feelings I had watching *All the President's Men* and *His Girl Friday* as a kid, and then later, when I grew up a little, reading about Florence Graves and the NSA surveillance whistleblower and *everything* about Vietnam. Sabina wasn't uncovering national scandals or solving murders, but her reporting felt like that to me. It reminded me of what made me want to become a reporter in the first place.

I wasn't surprised when I came to apply and found out Sabina had been made editor-in-chief. Christopher ran against her, but I heard he lost the votes when he got scooped by *Two Minute News* on a story about two girls who overdosed on fentanyl-laced fake Adderall last winter. One of the girls died and the other dropped out, and without in-depth coverage of the rise of laced study drugs on campus, both were painted as irresponsible party girls and everyone else moved on. No one even found out who they got the counterfeit pills from. I once overheard Angelica say that Christopher is carrying enough bitterness over the whole thing to fill a shipping container.

As for Sabina, being editor-in-chief means she doesn't really have time to spare for grunts like me, so I absorb any of her attention like a sponge that's been left in the desert.

"Hi," I say, rushing to her desk. "What's up? What do you need?"

Sabina beckons Three, who's slower to join us.

Sabina is effortlessly cool, with her dark hair cropped short, gold septum piercing, and the kind of artsy-grunge style that goes well with her collection of flannel. Beside her, Three, in his button-down and pullover sweater, looks extra dorky.

"I know you're both hoping for the Campus Life spot once Angelica leaves," Sabina says, leaning back in her chair. "I'm just gonna be real with you. We can't place you both. That means one of you will be working under the other, and I want some assurance you'll be able to deal with that."

"It won't be a problem. I'm with the paper for the long haul, no matter what." I glance at Three, already assembling a mental list of how I'll make his life hell when I get the Campus Life spot and he has to do my dirty work.

Three clocks the look, and his eyes crinkle at the corners like he's having a similar thought. "I'm serious about the *Torch* too," he says to Sabina. "I started at the bottom at my last paper. I was editor-in-chief when I graduated. I had to work under my friends, and then they had to work under me. I know how to handle both. I can be professional."

Of course he found a way to mention how he was editor-in-chief.

Sabina glances between us, assessing. "Then I guess it's the right time to have you both start submitting some stories for us. I know you've been eager, since you need samples for your application to the journalism program. I'll need to see what you can do too, if one of you is going to move up."

"I've already been working on something," I say quickly, because I want Sabina to know I've been proactive. "About the roach situation at Landing."

"I talked to Mel last week," Three says. "I have a Greek Row story I want to work on."

I scoff. "Of course you do." And of course he was enough of a suck-up to go to Mel, the Campus Life assistant editor who'll be taking over Angelica's spot next semester—moving up to a paid position, which is a real rarity around here.

Three shoots me a look of disdain. "A lot of attitude from a girl whose big story is about roaches."

"Well, I sit next to one every day, so I'm super well-versed."

Sabina rubs her forehead. "Okay, that's enough. Do the stories—both of you. If it's good, we'll run it. You can send your progress to Mel. Angelica has enough on her plate right now. And listen, I'm not your adviser or your RA or your big sister, but there've been a lot of people who've let their journalism app fall by the wayside because they thought it'd be easy. That's not a group you want to be a part of. Remember, if you flub it, you have to wait a whole semester to reapply. Getting stories done for your portfolio will be hard enough.

But you'll also have your essay, and you'll need at least one faculty recommendation letter. And we expect you to still be on top of your regular grunt duties. It may not feel like it, but the grunts are the backbone of this paper. We're relying on you to do your job and do it well. Okay?"

We nod.

"If you need anything, let me know," Sabina says, dropping her gaze back to her computer. "But try not to need anything."

On our way back to the grunt desk, I murmur to Three, "Have fun getting your recommendation. If you can get someone to stand in a room with you long enough to ask for one."

Three shoots me a bland smile. "Am I supposed to be worried?"

"True. I'm sure you've got a fat trust fund somewhere, and there's nothing like a good, old-fashioned bribe for a backup plan." I give him a sparkling grin. "Do me a favor and make sure you get caught, okay? I'd love to write that article."

"You wouldn't do it justice," Three says sharply. The insult lands, but I hardly feel the sting. I'm used to Three brushing me off as a joke. That I've gotten under his skin enough that he's biting back feels like a win.

"Writing about your downfall would be the highlight of my journalism career," I reply, dropping into my chair.

Three follows more slowly, and by the time he's seated beside me, his expression has cooled. "I'm glad to know you're so preoccupied by me, Evans. You must love getting to sit next to me like this. Is that why you haven't quit yet?"

My victory sours in my stomach, like taking a bite of something sweet only to realize it's rotten inside.

"Your presence is actually meaningless to me." I pluck up my headphones and pop them into my ears, blocking out whatever he says next.

It no longer feels like I've won anything, but at least I know I didn't lose. Still, I'm uncomfortable realizing that Three has a point—I am preoccupied by him.

With the Campus Life spot and potentially my entire journalism school application on the line, my attention is needed elsewhere.

I'm not surprised to find Ellie gone when I get back to my dorm. She spends a lot of time out of our room, and she doesn't have class tomorrow. She'll probably coast in sometime in the middle of the night, and even though she always returns smelling like beer and pot, I've yet to see her suffer a hangover or so much as stumble getting into bed.

The door has barely swung shut behind me when someone gives a series of quick, quiet taps on the bathroom door. Ellie is religious about keeping it locked, even though it's just Dara and Madison on the other side. I think it's some kind of sibling habit I don't understand. Apparently Ellie has three younger sisters who are always getting into her stuff.

I flip the lock and swing open the bathroom door. Dara waits on the other side.

"Hey," she whispers. "Can I hang out in here? Madison went to bed early."

A pathetic little part of me perks up. She wants to hang out with me!

And if it's because Madison went to bed early and her last resort is the lounge, I'll still take it.

"Yeah, of course," I say, pulling the door wide. "Sorry. I'd say you could always hang out in here, but Ellie's really weird about people touching her stuff."

Dara shoots me a smile, shutting the bathroom door behind her. "Ellie's, like, really weird in general."

I exhale. "Yeah. I'm glad I'm not the only one who noticed." I tug my hoodie over my head and toss it onto my bed, climbing up after it.

She moves to my desk, which is flush with the end of my bed, and perches sideways in my chair. "God love her, but so is Madison. She went to bed at, like, nine. And she's *such* a light sleeper. I've been hiding out in the bathroom waiting for you to get home." She smacks her forehead. "Which sounds really sad. But I've been talking to this guy I met on Buckonnect, and things are getting kind of"—she wiggles her shoulders, grinning—"and I felt a little weird with the pastor's daughter sleeping four feet away."

I try not to look uncomfortable. It's not that I'm morally opposed to consensual sexting, but the topic of sex always makes me freeze up. All people my age seem to care about is sex—who's having it and who isn't, who has and who hasn't, and, if nothing else, how far you've gone. My inexperience is a stamp of embarrassment. I have nothing to contribute to the conversation but one drunken makeout after prom where a guy I didn't even like groped my boob over my dress, and one innocent kiss at a party years ago with someone I *could* have liked, if he ever looked my way again, which he didn't.

It's not that I don't want kissing and sex and all the stuff that comes with it—dates and holding hands in public and having someone I'm dying to see at the end of each day. I'm a romance reader. Obviously I want romance.

But it's scary to put yourself out there. Especially when you're fat. *Especially* when you're fat and inexperienced and it feels like everyone else is on the fast track. Talking about it makes everyone wonder why I haven't done anything yet—or worse, *not* wonder—and I don't like giving people more brain fuel for the "fat people are undesirable and sexless" stereotype.

So I focus on what I *can* handle in this conversation. "What's Buckonnect?"

"*Where* have you been? *Buckonnect!*" Dara taps at her phone, then flips it around to show me. I crawl to the end of my bed and lie on my stomach, peering across my desk at her screen. It looks like a regular chat app, except there are no profile pictures. Dara pulls her phone back once I've gotten a good look. "It's a dating app this junior made as part of a project. He got some volunteers to beta test it, and it blew up. Everyone's using it. I started this week, because I think

Kayla and Yasmin—you know Kay and Yas, right? They're in my room all the time. I think they might be, like, getting together, you know? I don't want to be the third wheel, so I downloaded Buckonnect. It gives you a random username based on a campus building, so it's *super*-super anonymous, and you match based on your sexual preference. Other than your username, it only displays your preferred pronouns. Then you choose how much to share, and when. Like I exchanged numbers with this guy I'm talking to, but I haven't shown him my face yet."

"Huh. That's interesting, I guess. I'm surprised I haven't heard of it." And if I haven't, that means no one has done a story on it yet—not even *Two Minute News*. Light bulbs ding to life in my brain. "Hey, could you tell me more about it? I might write something for the newspaper."

I catch myself only once the words have left my mouth. Here I go again, turning every conversation into a potential story—the thing that ran off the few friends I had in the first place.

But I'm relieved when Dara's face brightens. "Would I be a source? Like, quoted?"

"Yeah, if you want to be," I reply, reaching over the side of my bed to grab my bag. I drag my laptop out and turn it on, sitting back against the wall. "This could be a really good story. I can't believe no one else has done it yet."

It sounds even better than my roach story, which I already knew was a risk. The issues in the older dorms are pretty widely known. It's not like anyone would be surprised to hear about roaches in Landing.

I've never imagined myself writing for the technology section at the *New York Times* or anything, but breaking the story on an app just as it begins to sweep campus would definitely get Sabina's attention.

"It's still pretty new," Dara says, "but I bet more than half the school is using it by the end of Saturday's game."

She's right—information spreads fast at football games. And by Sunday night, Dara confirms the Buckonnect usership has doubled, exactly as we expected.

When I get to the *Torch* office on Monday, I have an outline and a rough draft of my Buckonnect story ready. Dara's excitement over it has me optimistic, and that feeling intensifies when I spot the empty grunt desk. If Three isn't here, I'm definitely having a lucky day.

I drop my stuff at my seat and head straight for Mel's desk, where they're leaned over with their cheek resting on their fist, scrolling on their computer.

"Hey, do you have a minute?" I ask. "Because I have a really good idea for a Campus Life story I want to run by you."

Mel glances up, stretching as they recline a little in their chair. "The roach story?"

Their tone makes me glad I found a backup. Clearly Mel isn't interested in the roaches at Landing. It makes me wonder why Sabina didn't warn me off it. She had to have known it wasn't interesting if even the Campus Life assistant editor sounds ready to give it the ax. But maybe that was Sabina letting me learn the hard way.

God, I am ready to start learning things the easy way.

"No, way better than that." At least this way, Mel will know I can recognize what's newsworthy and what isn't. "Have you heard of Buckonnect?"

Mel's brow puckers. "Just as of yesterday."

"Right?" I can't keep my excitement from my voice. Getting my story into this week's edition is perfect timing if more people are hearing about Buckonnect after this weekend. "Its usership blew up after the football game—"

"I know," Mel says.

My smile freezes on my face, and I'm expecting a phrase uttered far too often in the *Torch* office: "You got scooped." Of course *Two Minute News* wouldn't have missed something like this. While I was toiling away at an outline to get all the facts, they were throwing together their typical slapdash update. I shouldn't even be surprised—

But then Mel says, "Three wrote a whole story on it over the weekend."

No. It's somehow worse than *Two Minute News*.

"He . . . what?"

"He sent me the outline Saturday night. Or technically early Sunday morning." Mel chuckles, shaking their head. "I don't think he sleeps. He had the whole thing finished and in my inbox yesterday afternoon."

I clench my teeth so I don't grimace. Everything in my stomach has turned to acid. I hate that I'm envious of the respect in Mel's voice. I hate that Three has somehow earned it. I hate that I don't know how to exit this conversation without giving myself away—that I had the exact same idea, that he beat me to it, that my only remaining pitch is about bugs.

I hate that I'm about to try anyway.

"You know what? Um, I think—maybe I should give this one a little more time." I plaster on a smile and pray it looks sincere. "Especially if Three just covered the basics. I'm sure we don't want to run two Buckonnect stories at the same time."

Mel blinks at me. "Maybe we could. We can always expand on his story if you've got something good."

Damn.

"I think it needs more work," I say quickly, backing away a step. "I can dig deeper."

Mel nods slowly. "Okay. Do you have something else for me?"

I swallow against my tightening throat. "Maybe!" My voice comes out a squeak. "I'll—I'll outline some stuff. Get a few ideas together."

"I can't ask them to save the space for you. I'd need to know soon."

"Yeah, for sure! I'll let you know." I give them a thumbs-up that I immediately regret. It does nothing to clear the uncertain look on Mel's face, and I imagine it only makes my forced smile seem even faker.

My only consolation as I head back to my seat is that the grunt desk is still empty and remains that way the rest of the afternoon. If Three found out he landed this story before me, I don't think I'd survive the shame.

THREE

"Why are you so down today?" my coworker Jennie asks, peeking at me over the library help desk. Of all the tasks I've done at the library since I got this job when school started, manning the help desk is the most low-maintenance and, thus, the best one. Unfortunately, it's usually covered by Susan, a full-time employee who's worked on campus for over twenty years, or occasionally Jennie, who, as a senior, has pull over most of the other student staff.

Right now I'm at the help desk only because Susan is on her break, and, as my boss, Scott, pointed out, "There won't be much for you to handle here."

Scott is not my biggest fan. Or anyone's fan, really. He's a pinched, perpetually red-faced man who seems to find joy in making our lives miserable, particularly mine. Every tiny mistake I've made since I started, from leaving a book cart in a walkway to forgetting to lock the bathrooms at closing has led to a firm and usually public reprimand from Scott. He loves to make even the most minor infractions into an example.

But he wasn't wrong about the help desk not being busy. With midterms over, the library is a ghost town. Everyone is out celebrating.

I should be celebrating something too, but after trashing my Buckonnect story today, I'm basically a husk of self-loathing and misery. I wish I were the type of person whose failures fuel them to do better, but my flops just take the wind out of my sails. I am a champion moper.

"The asshole I share the grunt desk with stole my story." I groan, dropping my head into my hands. "Of *course*. I should've emailed someone about it over the weekend, but it doesn't even matter. He had the whole thing ready to print. I heard someone say it barely needed editing."

Jennie makes a sympathetic noise. "I won't pretend to know what a grunt desk is, but I'm sorry—that sounds like it sucks."

I slump farther into my seat. "It *does* suck. I thought I was about to have my first feature. My first *anything* in the *Torch*."

"Well, maybe next time. How'd he steal it from you, anyway?"

I swallow. Okay, so technically he didn't steal it. No one even knew I was working on it. It's not like Three hacked my computer or something.

"It's not important," I say, waving her off. "What's done is done. I also bombed my stats midterm, which is what I should really be worried about."

"Ouch. Yeah, stats is tough. I took that when I was a freshman."

Jennie is in an intense engineering program, so I doubt statistics was as much a challenge for her as it is me.

"Hey, girls," Susan says when she returns. "Thanks for covering the desk, Wyn. Any problems?"

"Nope." I rise from her chair. "This place is deserted."

"Not entirely," Susan says uneasily. "Scott asked me to tell you the porn guy is on the fourth floor again."

I stare at her. "What does Scott want me to do about it?"

Susan gives me a tight smile. I turn a pleading look on Jennie, but she's gone—*poof*—like a magic trick.

"Why can't Scott go up there?" I complain. "He's a grown man."

Susan holds up her hands. "Sorry. I'm just the messenger."

I sigh, pulling open a few drawers until I find a ruler. Susan watches me with a confused frown, but I don't feel like explaining myself.

In the elevator, I fume. Scott should do this himself, or send one of the other staff, since I've already kicked this guy out once before.

I wonder if this is the library's version of hazing.

The elevator doors slide open on the silent fourth floor. Every table I pass is empty but for the man at the very last one, and I desperately hope the deserted floor doesn't mean he's doing something even worse than just *watching* porn up here. If I see a penis right now, I might actually quit my job.

The only bright side—if you can call it that—is that the porn perv watches his videos on mute. It's how he keeps getting away with it. If he caused a noise disturbance, Scott might deign to ban him.

"Hey." I don't bother to lower my voice. I smack the ruler on the edge of the table, and the sound echoes. "I've told you before. You can't do this here."

The guy lifts his eyes from his screen. They're glazed as he stares at me.

It is extremely unnerving.

I tap the ruler lightly on his laptop. "Get out. Next time, I'm calling the police for . . . indecent . . . stuff."

The man smiles without showing his teeth. He kind of looks like he could play a cannibal killer on TV.

I will myself not to back up a step.

"I'm dead serious," I whisper, putting some bite in my voice. "If I find out you're up here doing this one more time, I'll wallpaper this place with your picture and make sure you never step foot in here again. Get out." I point the ruler at him, then the elevator.

The man shuts his laptop slowly, his gaze locked on mine. I feel a burst of nerves, like I want to run. When he gets up, I keep my eyes on him, turning as he rounds the table and heads for the elevator. I never put my back to him.

As soon as the elevator doors slide shut on him, I sag

back against the wall. I don't understand how this keeps happening, or how the library Wi-Fi doesn't have porn blocked. Maybe he has porn saved to his computer, but . . .

I pull out my phone and open a new window, trying a couple of porn sites I know off the top of my head. Both go through without issue.

I close them out and slide my phone back into my pocket, an idea taking root.

It was surprisingly easy to get Mel on board with my story on public porn viewing. My outline covered all the basics about the campus Wi-Fi's access points, and some horror stories on the subject from larger publications across the country.

It was a lot of ground to cover—the age of the smartphone making porn accessible anywhere; the fear of retaliation or ridicule, particularly among women, when confronting a person watching porn in public; and quotes pulled from a story I found in the *Torch*'s online archive about a student who was interviewed about a guy watching porn in one of her classes. Finished, the story painted a picture of a growing issue with publicly viewed porn on campus. It highlighted the danger it puts people in when the goal of watching porn in public is sometimes to be seen doing it, and what could happen if that were to escalate to something much more . . . hands-on—and what that would mean for everyone's safety and comfort on campus.

I could feel Mel's enthusiasm as they read over my draft,

and when we brought the story to Sabina, she was immediately on board.

It felt like a huge win. When I was a kid, I wanted to be Nancy Drew or Harriet the Spy, uncovering the truth and catching the bad guys. As I got older, I realized that meant being Lucy Morgan, the first woman to win the Pulitzer Prize for Investigative Reporting, or a member of the *Boston Globe*'s Spotlight team, because nothing holds the bad guys accountable better than public outcry. And now, finally, people would be reading *my* words in the *Torch*—my first serious story as a hopeful for the journalism program.

But as it turns out, the "reading it" part of my story is what evades most people. I learn this when the new edition of the *Torch* goes out, and the headline I submitted—"Banning Public Porn Access: Is It the Key to a Safer Campus?"—goes in with a word missing: "Banning Porn Access: Is It the Key to a Safer Campus?"

We don't realize until it's already been printed in the physical paper and posted on our website. I thought fixing the digital version would take care of it. Most people don't read the physical copy of the *Torch* anyway.

Then two days later, I get back to my dorm after work and Ellie says, "Why are people texting me asking what my puritan roommate has against porn?" The door has barely shut behind me. She eyes me from her desk, brow furrowing. "I didn't even know you were religious."

"I'm not," I snap.

"Well, people are saying you're trying to get porn banned on campus. It's, like, all anyone's talking about."

My stomach bottoms out. "Please tell me you're joking."

Ellie's eyes widen slightly. "You didn't know?"

"*He-eey,*" Dara says, poking her head in from the bathroom, her smile almost a grimace. "How's it going?"

"Wyn, I should thank you," Madison says from behind her. "My parents are thrilled I have a suitemate whose morals are aligned with mine."

"My morals are not—I'm not trying to—Wait, your *parents*?" I set my bag on my desk and drop into my chair, stunned. "What is happening right now? No one even reads the *Torch*." It's normally painful to admit, but right now I'm numb to everything but pure panic.

"Some frat is, like, protesting," Dara says. "Tau Delt, I think?"

My breathing quickens. "What?"

"They posted an opinion piece on their website about how banning porn on campus is a personal rights infringement."

"And then *Two Minute News* covered the whole thing," Ellie says, pulling up the video on her phone. She lets the first few seconds play as the person on camera says, rapid-fire, "A freshman reporter at the *Torch* is proposing a campus porn ban that has at least one fraternity wading into the debate—"

"I'm not trying to ban porn on campus. I'm not even trying to get it banned! All I did was write a piece about how it's dangerous to have porn available on public access points, because it gives people the opportunity to watch in public places and be seen doing it." I look between my roommates, who all stare back blankly. *"None of you even read it?"*

"Well, okay, I was going to," Dara says quickly.

"I wasn't," says Ellie.

"My parents have restrictions on my internet browsing, so I can't technically," Madison says. "Since it has 'porn' in the title." She whispers the word "porn," like her parents might be listening even now. "But I told them all about it, and they're really happy."

"You told them all about an article you haven't read?"

Madison flushes. "Well, just what I've heard from other people."

I rub my forehead. "You do realize this is how misinformation spreads, right? I'm not trying to ban porn on campus. *Just* in public. I'm not even *trying*—I'm repeating myself. I'm literally talking in circles. Okay. I'm out."

"Hey, Wyn, don't—" Dara's protest is cut off as the door slams shut between us.

The lounge that the dorm rooms circle is full of people, and heads swivel in my direction. I can tell a few of them know who I am, and I'm sure as soon as I turn my back, the whispers will start.

"I'm not trying to get porn banned on campus," I say loudly. "*Please* read the whole article. *God.*"

I turn and storm into the stairwell, thundering down until I reach the ground floor and burst out into the chilly autumn night. I wander for a while until my feet take me past the gym, where people stream steadily in and out.

Then the door to the aquatic center swings open, and Three strolls out. Like the universe plucked him up and dropped him right here for me and my rage.

He has a gym bag slung over one shoulder and his hair is wet, and he doesn't notice me coming at a velocity last seen in a middle school math textbook.

Not until I move into his path and put us on a collision course.

"*Jeez*, Evans, come on," he says, catching my shoulders before we can crash into each other and create the next Big Bang, flinging fury into the universe to form a brand-new hellscape.

"It was you, wasn't it?" I advance a step, and he drops his hands and backs up until he hits the ramp railing behind him. "You changed my headline."

I don't miss the way the corners of his mouth twitch, even as his gaze remains serious. "I didn't do anything. Why would I mess with your headline?" His teeth come down on his lower lip, as though he can bite away the smile that's fighting to break free.

"To. Mess. With. Me." I punctuate each word with a poke to his chest.

Three catches my hand. "Okay, you're obviously having a night." He tucks my finger back into my fist. "I didn't mess with your headline, or with you."

But he's too smug for that to be entirely true. He's clearly riding the high of a win right now.

"Let go." I tug my hand out of his.

Three smiles. "You touched first."

"And you moved first." I point at him again but keep a few inches between us. "Remember that. You started it."

His smile widens. "I have no idea what you're talking about."

"Yeah, sure. Okay. Play dumb all you want. You think I'm going to fall for that when your stupid-ass fraternity is the one posting about my article?"

"Ah," he says, as though everything has just dawned on him. "Right. The porn ban thing. You know, I'm only a pledge, so I don't know if they're really *my* stupid-ass fraternity. But hey, I'm sorry they've got you so rattled."

Rattled. My heart gives a warning leap, like I've walked straight into a trap.

No wonder he seems so pleased right now. I'm giving him exactly what he wants.

I grind my teeth together, struggling to regain my composure. "You know what? I'm done talking to you. I've said what I wanted to say." I turn to walk away.

"And what did you say exactly?"

My tiny bubble of self-control bursts, and I snap over my shoulder, "It's fucking *on*, Wellborn. That's what I said."

"Wow, okay," he calls after me, laughing. "I'll keep that in mind!"

It's how flippant he sounds that really fires me up. All this time, I've thought I simply needed to prove myself the superior journalist. But it's clear Three's method for winning isn't just about out-reporting me—he's getting in my head and under my skin. And if I don't start playing his game, I may as well forfeit. I'm not about to win the Campus Life spot on the high road.

On the walk back to my dorm, I make a hundred different plans to ruin him, fueled by rage and that stupid, self-satisfied smile of his.

Until I arrive at my building and realize I left my room with nothing—no phone, key card, or even my ID. I stand at the front of the building, tipping my head back with a frustrated groan.

"Uh . . . you okay?"

My head snaps up. Lincoln has stopped beside me, still leaning in the direction of the door, like he was on his way around me.

"Oh, thank god." I sigh in relief. "I forgot my key card. And my phone. And literally anything else I should have grabbed on my way out."

Lincoln smiles, nodding toward the door. He unlocks it and holds it open for me.

"You're my hero," I say as I step inside. "Seriously, the only good thing to happen to me all day was running into you."

"You know, you don't have to flatter me. I already let

you inside." He shoots me a teasing smile as we head for the elevator.

"Well, I nearly maimed you the other day, and now I'm asking you for favors. It's only fair I give you something in return."

Someone knocks on the door behind us, and we both turn. A girl stands on the other side, wearing pajama pants and a sweatshirt, hair pulled up in a messy bun. She points at the door and mimes opening it.

Lincoln's smile slips a little as he heads over and pushes it open a crack. "You don't have your key card?" The elevator dings and the doors open, but I wait.

"I'm here to see someone," she says, moving to slip past him. I get a better look at her face this time, and I feel a tug of recognition. I'm pretty sure I've seen her stop by my room for Ellie, though it's hard to keep track of Ellie's long list of visitors.

Lincoln blocks the way. "I can't let you in if you don't live here."

She jerks back with a sneer. "What are you, a cop?"

"I'm an RA."

Her expression goes stony.

"Hey, wait," I say before she can walk off. "I think you're going to my room. Two-oh-two, right?"

The girl looks at me for the first time, and she brightens. "Yeah," she says, shifting to move past Lincoln. "Thanks."

He gives me a questioning look, but I wave her in. "It's cool. I know her."

Lincoln pushes the door wide, letting her pass, but he doesn't look entirely comfortable. I try to give him a reassuring smile, but his attention is on the new girl as we enter the elevator. I wonder if he's angry—if I somehow undermined his authority.

We ride up to the second floor in awkward silence, and then the girl and I exit the elevator together. I give Lincoln a wave goodbye and thank him again, which earns me a small smile in response.

Then the elevator doors slide shut, and the girl says to me, "Hey, aren't you the one trying to get porn banned on campus?"

And I instantly regret letting her into the building at all.

FOUR

For the next few days, I watch Three like he's my favorite TV show, my only interest, and the singular thought in my brain.

Which, to be honest, he might be.

I don't have a definitive plan. But when it comes to investigating, observation is key. If I want to learn how to beat Three, I need to know more about him—his strengths, his weaknesses, when he eats, where he lives. Right now I am a squirrel preparing for winter—gathering tiny morsels of information and stowing them away for later. And the longer I go without attacking, the more nervous he'll become, anticipating my next move, wondering when I'll strike.

Or at least, that's how it *should* be. But from what I've seen—and I've seen a lot, because it's really amazing the stuff you'll witness when you're halfway to stalker territory—Three isn't worried about me, despite my declaration of war.

Which sets my blood absolutely *boiling*.

I spend days sitting in stony silence at the grunt desk, not rising to his bait. It's a decent approach. With every snide comment that goes ignored, he tries harder to rile me up.

If nothing else, my silent treatment is god-tier.

And my patience pays off, because a few days into our cold war, he makes a grave error.

He enters his computer password while I'm looking.

We're in our stats lecture, so it's a reasonable mistake. He can't expect me to always be watching this closely. But I'm so hyper-focused, within minutes I have a list of potential passwords he just typed.

sick0522
sock0522
duck0522
dock0522
dick0522

Spotting the numbers was the easy part. But if the first four letters aren't even a word, then it's pointless. Still, I have to at least try.

So I bide my time. Three regularly leaves his computer unattended beside me, though always locked. It's habit by now.

Which is why later in the newsroom, while we're working

in complete silence, side by side, Three locks his computer without a second glance at me and gets up to leave. He could be going anywhere—to the restroom, to grab a snack, to take a walk. I can't waste any time.

With a quick glance around to make sure I'm not being watched, I slide closer to his laptop and open it.

I know I'll only have a few attempts at this. If I get him locked out, it'll be obvious it was me, and he'll know my silence all week has been a scam.

My fingers hover over the keyboard. I squeeze my hands into fists, then release and type *dock0522*.

Wrong.

I swipe a hand over my mouth, my heart hammering. I glance toward the door. Then I try again: *duck0522*.

Wrong.

My stomach turns. Below the password bar, a little message reads, *1 attempt left*.

If I get the next one wrong, I'm screwed. I take a deep breath, second-guessing myself. Maybe it wasn't *d*. Maybe it was *s*. "Sick" or "suck" or "sock."

I squeeze my eyes shut, going with my gut, and type *dick0522*.

When I open my eyes, I'm staring at Three's open browser, where he was doing research for a campus crime story for Angelica.

And like the official victory cheer of dicks everywhere, I have one singular thought: *I'm in.*

I navigate away from his browser, checking his minimized programs. I search his desktop, then his folders, until I find one labeled "Torch" and, inside, a document called "Ideas."

It's almost too easy.

The program bounces open, and I skim over the list. It's longer than I expected, and . . .

Different. Much different than I thought it'd be.

I hold my breath as I read line after line about the lack of diversity on campus, the benefits of counseling available in the health clinic, self-defense classes at the gym, campus safety developments, a university alum managing a project for further space exploration, a group of law students working to prevent Greek-life hazing.

It's all so good, it almost hurts to read. Not only is it clear he's a good reporter, but he's *focused* on reporting. While I've been focused on him.

Maybe I could have come up with some of these ideas too, if I hadn't been so single-minded in my mission to best him.

But I'm here now. I may as well finish what I started.

My gaze drops to the last item on the list: the planned demolition of one of the university's affiliated housing complexes, which is the most affordable housing option and partially dedicated to students with families.

A noise behind me makes me jump, and I turn toward the door. But Three isn't back yet. Brent, who does IT, is messing with one of the computers on a desk at the back of the room.

Still, it's enough to remind me that my time is limited.

I close the document and lock Three's laptop, my hammering heart slowing as I return to my work. I hear the door open at the exact moment I have a terrible thought.

His laptop was closed.

I shoot a quick glance at Three's computer, which sits open, screen black. I lose some dexterity in my panic, and every word I type next has an error. My screen becomes a collection of red squiggly lines.

Three drops a snack bag of salt-and-vinegar chips on the desk. Then he sits, pauses, and looks over at me.

I keep my gaze focused on my own computer, but his prolonged stare has an unexpected effect on me. My fingers stutter on my keyboard, seizing up.

"Stop looking at me," I mutter, squeezing my hands into fists and popping my knuckles. I muster some strength into my voice. "Yes, I have many thoughts about your choice in snack food. No, I don't want to engage long enough to voice them. Just know I'm silently judging you."

"I bet you've never even tried them," he says after a long moment, turning back to his computer. He grabs the bag and tears it open, the smell enough to burn my nose.

"Seriously?" I shove his chair with my leg. "Eat those somewhere else."

The bag rustles as he fishes out a chip and pops it in his mouth, crunching loudly. He makes a satisfied sound, then offers the bag to me.

I push his hand. "Get away."

"Try one."

"I'd rather drink bleach."

He shakes the bag. "I bet you won't be saying that once you try one."

"What makes you think I haven't?" I hiss, finally turning toward him.

Three dips his head, gazing at me from under his lashes. My heart gives a disloyal extra thump. "You seem like the type who'd judge without giving something a chance."

The way he's looking at me, I feel immediately defensive. Arguments claw their way into my mouth: *I gave you a chance, and you ruined it. We could have been friends. How dare you accuse me of being the problem here.*

I clamp my mouth shut against all of them. Because I'm starting to understand Three, and one thing I can't do is seem like I care. It's like Dara says about dating: *If you care, you lose.*

I shoot Three a cool look. "I don't have to eat shit to know it'll taste bad. Everything has a stench to it—even shit personalities."

Three's smile puckers, but he isn't mad—he's pleased. And I realize belatedly that in my panic about being caught, I broke my silent treatment. He got a rise out of me, putting me behind in our little war once again.

But that's just fine, I reason as I climb into bed that night. Because my next hit is going to be so huge, it'll send his head into space.

* * *

I draft the Buckeye Crossing story in a matter of days, using an interview with the only person I can get to talk to me. Her name is Kate, and she's a single mother on the brink of being kicked out of her building so they can replace it with luxury campus-affiliated apartments.

I'm surprised how deep this story ends up going. Beyond forcing people out of their homes, it hadn't occurred to me until she pointed it out just *who* the university is targeting: low-income and nontraditional students, who make up a significant portion of our diverse students. It reeks of hypocrisy from a school so vocal about improving its diversity, which is severely lacking in general but especially for a school of its size.

But of course, Kate and I both know the truth: money trumps all.

Mel loves the story so much, they show it to Angelica as soon as I turn it in.

"Calling out the school, especially about the diversity stuff—that's bold, Wyn," Angelica says, her mouth curled in a half grin. "You know, my first year, I was the only Black girl on my floor, and in the bathroom, this girl used to always make comments about how gross my hair was if she saw a strand on the shower tile or in the sink or something. After a few times, one of my friends I met in the BSA"—the Black Student Association—"told me I should report her to my RA. Tell me how the school made me sit down for mediation about the whole thing. *Mediation*. Like there was something to mediate, and not just—'hey, stop being racist.'" She shakes her head. "We try to publish a lot about the lack of diversity at this school. Highlighting the nontraditional students is an especially good move."

I flounder for something to say, but everything rings false. "I don't know if I deserve that much credit," I finally manage, my voice meek.

Angelica gives me a flat look. "It's important, and these students deserve a voice. That's what we're here for—to give people a voice. Maybe the *Torch* doesn't get as many readers as we used to, but it's still our responsibility to report. Your porn story was great—sorry about the typo."

"No problem," I say, even though it's pretty big talk on campus even now, especially after the Tau Delt piece, which is still on their website.

"But this is the stuff," Angelica continues, tapping her computer screen. "If you can keep up this kind of work, I think the Campus Life spot is yours. No joke."

Mel nods along. "That's what I said. One hundred percent."

"Wow, thank you. That really means a lot."

I can't quite swell up with pride the way I want to, though.

I try to stifle the guilt by reminding myself that it's *my* writing they're praising. And Three might not have gotten Kate, or anyone else, to speak to him about it in the first place. I can't imagine him sitting in her kitchen in the half-abandoned Buckeye Crossing complex, listening to her story and her worries, and handling both with the same level of care that I did. It might have been his idea, but it's still my work.

When I return to the grunt desk, I have Three's undivided attention.

"Can I help you?" I ask lightly as I open my browser to research some football stats for Aaron, one of the sports writers.

"Do I get to read it?" Three asks with a smile. "Your big story that's got everyone so hyped?"

I shoot him a withering look. "Yeah. When it goes out next week."

His smile curls up at the corners, almost cartoonish. "What's it about?"

"Oh, we've actually got a great headline planned. It'll just say, 'MYOB, Three.'"

He laughs. "Wow, okay. I get it. Worried I could whip up something better for them?"

I guffaw, turning to stare at him. "Are you kidding me? I don't worry about you at all, Wellborn."

FIVE

When school first started, I used to hang out in the lounge a lot, hoping to meet people on our floor. But no one seems to use the lounge alone unless they're studying, and the girls who'd come out here in groups were always too tight-knit for me to join naturally. It's not easy, making friends. I'm not practiced at meeting new people after years with the same group, all of us having met when friendships were forged over cartoons and parent-planned playdates. I must have missed the lesson on forging new friendships, and putting yourself out there for friends is as hard as dating—maybe harder.

Now I sometimes hang out in the lounge when I need a change of scenery to help me concentrate. Which is what I'm doing—working on an anthropology assignment—when Dara and Madison come in from the stairwell.

". . . use mine and they'll never even know," Dara is

saying as the door swings open. She waves her phone under Madison's nose.

Madison giggles as she pushes Dara's hand away. "That would be deceitful."

"The way I see it, the Lord put me in your path to help you get some fine ass in college." Dara twirls away from her with a flourish, grinning when she spots me. "The two of you—so resistant to getting your world rocked."

"Um, that's not what I'm resistant to," I say as Dara flops onto the couch across from me.

"I can't lie to my parents," Madison says, taking an open chair. "And I don't think I'll find a nice Christian boy who wants to have a serious relationship on Buckonnect."

I try not to let it show on my face how pleased I am that they're joining me in the lounge, and how quick I am to abandon my schoolwork to hang out. I'm so desperate for friends, I'd risk my GPA at this point.

"Maybe not," Dara cedes with a shrug. She looks at me. "But you're not looking for a nice Christian boy."

"I'm not really looking for anything."

"But that's the best part," Dara says. "You don't have to be *looking* for something. It's, like, harmless flirting at its very baseline. If you want to get railed four times a week, that's on the table too. Or on the bed, or in the shower . . ." She laughs at her own joke.

"Oh my god," I say, laughing, while Madison turns a shade of red last seen on a vine of ripe tomatoes.

"Please tell me you aren't getting railed in our shower," Ellie says from our doorway. She must have heard Dara's voice, because a few seconds ago, that door was firmly shut. Now she holds it wide, her foot shoved against it. "Or at least that you're cleaning it afterward."

Dara laughs, waving her off. "I haven't even met anyone for real. Seriously, I'm a"—she cups a hand around her mouth, whispering the last word—"virgin."

"That's not a bad thing," Madison says, scandalized.

I feel a rush of defensiveness. If Dara is admitting this, then I may as well back her up. If nothing else, at least from Madison's judgment. "No one said it is," I reply. "I am too."

"I am, obviously." Madison holds up her hand to show off her purity ring. It was one of the first things she told me about when we met on move-in day. She's had it since middle school, when she took her purity pledge.

Ellie props our door open and comes out into the lounge. "Is this our big teen-movie confession moment? I'm not a virgin, you fuckin' nerds." But she's grinning as she sits, softening the blow.

"Hey, I'm trying my best here!" says Dara. "I spent all of high school studying and doing extracurriculars and killing myself to get into college, and now that I'm here, I'm like . . . Tons of other people made it here and have already done everything I didn't do. I want *experiences*! I want to go on a date. I want to get laid *just once* in my life, at least!"

I'm startled to hear that Dara, who is so open about her

online dating life, might be as inexperienced as I am. It's a little comforting, but I also know that if she keeps going for it as hard as she is, it likely won't last. Dara is thin and pretty. She knows how to talk to people. She'll bag a boyfriend by the end of the semester, I bet.

When you're fat, dating is like shopping for jeans—most stores don't carry your size, and the ones that do are limited and often not the style you want, and even if you do manage to find the right style, they'll gape in the waist or sag in the bottom or hang low in the crotch. Finding the perfect fit sometimes feels impossible.

"Hopefully more than once," Ellie says to Dara. Then she looks at me. "You could probably use getting laid too. Stressed-out as you are all the time. Or weed does wonders for that if you aren't interested in sex."

"I didn't say I'm not interested in sex."

Dara brightens, but Madison speaks first, wide-eyed. "Have you all smoked weed?"

"No," I say at the same time Dara says, "I haven't." She doesn't even seem to hear me as she continues, lamenting, "God, I haven't done *anything*. This blows. Someone better offer me drugs or sex soon, or I'm gonna lose it."

Ellie snorts. "Keep saying that loud enough, and one of those douchebags down the hall will definitely offer you something."

"Ew, no." She slumps into the couch, lifting her phone. "I like Buckonnect better. More potential for something . . . *not* that." She flicks her hand in the direction of the boys' hall.

I shake my head at her. "Your Buckonnect obsession is a problem."

"You'd get it if you'd play."

I shoot her a flat look. "Do you know what guys who don't know what I look like will say when they find out? Majority of them would not like to be surprised by a fat girl—trust me."

Madison's eyes widen. "Don't say that!"

"Why not? It's true," I reply.

She flounders for a second. "You aren't *fat*."

"It's not a bad word. I'm fat. I'm not embarrassed by it. But I have to be realistic about how other people view fatness."

Madison flushes deep red. I feel Ellie's gaze on me, assessing.

Only Dara seems unaffected by my words.

"Well, I'm Black," she says, "and Buckonnect hasn't been all that bad for me. This school is super white, right? So I just tell them right off the bat that I'm Black."

Madison makes a choking sound.

I feel a rush of guilt for assuming dating will end up being easy for Dara. I hadn't considered what the experience is like for someone who, outside being thin and pretty, is also Black on a mostly white campus.

It makes me wonder about that early Buckonnect article I wanted to write, and if Three and I both missed the real story—the human aspect of Buckonnect, rather than the tech itself.

"And how does that work out?" Ellie asks Dara, looking genuinely curious.

Dara shrugs. "I get unmatched with a lot."

Madison gasps. "That's horrible!"

"I mean, yeah, but they were gonna be horrible either way. Better to learn the truth early before I get invested."

"And you don't find that at all upsetting?" I ask. "I don't think I could handle telling everyone I match with that I'm fat and having a bunch of them unmatch with me right away. I'd probably cry, no joke."

"But then you end up matched with someone who already knows, and it doesn't matter to them," Dara says. "That's the upside. And the other thing is, you only have to tell them if you're worried they'll ghost you once they see what you really look like. If you never plan to show them, then it's a—you know, a—"

"Moot point," Ellie supplies.

"Exactly," Dara says, pointing at her. "Moot point. If you're only looking to blow off steam with some harmless flirting, you don't have to say anything. Then it's just fun."

"Except flirting"—I swirl my hand at her—"is not fun for me."

She flattens her mouth. "Practice makes perfect."

"My humor translates better in person."

"I'm not sure your humor is translating anywhere," Ellie says.

"Okay," I say loudly. "*Wow*. Thank you."

Ellie shrugs. "Sorry."

"You'll see." Dara pushes to her feet. "When I get Madison talking to boys on my Buckonnect so her parents don't find out—"

"I'm not doing that," Madison says primly.

"—that's when you'll want in." Dara points at me. "You'll see how fun it is."

She retreats to their room. Madison trails her, shoulders stiff.

Ellie stands, watching them go. "Do you ever think we might be scarring Madison for life, living with the three of us?"

A laugh bursts out of me. "I think she's a month away from begging for a new room assignment."

Ellie shoots me a smile. And for the first time all semester, I feel a little bit like we might be becoming, if not friends, at least friendly.

The next edition of the *Torch* goes out right before fall break, as everyone is preparing to head home for the long weekend. Dara and Madison took off last night after classes, and Ellie is packing up to leave now.

For the next few days, I'll be the only one here. My parents will be working the Renaissance Faire for the entirety of our break, and I don't want to waste what little money I have on the bus to get there only to sit around, alone, exactly as I would at school.

My Buckeye Crossing story also went out in this week's

edition of the *Torch*, which has been bittersweet. After the porn ban story swept campus, I hoped this would do the same. I imagined people petitioning and writing emails to the administration about the treatment of the students living there.

That didn't happen, though someone did start a GoFundMe for Kate to buy a car, which has gained a little traction. I'm happy people want to help her, but it isn't nearly the impact I was hoping for. Kate is only one person affected by the Buckeye Crossing demolition.

Some people say news today is only considered newsworthy if it's sensational. And even though I know the story is good, and that it matters, and, most importantly, that it'll look great in my portfolio, I don't enjoy feeling like those people are right.

With nothing else to do and a long, lonely weekend ahead of me, I leave the dorm. It's nice, at least, to be the one going, rather than watching Ellie leave me behind in our quiet suite.

My feet take me to the *Torch* office, but as I near the room, I'm surprised to see a light shining from beneath the closed door.

I have it half open when it occurs to me that it could be Three inside. After statistics this morning, I should be avoiding him. From the narrow look he shot my way in our lecture, he's at least suspicious about the Buckeye Crossing story. And as much as I've been practicing the confident bravado of someone who *definitely got the idea on her own*, a rush of nerves chased me out of the classroom the second our professor stopped talking. I hid in the building across the street until I was sure he wouldn't be hanging around outside, waiting to confront me.

Now I've walked straight into his trap—or, I guess, the trap he didn't even know he'd set. Because when he looks up from the grunt desk, there's a brief flash of surprise across his face.

His expression instantly sours, not unlike my stomach suddenly.

"Don't look so guilty," he says, sounding smug despite the lid he's clearly holding on his rage. "I might think you did something wrong. Something . . . *dirty.*"

I give him a prim smile, hoping I don't seem as rattled as I feel. "I have no idea what you're talking about." The door swings shut behind me. I can't help but notice we're entirely alone.

"Really?" His brows arch up, the picture of shock. But I can tell he's biting down on the insides of his cheeks to keep his temper from showing. After a second, he gives me a knifelike smile and pats the chair beside his. "Then why are you hanging out by the door like you're about to run?"

I bark out a laugh, willing it not to shake. "Run? From what?" I approach the grunt desk and drop into my seat. "I was just deciding if I wanted to get a little space from you for once. But it seems like you've missed me."

"Like an infectious disease," he replies.

I shoot him a sideways look, smirking.

"I know you stole my idea." He swivels toward me, his gaze like lightning. The arm of his chair bashes into mine. "I'm even kind of impressed. I didn't expect you to stoop this low. So tell me, how'd you choose 'dick'? Over all the other possibilities?"

"I don't know what you're talking about, but it sounds . . ." I wiggle a hand, indicating the iffy direction this conversation is taking. And to someone without a clue what's going on, it would be *very* iffy.

"This is the part that's really getting me." He turns his computer toward me, showing an activity log. In the center is a highlighted group of lines detailing a couple of failed log-in attempts. "I had a weird feeling last week. It was the day with the salt-and-vinegar chips, wasn't it? I knew something was off."

I draw up every ounce of confidence I can muster, readying the words I've practiced for days, mouthing them to myself between classes and lying in bed at night. I had to be prepared for this moment, knowing Three wouldn't let it slide without the accusation.

"Three," I say sweetly. "Honey." I can tell I've earned the desired effect when his eyebrows slant down sharply. The pet name definitely rankles. "You think you were the only one who knew about Buckeye Crossing? Do you think you're *that much* smarter than everyone else here? You are not that special. When you wrote that Buckonnect story, I didn't accuse you of stealing from me, even though I had the same idea. It's called *news*, babe."

His gaze flattens, hardening. I feel a head rush so intense, I don't think I'll ever need to do drugs in my life. This high is enough for me.

"This is how the news *works*," I continue. "We all know how to find it. That's why we're here. Maybe when you were editor-in-chief at your little school, everyone felt the need to run every story by you, but we work for the *Torch* now. I don't need to run my stories by you, and I'm not desperate enough to steal from you." I reach over and tap the edge of his computer. "I see you leave this thing lying around all the time. And if I knew someone broke into my computer, I'd be a little less worried about my 'newsworthy ideas'"—I punctuate the finger quotes with a sweet smile—"and a little more worried about, I don't know, my saved passwords, my banking information, the pictures I don't want anyone to see . . ."

His cheeks go splotchy red, signaling I've hit my mark.

"Ah," I say, nodding. "Didn't think about your nudes, did you? Tough break." I reach over and pat him on the back, shocked to feel how hot his skin burns beneath his shirt.

Three shrugs me off, swiveling toward me with bright, angry eyes. "You know what? That's fine. Because if whoever broke into my computer was hoping to use any of my other ideas, they'll be pretty disappointed when they find out I've already written every story."

I try to keep the surprise off my face. "You—" I backpedal before I can say something stupid. "What, your big stories about how beneficial Greek life is to campus, and how legacy students deserve more respect?"

Three smirks, but there's an edge to it I've never seen before. "Sure, we'll go with that hard-hitting news." He pushes his chair back, gathering up his stuff. "By the way, that stats assignment was pretty tough, huh?"

My stomach dips with sudden dread. "Whatever."

"You looked sick when we got our scores. Not doing well?"

I suck in a breath, glaring up at him. "Don't even *look* at me in class."

His face breaks into a delighted grin. "Sure. You first."

He's halfway out the door when he stops and leans back in. His expression has lost all its fury, replaced with something wicked. "And if whoever broke into my computer stole my nudes, well, I guess I just hope they enjoy them. I'll sleep easy knowing they made it into the hands of someone so desperate to see me naked." His grin stretches impossibly wide as I gape at him.

Then the door swings shut, leaving me with nothing but my erratic, pounding heartbeat.

I feel like the last person left on campus.

I know it's not true. I see other people walking around, though few and very far between. My floor is empty, my RA gone, and at night, when everything is quiet, it feels like I'm the only one in the building.

By the second night, loneliness creeps in. I'm in my room,

a movie playing on my laptop and every light turned on, while I mindlessly scroll social media. I pass people from high school at a football game, someone in a pumpkin patch, so many pictures of falling leaves, Dara with a younger girl who looks just like her, Madison with some churchy quote, and, of course, nothing from Ellie.

Then I go to my recent searches and click the name at the top. The one I've looked at far too many times.

Three's profile is private, and I have enough pride not to request to follow. All I can see are his tiny profile picture and the description: *third*. Nothing else. Is his entire personality being the third?

"So annoying," I huff, rolling onto my side.

I'm starting to wish I'd gone home, even though the house would be empty too. But at least Mom and Dad would get back from working the Renaissance Faire before I went to bed. They'd arrive smelling like fried food and dusty dirt, using accents and lingo they no longer need away from the faire. One of them would have spent too much money buying something useless but pretty from a new vendor. The other would be toting a turkey leg for me, wrapped in greasy paper.

I miss my parents in a way I didn't quite expect. They've always been very hands-off, and I grew up doing a lot on my own. I learned how to pack my own lunch and do my laundry and use the stove long before anyone else I knew. But despite that, my parents still felt present in my life, especially in their influence over my interests. When I got older, I was dying to get away from the Ren Faire and their *Lord of the Rings* obsession. But right now I'm torn between my constant, niggling annoyance with them and my yearning for our old, broken-in couch and one of a thousand *Lord of the Rings* marathons, obsession or not.

I wonder what Three would do with the *Lord of the Rings* thing in his arsenal. He has to suspect *something*. But if he knew for sure, I bet I'd hear about it constantly, like I did back home—"my precious" and "POH-TAY-TOES" echoing down the halls of my school for years. Most of them didn't even know who Éowyn was, and probably still don't.

Bitterness floods my mouth, and I flop onto my back. I need to focus on something else—not my loneliness, or my surprising bout of homesickness, or my preoccupation with Three.

I stare at my screen for a long time before downloading the app I've been resisting for so long, Dara's words echoing in my head.

A harmless, fun distraction.

WELCOME TO BUCKONNECT

Buckeye nuts rain down my screen, bouncing as the app loads. I enter my gender identity and the gender or genders I'm seeking. Then it takes me to a basic campus map, where a few buildings are available to choose.

Pick your favorite campus landmark, the top of the page reads.

I tap a classroom building at random, and it generates a username: *pomerene1765*.

Then I'm bounced into a chat.

hitchcock444: hey wanna see my hitchcock

I wrinkle my nose, swiping away. I land in another chat.

morrill2012: hey
pomerene1765: hi
morrill2012: you on campus?
pomerene1765: yeah. you?
morrill2012: yeah. looking to link up. you hot?

I make a grossed-out noise and swipe away. How does Dara possibly enjoy this?

I'm about to close out the entire app when a line pops up in my new chat that makes me pause.

hayes6834: would you rather always have BO or always smell BO on everyone else?
pomerene1765: lol what??
hayes6834: idk I thought it'd be a good opener lmao
pomerene1765: I guess I'd rather smell BO on everyone else?
hayes6834: sounds miserable. I'd rather have it.
pomerene1765: yeah but then you're repelling everyone.

if everyone else smells bad at least it's EVERYONE. plus
then there's less expectation for you to shower regularly
and wear deodorant every day. imagine the time you'd
save.

hayes6834: that's a well thought out answer

pomerene1765: yeah I've been told I'm a really deep
thinker

When he doesn't respond right away, my heart sinks. Maybe
this is it.

I go back to the main page and block the other two users,
then delete our chat history.

My phone buzzes a second later. Hayes has responded.

hayes6834: would you rather spend a year in prison or a
year at war

pomerene1765: prison. I'm a pacifist.

hayes6834: I might be too soft for both

pomerene1765: that's very brave of you to admit. so
you're not one of those "I'm so badass, I'm so macho"
beating your chest, arm wrestling kind of guys?

hayes6834: nah I'd get snapped like a twig

I actually laugh out loud.

hayes6834: would you rather have a rumor go around
that's terrible but a lie or embarrassing but true?

pomerene1765: are we just playing would you rather all night?

hayes6834: oh sorry did you have something else in mind?

I freeze, expecting the worst.

hayes6834: I don't know any other games except twenty questions and that seems risky on this app. come on, humor me. do you have anything better to do?

Of course, *no*, I don't. And this is almost exactly what I was looking for, dropped into my lap just before a third strike. Like maybe I didn't hit a home run, but I at least got on base. Though I don't think this qualifies as even the most harmless flirting.

pomerene1765: probably the lie. I'd rather people think I'm terrible than know some of my embarrassments

pomerene1765: that's a long pause

hayes6834: yeah I'm a deep thinker too lol

hayes6834: this one's hard

pomerene1765: you can't hear me right now but I'm whistling the jeopardy music

hayes6834: probably the truth.

pomerene1765: spoken like someone who's never really been embarrassed before

hayes6834: spoken like someone who's never had anyone think the worst of them

pomerene1765: is this when you reveal you're secretly the softhearted yet misunderstood bad boy?

hayes6834: LOL

hayes6834: no, I'm not nearly that cool

pomerene1765: okay my turn. would you rather have all your texts leaked or your search history leaked?

pomerene1765: wow you really are a deep thinker with these long pauses

hayes6834: lol sorry, my mom needed something apparently right this second that couldn't wait

hayes6834: (she couldn't get her ipad to turn on. spoiler alert: the battery was dead.)

pomerene1765: you're home for break?

hayes6834: yeah it's a fucking joy. you?

pomerene1765: no, my parents had to work. I'm on campus.

pomerene1765: so texts or search history?

hayes6834: ughhhhh idk. probably my texts. I don't need everyone to know how many times I've googled how to spell accommodate.

hayes6834: one more on the books just to send that btw. so embarrassing.

We end up talking much longer than I expected, trading "would you rather" questions back and forth until my phone gives a low-battery warning and, blinking the screen-haze from my eyes, I realize it's after midnight.

pomerene1765: hey I should go to sleep

hayes6834: did I scare you off with the ketchup/mayo thing?

His last question: Would you rather drink a full glass of ketchup through a straw or eat half a jar of mayo with a spoon? Both instantly activated my gag reflex.

pomerene1765: yeah when I have nightmares I'll know who to blame

hayes6834: I've been blamed for much worse

pomerene1765: there's that misunderstood bad boy persona coming out again

hayes6834: I'm starting to think it might actually be my alter ego.

And somehow, despite my having every intention to go to sleep, we end up talking for another hour, until he finally admits he's exhausted.

But it's his parting message that really gets me.

hayes6834: I'll think of some good questions for tomorrow

And when I wake up late in the morning and grab my phone, I have a notification from Buckonnect waiting: *3 messages from hayes6834.*

SIX

When fall break ends, campus explodes with energy, and focus shifts to Halloween weekend. Suddenly all anyone can talk about is costumes, parties, and, most "importantly," the Greek Row haunted house competition.

My Halloween plans consist mostly of my bed and movies so scary, I'll have to watch through my fingers. Maybe talking to Hayes. We finished fall break with an endless scroll of messages between us, eventually shifting from "would you rather" to favorite anything. I couldn't tell you his favorite movie or what music he likes, but I know his favorite vegetable is asparagus, his favorite Olympic sport is swimming, and his favorite ride at Cedar Point is Blue Streak (*for the best Cedar Point souvenir: whiplash,* he said when he answered).

So you can imagine my surprise to find myself on Greek

Row, dressed like a sad birthday girl in a costume cobbled together by Dara using scraps of whatever she could find—a birthday sash borrowed from a girl down the hall and a party hat from the pack Madison used for the *Trolls* costume she did with her church group. Mascara is tracked down my face like I've been crying.

It wouldn't have taken much convincing for me to give up my non-plans for actual human interaction, but Dara still begged me to come. Apparently her friends Yasmin and Kayla are, in fact, dating now, and she didn't want to third-wheel. Because according to her, Halloween is a romantic holiday—even though her friends didn't do a couple costume. Instead, all three of them are dressed like Black Disney characters created before any of us were born—Yasmin as Larry Houdini from *Don't Look Under the Bed*, Kayla as Penny Proud from *The Proud Family*, and Dara as Nebula from *Zenon: Girl of the 21st Century*.

Kayla and Yasmin are easy to be around—the type of people who treat you like a friend they've known forever, even when you've met only a handful of times. They fold me into their group without hesitation.

"Which house do you think is the most unsettling?" Yasmin asks as we make our way from a sorority where the haunted house was a timed maze, and you only won candy if you made it through in under ten minutes. "Like, *haunted house aside, I would not go in either way*?"

I pop a piece of banana taffy into my mouth. "All of them."

Dara snorts, leaning around me to say to her friends, "Wyn is very anti-Greek."

"That's not true. I read the whole *Percy Jackson* series, like, six times."

Kayla and Yasmin blink at me, like twin owls.

"If you don't understand her jokes, don't beat yourself up about it," Dara says to them. "It's kind of the Wyn experience."

I frown, and it deepens as Dara and her friends make a turn up to the next house. We've been sticking to the sororities, but now we're standing in front of Tau Delta Pi, which, according to Kayla, has been lauded by *Two Minute News*'s Halloween update as *the* haunted house to see. At the front door, a tall guy in an LED mask with a big, scary smile and oversized round eyes monitors the line, letting groups through in intervals.

Inside, someone screams. I jump, bumping Kayla, and nearly choke on the banana taffy. I swallow it quickly, forcing it down my dry throat.

"Are you nervous?" Yasmin asks with a laugh.

"I'm fine," I lie. The truth is, I'm not good with scary stuff. The first three houses were tolerable, because they felt fake and harmless. But when we step through the front door of the Tau Delt house, it's pitch-black inside.

"Oh, I hate this," Kayla murmurs, and I think she's reaching for Yasmin's hand, but she gets mine instead.

We're two steps in when a mask lights up beside me, so close that I scream. The guy wearing it laughs.

Kayla squeezes my hand, inching closer. I use my free hand to feel across the wall until I find a door.

"Through?" Dara whispers.

"Through," a deep voice says from behind us.

The four of us shriek—even Yasmin, who *swore* when we started this night that she's not scared of anything. But when we rush through the door, I'm the last one into the next room, and my sash gets stuck on the doorknob. In the extra few seconds it takes me to unhook myself, I realize I've been deserted.

The door slams shut behind me.

The next room is big, and even though I can see enough to make my way through, there are two curtain-covered doorways to choose from. I have no idea which one the others just disappeared through.

A sound plays—a cackle, followed by a low siren—and masks start to light around the room: three, then seven, until I lose count. I'm frozen in place until I realize they're only hung on the walls, not worn by anyone.

As soon as I have the thought, one breaks from the wall and charges at me. I scream, sprinting for the next doorway and barreling through the curtain. My party hat is knocked askew, and I tear it off, crumpling it in my hand.

In the hall, Christmas lights flash on and off, briefly illuminating everything. Music starts playing—a garbled, demonic remix of "Sleigh Ride." Then a door opens, and a huge guy walks out in an LED Santa mask, dragging a body bag behind him.

I rush through the next doorway and into another dark room. The hall was so bright, my eyes need to readjust again, and I realize that's the point—they don't want us to be able to see too well.

What a nightmare.

In the kitchen, I'm harassed by two more masked guys, who chase me toward a staircase that takes me up to the second floor. As I make it to the top, I hear Dara yelp somewhere in the distance.

Getting close.

I pause to gauge whether I heard Dara from the right or left. I make a right, going with my gut. At the end of the hall, the next turn is blocked with furniture. I reach for the only door, but the knob is locked.

I whip around at a noise behind me. A figure turns the corner, carrying a baseball bat wrapped in LED barbed wire and wearing a mask with an eye patch made from three vertical lines. He whistles as he twirls the bat around in a lazy circle.

I try the door again, jiggling the knob hard. Then I give up, twisting into the dark corner, and put on the calmest voice I can muster.

"This is kind of cheesy."

The guy stops, the bat falling limp at his side. Then he laughs. "You *would* be the one to make this as little fun as possible."

My heart gives a jolt of recognition. "Seriously? Isn't that eye patch a little on the nose?"

Three pushes his mask up, his grin lit by the orange glow of the barbed wire. "It spoke to me."

"I'm sure it did. God, get a personality or something." I move to pass him, but he steps into my way, leaning an arm against the wall. When I try the other direction, he shifts, putting the bat out to trap me.

I glare at him, pressing back into the corner. "You're not allowed to touch me," I hiss. "I read the rules."

Three tosses his head back and laughs. "*Touch* you? Is that what you've been dreaming about, ogling my nudes every night before bed? You wish, Evans."

"I did not—I did not *steal*—" I splutter, rage curling my hands into fists. I blow out a harsh breath, straightening my shoulders. "You know, you're pretty obsessed with the idea of me having your nudes. Is that what you're into? Thinking about me, looking at you?"

It should have an ice bucket effect. Maybe he'll stop saying it if he thinks I might get the wrong idea.

Which is why I'm so surprised when his eyes narrow, and he ducks his head closer to murmur, "Maybe it is."

My heart lurches up into my throat, and my skin goes so hot, I'm afraid I might *actually* combust. Especially when his gaze drops—and I swear, I *swear* I'm not imagining that he's looking at my mouth.

The door to my left swings open suddenly, and someone yells. I scream, lunging forward, and smack straight into Three.

"Jesus—fuck—Kelly! What the hell?" Three snaps.

"Sorry," the other guy says, laughing. He sounds the least sorry I've ever heard someone sound in my life. "She wasn't moving, and someone else is coming."

I'm too distracted to absorb anything else, because I'm suddenly aware that I'm touching Three in many places—my hands fisted in his shirt, his arm caught around my shoulders, my thigh pressed between his. He's incredibly warm, and he smells *so* good. . . .

I shove him away hard enough that he drops the bat. It hits the rug with a thud that shatters the moment. With the orange glow gone, I can't read Three's expression. He pulls his mask back down, ensuring I never will.

He grabs the fallen bat and prods it into my back, urging me toward the opposite end of the hall. "Don't make me chase you."

I can't form a single coherent thought as I dash for the exit.

The rest of the haunted house passes in a blur, my brain caught up on the second floor, replaying those few seconds over and over again. I can practically still feel his arm around me, and the peppery, woodsy scent of him is fresh in my nose.

I'm still thinking about him long after I've caught up with Dara, Kayla, and Yasmin and we've navigated our way out. Even once we're clear of the house, my racing heart shows no signs of slowing, and I break off from our group before our next destination, begging exhaustion. Their protests that I stay feel nice, but I want to go home and sleep off this entire night.

Maybe I'm touch-starved—and truthfully, that is definitely the explanation—but coming in such close contact with Three, and those few seconds just before, has me feeling . . . a lot of things.

"No, no, stop it," I whisper to myself, smacking my cheeks hard as I make my way back to my dorm. He's the *enemy*.

I'm just lonely, that's it. College hasn't been the social extravaganza I expected, and I read romance webcomics every night before bed. I can admit I thought Three was cute when we first met. So it makes sense—*perfect* sense—that I spend my entire twelve-minute walk home imagining what it'd feel like to kiss him.

I take a long shower as soon as I get inside, then climb into bed in my fuzzy robe. I'm still burning hot and restless, but I can't do anything about it—not when Ellie could walk in at any moment, and not with Three's face lit by the orange glow of that bat so fresh in my mind.

I slide down in bed, pulling my blanket up over my head. I need something to distract me. Something anti-Three.

Hayes instantly comes to mind. A calming presence. The opposite of everything Three makes me feel.

pomerene1765: let me guess. your alter ego won and you dressed as one of the outsiders for halloween

pomerene1765: living out your bad boy dreams one costume at a time

pomerene1765: probably sodapop. tell me I'm right. you have sodapop energy.

But he doesn't respond. Not in the hour and a half it takes me to fall asleep. And not by the time I wake the next morning, sweating and breathing heavily. I'm half out of my pajama top, and my bottoms are twisted up. My face is mashed into my pillow, both of my hands fisted in it. I can still feel the burn of hot palms on my hips, can still see the orange glow in an otherwise dark hallway, and a mask pushed up just enough for our mouths to meet. The hard wall at my back and clothes pushed away as . . .

I sit up, scrubbing at my eyes.

A dream. Only a dream.

Only the hottest, dirtiest dream I've ever had in my life.

It should be the most shocking thing about my morning. But what startles me most is the banging on my door, which I realize is what woke me so abruptly.

And when I swing open the door to see who it is, campus police wait on the other side.

SEVEN

I spend two hours being questioned at the campus police department. It should have taken about thirty minutes, but at some point the cop has to leave the room, and I end up sitting by myself for a long time.

It's only in the last ten minutes of my interview that I learn why I'm here.

"Have you ever bought stimulants from anyone on campus?" the cop asks when he returns. I've finished the bottle of water and two cups of coffee they gave me, and now I have to pee, like, *really* badly. It makes it a little hard to focus.

"No. I don't even know what that is."

After that I get a lengthy explanation, and—plot twist—he just meant Adderall.

"Have you ever sold any drugs to anyone you know— your friends, your classmates, or people you've met on campus?" the cop asks. "Marijuana, ecstasy, cocaine?"

"*Cocaine?*" I bleat. "What is this, the eighties? No—seriously—I've never even *done* drugs! Not even pot! I know that sounds like a lie, but like, it's kind of embarrassing, so—no, I'm not *selling drugs*. Did someone name me?" I stop, going slack with understanding. "Oh my god. Did Three do this? Did he tell you I had drugs?"

The cop makes a note. "Three? Who's that?"

"He's—he's just a guy I've been . . ."

"Dating? Bad breakup?"

"No, oh my god. I shouldn't have even mentioned him."

The cop looks up from his notepad. "Why's that?"

"I'm just—I'm confused why I'm here. Because I'm not doing or selling drugs. I wouldn't even know where to *find* drugs. Where are you getting this from?"

"Were you aware that your roommate, Elizabeth Huffman, has been selling MDMA, Adderall, and cocaine on campus?"

"Ellie . . . *what*?"

They must decide after the big reveal that I couldn't possibly be a good enough actress to pull off that kind of lie.

Or at least that's what I think, until I arrive back at my dorm and find it ransacked. My drawers have been pulled open, my closet emptied, clothes piled on my floor and bed. My desk is trashed, the drawers removed completely.

I should have expected it, especially when the resident director accompanied me in to pack a bag. I'll be staying on a cot in Dara and Madison's room for the night while they get Ellie moved out, and the RD is adamant that we are not allowed to speak to her when she returns.

"My parents are freaking out," Madison says as she, Dara, and I make our way to a table in the dining hall that evening. I've barely eaten all day, and I'm irritable and hazy from lack of food.

"Mine too," says Dara. I feel her hesitant look. "Have you talked to yours?"

"Not yet." I twirl an unappetizing bite of pasta on my fork. "They're at work."

But even knowing my parents won't see any of my messages until late this evening, when the Renaissance Faire is over for the day, I check my texts again just in case.

Nothing from them, but I do have a notification from Buckonnect.

hayes6834: am I the only person in the world who didn't read the outsiders in middle school?
hayes6834: anyway I looked him up and idk if I want to be compared to rob lowe. that's my mom's celebrity crush.

I can't help my sigh of relief. Ellie is going to be all anyone asks me about for at least the next week. It's nice to know I have someone I can turn to if I need to talk about nothing at all.

pomerene1765: she sounds like a woman of taste
pomerene1765: we probably shouldn't share our

costumes anyway. flying a little too close to the sun.

hayes6834: you mean you aren't dying to know who I am?

pomerene1765: no I am. but I think I like it better this way

"We can help you clean up tomorrow," Dara says, drawing my attention back to her and Madison. "When they let you back in your room."

I exhale, finally finding a smile of my own. "Thanks. It was a total war zone in there."

Madison leans in, lowering her voice. "So, neither of you knew about Ellie? I knew she smoked weed, but I had no idea she was selling anything."

"Nope," Dara says. "But I will be holding a grudge that she never offered me any."

I nearly choke. Smacking my hand against my chest, I croak, "She was selling *hard drugs*!"

The table next to ours goes quiet, a few of them looking in our direction.

Madison flushes, shoveling a bite of her salad into her mouth.

Dara shrugs. "I'm just saying it would've been nice of her to offer. I didn't mean I wanted to try anything. But for real, she thought the three of us were such dorks, she never even asked? So rude."

* * *

That evening, our RA stops by Dara and Madison's room to let me know I'll be allowed back into mine by tomorrow afternoon. Dara is in the middle of a lengthy explanation about *Proper Southern Ladies: Baton Rouge* as we watch on her laptop, while Madison is on a video call with her parents, discussing her father's sermon for tomorrow morning's worship service.

I should call my own parents, but when they tried me earlier, I texted them and asked to talk tomorrow instead, feigning exhaustion. So far today, I've spoken to the police, my suitemates, my RA, and the resident director. I'm all talked out for now. And nothing I tell my parents will change anything. It's not like they'd pull me out of school or demand a new room. They aren't those types of parents, and anyway, Ellie is gone. The damage is already done.

With nothing else to do, and seeking a little reprieve from Dara and Madison's company, I leave to wander campus, hoping to clear my head.

As I exit the elevator, Lincoln steps through the front door, grinning when he sees me.

"Oh, hey," I say at the same time he blurts, "Hi!"

He adjusts his bag on his shoulder as he crosses the lobby to me. "How're you doing? I heard you can go back in your room soon."

I swallow. Of course Lincoln knows about Ellie. He probably knew before I did. "Yeah, I think tomorrow morning. I'm waiting for someone to give me the okay."

"Whenever she moves her stuff out, the RD will do one last inspection, and then you should be good."

I knew Ellie would be back in the room soon, but the thought of her moving out tomorrow, clearing away every trace of her presence, sends a pang through me like I've lost something.

"Hey, if you want something to do while you wait tomorrow, the library in the geological building opens early. I'm usually there in the morning."

I've worked in the main library since school started, but I've never been to the one in the geological museum. It's smaller, tailored more for the earth science majors.

"Do you go to that library a lot?" I ask.

Lincoln's mouth pulls up in a half smile. "Yeah. I'm in the major." At my stunned silence, he laughs. "Let me guess. You thought I was doing agriculture." He shakes his head, still smiling. "Farm Boy Lincoln strikes again."

"Farm Boy Lincoln?"

"I'm from Cleveland," he says. "My parents are teachers. But there's something about me that makes people think of—"

"Nebraska?"

He stops, gaping at me. "Yeah. It's the name, isn't it? My brother's name is Jason. I can't believe my parents did this to me."

I laugh. "My parents named me Éowyn. At least yours just gives a vibe. Mine is *actually* a character from *Lord of the Rings*."

I don't know why I volunteered this information. Even if someone guesses, I don't normally admit it. It's like saying, *yeah, my parents are obsessed super-freaks.*

"Hey, she's pretty cool, though," Lincoln says, as though he can sense my instant regret. "Éowyn. Not that it's a competition or anything, but if I had to pick a favorite female character from that series, she'd probably be it."

This is why it's nice talking to Lincoln. He's the type of person who makes it easy to volunteer information about yourself, and he *wants* you to feel comfortable doing it. My defenses are no match for him.

It helps that it feels like he wants to be talking to me too. That this could be something like flirting. It reminds me of the feeling I get talking to Hayes.

"Well, Tolkien doesn't give many options for favorite female characters," I say.

Lincoln winces. "I guess that's true."

"But most people would say Arwen, so I'll accept your answer." I duck my head to hide my smile, busying myself with a quick glance at my phone.

"Hey, I have to head up," he says. "I'm on duty tonight. But I'll see you later?"

I nod, moving to step around him. "See you later." It feels sweet, like a promise.

"Hey, Wyn?"

I pause, turning back. "Hmm?"

He shifts from foot to foot. "I should apologize. About . . .

Well, I'm the one who turned your roommate in."

"Oh." I hesitate, then shrug. "I mean, that's your job, right? You're an RA."

"Yeah, but I . . ." He bites his lip, fidgeting. "I told them they should check you too. Because of that girl that came by. We're kind of on high alert for drugs around here—there's been a lot of stuff circulating, and it's not weed. Someone had already reported your room for suspicious activity, and the RAs were supposed to keep an eye out. I thought it was a red flag, but I might have overreacted."

It takes me a minute to figure out what he's talking about. "The girl who tried to get in the building that one night? I only let her in because I'd seen her with Ellie."

He nods. "Yeah. Sorry. I got caught up in the whole thing once we found out she was dealing."

So this whole time he's been standing here talking to me, he's been feeling guilty. That's why he's being so nice. What I might have mistaken as the tiniest bit of flirting was actually his conscience looking for the right time to apologize.

I should've seen that coming. Historically, flirting with cute guys has not been in the cards for me. Normally I'm *too intense*. Today it's guilt and obligation. That tracks.

"It's fine. You were doing your job," I say at last, my voice flat. I fuss with my jacket as I head for the exit. "I'll see you later."

"Hey, Wyn, I really am—"

"It's fine!" My voice comes out too loud for the small

lobby. My smile feels like a grimace as I push my back into the door. "It's all good."

I catch a glimpse of his pained expression before I twist away again, letting the door swing shut between us.

As I replay my conversation with Lincoln, feeling hot with embarrassment and incredibly stupid, my feet carry me across campus to the *Torch* office. I don't have anything to work on, but at least it'll be empty.

Or so I think, until I step inside and spot Three at the grunt desk.

"I can't believe you're allowed out of the frat house on a weekend." As soon as the words leave my mouth, I remember our last encounter—the haunted house, and the dream I had after.

My face burns. I pray he doesn't notice.

"Oh, it's easy. You just put on your fraternity-issued ankle monitor before you go," Three replies. "No big deal."

"That little slice of freedom, and you chose to be here, alone, when you could be shotgunning beers with your bros?" I drop into my seat, eyeing him. "Seems like an odd choice."

"Does it?" He turns his computer away from me before I can see what he's working on. "Doesn't look like you had anywhere better to be either. At least I have things to do. Let me guess, you just missed me?"

I wish I had a witty comeback for this, but I'm not exactly

firing on all cylinders today, and all I can come up with is, "Mmmpf! Yeah, right!"

"Or maybe you're here to explain why the cops showed up at my door this afternoon saying you named me during a drug interrogation." When I jerk around to look at him, Three raises his eyebrows. "Talk about something I never thought I'd hear."

"That was an accident." I shouldn't even comment, but I'm so startled, I can't keep the words in.

He tilts his head. "Are you a drug dealer?"

"No! Of course not. Don't be ridiculous." I turn away from him, wishing I had my laptop. It looks highly suspicious that I have nothing to work on right now. I fiddle with my cup of pens, spilling them across my desk.

"You're seriously giving me nothing?" He shakes the arm of my chair. "Hello?"

"Stop that." I smack his hand lightly, not expecting the zing that shoots straight to my chest. I jerk my hand back, my gaze snapping up to his.

But it's not like an electric shock, where we both feel it. Three simply pulls away, his movements lazy as he shifts back in his seat.

It makes me angry. Why can't I hate him properly? Why don't I find him disgusting? His personality is terrible. He's smug and vindictive and bad at winning but worse at losing. So why do I want to kiss him so badly, I can barely see straight? It would take almost nothing to grab him by the front of his shirt and yank him toward me. The distance is so minimal, I can feel the warmth from his body even now.

My heart picks up speed as I imagine it—his brows jumping in surprise, eyes narrowing, gaze filling with heat as I pull him closer. The rough, frantic meeting of mouths. His gasp at the bite of my teeth on his lip.

"Why do you look like you're plotting my murder?"

It's like having reality grab me by the throat. Everything comes screaming back in twice as sharp—especially the smirk on Three's face.

"Or were you thinking about something else?" His mouth hitches up in a grin. "Hard to tell with you. Could be bloodlust or . . ." His lips twitch, and I get his meaning.

My frustration mounts. After my encounter with Lincoln, I'm already on edge. I came here to relax, but clearly that's off the table. I feel like I've been walking in circles, searching for silence. It figures that the first time all year I want to be truly alone, I can't seem to find an empty space.

I gather my pens, shoving them back into their mug. "My roommate got kicked out for selling drugs. I didn't know why I was being questioned—I thought you put them up to it somehow. Because you're sick and twisted and probably could blackmail campus police into making my life hell. That's why I mentioned your name."

"Sick and twisted," Three repeats, something changing in his expression—too quick to catch before he covers it with a smile. "I'm glad you think so highly of me. Hey, don't run off on my account."

"It's not on your account." I shove my chair back and stand. "I've already had a very long day. The last thing I need is to subject myself to the *literal* worst person I've ever met."

He lets out a halting laugh. "Not at all an overreaction. Perfectly reasonable, as always, Evans."

I don't look back as I leave the office, the door slamming shut behind me.

EIGHT

The resident director wakes Dara and me late the next morning to let us know Ellie and her parents are moving her things out. Madison is already long gone for morning worship service, and Dara and I both agree it's too weird to stay in the room with Ellie next door. She takes off to get lunch with Kayla and Yasmin, and even though she invites me along, for once I want to be alone.

It's a warm and sunny afternoon, despite now being November, so I head to the crowded Oval to soak up what will probably be our last nice day of the year.

And to finally talk to my parents, a long overdue phone call.

"I can't believe you didn't call us yesterday! We could have . . ." Mom's next words are lost under the swell of bagpipes. They're taking their lunch break at the faire, and there is no escaping the noise.

"Sorry!" Dad shouts, his voice so loud, the speaker crackles. I pull the phone from my ear. When I put it back, he's still speaking. ". . . for the closing ceremony this weekend."

"I didn't know they had bagpipes in medieval times."

"Of course they did!" says Dad. "The bagpipers are the biggest hit during Highland Weekend."

"And you know Highland Weekend is very popular now," Mom says. "Ever since *Outlander*." She whistles, and I imagine she's fanning herself.

"Okay, moving on from your kilt obsession," I say.

"Should I get a kilt?" Dad asks, and his voice is just quiet enough that I know he's turned toward Mom, the phone all but forgotten. "I could get a kilt. I bet I'd look pretty handsome."

Mom laughs.

"Hey, parents? Did you forget the part where I said my roommate was—" I stop short, glancing around. I'm sitting alone, but there are clumps of people close enough that anyone could overhear. Word of Ellie's arrest spread like a boulder rolling downhill in the dorm. I don't need to kick another one over the ledge.

"Of course we didn't forget," Dad says. "Are you okay, Wynnie? Do you want to come home this weekend?"

"No, it's fine. You'll be busy with the faire anyway."

"You could come to the faire!" Mom says. "It might take your mind off things. A turkey leg and some face painting."

"And you love the Washing Well Wenches!" says Dad.

"The bus only takes an hour and a half," Mom adds. "We could have you back home in no time."

To sit alone at the house while they're at the faire? Or worse, to sit alone at the faire while they're working? Pass. Double pass.

"It's okay. I have work this weekend." I yawn, sleepy from the warm sun. "And I'll be home for Thanksgiving soon anyway."

My parents go quiet, and I hear frantic whispering.

I sit up, my eyes snapping open. "What's going on?"

"Your dad was supposed to tell you," Mom says.

Dad makes a strangled sound. "That's not what we—"

Mom shushes him. Then, sighing, she says, "Wynnie, we have a con that weekend. The Duel of Dragons Convention."

"On *Thanksgiving*?" I can't keep the shock and hurt out of my voice.

"Well, it starts on Friday, but we planned to drive up Thursday night. It's in Chicago."

I swallow hard against the lump forming in my throat. Why am I so worked up over this? It's not like Thanksgiving is a huge tradition in our house. Sometimes we don't even eat turkey. We usually visit my grandma in the nursing home in the morning, and we finish off the night with whatever fantasy show or movie has caught their interest, or occasionally—you guessed it—a *Lord of the Rings* marathon.

Thanksgiving isn't that special in our house. So why do I feel like crying?

"You could come home the weekend before," Mom says quickly, reading the emotion in my silence. "We can do all the Thanksgiving stuff then!"

I clear my throat. "Yeah, maybe. I have to go. I have work."

"Oh—okay. Hey, Wynnie, if you change your mind about coming home this weekend, we can make it happen."

"I'm fine," I say. "Love you. Bye."

I hang up before either of them can respond.

With Ellie gone, work and class have somehow become my refuge. We may not have been friends, but the empty side of our room is unsettling to look at, especially the bare mattress. At least when I'm out of the dorm, I feel marginally less alone.

I'm in the library, pushing an empty cart back after restocking some shelves, when I spot Jennie at the front desk, a notebook open in front of her.

I redirect the cart. "Didn't midterms just end?"

Jennie glances up, then groans. "Try telling my professors that. It's all projects all the time for us, baby." She drops her highlighter and leans her chin in her hand. "When they invent time travel, I'm going back to warn high school Jennie to run. Run far away. Don't even think about college."

"I thought engineering was your passion."

Jennie's eyes narrow, and after a moment, she laughs. "I can never tell when you're joking."

Someone clears their throat loudly behind me, and I turn.

Our boss, Scott, stands a few feet away, fists on his hips.

Ah, damn.

"Wyn," he says, motioning me over.

Jennie quickly slides her study materials off the desk and into her lap.

"Hi," I say to Scott, grabbing the cart again. "I was just putting this back."

"I'll do that. You-know-who is up on the third floor. Could you go take care of it, please?"

I balk. "But—I did it—"

"Let him know if it happens again, we'll have to ban him from the library." Scott grabs my cart. "Please handle it discreetly."

I watch his retreating back, my fists curling at my sides. "Handle it discreetly?"

Jennie winces.

"Handle it *discreetly*." I push up the sleeves of my sweater, hot with rage. "Sure. I can be discreet."

"Wyn," Jennie says as I head toward the back office. I shove open the door and round the desk, dropping into the chair.

Jennie follows. "What are you doing?" she whispers, glancing over her shoulder in the direction Scott went.

"Handling it discreetly."

I unlock the computer and pull up the Wi-Fi access-point dashboard. Technically, I should not know how to do this. I'm not even authorized to use the dashboard—it's supposed to be accessible only to the library managers. But we had some issues with the library Wi-Fi a few weeks ago, and while the IT team was working on it, they gave the whole staff access so we can temporarily reset the access point.

Which is why I know exactly how to reset it, and how to shut it off completely.

"Scott is going to flip his lid," Jennie says.

"Then he can come up with the solution next time."

There isn't a noticeable change when the Wi-Fi goes down. Not right away, at least.

I shove back the chair and march past Jennie, heading for the stairs. The noise starts when I'm halfway up to the second floor, everyone realizing it isn't a glitch or a momentary drop of connection.

I find Porn Guy on the third floor, a frustrated sneer on his face, slamming at his computer keys. I saunter toward his table, shaking from the adrenaline rush. I put both hands on the back of the chair across from him and lean down.

"Having fun now?" I ask.

He looks up. Irritation melts from his face, and his mouth pulls into a closed-lip smile.

"I warned you," I say. "Get out, and don't come back."

I wait for him to pack his things, arms crossed and foot tapping out an erratic beat against the floor. People look in our direction, distracted from the loss of Wi-Fi when there's a bigger, better drama happening.

When Porn Guy reaches the elevator, I head for the stairs.

I'm waiting at the bottom when he leaves the elevator, strolling toward the exit.

"Wyn!" Scott hisses, emerging from the back office.

Jennie stands behind the desk, eyes wide.

"He's gone," I say as I approach them, willing into my voice a calmness I'm certainly not feeling.

"What were you thinking?" Scott's face reddens, and he points into the office. "In here. Now."

It occurs to me, as my bravado fades, that I can't afford to lose this job. So it's a relief when Scott spends the next ten minutes tearing into me for abusing my access to the Wi-Fi dashboard yet doesn't actually fire me. But I just *know* he's going to make me suffer for this one.

"Wyn," Sabina calls when I walk into the *Torch* office a couple days later. "Hey, perfect timing." She waves me over to her desk.

I drop my bag at the grunt desk, relieved that, for once, Three is nowhere to be seen. It's the only upside to my entire week. Between Ellie getting kicked out, my parents skipping Thanksgiving, all the penance Scott has had me doing since I shut off the Wi-Fi the other night, and the statistics quiz I bombed yesterday, I'm exhausted.

It must show, because Sabina does a double take as I approach her desk. She opens her mouth, then shuts it and glances at Christopher. He's hovering beside her, bent at the waist to peer at her laptop, but he straightens at her look.

"We wanted to give you a heads-up about next week's edition," he says.

Sabina clears her throat. "We heard the student who was caught dealing drugs out of her room was your roommate."

A flush warms my cheeks. "I didn't realize everyone knew about that already."

"They will soon," Christopher says. "That's what we wanted to tell you. Three pitched a story about your roommate's arrest. He's almost done, and we plan to run it."

Fury lights like a fuse in my chest, and I feel it burn all the way down. "Three pitched it. Of course."

"It's an important story," Sabina says. "This wasn't just pot on campus. These were hard drugs."

"And if we have a hard drug problem sprouting up, people need to know," Christopher adds. "It's dangerous, and we don't want a repeat of last year." At the hint of resentment in his voice, I'm not sure if he means the girls who overdosed or *Two Minute News* getting to the story first.

"Yeah, I know," I say, my voice sharp. Sabina and Christopher exchange a look, and I take a calming breath. "Sorry. I know it's an important story. It's fine."

"We want to make sure you won't feel hurt by this," Sabina says gently.

"It doesn't even say your name. So it shouldn't be a big deal. Plus, we need to run it before someone else does." Christopher gives me a look. "You know that'll be worse for you."

Well, that answers Christopher's motivation.

"I get it. Run the story." I take a step back, glancing toward the grunt desk. "Is Three around?"

I try not to betray my mounting rage. My hair could stand on end at any moment, and I want to be far from this office when it happens.

"He left a little while ago," says Christopher.

I nod slowly. "Okay. I gotta go. But thanks for the heads-up."

"Wyn, are you sure—" Sabina's words are cut off by the door as it swings shut behind me.

In the hall, my hands curl into such tight fists, my knuckles crack. I am one wrong step away from exploding. I trek across campus, my fury beating out a steady drumbeat: *Three. Three. Three. Three.*

I don't know where to start. I don't even know what I want from him. No one has ever ignited this kind of anger in me before, and I've never had someone push my buttons so precisely.

But maybe it's because I had a hidden Three button all along, designed just for him to push. He's the only one with my rage manual, and he knows exactly how to turn me on.

Wait, scratch that. My brain is running away with itself.

I'm standing outside the gym when I finally slow. The last time the universe dropped him in front of me for a fight, it was right here, just as he was walking out of the aquatic center. That was the day I declared that it's *on* between us. That

I'll ruin every chance he has—of winning the Campus Life spot or getting into journalism school at all. Over my dead body.

Or over his, I think as I push open the door to the aquatic center.

It's the longest shot in existence, expecting to find him here a second time. So I should be way more surprised when I step through the doors to the lap pool and spot his lone figure cutting a backstroke down one of the lanes.

When he reaches the end and turns, he pulls into a free-style stroke, face down in the water.

I could yell his name. I could wait until he's finished. But I do neither. I want to catch him off guard. I want him shocked.

I set my bag on the ground and whip off my shoe, weighing it in my hand, then chuck it into the pool. I miss by several feet, and it splashes into the next lane over.

Well, I never claimed to be much of an athlete.

It still gets the job done. Three pulls up short, yanking off his goggles. He whips his hair out of his face, breathing hard as he turns in a circle, his eyes finally landing on me. He looks sufficiently surprised to see me, which eases a small bit of the wrath that's squeezing my insides.

"Jeez, Evans, are you tracking me or something?"

"Lucky coincidence."

He ducks under the lane rope, diving down to the bottom of the pool. When he comes back up, he's holding my shoe. He swims toward me, pushing his hair back from his face before resting his elbows on the ledge. He gazes at my shoe, then up at me.

"Were you trying to maim me?"

"Worse."

He grins, hauling himself out of the pool. I find myself—stupidly—deeply distracted by the fact that he's both shirtless and wearing those tight, knee-length swim shorts professionals wear. I catch myself staring one beat too long, and my gaze flicks up to his face.

Before Three can say anything, I ask, "What, do you think you're Michael Phelps or something? What's with the Olympic swimwear?"

Three smiles. "Are you wishing it was a Speedo?"

"The only thing I wish about you is that you'd go missing." I make a grab for my shoe.

Three pulls it back, holding it out of my reach. "I don't think so," he says with a laugh, warding me off with his other arm. "So, I take it they told you about my next story?"

My anger rages anew. I clench my teeth so hard, my jaw pops. "What is your problem?"

"People deserve to know what's happening on campus," he says calmly, as though I'm the unreasonable one.

"And *you* had to be the one to write it? Give it to someone who can at least be objective!"

"I'm very objective." He drops his arm when he's sure I'm not going to make another move for my shoe. "I objectively think that if coke and Molly are being dealt on campus, the students deserve to know. This isn't some kid passing out his prescription Adderall for extra cash. It means there's probably some serious dealing happening, and that makes everything else a lot more dangerous."

I slap my hands together in a sarcastic clap. "Hero to the people."

He scowls. "Evans, someone died last year."

"I know that!"

"I'm also *objectively* interested to hear how the administration plans to handle Ellie's case, when a Black student was expelled and served thirty days in jail for dealing pot on campus last year. It's called holding the school accountable for how they plan to treat a white girl from the suburbs in comparison. The code of conduct says they can expel her for possession, yet I heard your roommate was in class three days ago." I'm about to admit I didn't know any of that when he holds up my shoe like a microphone. "Care to comment?"

"You're an asshole," I say into the shoe, then make another swipe for it. He holds it out of my reach with a smirk.

"It's called *news*, babe." That he somehow commits everything I say to memory is so completely irritating, I could scream. "Besides, I don't know why you're so surprised I wrote it. I'm the literal worst person you've ever met, remember? What did you expect?"

"Fine. Write the article. I don't care." I reach for my shoe again, but Three passes it behind his back and into his other hand. I fumble for it before I realize letting him see me struggle is another point in his ledger. I let out a growl of frustration, straightening. "And keep the fucking shoe." I put a hand on his chest, shoving him backward.

He drops my shoe and latches onto my forearm, yanking me with him. I don't even have time to struggle.

We both tumble into the pool.

I come up gasping, weighed down by my jacket. I manage to tread water with significant effort, reaching for the wall. Three must take pity—and probably doesn't want me to actually die, maybe, I think—because he loops an arm around my waist. He pulls me to the ledge, and I grab on, panting. I struggle out of my sopping jacket and haul it out of the pool. It slaps onto the tile like a dead fish.

Three hovers so close, his legs brush mine underwater.

"I hate you." I push him away from me, splashing him in the face for good measure. "I wish we'd never even met."

He shakes the water from his eyes, shoving his hair back again. "Yeah, I know."

As I put my hands on the ledge and try to pull myself out of the water, I'm hindered by my heavy clothes and—ah—embarrassing lack of upper-body strength. He drifts close again, his hand skimming my hip. When he loops his arm around my thighs, I grab onto him with a gasp, kicking against his hold. He loses his grip, and I slide back down until we're aligned, pressed together.

"Try something. I will take you down with me, I swear to god," I growl, arms tight around his shoulders. His skin is warm, a sharp contrast to the cold water. And he's *solid*. Not overwrought with muscle, but strong.

I didn't expect that.

His gaze on my face turns intense, and his jaw tightens briefly before he glances away. "Grab the wall," he says, using one hand to remove my arms from around him. "I'm trying to help you."

This time, when he bobs low to curl his arm around my thighs, I let him. With his free hand, he grabs the wall, leveraging me up. I flop onto the tile beside my jacket.

As I push myself up, Three's hand lingers on my calf. I feel it burning through my jeans. His gaze is heavy, sweeping down and catching. When he looks away quickly, I realize my wet clothes are clinging, every detail of my body cast in stark relief. I instantly regret having removed my jacket.

"Don't look at me." I put my socked foot on Three's chest and shove him away roughly, and his head bobs beneath the water.

I'm not ashamed of my body, but I'm only human. And I don't want to know what he was thinking—

It doesn't matter. I don't *care* what Three thinks of me, and especially not my body.

"If I freeze to death on my way home, just know I spent my last moments wishing for your demise," I say, grabbing my shoe from where he dropped it. I pull it on over my wet sock, then start wringing out my sweater, my hair, and the bottoms of my jeans.

Three hauls himself out of the pool, passing me on his way to the bleachers. All his intensity is gone, replaced by easy smugness. He grabs a towel lying on the lowest bleacher, then tosses it over my head. I scrabble for it, tearing it away from my face.

"Don't freeze to death, Evans." He backs away, heading toward the locker room. "Things would be so boring without you."

NINE

When the Ellie story comes out, it confirms Christopher was right: it doesn't say my name anywhere in the article, and it doesn't say Ellie's either. One small blip of light in an otherwise dark, dismal situation. Because while it doesn't name either of us, the article does name our building, and word of mouth takes care of the rest.

I spend days fielding questions from everyone who recognizes me. If I knew Ellie was dealing the whole time, if it was only coke, Molly, and Adderall, or if she had a bigger stash, if I knew who was buying from her. This includes a contributor for *Two Minute News*, who hounds me for a comment outside my dorm building one afternoon until I threaten to call campus security.

It's exhausting. Worse than the porn ban thing. At least with that, I could say it was a mistake and move on.

But this is the cold, hard truth. *The news, babe.*

The worst part isn't the questions or the whispers or the way everyone in my dorm suddenly wants to get stuck in the elevator with me, just for five minutes of gossip.

It's that Three is being treated like Anderson fucking Cooper around the newsroom now. Even Christopher, who normally avoids the grunt desk like we're diseased, stops by a few times this week to chat with Three about some story ideas.

I can feel myself losing ground on the Campus Life spot. The Buckeye Crossing story was good, albeit stolen, and the porn ban story blew up, but for all the wrong reasons. Even I have to admit Three has good instincts. He didn't only write about Ellie—he called out the administration for answers. His piece is both informative *and* thought-provoking. It puts more eyes on the situation than just ours. Now the whole school is watching.

As Three soaks up the glory, I stew in the seat beside him, wondering if I'll ever write something that outshines what he's produced so far, or what he has under his belt for later. I've seen his ideas. I know they're good.

What if I've been wrong all this time? What if he *is* actually a better reporter than I am?

I'm so caught up in my newly discovered inferiority complex that I've hit a wall on my own stories. I'm floundering in a sea of mediocrity.

But while I don't have any groundbreaking ideas, I do

have Hayes. He's the best salve to Three's burn. Whenever Three riles my life up, it's Hayes who brings me back down. Which is why this is how I traverse campus 90 percent of the time now: head down, phone in hand, either typing out a message to Hayes or reading one from him. If one of the only friends I'm going to make at college is through a dating app, then I may as well lean into it. And it's no chore talking to Hayes. Most of the time, he follows what I'm saying even when I have trouble putting words to it, or when I change subjects without warning.

Like now, when we're in the middle of a conversation about which campus dining hall is best.

hayes6834: but the STIR FRY

pomerene1765: do you feel like you caught imposter syndrome when you got to college?

hayes6834: oh I had it way before I got to college

pomerene1765: seriously? I thought I was so smart in high school. like easily the smartest person in my class

pomerene1765: I realize that sounds very.........

pomerene1765: hold on, I'd like that stricken from the record, your honor.

hayes6834: consider it stricken

hayes6834: but I'd believe you were

pomerene1765: flattery will get you far in life

hayes6834: but will it get me

hayes6834: wait I hit send too fast

hayes6834: on second thought I don't want to make the joke

hayes6834: is this what it feels like to give your jokes thought before you say them out loud?

I pause at a stoplight, waiting for the walk sign, and smile. This is what I love about talking to Hayes. His friends might think his sense of humor is bad, but he always makes me laugh. And better, he always takes my mind off whatever stressors are causing my recently discovered, university-stamped eye twitch to flare up.

pomerene1765: it's a whole brand new world out there now, huh?

hayes6834: but imagine all the long, uncomfortable silences I'll miss out on

pomerene1765: yeah you would be depriving yourself of those little moments of self reflection.

hayes6834: very important for growth

hayes6834: but we were talking about you. so imposter syndrome?

pomerene1765: right. so it's not that I was the SMARTEST. I wasn't valedictorian or anything. but I thought I was the best at what I do. you know what I mean?

hayes6834: I'm pretty sure that's part of the traditional college experience. getting here and realizing the competition wasn't all that steep in high school. but that doesn't mean you aren't smart or good at what you do. it just means college is a bigger challenge. wouldn't it be boring if college was as easy as high school?

pomerene1765: I've never complained when something came easily to me. I don't think I'd mind if college was one of those things. especially the things I WANT to be good at.

hayes6834: that's fair. I might be better off if I didn't look at everything that was a little hard as a challenge.

pomerene1765: are you one of those super competitive people who ruin game night?

hayes6834: I can't even LOOK at a monopoly board

hayes6834: I've been told I take things way too seriously. it does tend to drive people away.

pomerene1765: I think people could stand to take a few things more seriously.

hayes6834: now who's flattering who?

pomerene1765: gotta see if it'll get me anywhere.

hayes6834: pretty bold for someone who doesn't want to meet

He's right—I did say I think we're better off not meeting. It's come up once more since Halloween, though I can't tell if Hayes wants to or not. He's never said it straight, and I'm always the one to draw the line. Maybe that's what he's looking for, though—my line in the sand, setting a boundary I don't want him to cross.

But the longer we talk, the hazier that line gets. It feels like we're friends now, but Buckonnect is still a dating app. I don't know if this is a precursor to dating, per se, but my experience is pretty limited. If Dara were interacting with someone on Buckonnect this long, she'd probably say they were "talking." More than friends, less than dating.

It's possible we've been building expectations. After all, it's not like Hayes and I don't flirt, in our own way. (It's a relief, really, to find that he's not all that great at it either.)

But I don't know what I'd do if he found out what I look like and ghosted me. I like to think he wouldn't, but how well do I know someone I've talked to for only a few weeks, and anonymously at that? What would I do if he got angry at me when he found out? Some people's fatphobia is *that* bad, where he might feel tricked and embarrassed, and lash out as a result.

I know the deeper I delve in, the higher I build this rickety tower. One wrong move—one wrong word—and I'll topple the whole thing. And the longer I talk to Hayes, the more I like him, which means I could be setting myself up for some serious damage. But rather than slowing down, I keep picking up speed, liking him a little more with every conversation, even knowing everything I'm risking as I do.

I turn the corner and freeze, backing up a step. Lincoln stands outside our building, head tilted down to his phone.

I haven't spoken to him since we ran into each other in the lobby over a week ago. I did dodge him once, mostly because

I'm still embarrassed. And I'm frustrated that Lincoln naming me somehow led to Three writing the article that's the talk of campus now. I don't care about being inconvenienced by the police, but if I hadn't mentioned Three, he might never have known to write his article in the first place.

And truthfully, I'm worried Lincoln will try to apologize again the next time he sees me, prolonging my humiliation. I just want to pretend it never happened and let time heal the wounds.

Lincoln finishes typing and glances up as he turns, starting in the opposite direction as me. At the same time, my phone buzzes with an incoming message from Hayes.

hayes6834: so you haven't acknowledged that the stir fry is the best dining hall option which is the deciding factor in the best dining hall

I glance up from my phone, staring after Lincoln.

A coincidence, right? A total coincidence. I could probably find half a dozen people in the vicinity who are on their phones right now. He could have been looking up directions or the hours for a store downtown, or even been on Buckonnect talking to someone else!

But something pulls at a string in my brain, and I remember that first conversation I had with Lincoln, when I told him I'm the only one at the *Torch* who wasn't editor-in-chief in high school. He mentioned imposter syndrome then—what did he say exactly? That imposter syndrome is the first freshman-year souvenir you get, and that he's already had it and dealt with it.

I blink at his retreating back, my mind whirring as my phone buzzes with new messages.

> **hayes6834:** I probably shouldn't have said that about meeting. I was joking, not giving you a hard time. but you know me. I'm naturally good at saying the wrong thing.
>
> **hayes6834:** seriously I could win olympic gold in a foot in mouth event
>
> **pomerene1765:** sounds like you're pretty flexible
>
> **hayes6834:** I've definitely never heard that before. usually everyone says how rigid I am.
>
> **hayes6834:** okay I realize that could
>
> **hayes6834:** you know what
>
> **pomerene1765:** it's so impressive to see an olympic athlete in action.
>
> **hayes6834:** ha. thanks.

I stare in the direction Lincoln went. The puzzle fits, albeit loosely. After the stuff with Ellie, I can confidently say he takes things seriously, the same as Hayes. And when I think back to fall break, when Hayes and I first started talking, I don't remember seeing Lincoln around the building. Hayes wasn't on campus either.

I'm getting ahead of myself, as usual. My imagination is

running wild with possibilities that, simply put, are astronomically unlikely. I might be nearly failing statistics, but even I can see the probability is low. Lower than low, even.

Still, my stupid, romance-webcomic-reading heart wants to believe it could be possible.

"So, what'd you think of my article?" Three angles toward me, leaning his elbow beside his laptop. We've been working in silence at the grunt desk for at least an hour now—Three on some research for Christopher, and me on my next story. I'm covering the university's spending on new VR training equipment for the football team, which is nearly double the budget they denied the nursing school for similar equipment only a year ago. I emailed the pitch to Mel yesterday and got the green light in minutes. It soothed a bit of the sting that's lingered in the wake of Three's success with his story on Ellie. If he's going to beat me, it won't be because I didn't try.

Beside me, Three has been blessedly quiet, immersed in his task. But now I know it was all a ruse, luring me into a false sense of security so I wouldn't see it coming when he finally decided to strike.

"You've been awfully calm," he says when I don't respond. Out of the corner of my eye, I see him slide off his reading glasses and set them beside his computer, a sign he's settling in for a nice, long battle. "I figured it'd be on as soon as I walked in today. Especially after you tried to kill me last week."

I don't rise to his bait. Instead, I reach for my coffee and take a slow sip.

Three leans closer, sliding his arm along the edge of the desk. His fingers tap out a slow, steady beat an inch from my wrist.

I tuck my hair behind my ear and tap lightly at my earbud. Truthfully, I'm not listening to anything, because I don't want to risk missing something happening in the newsroom. But Three doesn't have to know that.

"Ah." His fingers brush my cheek as he plucks the earbud from my ear and whispers, "Can you hear me now?"

I freeze, feeling that whisper down to my toes. Which makes me furious, because *why* does he have this effect on me? I should be disgusted by him! I should not feel hot all the way to the bone.

"Keep your salt-and-vinegar breath on your side of the desk," I say, jerking to face him. But he's leaning closer than I anticipated, and we end up nose to nose.

I flinch, but Three doesn't react. Which means he wins by default.

He smiles as he relaxes back in his chair.

I make a grab for my earbud. "Give it back." Each word comes out bitten off.

Three closes his fist around it. "Admit you tried to kill me first."

I pry at his fingers. "You are such a child."

He grins, tightening his grip. "Just say that last week was attempted murder by shoe."

I would rather die than give him what he wants, even if it's ridiculous.

"Or you can keep trying to hold my hand," he says, one corner of his smile hitching higher.

I dig my fingers into the shell of his fist. It occurs to me that I'm playing right into his hand like this, but my next best bet is to ignore him until he caves, which would be hard to pull off now. Plus, I wouldn't put it past him to simply leave with one of my earbuds.

No, he'll have to be bested. And to do that, I have to match his energy.

"Is that what this is about?" I ask, putting on an *oh poor you* face. "Can't get anyone to hold your hand naturally, and so touch-starved you're this desperate? I'm happy to take on a charity case, Three." I close my hand over his fist, flattening my palm against his fingers. "You don't have to trick me into holding your hand. You just have to ask. *Very* nicely." I lean in, brushing my thumb over the underside of his wrist. *"Wyn, I'd do anything for you to hold my hand for a minute. I'm so, so lonely."*

To my dismay, Three smirks. "You know, Evans, you might be going into the wrong major. I think you could do great in a creative writing course. You're incredibly good at making stuff up in your head." His expression shifts, and it's like someone put him in italics. Everything turns suddenly pointed. "Unless you're projecting a little. 'I'm so, so lonely' sounded kind of like a confession."

Three opens his hand under mine, his fingers closing

around my wrist. I feel my earbud press right against my thudding pulse. My breathing turns shallow.

Three lowers his voice to a murmur. "Does that feel better?" He strokes his finger over my forearm for good measure.

My toes curl. Because the sad, pathetic truth of it is *yes*, it does feel better. It feels incredible. It feels almost as good as last week, when he had his hand on my calf in the pool, or when he looped his arm around my thighs. I am acutely aware of how warm he is, and after this, after the pool, after Halloween, I can perfectly imagine what it would feel like to curl into him and be held.

Three reaches up, pressing the backs of two fingers to the spot right between my eyes. My synapses start firing at hyperspeed. I imagine the inside of my head looks something like the finale of a fireworks show.

Three gives me a rueful smile. "Never go to Vegas, Evans. They'll clean you out."

"What the hell are you two doing?"

I flinch, and Three's hand falls from my brow. His other releases me slowly, like he's barely fazed by the fact that our managing editor is standing over us now, staring like he's caught us doing something salacious.

Three shakes my earbud in his palm like he's about to do a dice roll, then drops it unceremoniously on my side of the desk. "Wyn's a little feverish. I was just suggesting she go to the clinic. I mean, look at her." He jerks his chin in my direction, shooting me a sly look Christopher can't see. "She's all red."

My heartbeat ramps up, my blood boiling. "You know, he might be right," I say, my gaze never leaving Three's face. "I am feeling sick all of a sudden. Like I could throw up at any moment."

Christopher makes a grossed-out sound. "Okay, well, if that's the case, go home. I don't have anything else for you today."

"I can't—I have a story."

"Not anymore," Christopher says. "You got scooped."

Time slows as Christopher flips his phone around to show me his screen. *Two Minute News* is pulled up, a fast-talking girl with red hair relaying my own story to me, with about a hundred holes. She even gets the cost of the equipment wrong.

"But—but she didn't even get it right! I can still finish this. I can work on the nursing school angle—"

Christopher cuts me off. "It's old. Time to move on." As he pockets his phone again, his attention shifts. "Three, I want to talk to you about what you've been working on." He nods toward his own desk, which is on the other side of the room.

Three takes his time getting up, letting Christopher stalk a few feet away. I watch him go, speechless with blindsided shock, until Three leans a hand on the grunt desk and angles his face toward me. "Left your diary lying around, huh, Evans? Tough break."

My gaze flicks up, settling on his smug expression. "This was you."

He puts a hand to his chest, brows raised in silent question.

"Yes, *you*." I stand, because I can't let him look down at me another second. "You gave my story to *Two Minute News*!"

"Now, why would I do that?" He leans closer, lowering his voice. "And how would I even know what you're working on?"

That I don't know. But the look on his face says it all—this was him. And he wants me to know it. "I don't know why you'd do it. My guess is you're worried."

He snorts. "Worried? About your hard-hitting VR equipment story?"

"It *was* hard-hitting!"

"Come on, Evans, if you're going to try to beat me, at least make it fun." He motions to my bag. "I guess it's good Christopher's giving you the afternoon off. You'll have time to come up with a better story. Something worth writing that you didn't have to steal from me first." He taps a finger against his computer with a smile. "You can try breaking into this again if you want, but you'll never get the password this time."

That's what this is about. The Buckeye Crossing story. After the success of his Ellie story, I thought he was over it, but it's clear Three has the patience to pull a long con. He distracted me with these stupid daily battles that fill our ledgers in increments as small as a grain of rice. It's the big hits that truly tip the scales, and they're moving in Three's favor.

As he strolls away, my fury starts catching like dry kindling. He thinks he's so superior. So much better. *At least make it* fun?

I seethe as I pack my things. I'm sick of losing to him. I

want to see him so turned inside out, so upside down, he can't even function. I want to see him panicked.

And I know for a fact he has an exam this afternoon, because I heard him mention it to Christopher earlier.

So I do something truly diabolical. Something I know crosses some very serious lines. Something that, were I feeling just one iota less like my anger could propel me into space, I might hesitate over for at least a moment.

But I'm too furious to second-guess myself.

I grab Three's glasses from beside his computer and swiftly head for the door.

It doesn't take long for regret to set in, but by the time it does, I'm in too deep. There's no going back to the *Torch* office to return the glasses now—not when he could easily catch me. I have to see it through.

I don't go far. There's an elevated walkway between two buildings that overlooks the street, which I know Three passes on his way to class. I'll have a perfect view of him heading off at his usual easy pace and then, if I'm lucky, sprinting back to the *Torch* office in a panic once he realizes he's missing his readers.

As soon as I see him pass by, I'll sneak to the office to slip his glasses back where I found them. He'll assume it was me, but he'll never be able to prove it. Just like I can't prove he gave my story to *Two Minute News*.

However, I've overlooked one small potential snag in my

master plan. I realize it when my phone buzzes in my hand, and a message from a number I've always had but never used pops up on my screen.

THREE:
Give them back.

I glance up the road toward the building the *Torch* office is in, and then quickly in the other direction. He hasn't passed by, which can only mean he hasn't left yet.

I contemplate his message, deciding how to respond.

THREE:
I swear to god Evans

ME:
This feels a little bit like a threat. Maybe I should talk to my adviser. I feel distinctly unsafe.

I smirk as I send off the message, imagining his face turning redder with every passing second. Any lingering regret evaporates in a wisp of steam. He's playing right into my hands.

It's especially gratifying when his next text comes through.

THREE:
You should.

A thrill travels all the way to my toes. I've got him. I've *got* him. Oh, if only I could see his face—

I suck in a breath.

Because when I glance up from my phone, Three is standing down on the sidewalk. He isn't rushing by in a panic or frantically texting me. He's staring straight up at me, not moving, his expression stony.

I hiccup in surprise and slap my hand over my mouth. My heart picks up speed as I stare down at him. A cold sweat starts between my shoulder blades.

Three's expression is deceptively calm as he watches me. When he finally moves, it's a subtle shift. He angles to his right, never taking his eyes off me. I instinctively lean in the opposite direction.

His eyes narrow, and he moves the other way.

I change directions.

Three stops again. Then he seems to make up his mind, shifts to his right, and takes off.

I stumble in the opposite direction, scrambling into the best sprint I can manage. I know Three is in shape, but I hope he's not as fast on his feet as he is in the water.

I tear down the stairs, heart pounding, and shove open the door at the bottom. I don't know what my plan is—to keep running, to hide. But it doesn't matter either way, because when I bolt out the door, it's straight into Three's waiting hold.

As soon as we collide, his arms close around me, tight as a vise.

"Give them back," he says in my ear.

"I don't know what you're talking about." My voice comes out shaky and breathless. I try to push away from him. "Let go."

"Give them back first, and I will." He pulls his head back to look at my face. We're so close, I can see every individual eyelash, faint freckles I've never noticed before, and the dip in his lower lip.

"I don't have—hey—!" He has a hand around the strap of my bag, but my protest grabs the attention of a few people passing by. Three and I both notice at the same time, and he blanches.

He releases my bag, stepping back to put some distance between us. Red creeps up his neck in the most delicious way.

I consider running, but now that I have all the leverage—and knowing he'd catch me anyway—I stay put.

"Well, this is a nice change of pace," I murmur, giving the passersby a reassuring smile. "Is this how it feels to be you? Always having the upper hand?"

"I have an exam." He bites the words out through clenched teeth. "Give me my glasses."

"Hmm." I tighten my hold on the strap of my bag. "Maybe if you say 'please' very nicely, I'll think about helping you look for your . . . glasses, was it? At the very least, I'll check my bag. Maybe I picked them up by accident."

His nostrils flare. His jaw clenches so hard, something twitches in his cheek.

I sweeten my smile. "Or I can just go . . ." I move to leave, but Three catches my wrist. Despite the way his body has gone so tense, he might snap at the slightest pressure, his hold on me is gentle.

He takes in a slow breath, then lets it out through his nose. "*Please*, Wyn, can you give me my glasses back?"

I don't know what delights me more—the use of my first name, or the tremor in his voice when he says "please."

I smile. "I would be happy to check if I have your glasses." I swing my bag around and pop it open. I make a surprised sound as I pluck his glasses from where I've stashed them safely in a side pocket. "Oh, look! I did have them. So weird. I have no idea how those got in there."

I hold up the glasses, and Three snatches them, his expression positively murderous.

"Sorry about that," I say, putting all the sugar I can muster into my voice. As he turns away, white-knuckling the strap of his backpack, I add one final blow. "But you know, I could get used to hearing you beg a little."

Three stops, turning slowly back to face me. "You'll *never* hear that again," he says, his voice nearly a growl.

I shrug, trying not to betray the wild, giddy pace of my heartbeat. "We'll see about that."

Three steps toward me, and I force myself to stay rooted in place, not letting the surprise get the best of me. If we're playing a game of chicken, I won't be the one to blink first.

His gaze is cutting. I feel like he can see all the way into the deepest recesses of my brain—the very secret places where him standing this close to me inspires a lot of mental images I don't want to acknowledge.

I hope I look placid rather than lobotomized as I try to keep those thoughts from my face. If he's as good at reading me as he says—or if I'm as bad at hiding my feelings as he's suggested— then it might be a useless effort. Especially when he gets so close that I have to grab onto the front of his jacket or risk being thrown off balance. At least this way, if I go, he's going with me. But the space between us narrows to an inch, maybe less.

He's so *warm*. Especially now, off the rush of his anger. If there's one thing I've observed about Three, it's that his emotions may not show on his face, but they burn hot under his skin. Which is why I know he's not nearly as calm as he wants me to believe right now, because I can feel the heat of him straight through his sweatshirt.

"I thought you had an exam to get to." I tug lightly at his jacket, batting my eyes at him. "Now you've really set yourself up. Because you're on a time constraint, and the only way you're getting away from this is to knock me over or pull away first."

His expression scrunches in faux confusion. "Is that the only way?" He leans closer, ducking his head until we're eye level. I've never been so hyperaware of the inches he has on me.

My fists tighten on his jacket as he dips closer, gaze dropping to my mouth. I am barely breathing, my eyelids fluttering wildly. Three's lips are so close to mine, I can almost feel the brush of them. I squeeze my eyes shut, every muscle in my body coiled in anticipation.

Then he says, "I thought you hated my salt-and-vinegar breath."

My eyes fly open, and I stumble back a step. My fingers slip from his jacket.

Three smirks, straightening. He tucks his glasses into the collar of his sweatshirt, every inch of him smug, from his half-lidded gaze to the slope of his shoulders to the light kick of his feet as he half turns away. Over his shoulder, he tosses me a lazy "I win."

Then he walks away, leaving me standing here to catch my breath, swallow my stupid pride, and slink toward home to lick my wounds, feeling dumber than I ever have. Because now I've shown my hand—that I would have let him kiss me, like the worst kind of fool—and he'll have that knowledge forever, to use whenever he wants. All those snide, joking comments he makes about my wanting him have weight now. Because he knows it's at least a quarter true, and that's a quarter too much to give someone like Three.

I thought I crossed a line stealing his glasses, but I didn't even come close. In fact, I don't think I could find the line if I tried.

TEN

On Saturday, not only is the library deserted, but so is much of campus, everyone flocking to the stadium for the football game. Earlier, as I prepared for work and Dara got ready to meet her friends for the game, she admitted she's supposed to see one of her Buckonnect matches there too. And when she lamented that she doesn't know anything about football, I schooled her on talking points I've heard around the newsroom.

It was just the two of us, with Madison gone for the weekend for her cousin's baby shower, and spending time with Dara alone was *nice*—before she had to rush off to meet Kayla and Yasmin, reminding me that she has real friends, not just someone she shares a bathroom and a common wall with.

Now, in the library, I have far too much time to think—about what happened with Three the other day, how Scott makes my library shifts a living hell, the fact that I still haven't made any close friends, my declining statistics grade, and the rapid approach of my lonely Thanksgiving. Not to mention my distinct lack of ideas for the *Torch*, which my entire journalism school application is riding on. It's a small program, and those of us who want to do print media are being edged out in the day and age of digital news and short-form videos on social media. There are students in the pre-major with a successful fashion blog, a political podcast, and a popular true-crime channel on YouTube. I *have* to find a way to stand out for print journalism. These are the thoughts that consume me, day and night.

As a kid, cartoons make you worry a lot about quicksand, something you're astronomically unlikely to ever encounter. But no one tells you your brain has quicksand too.

Later, as Jennie and I leave the library after closing, we can hear cheers in the distance. The deserted library grounds are a far cry from what the stadium must look like right now—bursting with revelry after our team's win. If we were there, I'd probably be tripping over a grown man in face paint with a beer in his hand.

But it's quiet here. Separate.

I don't like football. I don't think I'd enjoy tailgating. But that feeling of being a part of something—I'd love that. I *want* that.

"I'm a little worried about you, Wyn," Jennie says as we start down the walkway together. My dorm and the lot where she parks are in the same direction.

"What do you mean? I'm fine."

Jennie shoots me a sideways look. "You're stressed beyond reason. Trust me, I'm an engineering major—I can tell on sight when someone's been pushed to the brink."

I blow out a breath. "Well, okay, I might be a little stressed, but that's college, right?"

Jennie's expression turns sympathetic. "Do you want to do something tonight? There's this party—*very* chill, nothing wild. Mostly just hanging out. I'm going there now. You're more than welcome to come." She smiles, reaching over to squeeze my shoulder. "Maybe it'll be nice for you to get out for a while. Relax? Meet new people?"

I'm itching so badly for company, there isn't a single moment of hesitation before I say, "I'd love to."

The house Jennie takes me to isn't far from the Greek houses I visited on Halloween with Dara and her friends. It's a shared house with several roommates, all of whom I met in a flurry of introductions and none of whom I could name now, not for a million dollars or with a gun to my head.

The party is mostly other engineering majors and some of their friends, and Jennie was right when she said it's more hangout than party. *Pulp Fiction* is on the living room TV, and two people are crowding the coffee table with their laptops open, playing some PC game while others watch like it's the Super Bowl.

Overall, it's very easy to be here, mostly because no one

pays attention to me. I sit on the couch and nurse the beer Jennie got me when we walked in, quietly observing everyone. I didn't think about the fact that they'd all be older than me—most of them seniors, like Jennie. There are definitely no other freshmen around.

When my stomach starts to growl, I wander into the kitchen, where Jennie told me to help myself to snacks. She disappeared with another girl a few minutes ago, leaving me to fend for myself.

There's an open bag of chips on the counter, a container of cookies with a little notecard taped to them that says *eat at your own risk*, and a pizza that's definitely been sitting out too long.

I hesitate over the options, then grab two cookies, hoping they'll be enough to at least stop the embarrassing sounds my stomach is making.

I shove both cookies in my mouth one after the other, then return to the couch.

I don't know how much time has passed when I start to feel myself sinking into the cushions.

"Huh," I say aloud. The person next to me shoots me a curious look, but I don't elaborate. Mostly because my tongue feels heavy in my mouth, and my mouth feels a little too stretched for my face, and words are . . .

A little tough at the moment.

I push to my feet, and I'm vaguely aware that my hand has landed atop someone's head as I try to balance myself.

I hear a distant laugh. "You good?"

I plaster on a smile, hoping no one notices anything is wrong.

Because something is definitely *deeply* wrong right now.

I find the bathroom, where I close myself inside and stare in the mirror. My limbs are heavy, and there's this buzzy, tingling feeling under my skin. I blink at my reflection until someone knocks.

I pull open the door. "Sorry," I say, stumbling past them into the hall.

I should not be here, I think. *I need to go home.*

There are three doors at the end of the hall, all of them closed. I knock lightly, whispering Jennie's name, until finally one swings open. Jennie pokes her head out as she tugs her shirt on.

"What's wrong?" she asks. "Are you okay? Did something happen?"

I stare at her, smacking my tongue against the roof of my mouth. "Um . . . I think I ate something . . . funny . . ."

"Oh, fuck," someone behind her says. "She ate the cookies."

"Oh my god," Jennie says, smothering a laugh with her hand. "Wyn! How many did you have?"

I hold up two fingers.

"Five?" Jennie bleats.

I look at my hand. "Oh. No. Um." I try again, managing two fingers this time.

"Oh, thank god," Jennie breathes. "Okay. Wyn, you're

high." She puts her hands on my shoulders, leaning down to look me in the eye. "You'll be fine. It'll pass. Just go hang out on the couch, okay? Hey, Connor, get her some water for me?"

I end up deposited on the couch again, this time with a big glass of water.

"I've never been high before," I say to the guy who sits me down. Or I think I'm saying it to him, until no one responds and I realize he's gone. I settle back against the cushions, resting my glass of water on my stomach. "My roommate was a drug dealer and everything! She never even offered me any."

Now I don't know who I'm talking to. Myself, I guess.

I drink the water, but the weird feeling doesn't subside. Instead, as time passes, it seems to worsen, and the water in my empty stomach sloshes until I feel nauseous.

I can't sit here forever. I want to go home. I know it's not far. The drive in Jennie's car was only a few minutes, and I remember the walk from the Greek houses. It won't take me long to get back to campus.

I push to my feet, setting the empty glass of water on the coffee table between the warring laptops. I unearth my jacket from one of the chairs at the kitchen table. Then I head for the door.

The cold November air bites at my skin as I step outside, and the brain fog clears slightly. I send a quick text to Jennie that I'm going home, along with an apology for eating the cookies.

I'm distantly aware that this is probably a bad idea, but

so is sitting in a house full of people I don't know while I feel progressively worse as time goes on.

I look up directions to my dorm and start on the fastest route. The streets are mostly deserted of pedestrians, and I pass a few other houses clearly in the midst of parties before I finally make it to the main road. No cars are coming, and I'm about to cross when something catches the back of my jacket.

"Hey, Evans, if you're going to get hit by a car, at least don't do it where I have to watch."

I try to whirl, but Three's grip on my collar holds me in place. I blink, realizing he is, in fact, correct—there are cars coming from my right. I don't know how I missed that.

"I figured you would've pushed me," I say, my words heavy and a little slurred.

"Nah, I'm easily traumatized." He tugs my jacket, pulling me back so I'm standing beside him. "Are you drunk?"

I put on the best sober face I can muster as I turn to look at him. He's wearing a university sweatshirt with jeans, his hair mussed under a backward Tau Delta Pi hat. His nose and cheeks are pink from the cold.

I haven't seen him since I stole his glasses—which is the only identifier I'm giving that day. What happened after is too much to even think about.

Not that it's stopped me from thinking about it. Often. With a lot of imagination in use.

Like right now, as I find myself staring at his mouth.

"Evans."

"I am," I say quickly.

Three looks bewildered. "You are . . . ? Drunk? Because you look blasted right now."

"I am . . . not at liberty to say," I decide, turning away from him again. When the walk sign blinks on the other side of the road, I start forward.

Three keeps a grip on my jacket. "You're out wandering at night, wasted?"

"I'm not *wandering*." As we start across the road, I pull at my jacket, twisting from side to side in an attempt to wrestle out of his grip. "I'm *walking*. Home."

"You're walking home, alone, at night, drunk. And you almost just *walked* into oncoming traffic. You could've been the next tragic *Two Minute News* update."

"Don't sell yourself short, Three. I'm sure you'd write it first." But the jab loses some of its impact when I miss the curb and nearly go sprawling onto the concrete.

Three swears as he catches me. "I'm not sure this even qualifies as walking."

"I tripped. That's different. Let me go, please. I'm not telling you where I live." I shoot him a disdainful look. Or what I hope is a disdainful look, anyway. I'm having trouble focusing on his face. "I would *never* give you that kind of leverage over me."

"I already know where you live."

I gasp. "Stalker!"

"I wrote an article about your roommate. Obviously I know where you live. But I'm happy to let someone else take you." He plucks my phone from my hand. "Which one of your friends will come get you?" He holds my phone to my face to unlock it, and I focus on him long enough to see his expression falter.

I grab for my phone but miss. "That's none of your business."

"Dara?" He peers at my phone. "She lives with you, right?"

"That's none of your business," I say like a doll whose string has been pulled.

Three puts my phone to his ear. He waits, waits, waits, and then finally hangs up. "She didn't answer. Who else?" He waves my phone at me. "Who am I calling?"

"I'm literally five minutes from my dorm," I say, reaching for my phone again. "I can make it. I don't need a babysitter."

His expression darkens. "Listen, I'm either walking you home, or someone's coming to get you. One or the other. So you better choose now, or we're walking."

And because Dara didn't answer, and Madison isn't here, and Ellie is a non-option, and I can never, ever let this be the first time Hayes sees me, I relent.

"Fine. But you're not coming inside, and if you use this knowledge against me"—I turn, poking my finger into his chest—"I will end you."

At that, he actually laughs. "I thought you were already trying to do that."

"Trying, sure," I reply as we start walking. "But you're way more diabolical than I am, so I'm kind of having a hard time."

"Well, you came pretty close with the shoe," he says. "Could've given me some kind of head injury."

"You are a head injury. Anyway, you pulled me into the pool! What if I couldn't swim? I could've *drowned*!"

He chuckles. "Oh, come on, Evans. I would've saved you."

I scoff. "Yeah, right. Maybe after letting me struggle a little. Or a lot. You're like those animals that play with their food before they eat it."

"I haven't eaten you yet," he says, giving me a long look from the corner of his eye.

My heart picks up speed. I don't know why—probably the drugs.

Three grins, dragging his gaze forward again. "So, were you at some big party? Smashing beers to celebrate that game?"

"Is that where *you* were?" I cover my mouth with both hands, gasping. "Or were you actually following me? Maybe you really are my stalker. I was kidding before, but I'm starting to buy it now." My words are cotton-stuffed and heavy. I think I might be deteriorating where I stand, but I can't let Three know that.

"I'm not stalking you. I was at the house. Do you even know where you are right now?"

"Ohio."

"You're across the street from Greek Row, Evans. You

probably walked past four frats to get to that intersection."

I ignore him. "If you were at the house, where's your pledge bro entourage?" I make a big show of looking behind him. "Don't you all travel in a pack?"

"Yeah, I'm not part of that pack." He runs a hand over his face, wincing slightly. "What about you? Where are all your friends?"

"All," I repeat with a laugh that trails off sadly. "They're on their way. I'll just wait right here for them." I stop walking and pat the air like it's a seat.

Three halts beside me. "Okay, I'm done joking around. It's late. How much did you drink?"

"I had one glass of water."

"Evans."

I purse my lips, looking away. "And I may have accidentally eaten some cookies."

"Cookies."

"Special cookies." I lick my lips. "I was hungry. I did not realize."

Three swears. "How many did you have?"

"Two, not five."

"Whatever that means. Two?"

I nod. "Two. They were chocolate chip."

"So you're not drunk."

I offer him a grin. "I'm high."

Three swears again.

* * *

When I wake up, my entire body feels weighted with stones. My mouth is heavy and dry, and I can barely force my eyes open. My room is bright, sunlight streaming in through the window.

My stomach lurches as I sit up, reminding me that I did something terrible last night. I groan, cupping my hands over my face.

But when I turn to climb out of bed, I let out a startled yelp at the sight on the other side of the room. I scramble back, slamming my elbow into the wall behind me.

Three is sprawled on Ellie's bed, my Middle-earth blanket bunched under his head like a pillow. He jerks awake at the commotion, rubbing his eyes with one hand. He blinks at me as he pushes himself up onto his elbow.

"Is life just one chaotic moment after the next for you, Evans?" His voice is low and sleep-rough, and my stomach jolts with something very different from nausea. "Can't even wake up quietly?"

"What the hell are you doing here?" I whisper, my voice raspy. My throat feels scratchy, like I'm coming down with something.

Three's eyebrows arch in disbelief. "What am I doing here? That's a really weird way to say 'thank you, Three.' Especially after you begged me not to leave you."

"Begged?" The word leaves me in a frog-like croak.

"Begged," Three confirms.

"That doesn't sound ri—Is that my shirt?" I can't keep the

indignation from my voice, even as it scrapes out of me like the last sparks from a fire.

He narrows his eyes. "What's the last thing you remember?"

I open my mouth, then shut it quickly. What do I remember from last night?

"I was walking home," I say slowly. "And . . . I ran into you."

Of course. The first time I'd seen him since he tricked me into thinking I was about to be kissed, and I was high on edibles. He must be feeling so smug right now.

"You almost ran into traffic, actually, but close enough."

I glare at him. "And you walked me home?"

Three nods and makes a motion like *keep going*.

"And . . ." I rack my brain, but it's useless. Now that I'm really trying, I remember walking with him, but only up to a certain point. I don't remember getting back to my building, coming inside, *bringing him with me*, or anything that happened after.

"Hey, you're awake!" Dara pokes her head in from the bathroom. She's wearing a fuzzy robe and her pink silk bonnet, and somehow seems not at all surprised to see Three. "How are you feeling? How'd you sleep?" The first question she directs to me, but the second is lobbed at Three.

"Good, thanks," Three says to her as he slides off Ellie's bed. He drags my Middle-earth blanket with him and starts folding it like some kind of polite house guest.

"What about you?" Dara asks, turning to me. "You were in pretty bad shape last night."

I glance from her to Three and back again, then give her

a look that I hope conveys my only thought: *What the fuck is going on right now?*

Dara's eyes widen. "You don't remember?"

"I think your edibles really kicked in around the time we got back," Three says without looking at me. "You said your heart was beating fast and kept asking me if you were going to be like that forever."

My face warms. "I did not. I was fine when I ran into you."

"And then you threw up on me." He motions to his borrowed shirt.

I look to Dara for confirmation.

She winces. "Yeah, I saw you'd called, and when I tried to call back, he answered. You were definitely . . . not doing well."

"You can go smell my shirt if you don't believe me," Three says, his voice cold. "It's hanging in your shower."

"I rinsed it for him," Dara says. "I came home right away."

"From your date? Oh god, Dara, I'm so sorry."

She waves me off. "It's fine! You needed help."

Three scoffs. "First apology of the morning, and it's not even to me. Okay. Sure."

If Dara came home early last night, I have no idea what Three is still doing here. He clearly isn't thrilled about it, either. So why wouldn't he have just gone home? Even if I asked him to stay—even if I begged—it doesn't make sense.

Unless he's hoarding everything that happened last night while he puts together an evil master plan to use it against me. I imagine it all went into the same little treasure trove where he's keeping the look I had on my face as I waited—stupidly, *so stupidly*—for him to kiss me the other day.

Idiot. I keep playing straight into his hands, like an animal walking into the same trap again and again.

I cross the room to him, poking my finger into his chest. "You better forget everything that happened last night."

"Yeah, you're welcome, Evans. No problem. I had a great time making sure you didn't trip on a curb and crack your head open or drown in your own vomit in the night."

"I'm being serious!"

Three pushes my hand away. "So am I. And since it seems like you're all better now, I'm leaving." He grabs a Tau Delta Pi baseball cap from Ellie's empty desk, fitting it over his bedhead as he moves to the door.

The image brings back a vague memory, the hazy sight of his back as he walked to the door. My hand grasping the back of his shirt.

"Please, please, don't leave. I'm really scared. What if I'm like this forever? What if those cookies altered something in my brain, and I'm like this for the rest of my life?"

"Come on, Evans, that's not going to happen. Just get in bed—okay, I'll stay a little while. Relax. It'll wear off. You're going to be fine."

I can practically feel the phantom brush of his hand against the back of my head, smoothing down my hair, rubbing the spot between my shoulder blades.

Three thanks Dara again before pulling open the door.

I charge after him, hesitating when I spot a few people in the lounge. Curious gazes swing in my direction, and I flush all the way to my hairline as I hurry after Three. When the elevator doors open, I follow him inside.

"You have to tell me everything that happened," I say, crossing my arms. "And *everything* I said."

He tips his head back against the wall, closing his eyes. "Do I? Why?"

"Because it's not fair! You shouldn't get to have this kind of leverage over me!"

Three sighs. "We came back here, you freaked out, I stayed to make sure you were okay, you threw up on me—really can't stress that one enough—and then you went to bed."

"And how did I end up in my pajamas?" I motion to my outfit. "Did . . . You didn't . . . Did I . . . ?"

Three opens his eyes, and I catch a flash of surprise. "Dara helped you."

I feel a small rush of relief. Not that I'm worried Three did anything weird, but I'm more worried I did. Imagine if I'd started changing in front of him. How mortifying.

"And I didn't say anything?" I can still hear my own voice, that *please, please* playing on a humiliating loop. What other embarrassing things might I have said? "I didn't . . . tell you anything?"

At that, Three smiles. He tips his head to the side, looking his usual smug self for the first time all morning. "You mean you want me to return my payment?"

"What payment?"

"The payment I decided to accept for taking care of you."

"Three."

The elevator dings, and the doors slide open.

He grins as he slips past me. "Sorry, Evans, but this one's nonrefundable."

"You can't do that!" I follow him, bare feet slapping against the gross lobby tile. "Seriously, you have to forget anything I said last night. None of it was real—it doesn't count!"

He backs up into the door, pushing it open a few inches. "I don't know. It sounded pretty real to me."

"Three!"

He gives me a salute as he turns and walks out. The door bangs shut behind him.

"Do you feel up for breakfast?" Dara asks when I return, dragging my feet and stupefied with shock. She's leaning into my mirror, checking a pimple on her chin.

I lurch forward, grabbing her arms. "I need you to tell me everything that happened last night."

Her eyes widen. "Oh. Um, well, you were getting ready for bed when I got home. Three tried to leave then, but . . ." She winces. "You did beg him to stay."

I groan, turning to bang my head against the wall. "You've got to be kidding me."

"You followed him to the door, and then you kind of, um, cried."

I stop banging my head. "Please tell me I'm having a

nightmare right now." Nausea creeps up again, swift and intense.

"He was really nice about it," Dara says quickly. "Said he didn't even need a pillow or anything. I got him the extra blanket from your closet."

Oh, right. He's seen my Middle-earth blanket.

"I don't know what happened before that, but . . ." Dara chooses her next words carefully. "I know you hate him. But for what it's worth, he took really good care of you."

What she doesn't realize is that Three does nothing for free. And whatever I said last night, he seemed far too pleased to accept it as payment.

ELEVEN

I spend the next couple of days trying everything I can to remember what happened after I ate the edibles. I got the most from Dara—that I was throwing up when she called, and she left her Buckonnect date to come take care of me. That I was brushing my teeth when she got home, and apparently had been at it for a long time. That I'd begged Three, mouth foamy with toothpaste, to stay the night.

It was mortifying to hear, again, that I'd begged.

I gathered a few more details from Jennie at work the next day. She apologized for not taking better care of me and swore she'd tried calling, and as she recounted what an asshole Three had been on the phone with her, I had a brief recovered memory of him leaning in my bathroom doorway, my phone pressed to his ear as he said, "Then fuck off."

My eyes fluttered wildly as I tried to reconcile the image.

Because there was no way, absolutely no way in hell, that he was standing there shirtless.

But I guess it aligns with the details of the night. I can't stop hearing the crystal clear disdain in his voice as he said, "You threw up on me." It played on a loop in my head as I double washed his sweatshirt last night, just in case he wants it back.

But when I arrive in the *Torch* office a couple days later, nervous-sweating with his sweatshirt tucked in my bag, he's not at the grunt desk. On my way here, I was dreading crossing the newsroom to him, but now I'm dreading watching him approach me when he arrives.

So I distract myself with Buckonnect for a few minutes, which is another stress all its own. I haven't heard from Hayes since Saturday night, when he messaged me five times in a row, then never responded—not that night or since.

hayes6834: at the risk of this sounding like a line...you up?

hayes6834: hoping you're not. it's pretty late.

hayes6834: but if you are...

hayes6834: we could play would you rather

hayes6834: like would you rather chew your own toenails or someone else's fingernails?

I'm especially worried I scared him off when I sent a nonsensical response back to his "would you rather" question that night, though I tried to explain Sunday morning.

pomerene1765: tornaols

pomerene1765: ok as it turns out I was asleep

pomerene1765: actually in the case of full disclosure I should tell you I wasn't entirely sober

pomerene1765: somehow entirely on accident! would you believe I'm not even cool enough to get intentionally blitzed?

pomerene1765: do people even say blitzed? have I been spending too much time with my parents?

When he didn't answer, I tried again yesterday.

pomerene1765: if you had to pick one secret in the world to know, what would it be?

pomerene1765: I realize this isn't a would you rather question lol

I stare at those unanswered messages, dread pooling in my stomach. Then I try once more.

pomerene1765: hey...is everything okay?

pomerene1765: I'm a little worried

Because now that I think about it, I *am* worried. He messaged me five times in a row in the middle of the night on Saturday. What if he was walking home from a party? What if he got hit by a car? What if he fell in the river? Or a ditch? Or into a kidnapper's trunk?

Or maybe the fact that I wasn't sober was a turnoff. I could see Lincoln, for instance, being a stickler for that kind of thing. I can't help but keep linking him to Hayes, the puzzle connecting loosely.

> **pomerene1765:** I could be overreacting and if you just don't want to talk anymore that's totally fine, but if you're planning to ghost me can you at least give me a sign you aren't dead?
>
> **pomerene1765:** or...well it's not fine lol I'd definitely not be fine if that's what's happening here, but I can't keep you against your will so I'd understand I guess

Nothing.

I'm about to message again when I hear the door open, and I swing around. Three steps into the newsroom, his gaze lifting from his phone and landing on me with surprising intensity. It lasts only a second before his expression clears, and he tucks his phone in his pocket.

He drops easily into the seat beside me without saying anything.

I pick up my headphones but hesitate. I should get the hard thing over with now. The longer I wait, the more people will arrive in the newsroom, and then I'll never be able to do this quietly.

"Hey, um," I whisper, angling toward Three without looking at him, "I wanted to say—uh . . ." I glance up as Three leans his elbow on the arm of his chair, putting our shoulders so close, they nearly touch. His face is turned down toward mine like we're sharing a secret.

His eyebrows arch in question, and my heart picks up speed. I tell myself it's just an allergic reaction to thanking him for something. "Well, I realized I was a little . . . flustered the other day. When I woke up." I glance around, checking to make sure no one else is paying attention. The last thing I need is the rest of the staff getting the wrong idea of Three and me. Dara said she's been fielding questions from the girls who were in the lounge when he left, wanting to know who he was and, Dara quoted, "where they could get them one of those."

I had to tamp down an intense flare of jealousy I definitely had no right feeling.

I lean a little closer, lowering my voice. "I should have said thank you. So, thank you."

His gaze flicks over my face, and something about this up-close, undivided attention makes my cheeks warm.

He turns away at last, putting some distance between us. "You're welcome."

With oxygen pumping to my brain again, I remember one more thing. "I have your shirt too," I whisper. "But I'd prefer everyone didn't see me returning your clothes to you. So maybe we could do that outside?"

The corner of his mouth gives a tug, like the ghost of a smirk. "Worried people will get the wrong idea about us?" The look he gives me says it all: *Yeah, right.*

Something like hurt cracks in my chest that he's so quick to brush it off as ridiculous. I mean, I get it—he's . . . traditionally good-looking. And I'm . . .

I feel a flare of anger, defensive and annoyed—with him and with myself. "Yeah, that'd be out of this world," I snipe, reaching into my bag. "You're an asshole." I shove his sweatshirt at him, and it falls out of the nicely folded square I labored over after washing it, landing in a heap in his lap.

"Evans," Three says.

I hold up a hand. "Don't speak to me. I have a lot of work to do." I pop in one earbud, then turn to glare at him. "I don't even know why I'd thank you for the other night. Like you said, you got paid. And if you try to tell anyone what happened or anything I said, I'll just deny it, and why would *anyone* believe you?"

I move to put in my second earbud, but he catches my wrist, palm burning hot against my skin.

"I don't need to tell anyone else what you said or did." His voice is low but casual, despite the way his eyes have darkened. "But I do have one question."

My heart gives a warning thump. I feel like a rabbit cornered by a fox. I might be fast, but he's faster. *"What?"* I ask, the word knife sharp.

Three smiles. "When are you going to tell me what we were doing in that dream you had about me?"

"What—what dream?"

He tilts his head, giving me a sly look. "I think you know what dream."

As he waits, the memory comes back, hazy at the edges but not enough to misunderstand. Three's catlike grin as he said, "If you've been dreaming about me, just say so."

And the way I stumbled over my answer: "How'd y—I mean—"

Which was as good as saying, *How'd you know?*

Now Three's expression shifts, like he can tell the memory just hit me like a bus. He could not look more smug than he does in this moment.

My heart goes haywire. Like the fox just took a leap and got its teeth around my throat.

Three's grip on my wrist slackens, but he doesn't let go. He doesn't want to end this until he knows he's well and truly won.

I might be bleeding out and on the verge of being eaten, but I'm not dead yet. I twist toward him, laying my free hand on his chest. He touched first, which means this is fair game. Until he releases my arm, there are no rules.

"You really want to know?" I murmur.

Unfortunately, Three doesn't lose his composure. If anything, he brightens. "That's why I asked, Evans."

"I'd rather show you." I move my hand up until my fingers cup his throat. "It went a little like this."

A thrill of power rushes through me when I feel his pulse thrumming wildly under my touch. I give the barest, lightest squeeze.

"So *that's* what you're into," he says, his voice so quiet, I barely hear him.

"Watching your face turn purple and the life leave your eyes?" I whisper back. *"Oh yeah."*

"You're sure that's how it went?" he asks, brushing his thumb over the base of my palm. When it passes my pulse point, I hope he doesn't notice how it's hammering. But I know I'm not lucky enough when his smile widens.

"What the hell are you two doing?" Christopher barks, appearing over the grunt desk.

I spring back, wrist still caught in Three's grasp. He releases it slowly.

"Nothing," I squeak, tucking my hands under my thighs. "He was bothering me."

Three clears his throat but doesn't speak.

Christopher's attention shifts to Three. "I want to talk to you about that story." He jerks his chin toward his desk on the other side of the room.

Three nods. "Yeah. Just give me a second. I'll be right over."

Christopher eyes him, brows arching, before he turns and walks off.

I still haven't put in my second earbud, and I can't help but ask, "What story?"

"Worry about yourself, Evans," Three says roughly.

I scowl, turning away. "I wasn't worried at all, Wellborn."

But when he gets up a few minutes later to head to Christopher's desk, my eyes trail him. Christopher has been pulling Three aside quite a bit lately, always about *some* story. If he's taking Three under his wing, that'll be a leg up Three has over me for the Campus Life spot. It started with the article on Ellie, Three carrying out Christopher's retribution for getting scooped by *Two Minute News* on that story about the girls who overdosed last year.

And if Christopher is imagining Three as his protégé, I can't help but wonder how I'll compete on my own.

"Hey, don't look so miserable," Dara says, reaching across the table to set a piece of her garlic bread on my plate. "You'll get other ideas."

I'm currently wallowing, my gold medal sport. Three working with Christopher on some mystery story had me keyed up, and after losing my VR equipment piece, I panic-pitched something new to Mel, eager to have another story on my plate. But Mel axed the idea before I could even prep an outline. It would have been about the soon-to-open campus package center owned by the largest online retailer in the world, but apparently the impact that would have on small businesses in the area isn't interesting to anyone but me.

I tried to play off my misery when I got back to my room tonight, but Madison was home alone and is one of those people who insist you should "talk about your feelings." So I told her what happened and was mid-story when Dara arrived. I worried they'd think this is all I talk or care about, but Dara was sympathetic, and they insisted we get dinner together to cheer me up.

"But will those ideas be worth anything?" I grumble, mindlessly stirring my soup. "What if all I can come up with are subpar stories no one wants to give the page space to?"

"I don't think it was subpar," Dara says. I don't miss the way she nudges Madison, who's been distracted picking pepperoni off her pizza slice. Apparently she didn't want to wait for a fresh cheese pizza to come out of the oven.

"What if you focus on something else?" She folds her pizza in half and takes a bite. "Instead of these serious pieces, something a little more fun?"

"I'll never beat Three that way," I mutter, breaking apart the garlic bread Dara gave me. I pop a piece into my mouth.

"Is that why you're on the school paper?" Dara asks. "To beat Three?"

I pause, startled by her question. "Well . . . no. Obviously not. I chose the school paper because people deserve more than the twenty-four-hour news cycle." I pull a face. "Or the *Two Minute News* cycle. But I'm also not *on* the school paper yet. Not unless I beat him. And he has such good ideas, it makes me sick."

"Maybe the problem is that you keep trying to write a Three story instead of a *Wyn* story," Dara says. "Like, instead of trying to *be* him, why don't you try to *not* be him? From what you've told us, everything he writes is big and scandalous. But you wrote something that ended up getting a woman a whole car."

I sit up straighter. "What?"

"Your Buckeye Crossing story," says Madison. "Didn't you ever check on that GoFundMe?"

"They raised enough for Kate to buy a car," Dara explains.

I feel a wave of shame that I never checked on Kate again after that first story. I knew about the GoFundMe, of course, but I didn't know it'd gained that much attention. I thought she'd end up with a few hundred dollars at most to get herself started.

Now, pulling it up, I see it raised quite a bit more, and there's an update picture of Kate and her daughter standing in front of an old gray sedan.

Pride begins to battle with shame, even though I had very little to do with this. I remember thinking that Kate was only one person losing her home in Buckeye Crossing. Now, looking at her and her daughter in front of their new car, I realize this didn't help one person—it helped two. It's not an entire group of students or a whole housing complex, but it's certainly a start. Two lives connected to the goodness of other people because of something I wrote.

"You made people care about someone," Dara says. "Why not write something Three would never waste his time on, like a human-interest piece?"

I hesitate. "Like . . . like what? If you were to read a story, what would you want to hear about?" It feels a little cheap, like cheating, asking Dara and Madison to hand-feed me ideas. But I can't write an interesting story like this without my finger on the pulse of what people want to read.

"They're tearing down the Whispering Wall," Madison says. "Outside the arts center? I heard about it at rehearsal last week. It's a campus landmark. Isn't that important?"

"Will people find that interesting?" I glance from her to Dara. "Like, enough that they'll actually read it?"

"A pastor conducts worship service whether his congregation is two or two hundred," Madison says.

"Yeah, but the *Torch* won't put me on the pulpit if I've only got two people in the pews."

"The Whispering Wall is a campus staple," Dara says. "You should at least pitch it."

"I bet you could get a lot of stories from students and faculty," says Madison. "Maybe even alumni if you know who to reach out to. I could ask my prayer group and the glee club if they know anyone who wants to talk about it."

"I can ask my friends too," says Dara.

It's not the most compelling story ever, and I don't know how I'll spin it. Worse, I don't know if I can handle another rejection right now.

Dara senses my hesitation and gives me a gentle smile. "Would *Humans of New York* or *This American Life* have gotten so huge if people didn't want to hear about stuff like this? We talk about them all the time in my marketing classes."

Well, I hadn't considered that. "Maybe I could check the school's social media and see who commented on the announcement. If people are upset about it, they might have stories."

I'll think of something—some way to make people care about this that Mel will have to acknowledge.

I pick up my phone, pausing when I see I have a notification. One I've been waiting for.

> **hayes6834:** sorry I've been MIA
>
> **hayes6834:** I'd explain it but it'd take a lot of anonymity out of this whole thing

I exhale in relief. At least he's not dead. Or ghosting me.

> **pomerene1765:** why? is there some viral two minute news update about how they found you half dead in a ditch over the weekend?
>
> **hayes6834:** lol sure let's go with that
>
> **hayes6834:** makes me seem way more interesting than the truth
>
> **pomerene1765:** no, your secret bad boy persona makes you seem interesting
>
> **pomerene1765:** finding you half dead in a ditch is just seasoning
>
> **hayes6834:** oh right, how could I forget

Then another message comes through—one that sends warmth bubbling through me.

> **hayes6834:** I'm in this with you btw. no ghosting.

TWELVE

Over the next few days, I scour the comments on the school's posts about the Whispering Wall demolition and send dozens of DMs. A handful of people get back to me, and by Friday, I have enough notes from my interviews and a decent outline to send to Mel. I'm on my way home from my shift at the library that evening when their response comes through: *How fast can you have it done?*

So, there goes my weekend. It's not an enthusiastic yes, gushing with praise, but it's still a yes. And it feels good to have something to focus on other than the statistics assignment I scored dismally low on and the crushing reality that if I don't do something to improve my grade, I might have to retake it next semester. The thought of the money wasted if that happens turns my stomach—not to mention the time lost.

I stretch my neck, sighing as I reach the door to my building. But as I wave my ID over the reader, the elevator doors slide open, and Lincoln steps out.

Can't run now, I think as I pull the door open. I've seen him in passing but haven't really spoken to him since the day I was questioned by the police, when he admitted to turning me in along with Ellie. I expect him to look uncomfortable, but his expression brightens when he spots me.

"Hey," he says as the door swings shut behind me. "How's it going?"

Relief floods me as the awkwardness dissipates. "Not bad." I pause at the elevator, then turn to him without pressing the button. "Are you on duty?"

He smiles. "No, I have a kickball game."

"You play kickball?"

"Yeah, in the intramural league."

I blink at him. "Enough people play kickball at this school that we have a *league*?"

He laughs. "Yeah, some of the fraternities play, so we managed to scrape one together." He nods toward the door. "Do you want to come watch?"

I hesitate. I do want to, but when I think of my unwritten Whispering Wall story, something like panic squeezes at my insides. I'll never win the Campus Life spot if I don't buckle down and focus.

In my silence, Lincoln's smile droops a little. "It's okay," he says quickly. "I guess it probably would be kind of boring."

"No, it's not that! I just have this story I have to write. The *Torch* is letting me do *real* reporting now."

"Oh, yeah. I read the, uh, porn ban one."

I groan. "God, I hope that's not my legacy."

"You've got three and a half years to outdo yourself. And you know, it might be better if you don't see me play kickball, anyway. I'm kind of embarrassingly competitive."

"Over *kickball*?"

Lincoln grins. "Oh, I'm competitive over everything. I think my inability to play Clue without making lifelong enemies is the reason my last girlfriend broke up with me." He pauses, flushing. "Not that you needed to know that. *Anyway*, kickball is great—it's the sport for all of us who are too intense for board game night but who lack real athletic talent."

I didn't expect this from him, and something about it makes me pause. Lincoln is competitive.

Hayes is competitive. Ultra-competitive. Ruins Monopoly kind of competitive.

It's one more coincidence in a sea of coincidences lately. But each one connects, like a quilt of Hayes.

I'm silent for too long, and Lincoln must read it as the end of the conversation. He starts to turn toward the door but stops. "Hey, are we good? After—"

I cut him off. "Absolutely. I was just having a rough day. I'm over it now. I mean, there was nothing to even *be* over. You were doing your job."

"Well, I am sorry, for what it's worth."

"Don't worry about it."

He gives a wave as he turns to go, pushing out into the night.

I stand in the lobby for a few extra seconds, mind racing. If Lincoln really is Hayes—and I know it's a stretch, but I can't stop myself from considering it—then maybe I do want to know. If it's him, maybe I'd be okay with him knowing I'm Pomerene. I don't think it would send him running.

And if he's not Hayes, do I really care? The worst thing that happens is I make a friend. Something I've been desperate for since I got here. And I'll never make any friends at all if I keep holing up in my room, frantically writing story after story for the *Torch*.

"Lincoln!" I call, rushing out the door after him.

He hasn't made it very far, and I jog the rest of the way to him, even though it's kind of embarrassing.

"I'll come watch."

My bed is a sea of granola bar wrappers after I skipped dinner to get through the rest of my statistics assignment, which took a back seat to the Whispering Wall story I worked on all day.

I should deeply regret spending so much time at Lincoln's kickball game last night, but it doesn't feel like a waste. Afterward, I grabbed pizza with him and his friends, and I think he might have even been flirting with me at one point. The more time I spend with him, the more I think, with his awkward sense of humor and that mature older-boy thing he has going for him, where everything he says is with authority, he could very well be Hayes. And that is definitely worth losing my entire Saturday over.

Somewhere beneath my collection of wrappers, my phone buzzes with an incoming call. When I finally unearth it and see the name on the screen, I gasp and immediately choke on granola remnants.

I scramble to answer, wheezing to clear my airway. "Hello?"

"Come let me in."

I blink and check the screen again. "Did you call the wrong person?"

"I know who I called. Come downstairs and let me into your building."

"Um, no?"

"Evans, I need your help. Let me in."

I slide off my bed, bringing a handful of granola wrappers with me. They flutter to the floor like helicopters from a maple tree.

"What do you mean, you need my help?" I'm struck with the image of him being shot or stabbed, bleeding out at the door to my building, having barely made it here.

I must sound panicked, because Three exhales a laugh. "No one's dying. But it's nice to know you'd be worried about me."

I scoff as I push into the stairwell, dashing down to the first floor. "I wouldn't be worried," I spit out as I reach the lobby. "I was hoping I'd be able to watch."

Three waits on the other side of the door. He's wearing a hooded sweatshirt underneath his jacket, and it's zipped over a misshapen bundle—like a backpack worn the wrong way. He has one arm around it, the other holding his phone to his ear. He's hunched weirdly, his hood pulled up so I can't see his eyes.

As soon as I push the door open, he rushes past me, heading for the elevator.

"Gee, hello to you too," I say.

He hits the button with his elbow, and the doors slide open.

"Do you plan to tell me what's going on? And why it looks like you're smuggling a frozen turkey under your shirt? It's a little early for Thanksgiving." I blink at him as his sweatshirt *moves*. "What the f—"

"Inside," he says roughly, using his body to usher me into the elevator. He elbows the button for my floor.

"Why is it *moving*? What did you do?"

He crowds me into the corner of the elevator, leaning so close, our foreheads nearly touch. I'm acutely aware of his thigh pressing against mine, holding me in place. He has one arm cupped under the bundle in his sweatshirt, and when he lowers the zipper, a little head pops out.

"Is that a *go*—"

He covers my mouth with his hand.

I shake him off, making a gagging sound. "Gross! Don't touch my face with your *dirty* hand! Who knows where you've been and what you've touched tonight!" I motion to his hoodie, where he's zipping the goat back inside in preparation to leave the elevator. "Case in point!"

He ignores me, stepping out as the elevator doors open and making a beeline for my room.

"Hey, I don't think so," I whisper, quickening my pace as I follow him. "I don't know why you thought you should come here, but I am absolutely not—"

"Open it," he says, kicking my door lightly.

I glare at him. "You don't get to show up here and start bossing me around!"

"You owe me."

"I don't *owe you*," I hiss, but I unlock my door and push it open anyway, because it's at least safer to argue with him in my room than out in the hall.

Inside, he pokes his head into the bathroom, then pulls the door shut and locks it. Dara is with Kayla and Yasmin, but Madison got home a little while ago. I can hear her music playing softly from their room.

"I just need you to watch him for a little while. I'll be back in, like, two hours."

"Two *hours*?"

He's crouched down to let the goat out of his sweatshirt, and when he looks at me over his shoulder, my heart gives an extra thump. I don't know if it's a warning or . . . something else. He looks more serious than I've ever seen him, and there's a trace of panic beneath it, badly hidden.

"You owe me," he says as he straightens. "You threw up on me, remember? And I stayed with you. So this is how you can repay me." He waves the goat away from one of the fallen granola wrappers. As he picks up the ones from the floor, he glances at the others littered across my duvet, and his brows arch up. "Jesus, Evans, are you making a blanket out of these things?"

I move between him and my bed, blocking his view with both arms out. "This is an invasion of privacy."

"That's fine, keep your weird art project or whatever the hell this is." He tosses the wrappers into the trash can next to my desk. "Just make sure he doesn't eat those."

I catch his elbow as he heads for the door. "Hold on a second! You said you were taking whatever I did and said that night as payment. It's one or the other—you can't have both."

He blows out an exasperated breath, pushing a hand through his hair. His hood falls back. "Fine. What, you want me to tell you everything that happened?"

"Obviously, yes!"

He nods quickly. "So the part where you admitted you had a dream about me? And how you cried and grabbed onto me and begged me not to leave you? And when you threw up on my shirt? And how you told me I'm distracting?"

"You're lying! I knew you'd do this. You're taking advantage of the fact that I can't remember so you can make stuff up!"

"And you said you don't have friends." His voice comes out twisted with frustration, and I'm surprised to see a flash of regret as soon as he says it.

My stomach gives a nauseating kick, and I stare at Three in horror.

His mouth presses into a grim line. "I have to go. If I'm not back in a few minutes, someone will figure out I'm the one who took him. I promise I'll come back as soon as I can. Two hours at most. Hopefully sooner, and then he'll be out of your hair."

He turns to leave but stops once more with the door cracked open an inch. He looks back at me, then down at my arm, stretched out to where I've caught the back of his jacket.

"We're even," I say. "Whatever else we've done up to now, this makes us even."

He hesitates long enough that I glance at his face. His expression is hard.

I tug his jacket. "Say it."

"Fine," he bites out, sounding angrier than I expected. "We're even."

I release him. "I knew you hated to lose, but I didn't think you hated it that much."

"Yeah, well, we've all got our flaws." He pulls the door open wider and steps out, yanking it shut before I can say another word.

There's a small crash behind me, and I turn. "Oh *no*," I whisper, rushing across the room.

Because the goat is standing on my nightstand, poised to jump onto my bed.

Somehow I think two hours of this should have been worth a little more from Three, but it's too late now.

* * *

I've sent Three six texts since the exact two-hour mark, all of which went unanswered. Now it's after midnight, nearing the third hour.

Chewy, which is what I've named the goat since he ate some paper out of my trash, the edge of my blanket, and part of the curtain hanging over my closet, is nowhere near tiring. He spent the first hour wandering my room, looking for new things to eat, destroy, or headbutt. The last one got some attention from Madison, who insisted on being let in so she could confirm I wasn't being held hostage. As soon as she saw Chewy, she shifted into babysitter mode and grabbed a glittery baton from one of her glee club performances and some floral scarves she tied together like a rope.

We have Chewy chasing the scarves in what must be his ten thousandth circle when there's a knock at the bathroom door and Dara pokes her head in.

"Hey, I hope you don't mind. I ran into him outside." She's barely finished speaking before Three pushes into the room.

"Where the hell have you been?" I demand. "I've been texting you!"

"Yeah, I know." He's carrying an empty backpack, which he sets on the floor. "I got stuck at the house."

It's no mystery which house he means—obviously he was at Tau Delt.

When Chewy ventures close enough, Three scoops him into the backpack. For the most part, Chewy doesn't struggle, and Three zips it just enough that he can still poke his head out.

"Thanks for watching him." He glances up, briefly meeting my gaze. "But I need another favor."

"You're joking."

"Not even a little." He pulls a key fob from his pocket and holds it out to me. "I need you to drive."

I push his hand back to him. "*You* drive."

"I can't," he says, and as he stares at me, I get what he means. His gaze is a little unfocused and slightly glazed. If he were wearing his glasses, I might not have noticed, but he's missing that extra layer of protection tonight.

"You got *drunk*?" Disdain saturates my voice. "Are you kidding me right now?"

Madison clears her throat, pushing to her feet. "I should go to bed. I have church in the morning."

"Thanks for your help," I say as she retreats. She shoots me a smile before slipping past Dara into the bathroom.

Dara waits in the doorway, her expression questioning. When I give her a reassuring nod, she mimes to text her before following Madison.

"I told you I was stuck at the house," Three says once they're gone. "I couldn't exactly be like *no, sorry, I can't drink tonight, I have to drive a goat I stole to a farm an hour and a half away*." He sighs, rubbing a hand down his face. "I'll never ask you for anything again."

"How did you even get the car here if you're wasted? Don't tell me you drove drunk."

Three jerks back, looking appalled. "No! I got the keys earlier. It's already on campus. And I'm not *wasted*. I had to go back to the house so I had an alibi, and they made me drink—yeah, I'm a fucking pledge, Evans. What do you expect?"

"Sounds like being in a frat is a real fun time. You haven't even told me where you stole him from."

"Another frat. Obviously."

"Why would a frat have a goat?" I lean back, giving him a dark look. "Why does this feel like a setup? Are you messing with me? Am I about to—"

"They make the pledges raise it! They get a goat, and the pledges raise it, and then . . ."

I blanch. "And then *what*?"

"I don't know!" he explodes, throwing his hands up. "I don't know, but I didn't want to find out!"

Chewy makes an agitated noise, rustling in the backpack.

Three sighs, hanging his head. I reach out, hit with the overwhelming urge to smooth my hand over his hair. But I change course halfway there, knowing what a bad idea it would be, and take the key fob instead.

Three looks up, his whole body slackening with something like shock. Then he says, "I just need you to drive. Please. I'll—I'll owe—"

I hold up a hand, not quite covering his mouth. But it's enough to make him stop, and his eyebrows arch in question.

"I don't make deals with drunk people." I grab my bag

from my desk chair. "Right now I'm just doing this. If you want to talk about payment, we can do it tomorrow. Or later. Whenever you're sober."

He doesn't get up right away, remaining hunched over Chewy. Then he slips the backpack on so it hangs down his front, zips his hoodie over it, and stands.

"Who'd you borrow a car from, anyway?" I ask as I follow him to the elevator. "One of your frat bros?" I can't even say the words without putting a sarcastic twist on it, like a garnish in a drink.

Three snorts. "Yeah, right. They cannot know I had anything to do with this." The doors slide open as he answers. "I borrowed it from Christopher."

"Christopher?" I yelp.

THIRTEEN

M e, my drunk enemy, a stolen goat, and my managing
editor's car.

There's a joke in there somewhere, but I'm too exhausted
to find it. Between the trek to Christopher's apartment, which
isn't far from my building but felt as long as the journey to
Mordor with Three and Chewy, and wrangling Chewy into
the back seat—he was not pleased and bleated loudly to make
it known—I'm ready to turn straight around and fall into bed
for the next twelve hours.

But the night is far from over. We still have the three-hour
round-trip drive to get through.

"How the hell did you get Christopher to lend you his
car?" I demand while Three fumbles to start the directions. It
takes him longer than it should, and I get the sense he might
be more drunk than he seems. He's probably one of those

people who can be blacked out but still hold a completely normal conversation with you.

Three sighs, resting his head back against the seat and closing his eyes. "I asked."

"You *asked*." I flip on the blinker with a little more force than necessary and merge onto the deserted highway. I glance over at Three. The fact that most of the agitation has left his body and he looks almost relaxed for the first time all night should make me angry when I'm still wound up, overtired, and doing all the work now.

But for some reason, I'm relieved to see that the tension has left him. I'm trying very hard not to be charmed by him right now, but . . . *he saved a goat*. Not because it was easy, but because he didn't want to leave Chewy to whatever fate was planned for him, no matter how hard it would be to pull off. Despite having to ask me, of all people, for help.

I reach down and pinch my thigh. *Absolutely not*. He's still evil.

"So, you asked, and Christopher just . . . agreed. Because you're such great friends."

Three snorts. "Does it seem like Christopher has the capacity for friendship to you?" His voice sounds different than usual—less polished, more of a drawl, and husky. The way you might sound right before a bad cold.

"And you do?" I shoot him a look. "It sounds like a match made in heaven to me."

"I have friends."

"Oh, right. I forgot—fraternity friendships are forged in fire." I tilt my head toward Chewy in the back seat. "Must be why your pledge pals are here helping you right now."

"They're not my—" He stops abruptly, clamping his mouth shut so hard, his teeth clack together. "You want me to answer this? I thought you didn't make deals with drunk people."

"Does answering a question have to be part of a deal?"

"It does with me," says Three.

"You're so annoying. How do you not even seem drunk right now? How are you in your right enough mind to remember to make deals before you answer a question, when I—" I stop abruptly. *When I spilled every single thought that came into my head the other night,* I wanted to say.

"It's not that hard when it's already second nature." He huffs out a laugh. "There, you can have that as a bonus."

"I don't even know what that means."

"How many questions do you want for the drive? I'll give you—"

"Five."

"Two."

I scoff. *"Five."*

"Three," he tries again.

"I guess that's only fitting."

When I look over at him, he grins. His gaze has turned lazy, and he leans an elbow on the center console, long legs stretched out under the dash.

I pucker my lips like I've tasted something sour. "Why did Christopher lend you his car? And don't say it's because you asked," I add quickly. "I want the real answer."

"I've been working on a story," Three says. "For a while now. It's a big one, so Christopher's been helping me, and he gets all my status updates."

"Oh my god." I bark out a laugh. "You *would* take this opportunity to try to intimidate me. Why should I believe anything you say right now?"

"As much fun as it is to freak you out, Evans, I don't have to lie to do it." He reaches down to recline his seat a little.

I let this slide because I realize arguing with a drunk person is a bit of a lost cause. And also because he's struggling with the lever, and his seat keeps popping back up and knocking him in the shoulders. I watch him from the corner of my eye, biting back laughter.

When he finally settles, I say, "So you and Christopher *are* friends."

"Is that a question? Because I hate to help you, but it's hard to watch you waste your questions on things I've already answered."

"No, that's not a question," I snap, annoyed at how haughty he manages to sound, even drunk. I don't need to ask this, anyway. I can simply assume that Three and Christopher are, at the very least, closer than I realized. "Let me think."

"We've got time." He motions to the road.

"Do you like being in a frat?"

His head whips around. "Why would you ask that?" His voice is cautious.

"Well, they were going to do god knows what to Chewy—"

"Who the hell is Chewy?"

In the back seat, Chewy bleats in response.

Three twists around to look at him. When we got Chewy in the back seat, Three used the backpack to create a harness so we could secure him. Chewy is not happy about being buckled in. When I glance in the rearview mirror, he's chewing on the seat belt.

Three swears, stretching into the back seat to wrestle it from Chewy's mouth.

"Have fun explaining that to your best friend Christopher." I keep my eyes firmly focused on the road so I won't be tempted to stare at the strip of skin exposed when his shirt rides up.

"You named the goat?" Three demands, his voice strained.

"You left me with him for almost three hours!"

"It wasn't three hours."

"Oh, were you keeping count? No? Because I was."

He rolls his eyes so hard, his head falls back against the seat.

"So, do your penance. Do you like being in a frat?" I catch the edge of his conflicted expression before he manages to stow it.

"It wasn't *my* frat that had the goat. I want to make that clear."

"Right, yours just forces you to binge drink even when you don't want to."

He starts to respond, stops, and sighs. "Yeah," he says tightly. "I guess so."

"You guess you like it?"

"No, I guess you're right." He shoves his hand through his hair. Then he laughs. "Of course this is the question you picked. . . . No, I don't like being in a frat."

"Then why do you do it?"

"Is that your next question?"

"No! Come on, just tell me. I didn't sign on for yes-or-no answers."

Three stalls. Then he says, "My dad wanted me to join. He was in Tau Delt when he went to school here, and he says it helped him a lot after boarding school. More of that brotherhood thing." He clears his throat, and I feel his attention turn toward me. "And you know I also went to boarding school."

"You've mentioned it once or twice . . . or ten times."

"Well, being in a frat isn't like that," Three says. "Maybe it was for my dad, but then again, I'm not my dad." The last bit comes out bitter, like the dregs of tea from the bottom of a cup.

I sense we're venturing into something real, and Three must feel it too, because he says, "So, there's your answer. Next question?"

I want to ask more about his family—especially his dad—but I don't want him to know how curious I am about him.

So I change direction, veering back to safer waters.

"What's the story about? The one you've been working on with Christopher."

"Pass."

"You can't pass!"

"I can do whatever I want. Pass. Pick something else."

"There's nothing else I want to know."

Three shoots me a look. "I know that's not true."

"There's nothing else I want to know right now. That's it—that's all I want."

"Pass," Three says again.

"You are so—"

"I'll tell you later. When I'm sober."

"So I have to wait for my third answer?"

"Call it another bonus," he says. "Pick a different question. I don't want to talk about the story right now. There's too much—" He stops and shakes his head. "Just pick something else."

Of course, there are a hundred things I want to know about Three. Maybe a thousand now. But I don't want to be rushed into asking. I want to take my time and think of the perfect question.

"I want a deferral. To keep my question for a later date."

"No."

"Then answer the question I want. If you get to defer an answer—"

"It's not an answer. It's a bonus."

"Regardless. You don't get to make all the rules, Three. I want a deferral. I think it's only fair. It's the middle of the night, I'm exhausted, I can barely think of my own name let alone something to ask you."

"That's the point. If it was that easy, you'd only be getting two questions."

"Fine! So ask it now, or I lose it?"

"Exactly."

"And you won't lie."

"I won't lie."

"Don't forget you did this to yourself," I say through my teeth, gripping the steering wheel tighter. I glance over at him as I spit out a question I'm already half regretting before it leaves my mouth. "Have you ever been turned on by me?"

Three freezes, mouth flattening into a tense line. He doesn't look at me.

My heart picks up speed. If he says no, I'll be mortified. But if he says yes . . . it'd be nice to know we're on an even playing field. If he gets to know I had a dream about him, then I should get this. It doesn't have to mean anything except to soothe the sting of my own embarrassment. I know nothing real would ever happen between us, and I have Lincoln who might be Hayes and Hayes who . . . I really like. A lot.

And if he says no, then at least I have the truth. I won't be upset by it. I certainly won't cry.

"Yes." His voice comes out clipped, bitten off at the end.

I nearly swerve off the road. *"What?"*

He stares straight ahead. "I'm not repeating myself. I know you said you didn't sign on for yes-or-no answers, but that's all you're getting."

I suck in a slow, calming breath.

"It doesn't mean anything," he says quickly. "I get turned on when I argue. We argue a lot."

"So you're turned on by me a lot." I simply can't help myself.

He lets out an irritated sigh, fumbling for the lever to recline his seat further. "Wake me when we get there."

"Hey, you can't go to sleep!"

"I can do whatever I want." He's thrown an arm over his eyes, but he lifts it briefly to look at me. "I paid for the trip."

I clench my jaw. I'm not sure if he actually sleeps or not, but he doesn't speak again. I spend the rest of the drive blasting the AC in my face to stay awake and flipping through radio stations to keep busy.

I absolutely do not—*do not*—think about how he answered that question.

It's past two in the morning when we surrender Chewy to a woman named Sarah, who meets us on her porch in a bathrobe thrown over flannel pajamas. As he thanks her for letting us come so late, Three manages his perfect manners, even drunk, while I droop beside him, an ode to exhaustion.

He did, in fact, fall asleep earlier, and it took herculean effort not to reach over and smother him while he was out.

"I don't think I can make it all the way back," I say as Sarah and Chewy disappear around the side of the house.

Three winces, looking apologetic. "I can't get us a hotel. My parents watch my spending."

"We don't need a hotel. I just need you to promise whatever you see tonight, you won't use it against me later." I point at him. "Not one single joke."

He holds up his hands.

In the car, I fumble for my phone and dial, setting it to speaker as I maneuver out of the driveway.

"Don't panic," I say when my mom answers.

"Why would I panic?" Mom asks, voice scratchy with sleep. "A call from my only daughter at two in the morning? No cause for concern there."

Dad snores in the background.

"I just wanted to warn you I'll be home in, like, fifteen minutes."

Three's head whips toward me, and I do my best to ignore him as I offer the barest explanation to my mom before hanging up. The energy in the car begins to crackle, his curiosity like a live wire.

As I pull Christopher's car into the driveway, I try to see my home through Three's eyes. The cottage-style house with a rounded-edge roof that looks straight out of a storybook. My parents have worked years to make our house seem out of this time, and often out of this world.

The front door, which my dad painstakingly hand-carved

to look elvish, swings open as we come up the front steps.

"Wynnie," Mom says, catching me in a hug on the porch. Three lingers at my back, hesitant. "You two look exhausted! Why are you out driving so late?" She reaches past me to grab Three and hugs him too. "Hi, Wyn's friend. It's so nice to meet you."

Three chokes a little in surprise, eyes widening. "Um, nice to meet you too. I'm Three."

"Three." She sniffs, then pulls back, frowning. "You smell like a bar and a barn, Three."

His cheeks turn pink. "Ah. Yeah, there—there was—"

"A circumstance," I say.

I'm saved from further explanation when Dad comes around the corner, poking his head out the door. "Get in the house. It's freezing."

Mom quickly ushers us inside, where Dad hugs me and doesn't let go for a long time, not even as he shakes Three's hand and introduces himself.

"I think we have some extra toothbrushes around here. Do you want me to wash those clothes for you, honey?" Mom directs this question to Three. "You can borrow some of Wilson's."

"Oh, that's okay," Three says quickly, holding up his hands. "Thank you. And thank you for having me. I know it's inconvenient. I appreciate it."

"Suck-up," I grumble, shoving him with my elbow as I move toward the hall. If Three is at all thrown by how small our house is or, more glaringly, the fact that it's decorated like a museum of fantasy media, he doesn't show it. He's polite to my parents as I pull out some blankets for him, and when I start setting up the couch, he's quick to help—and to compliment the coffee table, which Dad made himself.

Mom finally unearths some toothbrushes, and Three and I stand over the sink together, bumping elbows as we brush.

"Your parents are nice," he says around a mouthful of foam.

I lean over to spit into the sink and rinse my mouth. "Yeah, I know."

It must come out defensive, because Three says, "That's a good thing, Evans. If we showed up at my house at two in the morning, I'd never hear the end of it." He spits next, then rinses. "It'd be the Wellborn special—interrogate, berate, and . . . what's a word for giving someone the silent treatment while conveying your utter disappointment in their choices?"

I raise my eyebrows at him in the mirror. He arches his own eyebrows back at me.

"I'll get you a pillow," I say, steering the conversation elsewhere before I have the terrible sense to feel bad for him or something. I move into the hall, and it isn't until I reach my bedroom that I realize he's followed me.

I put my arms out to block him. "No."

But his eyes are already wandering.

"What is that?" He laughs as he ducks under my arm. I

catch him at the same time he gets a hand around the stuffed chicken on my bed.

I snatch her back. "*Don't* touch anything."

"You still sleep with stuffed animals, Evans?" he asks, leaning back against my desk. It's neater than it ever was when I lived here, but the hutch is still packed with my favorite romance manga and graphic novels.

Please god, don't turn around, I try to will him with my mind. If he figures out I'm secretly a super romantic, I will simply pass away.

"I see you found Fat Chick," Dad says, leaning in the doorway. "Right where you left her."

"Fat Chick," Three repeats, looking delighted.

I angle toward him, putting my back to my dad as I whisper, "I will murder you in your sleep."

His smile widens.

I pivot toward Dad. "Yep. Found her." I grab a pillow from my bed and thwack it hard into Three's chest. He jolts into my desk, and one of the books falls off the top shelf.

Before Three can reach for it, I shove him toward the door, pushing at his back even as he digs his heels in.

"Dad, please show him to the guest accommodations," I say primly.

Dad falls right into character, bowing at the waist and putting an arm out toward the living room. "Right this way, good sir," he says in his best Ren Faire accent.

When I catch a glimpse of Three's face, I'm surprised to

see he's smiling. And not in his usual smug, superior way, but simply smiling. Like he's having a good time.

As soon as they're gone, I shut off the light and fall face down into bed, worm-crawling my way up to my remaining pillow.

I don't think I'll sleep at all knowing Three is just down the hall, but then I blink, and when I open my eyes, the sun is streaming in my window.

It takes a lot of effort to drag myself out of bed, and when I shuffle into the living room, Three is still asleep on the couch. He's sprawled on his stomach, one arm curled around his pillow, blankets twisted around his legs. His shirt has ridden half-way up his back, and he's wearing a pair of sweatpants Dad must have lent him after I went to bed. His jeans are folded neatly on the coffee table, right next to a nearly empty glass of water.

When I poke my head into the kitchen, Mom is at the table with her tablet. The clock on the stove reads 8:17 a.m.

"Hey," Mom whispers, flapping a hand for me to sit. She gets up and moves to the coffee maker. As she pours me a mug, she glances into the living room, her mouth quirking in a little smile.

"Don't," I say.

She shoots me an innocent look. "What?"

"You know what."

Mom ignores me, returning her attention to the coffee. Like me, she's a big romantic, the type who religiously reads fantasy romance novels and wrote piles of Aragorn/Arwen fanfic in college—among other ships—all of which she swears was terrible and has never let me read. Though I suspect when she says "terrible," it's code for "smutty."

So of course, for her, if I bring a cute boy home, she automatically assumes something is going on that *very* definitely is not.

I get down a few sips of coffee before I hear rustling from the living room, and Three appears in the doorway. My dad is quite a bit bigger than Three, so even though the sweatpants are pulled as tight as they go and the string knotted, they still hang low on his hips, showing the band of his boxers.

I do my best not to stare, but I'm still getting my faculties up and running, and I hit a small processing delay. When I look up, Three is watching me.

"You look ridiculous," I say.

"Good morning to you too," he says, his voice hoarse. He clears his throat and smiles at Mom.

"Good morning," she says. "Wilson should be back in a few minutes with breakfast. I didn't want to wake you, so he got you a bacon, egg, and cheese." She freezes, looking horrified. "Oh my god, you aren't vegetarian, are you? Or kosher?"

Three waves his hands in front of him. "No, ma'am, that's perfect, thank you. I can—I have money I can—" He pats his pockets, then seems to remember where he left his jeans, half turning toward the living room.

"Absolutely not," Mom says. "Do you drink coffee?"

His shoulders sag with relief. "I'd love coffee."

As soon as he sinks into the seat next to me, I kick him in the ankle. "Ma'am," I mimic, rolling my eyes.

"It's called manners," he says quietly, nudging me with his elbow.

"So, what brought you all the way out here last night?" Mom asks as she returns to the table with Three's coffee.

"Newspaper stuff," I say before Three can answer. I don't want the third degree from Mom when she finds out Three is in a frat. She is extremely anti–Greek life.

Mom brightens at my answer, turning to Three. "Are you another lifelong reporter? Wynnie used to go all over the neighborhood like a little Harriet the Spy. She had so many notebooks—I wonder if we still have those."

"Mom."

She ignores me. "I swear, she knew everything about our neighbors. When they went to work, when they came home, when they did their yard work and got the newspaper from the driveway. We used to call her Neighborhood Watch."

Three looks positively delighted to learn this.

"Please, I'm begging you," I say to Mom. "Do you have any idea how much therapy costs?"

I'm saved by Dad's arrival. He comes through the front door, whistling merrily, as though we didn't interrupt his sleep in the dead of night. He passes out breakfast sandwiches, regaling us all with a story of the extra-long drive-through line that could put me back to sleep.

I eat quickly, avoiding Three's eye. I've worked very hard not to feel weird eating in front of people, especially when it's fast food. I had a big setback moment in high school, when I went through a drive-through with two of my friends, and after I ordered, they ordered the same thing, but only one, to split, because it was "just too much food."

I avoided eating much around them after that, even if it meant taking smaller portions than would satisfy me, or not eating at all and going hungry until I got home.

Luckily, I mostly worked through it before I got to college, so eating in the dining hall is much less stressful for me than it would have been a year and a half ago. But I've never eaten in front of Three, and even though he's been unpleasant in every way *but* this one, I still worry about his perception of me.

"We have to go soon," he says, mouth full as he finishes scarfing his own sandwich. "Christopher needs his car back."

Ah, Christopher. I forgot we're on borrowed time.

Not that I thought Three and I would spend the day loafing around with my parents or something. But I thought . . .

I guess I thought I'd get a little more time with them.

Three's gaze flicks away from my face, and he scratches the back of his neck as he leaves the kitchen, heading for the bathroom.

"I'm glad we got to see you," Dad says. "Even just for a few hours."

"We'll miss you next weekend," Mom adds.

Next weekend. *Right*. Thanksgiving.

"I'll be home soon after that." I take a long pull of my coffee. "The semester only goes a few more weeks." I try to sound like it doesn't bother me, but the feeling of being left behind is sharp.

When Three returns, his hair is damp and pushed back like he ran his hands through it. He thanks my parents for letting him stay, and for breakfast.

And then we're leaving.

"You don't want to bring Fat Chick with you?" Three asks as we step out the front door.

It takes all the willpower I have not to shove him down the porch steps. "I told you, you can't use anything you saw in there against me."

Three chuckles as we head to the car. "Like what? That you have really nice parents and a comfortable house?"

"Is 'comfortable' your way of saying 'small'?" I shoot him a look as I fish the key fob from my bag and unlock the car.

"Stop putting words in my mouth." He plucks the fob from my hand.

"Hey, are you—"

"I wouldn't drive if I wasn't," he says, cutting me off. Once we're buckled in and backing down the driveway, he adds, "You can sleep on the way there if you want."

I glance over at him, surprised. His hair is already drying, turning to soft waves that fall in his face, and I'm startled by how good his hands look on the steering wheel.

I face forward again. "Like I could ever fall asleep with you sitting next to me."

"Worried you'll have another dream about me?" he asks, his voice smug and teasing.

"I will kill you."

"Uh-huh." He grins, pulling his phone from the cup holder so he can start the directions. I didn't notice last night, but his lock screen is a picture of a fluffy gray cat.

"You have a cat." It comes out more a stunned statement than a question.

"My family has a cat. But yes." He flicks a look at me. "Her name is Dick."

"You named your cat *Dick*?"

He grins. "My sister named her Emily Dickinson. I call her Dick. It's very fitting."

"Wait, so that's—" I stop short, clamping my mouth shut. *Stupid, stupid, stupid.*

Three catches it anyway. We're pulling up to a stoplight, and he turns all the way toward me. "I knew it. I *knew* you did it."

"You don't know anything." I point to the road. "The light changed."

Someone behind us honks, but Three doesn't move. He's still staring at me with this irritated yet kind of impressed look on his face.

Someone honks again. "Three!"

He faces forward with all the urgency of a snail, finally stepping on the gas.

"So, did you just steal my story, or did you really have a look at my nudes?" he asks a few minutes later as he merges onto the highway. "Is that what inspired that dream you had?"

"I'm not participating in this line of questioning."

"That's fine," he says, a note of resolve in his voice. "I changed your porn ban headline and posted that opinion piece on the Tau Delt site. I also tipped off *Two Minute News* on your VR equipment story, but honestly, Evans, that was so boring; I did you a favor—"

"*Nathaniel!*" I screech, whipping to face him.

Three's mouth curls into a slow smirk. "I didn't know you knew my first name."

I splutter, rage-red and fuming. "Of course I know your first name! You really think I don't know how to do basic research."

"You researched me?" he asks, sounding pleased.

I ignore him. "God, I *knew* you did that! You were so smug—"

"I couldn't help it. It was funny. And hey, the porn ban thing got you the most readers you'll probably ever get, so you should thank me."

"You wish that were the case."

His smirk deepens. "You'll never top my best, that's for sure."

I eye him. "You mean your new story, don't you? The one you're working on with Christopher."

He gives a noncommittal shrug.

"You said you'd tell me."

"I guess I did say that." He exhales, stretching his neck. "Fine. It started with the story on your roommate."

"You're writing about Ellie?" It's enough to shock the anger right out of me.

"Sort of. I started looking into it after she got arrested. How a freshman from Akron ended up selling drugs. It's not like she would have had that many contacts in the area. I wanted to track down her supplier and see if it was worth pursuing."

I stare at him, dumbfounded. "You really think you're writing for the fucking *Post*, don't you?"

To my surprise, Three's ears redden. "It's important. Why shouldn't I be the one to write it?"

"Why are you even telling me this? You've never shared your stories with me before."

Three's hands tighten on the steering wheel. "I've been trying to figure out how to ask you . . ."

I narrow my eyes. "This feels like a trick."

"It's not a trick. You're so suspicious."

"Sorry, have you *met* you?"

He laughs. "Okay, that's fair, I guess. But I really do need your help. Ellie won't talk to me. I've emailed her half a dozen times. She only responded to the first one to tell me to fuck off, and then I think she blocked me, because I didn't hear anything else. Christopher got basically the same response."

"Gee, I can't imagine why."

"If I'd known looking into your roommate could lead me

to a campus drug ring, I might've held off on writing that article. But it's done now."

"So this is Christopher's big 'fuck you' to *Two Minute News*? You two bust a big time drug dealer, and he gets his revenge on them for scooping the laced Adderall story?"

"Christopher isn't that involved, and I don't think he's worried about getting revenge."

I give him a long look. There's no way he believes that.

"So what do you need me for?" I ask. "I don't know anything about it. I didn't even know she was selling until she got arrested."

Three's lips purse in a small smile. "Quite the investigative reporter, aren't you, Evans?"

"Screw you."

"Sorry. I'm kidding—sorry."

It's unsettling to hear him apologize for something, even casually like this.

"I was hoping you would talk to her," he says. "Maybe if it's with you, she'll do the interview."

"You want me to help with your story?" I continue to be dumbfounded by this conversation.

"Just with the interview," says Three.

It's a small clarification, but I don't miss the implication: *just* the interview. Not the story. Which means my credit is nonexistent.

"I want on the byline."

"No." His answer is lightning quick.

"Then I guess you'll have to work with what you've got."

"I'm not putting you on the byline for doing one interview. I've been working on this for weeks, and will probably have to keep working on it even longer."

I shrug. "Okay."

He sighs heavily, his jaw set. "Come on, this isn't some throwaway story. If I end up being right, it could be huge."

"Then I guess you'll be super happy to have your name alone on the byline."

Three swears. I can tell he's angry, and I'm almost giddy over it. Finally I have a little power here.

The drive back to campus goes by much faster than the one to the farm. Maybe it's because I get to sit smugly in the passenger seat while Three seethes beside me. Maybe it's because I'm not bone-tired the way I was last night. But whatever the reason, it feels like almost no time has passed before Three pulls up outside my building.

"Wyn," he says when I reach for the door.

I pause, turning back. It is extremely odd to hear him say my name to me. Sometimes he says it in the newsroom if he's mentioning me to someone else. But to me, it's always "Evans."

He lets out a long breath, staring straight ahead. "If you want your name on the byline, you'll have to do the work."

I tilt my head. "How so?"

He slides his hands down the steering wheel, a slow drag, and I try to blink away the image. I do not need that stored in my brain.

"I'm not giving you credit for doing one interview," he says. "If you want to work on it, you have to *work* on it. With me. Writing, interviewing. Investigating. All of it."

"What, you think I'm scared? That it'll be too hard for me?"

He turns his head toward me, resting it back against his seat. "You tell me. I think Ellie's supplier is on Greek Row. In the Sigma Rho house, specifically. And I think they're more than some small-time operation. I already know about two other houses that are definitely involved, and there are probably more. I want to know what they're selling, who's involved, and how they haven't gotten caught. It won't be easy, and it might be dangerous."

I stare at him, my mouth going dry.

"I only need the interview. But if you want credit, you're doing the work."

I hesitate. I don't want to help him, and I certainly don't want to do it without credit. But he's not wrong—it's an important story. Especially if it goes as far as he thinks.

"I . . ."

His brows arch expectantly.

"I'll let you know." I pop open the door and climb out of the car.

Three rolls down the window. "I can't wait forever. I need an answer soon."

"And you'll get one," I snap over my shoulder. "Just give me a little time."

As I swipe into the building, I glance back. Three still waits at the curb, watching me.

Only when the door swings shut between us does he pull away.

FOURTEEN

My Whispering Wall story is a hit by the *Torch*'s standards. Not a viral sensation like the Great Porn Ban, but widely read enough—or at least widely talked about enough—that when I walked past the Whispering Wall on Tuesday, there was a large group of people waiting to try it. For two days now, they've whispered secrets, confessions, and jokes to friends, lovers, and complete strangers at the other end of the curved wall, their words carried across the stone to waiting ears. A couple I interviewed who got engaged at the Whispering Wall is even coming back to do a photoshoot with it for their ten-year anniversary, and their story is making the rounds on social media.

Sabina is thrilled by the reaction, and she already wants something else like it.

I'm a little embarrassed that I'm so surprised by the story's success. But it reminds me of what Dara said about people liking stories about other people—and what my mom said about how they called me Neighborhood Watch when I was a kid. I was always fascinated by our neighbors. When one family lost their dog, I helped get the word out. When another had their house broken into, I tried to take statements from the neighbors. And when one lost his wife to cancer, I went door-to-door to make sure everyone knew. That was all about the *people*. I was getting the story out, but it wasn't sensation or scandal. That was probably my first brush with journalism.

Maybe all those things are the reason I want to do this in the first place. It makes me wonder how that couple who got engaged at the Whispering Wall would have felt if they'd found out it'd been torn down too late to get a few last photos. I can suddenly see the value, the way Dara and Madison do, in these types of stories. And maybe this is an angle the Campus Life column has been missing for a while—stories focused on people rather than scandal.

I'm excited to think of more, and brainstorming new ideas will be a nice distraction over my long, lonely Thanksgiving break.

I'll have time to think about Three's story too. Luckily, he isn't in the newsroom today, already out for the holiday weekend like most of the staff. I spent over an hour yesterday ignoring that penetrating gaze of his, until Madison texted me a link to a *Two Minute News* update about a fraternity under investigation for hazing involving a goat.

"Hey, hey, this is—this is—" I smacked at his arm, holding my phone out to him. "Do they know? Are we—is this—will they—?" The thought of being caught stealing a goat from a fraternity robbed me of my ability to form a complete sentence.

Three put a hand on my phone, lowering it. "Don't let Christopher see you watching *Two Minute News* in here."

"Three!"

He smirked. "Relax, Evans. That was me."

I stared at him, heart rate slowing. "This was . . . you."

He tipped his head toward me, lowering his voice. "I mean, would you have rather covered it? Someone needed to get the hazing investigation going. I wasn't really into it being me, and if you're public enemy number one on Greek Row, you can't exactly help me with my story, so . . ." He gave me a long look.

"And when *Two Minute News* connects it to us?"

"In the unlikely event they decide to actually investigate something instead of just regurgitating gossip they hear on campus, then that tip will lead them to an animal rights group that will happily claim responsibility for Chewy's kidnapping."

"Well." I gave a little sniff. "I guess you've got it covered." Then, unable to resist one last jab, I added, "Of course, I should've guessed, since you're an expert at tipping off *Two Minute News*."

He only laughed, returning to his work, and didn't bother

me again the rest of the day. Now he'll be off to wherever he's from—Cincinnati, I think—and I'll have the whole break to decide if I want to lean fully into this human-interest thing, or if I still want to be the investigative journalist I've always dreamed of.

Despite my various distractions and decisions to be made, the prospect of being truly alone for the next four days is daunting. My roommates are gone. My coworkers are gone. The *Torch* staff has cleared out. Campus is slowly shutting down, not to reopen until Monday.

At my desk, in the quiet, empty newsroom, I pull out my phone and open Buckonnect.

pomerene1765: in your opinion, what is the most depressing holiday?

His response comes almost immediately.

hayes6834: all of them
pomerene1765: oh are you one of those anti-holiday people?
hayes6834: I'm one of those anti-family time people
pomerene1765: most people would say valentine's day
hayes6834: one of the only holidays I'm NOT expected to sit at a table with my parents? I don't think so
hayes6834: I can tell you the least depressing holiday though

pomerene1765: what's that?

hayes6834: mardi gras

pomerene1765: ...

hayes6834: lol what?

pomerene1765: just say you love boobs and move on

hayes6834: ok that's not

hayes6834: well actually

hayes6834: listen I can't LIE but that's not why I like it

pomerene1765: it's great to see you place in your event again

hayes6834: my event?

pomerene1765: yeah the foot in mouth event

hayes6834: lol right

hayes6834: all I meant was I love king cake

hayes6834: also has anyone ever really been sad at a parade?

pomerene1765: I think I could be sad anywhere

I've hit send before I can think about it. Talking to Hayes is so easy, I didn't even hesitate to type it.

But now that I'm staring at the words, I feel the squeeze of regret. I shouldn't have said that. It's too real. Too raw. My throat aches suddenly with tears.

pomerene1765: lol maybe that's my olympic event

pomerene1765: anyway I've never had king cake before

His message comes through at the same time.

hayes6834: sometimes I really wish I could hold you

My heart jolts up into my throat. Whatever tears might have been coming dry up instantly.

When I don't respond right away, another message comes through.

hayes6834: it's kind of like coffee cake and a cinnamon roll had a baby
hayes6834: king cake
hayes6834: and the cake sometimes has a baby in it
hayes6834: not a real baby. like a toy
hayes6834: and if you get the baby in your piece it's supposed to be good luck
hayes6834: I freaked you out, didn't I?
pomerene1765: no I love the thought of a petit l'enfant in my cake
hayes6834: ha
hayes6834: you know that's not what I mean
pomerene1765: I'd actually kill to be held
pomerene1765: so no. you didn't freak me out.

When he doesn't say anything, I try to put us both out of our misery. Because being vulnerable is hard, even anonymously.

pomerene1765: if I don't talk to you tomorrow, I hope
you have a nice thanksgiving

hayes6834: you too

hayes6834: I hope you can recharge a little. I bet your
family will be happy to have you home

A dull ache blooms in my chest. But I don't want him to
think I'm pathetic, or to talk about my parents and where they'll
be instead this weekend.

pomerene1765: a little recharge would be nice

But when I think about recharging alone in my dorm room
for the next four days, I really, truly want to cry.

By the time Thanksgiving Day rolls around, the weight of my
loneliness is crushing. It shouldn't be, after only one day. But
I'm like a ship riddled with holes, taking on sadness fast enough
to capsize. I stay in bed until I can no longer stand it, and then
I get up and shower. I dry my hair with an actual hair dryer. I
do my makeup, curl my hair, spritz on my favorite perfume,
and then pick my nicest dress out of my closet. It is effort wildly
unfit for where I'm headed, but it feels fun. I'll breeze in like
someone mysterious, who might have come from any Thanksgiving table across town, but now she's had a craving for hash
browns, smothered and covered, that she cannot ignore.

The Waffle House near campus is much busier than I

expected. When I imagined this, I thought I'd be sitting alone at a table, gazing out the window at the passing cars while I sip bottomless cups of coffee.

Instead, I barely snag a spot at the crowded counter between a large man and a couple that's arguing loudly. I tune in as I place my order, happy for the distraction. Apparently, the woman was rude to the man's mother during their visit for Thanksgiving, and then the mother refused to feed them, and the woman insists his mother took something she said the wrong way, and *it is cruel and unusual not to feed someone on Thanksgiving.*

My plate is plunked down, and I cut into my waffle as the argument continues.

"Excuse me," I whisper to the man on my right, reaching for the syrup basket in front of him. At the same time, someone on his other side says, "Pardon me." A hand lands beside mine on the basket.

"Sorry," I say, leaning around my neighbor.

I freeze, and my jaw practically lands in my lap.

One seat over, Three mirrors me.

I draw my hand back from the syrup like I've been burned.

Then through the din of the shock buzzing in my ears, I hear the woman behind me shout, "You are *such* an asshole!"

And the man she's with gives a warning yelp as an ice-cold drink splashes across the back of my head and down my dress.

I jolt to my feet, tripping into the man between Three and me as I shake the ice out of the back of my dress.

"Uh-uh," the woman behind the counter says, pointing at the couple. Her name tag says *Marie*. "You two are out. *Now*."

While the couple is ushered out, I rush to the bathroom. I hunch over the sink, rinsing sticky soda from my hair.

Great, I think as I stare at my reflection. *Glad I went to all the trouble.* Most of the curls are already washed away, and I quickly take care of the rest. I unzip my dress and roll it to my waist so I can wipe down my back as best as possible using a wet paper towel. When I'm done, I struggle with tired arms to get the zipper back up, and it's still hanging open a couple of inches when I give up.

I return to my seat to find Three has moved to the empty stool on my left, bringing his plate and coffee with him. I hesitate as I get closer.

He glances up, his soft expression flattening at whatever he sees on my face. He looks pointedly at my empty seat.

My coffee is still there, but my plate is gone.

"They got your food too," Marie says as she pours some coffee for someone down the counter. "You just sit tight, okay?"

"Thank you," I reply.

"Can I get a small plate, please?" Three asks.

She produces one, and he starts shuffling some of his waffle onto it. He slides the plate over to me. I try to push it back, but he holds it in place.

"Eat," he says.

"Don't tell me what to do."

His gaze flicks to the back of my dress, and he reaches

behind me and yanks my zipper up the rest of the way in one quick movement. I nearly gasp, which is possibly the most embarrassing thing to happen tonight. And that's clearly saying something.

"Eat," he repeats.

I shovel a few bites of waffle into my mouth while I gather my bearings.

After a long moment, he asks quietly, "What are you doing here?"

I glance at him as I chew. He's eyeing my outfit, which makes me angry for some reason. I push his face away. "Don't look at me," I say around a mouthful of waffle. "What are *you* doing here?"

"I asked you first."

"I just got soda dumped down the back of my dress."

Three huffs out a laugh. "And?"

"You're supposed to take pity."

He levels me with a serious look. "I would never be dumb enough to take pity on you, Evans." He turns toward me, nudging his knee against my thigh. "When did you get back?"

"I never went anywhere." My new plate arrives, and I busy myself cutting into my own waffle and mixing up my hash browns. "Your turn."

"Me either. Why didn't you go home?"

I glare at my plate, spearing a few bites onto my fork. "There was a circumstance."

"That's your favorite explanation, isn't it?"

"And you?" I circle my fork, prompting him to answer.

"Several circumstances."

I roll my eyes. "What a thrilling conversation."

"Should we get in an argument, and you can throw your drink on me?"

I try not to remember how he said he gets turned on when he argues.

"You'd better not," Marie says. She's returned to put some plates down for the person on Three's other side.

Three tosses her a grin, and she smiles, clearly immediately charmed.

"Don't look him in the eye," I say. "He sold his soul for that smile."

Marie chuckles. "Might've been worth it."

Three positively preens. "Thank you very much," he says, laying it on thick.

"I am throwing up in my mouth," I mutter.

"So, what's with the dress?" Three asks as Marie moves down the counter. "Big plans tonight?"

"Oh yeah," I reply. "Huge. Huge plans."

"A date?" It comes out glib, and I bristle.

"You bet. Just wanted to get some food first." I shove another bite of waffle into my mouth. "Could be a long night."

"I would've skipped the onions, then," he says, pointing his fork at my smothered-and-covered hash browns.

"I hope I never see the day I want your opinion on how I approach a date."

"Anyone I know?" he asks, leaning an elbow on the counter.

"Sure, but not super well." I hold up my right hand and wiggle my first two fingers at him.

Three stops, then turns slowly and drops his head to the counter.

I grin at my plate, victorious. It's nice to see Three squirm for once.

"Is he dead?" Marie asks when she walks by again.

"God, I hope so," I reply.

Three doesn't move.

"So, what are your plans tonight?" I ask him. "Something similar, I assume."

When he sits up, his cheeks are pink. "Not exactly."

"Oh, a real date, then?"

"I'd tell you, but you haven't given me an answer about interviewing your roommate yet."

I focus on my food again. "I haven't decided."

"Decide now."

But it's not that easy. I think I'm starting to find my voice at the *Torch*, and I don't want to lose that to Three's story.

"It's a holiday," I say. "I'm off the clock."

"Then I guess you're out of questions."

I take a few more bites, clearing my plate. The silence is weighted as Three does the same.

When Marie drops my check, Three snatches it, folding it inside a big bill, which he passes to Marie before I can protest.

"Happy Thanksgiving," he says to her.

I gape at him. "What—Why—"

He hops off his stool. "Happy Thanksgiving, Evans." He ruffles my hair in an infuriating gesture, then turns and heads to the door, shrugging on his coat.

I blink at Marie.

She raises her eyebrows, nodding in the direction of the door.

"Happy Thanksgiving," I say to her, jumping down from my stool.

By the time I make it out the door, Three is a few store-fronts away.

"Tell me what you're doing tonight," I call, shoving my arms into my coat.

Three turns, walking backward. "I don't think I will." He tucks his hands into his pockets, and I'm certain he's enjoying himself right now.

"Call it a trial run," I say as I get closer. He's slowed to let me catch up, so I know he hasn't written me off entirely. "I'll come with you. To see if I really want to do this story or not."

I want to—badly. But I'm worried about the balancing act—this story, work, my new human-interest angle on Campus Life, and somehow not failing all my classes, particularly statistics.

I need to know this is worth how hard I'll have to work.

Three laughs. "How generous." He turns, speeding up again. "Go home, Evans."

I let out a frustrated growl. I know he's probably playing

with me, backing me into a corner until I can no longer fight my curiosity. Because he isn't heading toward campus, and when he gets to the end of the block, he makes a right toward Greek Row.

I start after him, resolving that if he won't tell me, I'll just have to follow him.

But when I turn the corner, he's waiting, leaning up against the side of the building. He tilts his head toward me lazily, his expression amused.

"Fine," I say.

He raises his eyebrows.

"Fine, I'll do the interview. Fine." I pause, considering this. "I mean, I'll give it my best shot. I told you we aren't friends."

"Text her."

I balk. "Right now?"

"I need proof you'll actually do it."

I take my phone out, holding it up to show him as I open my texts with Ellie. She's still embarrassingly high in my messages list, even though we haven't texted in months.

I start typing: *Hey, Ellie. Are you available*

Three grabs the phone. "No. Jesus, Evans, do you have no idea how to talk to people?"

I bristle, snatching it back. We both fumble for the phone, yanking it back and forth, and when I finally get a look at the screen, I yelp in dismay.

"Three!" I hold up the phone, both our hands still clasped around it.

ME:

He

He jerks it out of my hands and starts typing, thumbs flying across the screen. When I peek over his shoulder, he has a block of text written.

ME:

Hey. Sorry. I hit send too fast. I just wanted to say hi and Happy Thanksgiving. I hope you're doing well. I've been thinking a lot about you and the story the Torch did. I'm really sorry if you were hurt by it. I would have warned you but I didn't know about it until it was too late. But I should have reached out then anyway.

I guess he can clearly see I haven't texted Ellie since September, when I sent, *Did I leave a blue notebook on my bed?* and Ellie responded, *No.*

Three keeps typing.

ME:

I want to try to make it right if you're up for it. I'd like to get your side of things. It can be as short an interview as you want. I don't think you started selling on your own and it's not fair that you're going down alone now.

I stare at the messages, then look at him. "You are a master manipulator, aren't you?"

I don't say what I'm really thinking: How does he manage to *sound* like me?

He passes my phone back to me. "I didn't say anything that isn't true."

"Right. Of course. Because you're so worried about the people your articles might hurt."

"I know you'll hate to hear this, Evans, but I do actually worry." He scrapes his hand through his hair. "I joined the *Torch* because I want to write stories that help people. I'm sorry your roommate had a tough time because of me, but she did that to herself. She was selling drugs. *Hard drugs.* So I'm a little confused how you've made me out to be the bad guy in all this."

I bite my lip, my chest squeezing with embarrassment. Because he's right, to a point. I don't know if I believe he's on the *Torch* to do good so much as he is chasing glory, but he's right about Ellie. Whatever has happened to her, it's because she made a very bad choice. One that had the potential to hurt a lot of other people.

I look away, mumbling out a quiet, "Sorry."

I feel Three's attention swivel back to me. "What was that?"

I hold up a hand. "Don't push it." When I look over, he's grinning, delighted. I groan. "Ugh. That's pushing it."

His grin widens somehow, even though it's already stretched far enough to crack his face in two.

"So, what are you doing? I did my part. You have to tell me your plans."

Three coughs into his fist, glancing down the street. Then he inches closer, leaning down to whisper in my ear.

"I'm breaking into the Sigma Rho house."

The Sigma Rho house is at the center of Greek Row, a few doors down from Tau Delta Pi. The windows are dark, and Three leads me around the side to the empty parking lot in back. He walks with the confidence of someone who's sure we won't get caught.

"'Breaking in'?" I whisper, lifting my hands to give it air quotes when he produces a key to the back door.

Three flashes me a grin, pushing the door open with his shoulder. "I grabbed it at a party last week. You'd be shocked how many of these guys leave their shit just lying around."

As we step inside, I observe the state of the kitchen, which has dishes piled high in the sink, an old pizza box on the island, and, sitting by the door, two trash bags that, judging by the smell, have been here awhile.

I press my nose into my sleeve. "Yeah, no, that's not taking a stretch of the imagination, actually."

He motions for me to follow him through the kitchen

into the hall. We pass a great room with two large couches, big enough to easily seat twenty but littered with discarded clothes, a blanket I could not be paid to touch, and a single boat shoe inexplicably tied to the ceiling fan.

"Please tell me your frat house isn't this disgusting," I whisper to Three as we start up the stairs.

He shoots me an insulted look over his shoulder, shaking his head.

"Oh please, you said you don't even like it," I hiss as we reach the second floor.

He puts a finger to his lips, and my eyes pop wide.

Is someone here? I mouth.

He rolls his eyes. "No, but I'm trying to focus."

He points toward a door down the hall. I follow him, my heart hammering harder with each creak of the floor.

Inside, Three motions to the desk, which is strewn with every piece of junk imaginable, though no schoolwork. "We're looking for a stash. Bags, bottles, anything." He pulls open the curtains, letting in light from the moon and the streetlamps outside. "I think he's Ellie's supplier, but I can't link him to the guys at the other houses unless I find what he's dealing."

I start pulling open drawers, rifling through their contents and checking for false bottoms like I'm Sherlock Holmes or something. Three opens the closet, flicking on his phone flashlight as he pushes around the clothes and shoes inside. I exhaust myself on the desk and move to check under the bed, but I end up touching something fuzzy and immediately start to gag.

"So dramatic," Three mutters.

"Oh, you touch it, then!"

"If you can't handle it, I guess I'll have to—*oh*. Scratch that." He waves me over.

He's unearthed a backpack from beneath a pile of clothes, and inside are several plastic bags. Most are filled with different-colored pills, and a few more with pot.

Three snaps some pictures, flipping through each bag carefully to make sure he gets every variety and quantity. As I hold one up for him, I have the good sense to ask, "Um, should I be worried about leaving fingerprints on these?"

He huffs out a laugh. "Jesus, Evans, you watch too much TV."

"It's a reasonable question!" I start returning some of the bags to the backpack, frowning at the stash. It's certainly a lot of drugs. "Why would he leave this here when he's out of town?"

"He's not out of town," says Three. "He's from here."

"*What?*" The word leaves my mouth on a hiccup.

Downstairs, a door slams.

Three's eyes widen.

"I'm gonna throw up," I moan.

Three quickly piles everything back into the closet, then grabs me and pulls me out the door. He leaves it open behind us, exactly how we found it.

We duck into a room across the hall, where he tugs me into another closet and slides the door shut behind us. I grab onto him like he's the last life raft and the ship is sinking. At the very least, I can fling him at whoever finds us as a distraction while I make a run for it.

"Cozy," Three murmurs.

"If you don't shut the hell up," I hiss back.

Feet thunder up the stairs, and I close my eyes, dropping my forehead to Three's shoulder. I've lost all sense of reality beyond what's happening on the other side of this door. Three must have too, because he puts his arms around me and gently smooths his hand down my back.

"It'll be fine," he whispers, tilting his head down so his mouth is right by my ear. "We won't get caught."

I swallow down my nerves and let out a slow, shaky breath.

I don't know how much time passes before I hear a bedroom door shut. Music starts up loudly on the other side.

Three maneuvers us, keeping his arms around me. He leans back against the wall, using one hand to crack the door a sliver. It lets in a dim, orange glow. The hall light must be on now.

"Come on," he whispers, pushing the closet door open.

I widen my eyes at him, shaking my head. But he steps out into the room, pulling me with him. I try to take several calming breaths as we move to the door. He leans out, keeping one arm stretched back toward me. Then he waves me forward as he steps out into the hall.

I freeze in the doorway.

He looks back, motioning for me to move.

I shake my head, heart pounding.

Three's expression darkens, and he grabs my wrist, yanking me into the hall. We tiptoe past the room we were just searching, music rattling the closed door. We take the stairs as quietly as possible, and I wince at every creak and groan of the wood beneath our feet.

Outside, Three leads me along the back of the house, keeping close to the wall, before we slip down the yard and to the street.

"Oh my god," I whisper when we reach the sidewalk. Three keeps moving, pulling me along at a clip. "I thought I was gonna die."

"You froze," Three says, accusation in his voice. His hand on my wrist is burning hot.

"I was *scared*!" I jerk my arm out of his grasp. "You gave me zero warning going in there! If I'd known he could come home at any second—"

"He shouldn't have. His parents live in town, but he was supposed to be there late." He rushes a hand through his hair. "I don't know why he came back so early."

"And I had no way of knowing you wouldn't abandon me in there! You'd be guaranteed the Campus Life spot if I got picked up for a fucking B and E."

"B and E." He rolls his eyes. "You really do watch way too much TV."

I speed up until he's several feet behind me.

"Oh, come on," he calls, jogging to catch up. "I wouldn't

have left you. You would've immediately sold me out, and Christopher would know you weren't lying, so—"

I let out a high, outraged sound. "I'm so glad to know that's your reasoning! Not because it would be a horrible thing to do!"

"Hey, I got you out of there, didn't I?" He catches my elbow, pulling me back beside him. "I wouldn't have left you. I had four different plans to get you out of that house. I might mess with you, but I wouldn't abandon you like that."

He's loosened up now, likely coming off an adrenaline rush. I'm still on edge, but his calm is rubbing off on me.

"Four different plans?" I eye him. "Are you some kind of criminal mastermind?"

"I developed some specialized skills at boarding school."

"Right. Boarding school again."

"I can't change that I went there."

"You can change how often you bring it up. Although I'm sure it's hard not to think about it when you're still using your boarding school nickname."

I mean it as a jab, but Three responds sincerely. "Three isn't a boarding school nickname." At my incredulous look, he grins. "I've always gone by Three. Wells was the first one to get a boarding school nickname. Three's a family nickname."

"Wells?"

His expression shifts, and he coughs lightly. "My, uh, cousin." He looks out to the road, and I miss whatever happens next on his face. When he lets me see his eyes again, whatever clouded in them has gone. He tucks his hands into his pockets and smiles. "Anyway, it probably is annoying to hear about it, but I can't help it today. Thanksgiving always makes me think of them."

"Your school?"

"My friends." He shrugs. "My cousins."

"Why didn't you go home, then? See your cousins, at least. I know your boarding school friends probably aren't all from whatever hell town you crawled out of."

"Cincinnati," he says.

"So why didn't you go back to Cincinnati for Thanksgiving? Reminisce about your boarding school days with someone who cares?"

"Because I needed to do this." He jerks his thumb over his shoulder, indicating the Sigma Rho house. His gaze slides straight ahead, almost like he's avoiding my eyes. "And because I didn't want to be at home."

"Don't you miss your cat? And your sister?"

He sighs. "Yeah. Look, Evans, the truth sucks. I ditched my sister and my cat and my cousins because I didn't want to deal with my parents. Wells has already given me a hard enough time for it, so I really don't need to hear it from you too. I know you think I've got this bright and shiny life, and I guess I do for the most part, but it's not always nice. It's rarely ever fun. And Thanksgiving is just a big table where you get served expectations with a side of expectations, and for dessert it's expectations pie. It's not the worst thing in the world, and I'm grateful to have somewhere to go, but I couldn't deal this year. And clearly"—he circles a hand in the direction of the Sigma Rho house again—"I had shit to do."

His frown deepens, and I wonder if he feels the instant regret of sharing so much truth with me. I want to give him a hard time—I had *nowhere* to go, and a lot of people have it way worse than I did this year. But he's clearly already aware of that, and it's not his responsibility to make himself miserable just because he had somewhere to go and chose not to.

So instead I say, "Thanks for not leaving me. In the house. I won't freeze up next time."

"You better not," he says, but it's lacking bite. I get the sense he appreciates the change in subject.

"So there *will* be a next time?"

"Wasn't this your trial run?"

"Does it still count if I can't get your interview?" I pull my phone from my bag and show him the blank screen. Nothing from Ellie yet.

"Give it time," he says.

"I guess that's a no."

"It's not a no. This was your tryout." He grins over at me. "I *might* let you on the team."

"You and me, on a team?"

"Just for this," he says quickly. "I still plan to destroy you to get the Campus Life spot."

"Glad to know you haven't been body snatched, then."

He leaves me at the front of my building, waiting to see me inside before he turns and starts toward his dorm.

I realize when I'm lying in bed later, recovering from the adrenaline, that I can still feel the ghost of Three's embrace. And what I told Hayes is true—I would kill to be held like that again.

Even if it had to be Three.

FIFTEEN

I get a response from Ellie the next afternoon. I'm four episodes into a show I've been meaning to watch all semester while I jot down some new ideas for the *Torch* and try not to think about Three's story—*our* story, hopefully.

Her message says two words: *Happy Thanksgiving.*

I wait awhile, convincing myself she's just nervous and will agree any second now. But it's hours later when I finally realize I'm fooling myself and send the screenshot to Three.

I've just sat down at my desk with a bowl of instant ramen, my Thanksgiving-break staple since the dining halls are closed, when my phone rings, his name flashing on the screen.

"She said no?" he says in place of a greeting.

"Hello, Three."

"She didn't say anything else? That was it? That's time-stamped two seventeen. You waited *five hours* to tell me?"

"I thought she might change her mind. I wanted to give her some time." I blow steam off my bowl. "This is kind of weird, you calling me. I don't think I like the sound of your voice right in my ear."

He huffs out a laugh, and it's so soft, I almost feel the brush of it through the phone. "I'm sure you'll be dreaming about it later."

I clamp my teeth down on the ends of my chopsticks in a grimace. "You know, you make that joke a lot for someone whose secrets I know too."

The other end of the line goes deliciously quiet.

"So, am I still allowed to be in?" I twirl up a clump of noodles and shove them in my mouth.

"Do you have to slurp *directly* into the phone?"

"Are you one of those people who hates the sound of other people eating?"

"Yes," he answers tightly.

I slurp louder.

"You're still allowed to be in if you stop doing that. Right now."

"Fine. Is that all? My noodles are getting soggy."

"We should meet up," he says.

I drop my chopsticks.

In the following silence, Three clears his throat. "Stop making it weird."

"I'm not. You want to meet?"

Three goes quiet for a minute. Then he says, "Never mind.

We can talk about it with Christopher when he's back."

"I can meet," I say quickly.

"I gotta go. Bye."

"Hey—" But the call ends abruptly.

I'm still reeling when my phone buzzes a few minutes later.

I scramble to grab it, but I stop when I see it isn't Three.
I'm shocked to find I'm disappointed, but the feeling quickly
dissipates when I realize it's a Buckonnect notification.

hayes6834: happy thanksgiving

hayes6834: I forgot to say it yesterday

pomerene1765: happy thanksgiving

pomerene1765: clearly I forgot too

hayes6834: I hope that means you were having too good
a time to think about anything else

hayes6834: hold on that sounded passive aggressive

pomerene1765: lol no it didn't!

hayes6834: pom. trust me. you know that scene from
lion king when mufasa tells simba that everything the
light touches is their kingdom?

pomerene1765: yes?

hayes6834: in my family it's everything the passive
aggression touches. I know it when I see it. let me try that
again.

pomerene1765: if you must

hayes6834: I hope you had such a great thanksgiving
you couldn't think about your various...stresses

pomerene1765: thank you. I hope you did too.

hayes6834: now what would make you think I'm stressed out?

pomerene1765: it couldn't be the intense need to not be even a little bit misunderstood.

hayes6834: ah. I guess you have a point.

pomerene1765: so did you have a good thanksgiving?

He doesn't respond right away, and when I look down, I notice my noodles are bloated. I quickly finish the rest, grimacing at the loss of chewiness.

I'm slurping down the broth when my phone finally buzzes again.

hayes6834: definitely up there

hayes6834: maybe the best

pomerene1765: wow. must've been some pie.

hayes6834: I prefer the cranberry sauce

pomerene1765: oh so you're a serial killer

hayes6834: I thought we already established that

hayes6834: so how was yours?

pomerene1765: my thanksgiving?

hayes6834: yeah. top five? top ten?

pomerene1765: hmm

I think about yesterday. The sadness that followed me all day. The soda thrown down my back. Sharing a meal with

Three. The gripping terror that we might get caught in the Sigma Rho house.

The weight of his arms around me, and his hand smoothing down my back.

I let out a slow breath. *Nope*. Not going down that road again.

> **hayes6834:** that bad?
> **pomerene1765:** not at all! it was good
> **pomerene1765:** surprisingly good
> **hayes6834:** I'm really glad to hear that
> **hayes6834:** so would you rather drink the entire gravy boat or eat a whole bowl of cranberry sauce?
> **pomerene1765:** there is a special place in hell for you
> **hayes6834:** so I've been told

Late that night, I lift my self-imposed social media ban and find myself staring at that familiar private profile.

third.

My finger hovers over that *request to follow* button for a long time before I finally give into my months-long curiosity and click it.

Then I throw my phone facedown on my bed and begin to hyperventilate a little.

It's only research. It's not because I want to know about his cousins and his sister and his cat. We're still competitors, and knowing about his life gives me an advantage. He's probably already seen my profile, which has always been public, because I didn't think of it until long after our war began. Three is no dummy. My only comfort is that I've never been very active on social media, and there's nothing he could possibly have learned about me that I hadn't already freely given him in those first few weeks of school.

When my phone buzzes a few minutes later, I dive for it, heart lodged in my throat.

THREE:

I'm flattered

ME:

ME: Know your enemy and all that

Sun Tzu??

Rage against the machine

After a few minutes, I get a response.

THREE:

These guys are really good at spelling

ME:

Hilarious

A second later, I get a notification that he's approved my follow request. I immediately open his profile and begin to scroll with the frenzy of someone worried she might be blocked in the next thirty seconds, just for fun. I certainly wouldn't put it past him.

Three texts again.

THREE:

Enjoy

But I think you already got the best pictures off my computer

I don't respond, because I will not be baited into arguing about whether or not I looked at his nudes.

Besides, I'm busy.

Three isn't very active on social media either. His last post is from earlier this semester, where he's pictured at a football game with some guys from Tau Delta Pi. One of them is shirtless, banging his chest, and Three is grinning at the camera. I think it's the same day he found me walking home high on edibles, judging by his outfit and the date.

There's another of him at a frat party. Then one from summer, standing on the edge of a boat in a pair of swim trunks, about to jump off into dark blue water. Before that, it's a close-up selfie with that fluffy gray cat lying horizontal across the bottom half of his face, only his eyes visible.

He posted more often before college, documenting his boarding school days. I scour the public profiles of people he tagged and find Three in snaps from a Halloween party, at a carnival, in a bookstore. Laughing over pizza, over coffee, over ice cream.

A lot of laughter.

On a girl's profile, I discover a photo of him from graduation, his arm around another boy. Three is grinning, still wearing his cap. The other boy holds his cap in one hand, ruffling his dark, messy hair. His head is ducked slightly, but he's smiling.

The caption reads: *ewww wellborns (affectionate)*

I click the other boy's tag, and it takes me to a new profile, this one private. There is no full name or profile description, only: *Wells.*

This is the first photo I've found of the elusive cousin, and I study it for a long time. There's an easiness between them—Wells's playful exasperation and Three's unguarded smile. It reminds me of looking at pictures of my parents from high school—finding all the subtle differences in their faces, marveling at how they've changed. This feels like seeing a photo of my mom at twenty, surrounded by her friends, and realizing she had a life before me.

I don't know what it is that's different in Three now, but I can feel it. That the Three I know isn't entirely the boy in these photos. And I can't pinpoint exactly what has changed.

* * *

I spend the rest of the weekend messaging Hayes to distract myself from obsessively scrolling the profiles of Three's boarding school friends or panicking about what angle I'll take on his story if Ellie refuses to speak to me.

Then Sunday morning, as I'm crunching on my last granola bar and despairing about how I need to buy more, I get a surprising text.

ELLIE:

If you can meet today far off campus and alone I'll talk

But it's off the record

Fuck that sounds so STUPID

You're not publishing anything I say but I'll talk to you

ONLY you. I'm not talking to that asshole.

There's no question which asshole she means.

When Ellie walks into the coffee shop in German Village, I'm already seated at a table with my coffee, alone. She stops inside the door, scans the room, then makes her way to my table.

"Don't you want to order?" I ask as she drops into the seat across from me.

"No," she says. "I won't be here long."

I blink at her. "O . . . kay. Um, it's good to see you."

She slides off her sunglasses and arches a brow. "Let's not pretend we're meeting up because we missed each other."

I pick up my phone and open the questions I prepared with Three on the Uber ride here. "Should I just start, then?"

"No, I'll start." She eyes my phone. "You aren't recording me, right? And you won't publish this?"

I shake my head.

She raises her eyebrows. "I'm gonna need a verbal *no* on that."

"No, I'm not recording you, and I won't publish anything you say. I swear." I hesitate, leaning in a little. "But I could keep you anonymous. If you wanted—"

"They'd know."

"Who?"

"You should drop this story. You, or whoever it is that's doing it." She glances over her shoulder like we're in some kind of spy movie and someone might be following her. "I got my stash from a frat on campus. I'm sure you've already gotten that far."

I nod.

She waves a hand at my phone. "Forget those questions. Forget the whole thing. I'm not the only person on campus who was dealing, and it's not just one or two frats. It goes higher than you think." She lowers her voice, leaning in. "These are dangerous people."

"Will they, like, kill you for talking to me?" I whisper, panic rearing up.

Ellie blinks at me. "You watch way too much TV."

I glower at her. "I am so sick of hearing that. You're the one who keeps looking around like you're being followed."

"That's because I know you brought that snake from the *Torch* with you. I just don't know where he's hiding." She shoulders her bag. "But you can let him know that despite his best efforts, I didn't get kicked out of school."

"I don't think that's what he—"

"It *is*. It is what he wanted. I'm sure he'll be thrilled to know I'm on probation. But why don't you tell him and see what he thinks?" She stands. "I shouldn't have even warned you. If he gets his ass kicked, I'd just wish I could watch. But I don't want you to get caught up in it too. Let him catch hell all on his own. You don't need to help him."

I watch her as she angles to leave.

"I do miss you, you know," I say.

Ellie stops, half turning back to the table.

I stand. "I miss having you around."

She sighs, her expression softening. "You'd miss having anyone around, Wyn. It didn't have to be me."

I watch her leave, discomfort sharp in my chest. I never thought Ellie was paying attention to me, but she clocked my desperation either way.

I pick up my coffee and walk to a booth at the back of the café, sliding in across from Three. He had his back to our table, but as I approach, I see he's been using his phone to record us.

"We can't use that."

He gives me a flat look. "I know. It's not like I got any sound. I just wanted to see what her body language was like."

I'm not happy knowing he was recording me too. Not only because he didn't ask, but because I'm struck with sudden awareness of how my body looks from the side when I sit. Try as I might to love my body all the time, at every angle, sometimes insecurities can catch you like a fox in a trap. I'm only human. I hate that he has this now, immortalized on his phone for as long as he wishes to keep it. And I hate even more how it makes my own internalized fatphobia, which I battle so hard every day, rear its ugly head.

"Delete it."

His brows arch in surprise. "Now?"

"You didn't ask me." I can't look at him as I say it, ashamed that I've let my insecurity get the best of me, but unable to stop it.

Three blinks. Then he turns his screen toward me and hits the delete button. I watch the video disappear.

"Start from the beginning," he says, setting his phone in the middle of the table. His finger hovers over the button to record our conversation, but he stops and gives me a questioning look.

I nod.

"Sorry," he says as he hits record. "About the video. I should've asked."

Normally I love when he humbles himself—mostly because I know he hates to do it. But right now I can't even enjoy it. I wish I hadn't said anything. I feel like I've flayed myself open for Three to see where I'm weakest, and he has to guess—it must be so obvious—that this moment was about the way I look.

"It's fine," I reply.

He levels me with a look. "Don't say 'it's fine' when people apologize to you, Evans. It minimizes your feelings."

I open my mouth, then slowly shut it. After a moment, I say, "That was surprisingly insightful."

"Surprisingly," he says with a snort.

"You don't seem like someone all that worried about other people's feelings."

His small smile evaporates. He lifts his coffee and takes a sip. "Let's start from the first question."

"Well, we didn't exactly do the questions."

Three sighs.

SIXTEEN

Monday afternoon, Three and I meet with Christopher to talk about what we found in the Sigma Rho house and the interview with Ellie.

"So with Ellie's confirmation and what you've found, that's three houses involved. Is this enough for you to write it up?" he asks Three, who leans against the edge of Christopher's desk. "Do you think we could put it in the next edition?"

Three rubs a hand over his face. "I don't want to rush it. If we believe what Ellie says, then there might be more to it. It'd explain why her suppliers have been able to get so big without anyone getting caught. This could go higher than we thought, and right now we don't have anyone on the record to substantiate that. Once we publish, it's over."

Christopher turns his attention to me, where I sit in the

chair on the other side of his desk. "And there's no way your roommate will go on the record?"

"Not a chance, and especially not for him." I jerk my thumb at Three.

"Then what's your next move?" Christopher asks. "If we can't publish now, we'll have to wait until next semester."

"Will that delay the decision on the Campus Life spot?" I ask, purposely not looking at Three.

Christopher hesitates. "Sabina and I talked about that. You're both already contributing to the column, so . . . we may wait to decide."

"*What?*" Three and I say in unison.

"That's not fair!" I say. We have only so much time before our applications to the journalism school are due. I've been so worried about finishing our drug story in time to include it, I didn't consider what would happen if Sabina delayed the decision on Campus Life. If I lose the Campus Life spot, I won't have time to come up with anything else to pad my résumé—I'll have to rely on the articles I've written so far and this drug story, shared with Three. I don't want to end up looking like his assistant, and I don't know what they'll think of the rest of my material. I know my human-interest pieces are good, but what if the print journalism they're looking for is the pull-no-punches type of reporting Three has been doing?

Christopher shrugs. "We don't have enough to make a decision right now, and we really can't give one of you up yet. We'll bring on another grunt in the spring and announce after that. Until then, with both of you contributing, we won't have any lapse in coverage when Angelica leaves, so . . ." He frowns, looking from Three's tight expression to my furious one. "Hey, take your complaints to Sabina. She's editor-in-chief."

I don't move, glancing at Three. If one of us is going to complain to Sabina, it'll have to be him. I certainly won't risk it.

He returns my look with an unimpressed arch of his brows.

I shrug. Worth a shot—if not to get an answer, then at least to get him on her bad side.

"We can publish this next semester," Three says. "I think we'll have a bigger story by then."

As we make our way back to the grunt desk, Three leans down at my shoulder and says, "Hey, don't be too upset about the Campus Life spot." He pats me lightly on the back. "You weren't getting it either way. So this doesn't really affect you."

I stop, a sucked-a-lemon smile on my face.

Three drops into his seat, grinning up at me. He clearly has no issues letting me have the extra height on him, which irritates me to no end. He *really* thinks I'm not a threat. And if it weren't for Ellie, he would have never considered letting me work on this story with him.

He thinks her interview is all I bring to the table.

I can hardly focus on anything else for the rest of the day. Not as I work on my story for tonight's deadline—an in-depth article on a campus organization for Native American and

Indigenous students, the first of its kind and run by the university's only Native American faculty member. And not later, as I go through the motions of my shift at the library—mostly avoiding Scott, who did not forget in the five days the library was closed that he hates my guts.

I'm still seething and trying, without luck, to plan how I can make myself a major player in this story, when I leave the library that evening and run into Lincoln outside.

"Hey," he says when he spots me. He's coming up the path, backpack slung over one shoulder. "How was your break?"

"It was good," I answer. "How was yours? Relax, recharge?" I study his face for any reaction to the word "recharge."

But he only smiles. "As much as I could. But the whole family was in town, so . . . not as much as I wanted. Two of my cousins just had kids, so it was the whole baby parade thing."

"Was it fun, at least? If not restful?" My heart hammers as I wait for confirmation, remembering what Hayes said about his Thanksgiving: *maybe the best.*

"Oh yeah, it was great," he says. "It's always good being home."

But that doesn't quite fit. I think back on what Hayes said about the holidays: *I'm one of those anti–family time people.*

Maybe I'm reading too much into it. Hayes might have only meant his parents. He clearly has a complicated relationship with them.

I realize I've let the silence stretch too long and clear

my throat. "So, the library? First day after break?"

Lincoln sighs. "Well, finals are coming, and I've got a kickball tournament this weekend. Last one of the year. Gotta manage my time right."

"Yeah, you'd hate to get the gold medal in kickball only to fail your exams."

"My parents would murder me," he says with a smile. "My mom's already pissed I'm doing this. But, you know, what's a little parental disappointment for the sake of a win?" His smile rings false now, like something might be eating at him.

That sounds more like Hayes. The strings connecting them remind me of fishing wire—perfectly visible only in the right light.

I tuck my hands into my coat pockets. "Well, you can sleep easy knowing *I* won't be disappointed in you." I pause, pretending to think. "Unless you lose. In which case, I'm not sure I can continue to be seen with you."

His gaze brightens again. "You know what? You should come. I think I'd play better knowing I can get these kinds of inspirational pep talks between games." He changes course quickly, his expression turning sensible. I'm talking to RA Lincoln now. "Ah, but you should be studying for finals. So maybe just one game. Half a game, even, if it's boring."

I laugh. "You're really selling it."

"Well, you've been to one, so you know what it's about," he says, that ever-present smile crinkling the corners of his eyes.

It would be a nice distraction from everything else—finals, the delay on the Campus Life decision, this story with Three. Especially how much he underestimates me.

Plus, Lincoln might be Hayes. And if I want to know for sure—turn that fishing wire to rope—then I need to spend more time with him.

"Count me in."

I spend the next week alternating between studying and planning my next move. Finals are coming, and whether I pass or fail statistics relies entirely on how well I do on this exam. I also have only one more chance to get a good story into the *Torch* before winter break. And I'm still so angry at Three, just seeing his smug face makes me want to scream. Even Lincoln's kickball tournament, which was cold, rainy, and miserable, wasn't enough to distract me. Although the fraternity team they played against was terrible—possibly drunk—and watching them wipe out every few minutes on the muddy field cheered me up slightly.

But a real bright spot opens up in my weekend when I hear about a party at Theta Kappa Alpha, one of the fraternities on my and Three's short list of potential dealers, and I begin to hatch a plan.

One I am far too chicken to attempt without help.

"A frat party?" Dara stares at me, mouth ajar. She's perched at her desk, tablet propped in front of her. Everyone is getting into finals mode now.

Madison is sprawled on her stomach on her bed, head-phones in, as she clacks away at her computer. Her fingers still at Dara's words, and she pops an earbud out, looking over at us. "Did you just say you want to go to a frat party?"

I should spend the night studying, or working on my next human-interest piece for the *Torch*—a story about a twenty-four-hour diner called Claude's that used to be a campus-adjacent staple, especially during finals. It closed a few years ago after the owner, Claude Jacobson, passed away. He was famous for hosting Holidays for Everyone, a party and dinner for unhoused folks in the area. Since the diner's closure, restaurants across the city have taken up the tradition in Claude's honor—they call it Claude's Holidays for Everyone.

It runs entirely off donations, the rest of the costs covered by the restaurants, and I'm hoping my story might help inspire new donors, especially after Kate's GoFundMe was so successful.

I have great notes and some interviews done, but the draft itself is bare-bones. Finishing it will definitely eat into my studying time for finals.

But I *need* to go to this party.

I turn a big, cheesy smile on Dara. "I was hoping you'd go with me?"

Dara continues to stare at me. "To a *frat party*?"

Madison sits up on her knees, popping out her other earbud. "Can I come?"

Dara's look of shock swings toward Madison. I follow with an identical expression.

"What?" Madison brushes at her face, as though a stray crumb might be the source of our deep disbelief.

"*You* want to go to a party," Dara says.

"If you're both going," says Madison.

I look at Dara. "Are we both going?"

"Am I dreaming right now? Why would you want to do this?" Dara leans back in her chair and crosses her arms. "You hate frats."

"I thought it'd be fun."

"I'm sure it will be. I don't trust whatever this is, though." She swivels a finger at me.

I'm hesitant to admit I'm only interested in going for a story. I don't want Dara and Madison to think I only care about the *Torch*, the way my friends in high school thought I only cared about our school paper. Especially since I've already relied on them both so much with the human-interest pieces I've been working on. They're the ones who got me started on that path in the first place.

But I also don't want to lie. "Well, I need to get in for this thing I'm doing for the *Torch*, and if I'm going to be turned away at the door for being fat or ugly, I don't want to be alone when it happens." There. I said it. I could go alone, but I'm scared.

Madison makes a choked sound. "*Wyn*, oh my gosh."

"No one would do that," Dara says at the same time. "That does not happen. Wyn, what the fuck?"

Madison climbs off her bed. "You're *not*—"

"Don't say I'm not fat," I say with a brittle laugh. "I am, and I don't want or need to be told that I'm not."

Madison looks at Dara, who gets to her feet.

"You're not going to get turned away," Dara says. "They want those things looking as crowded as possible, and they aren't going to turn away a girl they think isn't attractive just so all the other girls can see it or hear about it and decide to never come back." She bops the side of her fist against my shoulder. "And you'll see that—when we go to this party."

I glance at Madison, whose cheeks are red. She opens her mouth, then shuts it quickly.

To Dara, I say, "So, you've been to a lot of frat parties, then?"

"Well, not in the technical sense, no," Dara says.

"What does that mean?"

"I've never actually *attended* one, but—"

I groan. "Dara—"

"It'll be fine! Look, this isn't totally my friends' scene, but we've been to a lot of other parties, so I stand by my logic. In fact, I'm inviting Kayla and Yasmin," Dara says, grabbing her phone. "Three Black women, two of whom are queer, a church girl, and a fat hottie walk into a frat party." At that, I laugh. Dara grins at us, reaching over to smack Madison's shoulder. "They're gonna *love* us."

* * *

Anxiety has me in a chokehold as we make our way up the front walk to the Theta Kappa Alpha house. I have to fight my teeth not to chatter, a combination of my nerves and the fact that none of us wore coats, not wanting to worry about finding them again at the end of the night. It's officially December, and the night air is frigid and clouded by our breath.

We follow another group of girls to the door, where a brother waves us in. Within seconds, the worst part of my night is over. Even as I pass him, he doesn't give me a second glance, and I have a brief flash of embarrassment for being so worried.

"Are we having the traditional college experience now?" Yasmin asks, curling her arm around Kayla's shoulders.

"Yes, I think the traditional college experience does hinge on bad beer and eau de unwashed boy," Kayla says, eyeing the pile of shoes by the front door. It smells like a locker room in here.

"Hey, it was on your list!" Yasmin argues. "You said you wanted to see a frat party."

"For science," Kayla says, inspecting her nails. "I like to observe."

"I'm very happy to tick this off my list too," Madison says cheerfully.

Dara looks at her in surprise. "What else is on your list?"

Madison flushes in the low light. "I'm sort of . . . making it up as I go."

"Just don't drink anything you didn't pour yourself,"

says Yasmin, "and never take drugs from strangers."

As Yasmin leads us in search of drinks, Dara says to me, "You're quiet."

"I'm thawing out," I reply, sticking close to her as we make our way through the crowd. I'm grateful Yasmin and Kayla are with us. They're both so outgoing, I can easily fade into the background. It's what I really need tonight. Because now that my nerves have subsided, my focus is entirely on finding the right moment to sneak upstairs.

I'm also keeping an eye out for Three, who would know as soon as he saw me that I'm up to something. There's no guarantee he'll be here, but there's even less a guarantee he won't.

We hunt down the keg, where I get a beer to nurse so I blend. Madison politely asks one of the guys at the keg if there's water available, which makes them howl with laughter.

"This beer's so cheap, it practically is water," one of them says to her, holding out the keg hose.

Madison hesitates, looking to Dara and me.

"You don't have to," I say.

"But you can if you want," Dara adds. "We'll take care of you."

Madison licks her lips, glancing at the guys around the keg. Then she takes a deep breath, lets it out, and says, "Sure! Okay!" She grabs a cup and holds it out. "Traditional college experience!"

Dara turns to me with wide eyes. "We've totally corrupted her."

"I wonder if she'll tell her parents," I reply. "Sunday's sermon will be all about how Jesus may have turned water to wine, but it wasn't to party with underage drinkers."

Dara snorts, smothering her laugh against my shoulder.

It takes a while for the party to get into full swing. I need everyone a little more drunk than they are at present, but not so drunk that the party ends and people start heading upstairs. It's a fine line, and one I'm not sure I'll be able to find with my very limited knowledge of frat parties, which I've really only learned from movies.

And yes, okay, maybe everyone is right that I watch too much TV.

I'm still waiting for the perfect moment when I spot Three through the crowd.

I don't know how I notice him in a sea of people, especially when most of the guys look just like him. But maybe . . . they don't look like him. Not really. Not to me.

Or maybe I'm so attuned to his presence, I can feel him enter a room.

Whatever it is, it's like an alarm. *Time to move.*

I leave the others where they're watching a game of beer pong, slipping out another doorway before Three spots me. I make my way around to the front of the house, where I wait until I'm sure no one is looking before I sneak upstairs.

The second floor is quieter, and all the doors are shut. I try the first one and poke my head in—*empty.*

I don't have Three's insider knowledge of who within the

frat might be involved, but I'll search every room if I have to. I know what I'm looking for now, and if I can confirm the involvement of brothers at TKA, Three will have to acknowledge I've contributed more to this story than just following him around, gathering scraps.

It's time-consuming and high-risk, but I don't have a choice if I want to prove myself. If I get caught, I'll just play drunk. I'll act like I'm looking for the bathroom. Or better yet, I'll simply slur my words so they're completely indecipherable and let that do the work.

Inside the room, I do a quick search of the drawers, unearth some dirty laundry, and pick through the closet. When I find nothing, I try the next room. I look under the dresser, check more drawers, reach under the bed despite all my brain's warnings to *not do that*. I find nothing. No indication of anything more nefarious than a lack of regular cleaning.

I'm silently cursing, wondering if this is all a waste, when I step into the hall and gasp.

Three waits on the other side of the door, back against the wall and arms folded.

"What the hell are you doing?" His voice is low and unhappy, and the look on his face is anything but playful. Like the day I stole his glasses, there's no question—he's truly angry right now.

I quickly shut the door behind me and glance around.

"Just me," he says. "Lucky for you, or you'd be screwed right now. What were you thinking?"

"I'm investigating," I whisper. "You seem to think I can't—"

He groans, knocking his head back against the wall. "That's not what I think—"

"You basically said as much!"

"Okay, fine, can we fight about this somewhere el—*shit*." He freezes as voices boom up the stairs. The panic in his eyes is quickly snuffed out by the light of an idea, and he grabs my arms, flipping us around. "Put your hand up my shirt."

"*What?*"

The voices grow closer. They're about to turn the corner.

"Unless you want it the other way around," he whispers urgently.

I shove my hand up his shirt so quickly, it bunches in the crook of my elbow. My fingers close around his bare shoulder, skin burning hot. And as he presses me into the wall with his hips and buries his face in my neck, I burn just as hot, if not hotter.

What the fuck.

He doesn't kiss me. Even as he nuzzles into my neck, his mouth never touches me.

"Hey, hey, hey," one of them slurs.

Someone else laughs.

Three pulls back slowly, lifting his head. His gaze is a little unfocused, and the anger has melted from his expression. My hand slips from beneath his shirt as he turns toward the voices, smiling sheepishly. "Ah. Sorry."

I hate that he's such a great actor, because he has that

blushing, *aw-shucks, who-me* thing perfected.

I don't dare look over, and not only because I don't want them reading my face.

"Don't mind us," the second guy says, laughter still in his voice. From the corner of my eye, I count three of them.

"Do mind us," says the third, a little more stern. "You wanna hook up, take her home, bro."

I stare at Three's profile as he replies, but the first two guys' laughter has turned to buzzing in my ears.

At me, I think. *They're laughing at me.*

They're laughing at *this*. Three and me. Because clearly I'm not—

Because I'm not the type of girl that gets brought upstairs at a party.

It's worse than being turned away at the door. And I want to tell myself I'm overreacting. That it's baseless anxiety again.

But when I finally get up the nerve to turn my head, the two of them are nudging each other and laughing, and when they catch me looking, they cover their mouths in a half-assed disguise. Because they don't care if I know they're laughing at me.

I shove Three away from me and turn, starting for the stairs. The third guy, who's in the middle of telling Three off for being disrespectful after they let him into the party as another frat's pledge—*blah, blah, blah*—doesn't stop talking as I start down the stairs.

I hear the guy shout in outrage a moment later, and I'm halfway down when a hand catches my elbow.

"You're welcome," Three says, pulling me along with him.

I yank my arm out of his grip. "I do not—and will not, and will *never*—thank you for that." We reach the bottom of the stairs, and I shoulder past him.

"Oh, I'm sorry I saved your ass." He follows so close, I can feel the heat of him at my back.

I whirl to face him. "I had it under control. I didn't need you to intervene, and I certainly didn't need you to do—*that*."

He gapes at me. "You mean convince a bunch of brothers you were harmless? So they wouldn't throw you out on your ass or *worse* when they caught you doing—whatever the hell you were doing—I have no idea, honestly!"

"I was investigating," I whisper fiercely. "Doing the exact thing you think I can't do without you, and I was *fine*—"

"You were about to get caught!"

"If anyone suspected I was up there, it's because they saw you follow me." I notice a few people looking our way, sensing the drama, and try to smooth my expression. "And I don't know how you knew I was here, or where I went—"

"You thought I wouldn't notice you the second I walked in?" He levels me with a disbelieving look.

"Of course. I'm sure you'd notice me right away, wouldn't you?" I bite my lip, turning my face away briefly. When I look at him again, his expression has shifted, confusion creeping in. "I know I don't belong at a party like this. I knew it before

I even got here. But I'm not some useless hanger-on for this story, and I won't let you treat me like one. I think you and me being up there to do—*that*—is just as unbelievable as me being up there, alone, wasted. And if it's all the same to you, I'd rather worry about saving myself than be humiliated by you."

I turn to go, but Three skirts past me, blocking my way. "Hey," he says, dipping his head close to mine. "There is nothing unbelievable about you and me."

I drop my gaze, glancing away.

Three catches my jaw in his hand, turning my face toward him again. The intensity in his eyes is jarring, and I flick my attention down, catching on his mouth before quickly settling on his throat.

"Sure," I whisper. "Except that you hate me."

"Right." His voice has sobered, losing its heat. He gives my jaw a brief squeeze before dropping his hand. "Except that you hate me."

I frown, opening my mouth to protest—that's *not* what I said.

But he's already moving past me, melting into the crowd, disappearing from my sight no matter how hard I search.

I end up finding Dara and Madison instead, where they're dancing in the living room. Madison's cheeks are flushed, her eyes glassy.

"Oh good, you're back!" Dara grabs me. "She's totally drunk. We should get her home." She pauses, glancing over my face. Then she smirks. "Were you with Three?"

"No." I look around, searching for Yasmin and Kayla.

"They left," Dara says without needing to ask who I'm looking for. "I guess some people are doing coke in the den, and they didn't want to be around if that gets out of control."

I look toward the stairs, a stabbing in my gut. I *know* there's something up there. But whatever chance I had to link TKA to the other houses involved has withered up and died.

"They said to tell you bye, since we didn't know where you went," Dara continues.

I drag my gaze back to her. "Sorry. I didn't mean to leave you."

She grins. "All good. I got to watch our girl have the time of her life." She nods at Madison, who's still dancing. "But I think we should probably head out before it gets intense in here." Dara waves to get Madison's attention. "You good to go?"

Madison nods, beaming. She throws her arms around both of us. "I just love you two!"

I shoot Dara a look over her head, and Dara laughs.

"We love you too, Mads," Dara says. "Let's go home."

"I love drinking," Madison says as we head for the door. "I don't know why some people in my church act like it'll—it'll—ruin your life or something!" At the door, she throws her arms up. "I drink alcohol and Jesus *still loves me!*"

A few people nearby whoop.

Dara and I wrangle her out the door and into the cold.

On the way home, it seems like every thought that enters

Madison's head immediately exits by way of her mouth. "I've never had a hangover before. Are you supposed to eat a raw egg in the morning? I think I saw that in a movie once. Ooh, can we watch a movie when we get home? I want to watch *Mamma Mia!* You know, my parents wouldn't even let me watch it because it glorifies premarital sex and it's— well, it's very sexy at times! I didn't know ABBA was so sexy. Oh my god, I can't stop saying 'sexy'—what's happening to me?" She starts giggling, covering her mouth. "I used to sneak-watch it with my friends from choir. I'm not normally sneaky, but I just love musicals! I really want to try out for the musical next semester. I *know* my parents don't agree, but I want to do it!"

"You absolutely should," Dara says, always encouraging.

Madison chatters away about the musical until we near the dorm, but when we step into the lobby, she promptly loses her energy. In the elevator, I feel her drooping against my side.

"You want help getting her into bed?" I ask Dara as we enter the suite through their door.

"Nah, I got her," Dara says. "Did you get everything you needed tonight?"

I think of touching Three's bare chest, his hot skin under my hand. The way he looked at me afterward, those blue eyes so dark and intense.

Then Dara adds, "For the *Torch*?"

I nearly choke out a laugh, but I'm too exhausted. "It was

a bust." I swallow, forcing a smile. "Thanks for coming with me. I really appreciate it."

Dara nods, but there's a thread of unease in her gaze that makes me wonder how much of the night she can see on my face right now.

"Hey, Wyn!" Madison catches me in the bathroom, grabbing my arm.

I turn back. "What's up?"

"Thank you for inviting me tonight," she says, leaning in to hug me.

"No problem." I pat her back lightly. "I'm glad you had a good time."

She pulls away, putting her hands on my shoulders. "And I want you to know—when I said you aren't fat—I didn't mean—"

"It's fine." The words scrape out of me, raw.

"You're *beautiful*." She takes both my hands and holds them to her chest. "You're beautiful, Wyn. And I'm so sorry if I've ever made you feel less beautiful than you are."

Something in me is cracking.

I open my mouth to give the knee-jerk answer again. *It's fine. It's okay.* But then I hear Three's voice: *Don't say "it's fine" when people apologize to you, Evans. It minimizes your feelings.*

"Thank you," I say instead, squeezing her hands. "I appreciate that."

She smiles, nodding as she releases me. She makes it one

step back into her room before she turns again and adds, "And Jesus thinks you're beautiful too!"

On the other side of the wall, Dara laughs.

Madison giggles.

And I find myself smiling, despite the deepening ache in my chest.

I manage to keep smiling as I get ready for bed, washing the makeup from my face and brushing my teeth. I smile right up to the moment I climb under my sheets and roll toward the wall.

And then I promptly burst into tears.

SEVENTEEN

I know there's no escaping Three, especially when I'm trying to finish my article on Claude's Holidays for Everyone for the next edition—and last of the semester. So after my final round of interviews for my story, I head to the *Torch* office to put the finishing touches on it. And it has nothing to do with knowing Three spends Monday afternoons in the newsroom, and I want him to know I'm not avoiding him.

The office is busy when I step inside. Three is at the grunt desk, hunched over his computer. I take in a deep breath through my nose as I start toward my seat, pausing to set my bag on the floor.

"I would weep to be your chiropractor," I say as I drop into my chair.

Three's fingers freeze on his keyboard. Then he straightens and yawns, stretching his arms above his head. "You know, Evans, I think you might've been one of those Catholic schoolteachers in a past life." He settles in his seat, angling toward me. "All that *sit up straight*, ruler-over-the-knuckles type of stuff."

"If you can find a ruler, I'd be happy to try it on you," I reply sweetly.

He mock gasps, clutching his hands to his chest. "Not my moneymakers."

I roll my eyes, leaning over to grab my laptop from my bag. As I set up, I notice Three is smiling to himself.

I'm relieved. Clearly Three and I are on the same page: we are not talking about Friday night.

We work side by side in silence as the office empties. Mel stops by briefly to get an update on my article, and then Sabina pauses on her way out the door to mention she'll be posting an ad for a new grunt first thing next semester. The others follow slowly, until it's just Christopher, Three, and me remaining.

"How late can you stay tonight?"

My heart jolts at the sound of Three's voice. When I glance over, his expression is bland, fingers moving swiftly over his keyboard.

His gaze slides toward me, hands stilling. "Do you need to check your schedule?"

"I'm free," I say. "Why?"

"We have a story to work on." He taps his computer. "I have new stuff to show you. And I want you to write up the portions about your roommate. You know more than I do, and you can pull from my original article for anything else you need."

I almost sigh in relief but catch it just in time. The last thing I need is for Three to think my mind went anywhere else. "Fine."

Christopher stops at our desk then, glancing from Three to me and back. "Aren't you two leaving?"

"We have a lot to do," Three replies.

Christopher eyes us. Reluctantly, he says, "Fine. Please remember to lock up before you go."

"We do this all the time," I say.

Christopher stares at me, then turns to Three with an unreadable expression. Three smiles back.

Christopher sighs, turning toward the door. "What do I care? Just don't go near my desk."

"Wouldn't dream of it," says Three.

Christopher shoots him one last look from the door, then leaves.

"So, what new stuff?" I ask as soon as we're alone.

Three leans his elbow on the arm of his chair, angling toward me. "I was thinking about what Ellie said. Theta Kappa just had an alumni weekend, and if this goes higher than the brothers, there might've been something in the house to point at who's involved. So after you left the other night"—I hold my breath, but he doesn't even pause—"I started looking around."

I hold up a hand. "Wait a second—"

Three keeps speaking. "I gave it some thought, and it wasn't the worst idea—"

I stand, my chair flying back and hitting the desk behind us. "You gave me all that shit about how stupid and dangerous it was, and then you turned around to steal all the glory—"

"I can't *steal glory* on my own story, Evans," Three says, getting to his feet. "You didn't find anything anyway, and you were about five seconds from getting caught on your own when I found you—"

"Thank god you were there to rescue me." I put a hand over my heart. "My hero."

"I guess next time I should let you get caught."

"Assuming there's a next time you even know about."

"A next time you do something stupid that'll get you into trouble?" His smile is arrogant as he leans back against the desk, crossing his arms. "I'm sure it'll be soon and impossible to miss."

"You act pretty superior for someone whose big idea was *put your hand up my shirt.*"

His smile drops. "It worked, didn't it?"

"Slightly better than kissing me outright. I guess I should thank you for sparing me the nightmares."

"Nightmares!" He barks out a laugh, tossing his head back. I look away so I don't have to stare at his exposed throat. I can't tell if I want to kiss it or tear it out with my teeth. He drops his chin again, so I don't have to dwell on it too long.

Except now he's fixed me with a dark look that makes something warm flash through me. *"Nightmares?"*

I shrug, giving him a bland smile as I lean in, bracing my hands on the desk so he won't notice they're shaking. "Just being honest with you."

"Oh, is that what you're doing?" He tilts his head, the corner of his mouth pulling into a smirk. "And what's this?" He indicates the dwindling space between us. "Is this you angling for nightmare fuel?"

We're so close, we're nearly touching. I can't look away from his face, even though I know my brain is writing everything out on mine: *Touch me, touch me, touch me* in big, bright, bold letters across my forehead.

He huffs out a laugh that brushes along my neck like a touch. "You could have just asked nicely, Evans."

I let out the smallest, tiniest gasp as I feel the slow slide of his tongue along the curve of my jaw. Then his teeth come down lightly on my earlobe, and I grip the edge of the desk so hard, I'm worried it might crumble in my hands.

His cheek brushes mine as he murmurs, "That should keep you rich in nightmares for weeks."

He pushes my arm aside, moving from between me and the desk. I collapse back against it, flushed and winded. As he starts packing his things, I feel the flare of nerves that he's messing with me again, pushing our game of chicken beyond the limit. But the red creeping up the back of his neck gives him away.

I need to see his face.

I'm not sure which of us is more surprised when I grab his sleeve. As he turns, I'm gratified to see the flush in his cheeks and the rapid rise and fall of his chest.

You can't hide from me, I want to say.

But I don't get the chance to speak, because Three drops what he's holding, backs me up against the desk, and kisses me.

I think my knees evaporate completely. It's the only explanation I have for how I end up perched on the edge of the grunt desk with my legs curled around his hips. We are frantic hands and small gasps of breath, and I am carefully cataloging the way he flicks his tongue against mine and how he groans into my mouth when I tug his hair between my fingers and the pressure of his hands cupping the backs of my knees and sliding up my thighs and trailing around to my back just to press me closer.

And I think maybe it might be nightmare fuel after all. Because when I finally push him away—if only to save myself the humiliation of having him pull back first—and grab my stuff—if only to spare myself having to watch him leave—I realize that this will probably never happen again. That I *can't* let it happen again. Because a kiss in the middle of an argument with a boy who has admitted to getting turned on during arguments is not a real kiss. I knew what I was doing. *Angling for nightmare fuel?*

Absolutely.

And as the door to the office swings shut behind me, I

can't decide if it was a mistake. Not because I regret it.

But because I know I will probably never get another kiss that good in my entire life.

During finals week, the library turns into Grand Central Station, people coming and going in droves. Table space becomes prime real estate, and reserving seats is strictly prohibited. I've witnessed few places more cutthroat, and the extended hours seem to only make it worse. Now we're aggressively studying *and* sleep-deprived. No one more than me, after I finished my shift at midnight last night, had two finals today, and was back in for another late night shift.

Now I'm discreetly trying to study for statistics while I monitor the help desk, splitting my concentration between ignoring the painful awareness that this final will decide whether I pass or fail the class and looking out for Scott, who could appear at any moment and catch me in a lack of dedication to my job.

I'm clearly very bad at splitting my concentration, because I'm in a full-on nervous sweat about the dwindling number of days I have to gain an understanding of a subject that is an entire mystery to me when Scott comes up behind me and says, "You're not supposed to be studying while clocked in."

I whip around, flipping my notes shut at the same time. "Sorry. I was just checking one thing—you know—to make sure I was remembering correctly."

He isn't swayed. "Put it away, please."

I'm crouched down, stowing my notes in my bag, when a quiet voice squeaks, "Excuse me."

I straighten, nearly bumping my head on the underside of the desk. A girl stands on the other side, chewing at her lip.

"Can we help you?" Scott asks. He's lingering now to keep an eye on me.

I'm starting to think things can't get worse when I catch movement out of the corner of my eye and spot Three crossing the lobby, heading straight for the help desk.

Then the girl says, "Um, there's a man on the third floor. He's, uh, watching something . . ."

My stomach drops. So not just worse but much, *much* worse.

I look over at Scott, who sighs.

". . . inappropriate," the girl finishes. Three steps up behind her, waiting patiently. I avoid his gaze like it might turn me to stone.

"Thank you for letting us know," Scott says to the girl. He turns to me. "Please go ask him to leave."

"But I'm . . . working the help desk," I say weakly. My cheeks burn as Three witnesses this particular humiliation.

"I think I can manage for a few minutes." Scott waves me toward the elevators. "Go on."

I look at the girl, whose eyes have widened.

Three clears his throat. "Sorry, what's going on?" His voice sounds different than usual, a thread of authority in it that makes even Scott pause.

He recovers quickly, though, offering Three a professional smile. "Nothing to worry about. What can I help you with?"

Three doesn't answer, directing his next question to the girl. "What happened?"

She clearly has zero defenses against someone like him, because she answers right away. "There's a man on the third floor watching . . . *porn*." She whispers the last part, glancing worriedly at me.

Three's brow furrows as he takes this in, nodding slowly. He turns, pinning Scott with that look that has, many times, made me feel like a cornered animal. But now I'm the rabbit spared, watching him close in on other prey.

"So there's a man on the third floor watching porn," he says in that same voice. "And you think this"—he indicates me with one hand—"is the best person to handle that?"

"It's fine," I say quickly, rounding the desk. I'm worried how this might bounce back onto me when Three finally lets Scott out of this conversational chokehold. "I've done it before."

Three's expression narrows further. "How many times?"

I don't dare look at Scott. "This is the fourth."

Three blinks at me, disbelief washing away everything else on his face. He turns to Scott again. "*Four* times, you've had her do this?" He doesn't give Scott a chance to answer before he looks at me again. "And did you find out if he's a student? Did you get his ID? Report him to campus security?"

I gape at him. "I . . ." This time, I do look at Scott.

"He's been told that if he continues this behavior, he'll be banned," Scott says. "Now, I don't think we need to—"

"Don't move," Three says, pointing at me. He pulls out his phone, taps at the screen, then lifts it to his ear. "Hi, I'm in the main library, and there's a man here watching porn. The employees said he's been warned several times. How do we go about having him removed?" He listens for a moment, nodding. "And you'd just need to speak to—sure, of course. Actually, if you hold on a second . . ." He holds the phone out to Scott. "It's for you."

I'm rooted to the spot as Scott takes the phone, turning away to speak quietly. Three leans over the desk, listening.

The girl beside me whispers, "Um, do you think I need to wait here?"

I shrug. I'm not even sure who's in charge now—Scott or Three. Judging by the look on Scott's face as he returns Three's phone, I think it might be Three.

"Campus security is on the way," Scott says tightly.

"Great, thanks!" the girl squeaks, the words nearly lost as she rushes to the elevator.

Three gives Scott his best *fuck you* smile. He leans against the help desk, making it clear he isn't going anywhere until this is resolved.

I do my best to look like I don't know him.

A campus security guard comes through the front doors a few minutes later, a man who looks a little older than my parents. He heads toward the desk, nodding at all of us. "Which one of you called?"

Three raises a hand. "But she's the one who's been dealing with him." He tilts his head at me.

I hate that it feels nice to have him defer authority to me. It's especially sweet when Scott's face reddens.

"He's on the third floor. I can show you."

"How many times has he done this?" the guard asks.

"This is the fourth, but he's escalating." Out of the corner of my eye, I watch Three suppress a smile. I ignore him. "The first few times, there was no one around, or only a few people. But now he's doing it in the middle of a crowd during finals week. That's a huge audience." I glance at Scott, feeling, for once, a little powerful. "I'd hate to guess what he might do next, and I don't want to be the one to kick him out when he does."

"No, you call us if he comes back." The guard looks at Scott. "Like you should have done to begin with."

Scott's face reddens even further. It feels like a victory, even knowing all I've done is dig myself into a deeper hole of his dislike.

Or, I guess Three started digging for me. I simply accepted the second shovel.

Three trails us to the elevator. While we wait, he leans down and murmurs, "*Escalating.* You really do watch too much TV."

I glance at the security guard, whose mouth presses into a small smile.

"Don't you have somewhere else to be?" I whisper over my shoulder.

"Nowhere in particular," Three replies pleasantly.

When the elevator delivers us to the third floor, the guard steps out first. I spot Porn Guy immediately at a back table, one of the security cameras' only blind spots, and discreetly point him out. The girl who reported him is at the table beside his, and her eyes widen when she sees the guard coming.

Three takes my hand and pulls me around the corner, silencing me with a look when I start to protest.

"You can report him to security if he comes back," he says, "but if he thinks about retaliating, I don't want your face to be what he remembers."

I peek past him as the guard marches the man to the elevator. "I've kicked him out before. He already knows my face."

"And now he knows it one less time, which can't hurt anything."

"How nice of you to worry about me."

"It's not about you," he says. "It should've never been you to begin with. I don't understand how they don't have a fucking protocol for this." He blows out an agitated breath. He won't meet my eyes, his gaze focused straight over my head.

"They're gone," I say.

Three waits a moment, visibly calming. Then he says, "I have something for you." He swings his backpack around and unzips it, digging out a packet of papers.

I blink down at it as he passes it to me.

"It's my study guide for stats." He clears his throat. "I made a copy."

"For me," I say slowly. I lift my gaze to his face.

He nods, his mouth tightening.

I purse my lips, offering it back to him. "No thanks."

He frowns, catching it before I drop it. *"No thanks?"* I turn toward the stairs, and he follows. "You're not taking it?"

"I don't need it."

He lets out a disbelieving laugh. "Come on, Evans, I know that's not true. I have an A. Let me help—"

I whirl on him as we reach the next landing, whispering fiercely, "*Stop* trying to apologize."

He jerks his chin back. "What are you talking about?"

"This"—I motion to the study guide—"and that." I wave a hand at the floor above us. "I don't need your help, and I don't want your apology."

I start to turn, but he blocks my way, ducking his head so we're eye level. "What exactly do you think I'm trying to apologize for?"

I open my mouth, then shut it quickly. Glancing away, I mutter, "You know what."

"I definitely don't, because I have nothing I'm sorry about." He grabs my wrist and shoves the study guide into my hand again. "Your pride isn't worth retaking this class. Follow this exactly, and you'll pull at least a C on the exam. You don't even have to thank me."

He turns and starts down the next flight of stairs. I stare after him, any retort locked in my dry throat. By the time I stagger down to the first floor, he's long gone, leaving me with nothing but my angry boss awaiting my return and a hundred million thoughts running through my head, most of them starting and ending with the words *I have nothing I'm sorry about.*

EIGHTEEN

WINTER BREAK, DAY 1

hayes6834: so is it too early to talk about finals

pomerene1765: no content warning? just jumping right in?

hayes6834: hmm. that bad?

pomerene1765: not as bad as I thought but...we'll see. I've only gotten one score back.

hayes6834: and?

pomerene1765: surprisingly...good

WINTER BREAK, DAY 1

ME:

Thanks for the study guide

THREE:

You're giving me nothing? Not even a pass/fail?

I got a B

So. I passed.

Because of you

I hope you know how annoying that is to me

You already said thank you so I'll just pretend I didn't read the rest of that

WINTER BREAK, DAY 4

pomerene1765: well I knew it was coming but the inevitable parental breakdown has arrived

hayes6834: ?

pomerene1765: I had a fight with my parents

pomerene1765: well, not so much a fight...

hayes6834: an airing of grievances?

pomerene1765: yes exactly

hayes6834: we do that all the time at my house

hayes6834: was it a specific grievance?

pomerene1765: yeah it's been festering. they sort of left me on thanksgiving

pomerene1765: they're super into fantasy stuff like lord of the rings, game of thrones, and all that. there was a convention thanksgiving weekend and they went

hayes6834: you said you had a good thanksgiving though

pomerene1765: yeah that was a different reason. I stayed on campus but there were some bright spots.

hayes6834: you weren't alone?

hayes6834: long silence...

pomerene1765: sorry

hayes6834: you know there's no pressure here right? if there's someone you like

hayes6834: you said you don't want to meet. we can't really go anywhere from here

pomerene1765: I'm just thinking

hayes6834: it's winter break. you don't need to think about anything

WINTER BREAK, DAY 4

hayes6834: recovering from the parental breakdown?

pomerene1765: yeah...we're watching a movie

pomerene1765: lord of the rings extended edition. it's kind of our thing.

hayes6834: you okay?

pomerene1765: I'm getting there. I think they understood where I was coming from. they definitely felt bad and they apologized, so that was nice

pomerene1765: thanks for checking on me

hayes6834: that's what I'm here for

pomerene1765: I'd send a heart but that feels cheesy. and also there are no hearts on this app which feels weird for an app intended for dating, right?

pomerene1765: heart

pomerene1765: pretend you didn't see that

hayes6834: you can't take it back now

pomerene1765: god that's embarrassing

hayes6834: I won't mention it

hayes6834: but same

WINTER BREAK, DAY 8

pomerene1765: so are you ever going to tell me how you did on YOUR finals?

hayes6834: lol I did fine

pomerene1765: you're on the dean's list aren't you

pomerene1765: extremely long silence says yes

hayes6834: listen. not doing well really isn't an option for me

pomerene1765: so that's where your bad boy persona comes from. the expectations that run your life

hayes6834: dr. pom with the analysis

hayes6834: you're probably right

pomerene1765: I don't get tired of hearing that so feel free to say it whenever you want

WINTER BREAK, DAY 10

pomerene1765: merry christmas!

hayes6834: merry christmas

hayes6834: how's your day?

pomerene1765: good! how's yours?

hayes6834: get anything good?

pomerene1765: I will pretend I didn't notice the deflection

pomerene1765: I got a new computer. which is like a very big deal because I had my dad's old work computer for a really long time

hayes6834: what does your dad do?

pomerene1765: ah that's a trick question.

hayes6834: interesting

pomerene1765: my parents work at the renaissance faire. it's their dream job. but they also have boring day jobs that pay for our house and stuff. he works in an accounting department for a construction company and she does HR for...wait for it...a competing construction company.

hayes6834: a little competition keeps the romance alive

pomerene1765: I'm throwing up

pomerene1765: did you get anything good?

hayes6834: yeah I was the sibling that didn't get in a fight with my parents this year

hayes6834: a gift for us all

pomerene1765: geez. I'm sorry.

hayes6834: don't be. I got to eat breakfast in peace. it's a christmas miracle.

WINTER BREAK, DAY 12

hayes6834: my turn for a total parental breakdown

hayes6834: and it's not a competition or anything but I AM considering moving to a remote island in the pacific never to be heard from again

pomerene1765: does the remote island have wifi?

hayes6834: obviously. how would we talk if it didn't?

pomerene1765: glad to know I'm invited

hayes6834: you could come in person but you don't want to meet.

hayes6834: sorry. I take that back. I'm not trying to pressure you

pomerene1765: you really want to meet?

hayes6834: I wanted to meet from the start

hayes6834: is it something about me?

pomerene1765: definitely not. it's about me.

hayes6834: what are you worried about? I already like you

pomerene1765: yeah that's the problem. I like you too.

hayes6834: that sounds like the opposite of a problem. most people would call that a success.

pomerene1765: I'm worried you won't like me once we meet.

pomerene1765: I've been thinking about it a lot. and about who you are.

hayes6834: me too

pomerene1765: but if we met and you were disappointed, I don't think I'd recover

hayes6834: you know it could very easily be the other way around

hayes6834: what if we meet and you're disgusted by me?

pomerene1765: that would never happen

hayes6834: I could never be disappointed by you

pomerene1765: you don't know what I look like

hayes6834: I know what you feel like

hayes6834: I've known it since we started talking

pomerene1765: oh, was it my well thought out answer to the BO question?

hayes6834: don't fight with me right now

hayes6834: I'm telling you I like you. so whatever you're worried about, don't.

WINTER BREAK, DAY 16

pomerene1765: did you ever work things out with your parents?

pomerene1765: you never really said what happened. and I'm sorry if I'm being nosy, but I didn't want to go into the new year without saying something. I think you should start next year with a clean slate. and if you can do that by talking to me about whatever is going on, I want to be here for you.

pomerene1765: I'm always here for you but I especially want to be now

hayes6834: have you been drinking?

pomerene1765: hayes

hayes6834: that's not my name so it doesn't really have the same effect

pomerene1765: no I'm not drinking

hayes6834: you really don't need to worry about me

pomerene1765: for some reason I don't believe that

hayes6834: it's just complicated. my parents have given me a really good life but they expect a lot from me in return. I started to get off this path they have me on and couldn't make it happen because it's hard to disappoint your parents. then my girlfriend dumped me this summer because I was "regressing" which she was probably right to do and now idk. I keep getting brave but can't seem to get a grip on it and every plan I've come up with to fix it has either fizzled out or imploded completely.

pomerene1765: I'm sorry

hayes6834: don't be. I'm not sad about it.

pomerene1765: you don't seem sad. you seem angry.

hayes6834: great

hayes6834: I'm not angry

pomerene1765: there's nothing wrong with it. it's no worse emotion than any other. people think they aren't allowed to be angry because it's ugly, but anger is just like the rest. you can't go through life without feeling it.

hayes6834: that's not what it is. I'm disappointed in myself.

pomerene1765: do you ever think you're being hard on yourself?

hayes6834: I don't think I'm being hard enough on myself actually

pomerene1765: I find that very hard to believe

hayes6834: well to be honest, you don't even know me

pomerene1765: wow.

pomerene1765: ok.

hayes6834: hold on

pomerene1765: no that's great

hayes6834: that's not what I meant

hayes6834: I just meant you don't really know what I'm like outside of this

hayes6834: I'm not explaining myself well

hayes6834: can we start this conversation over?

hayes6834: pom?

WINTER BREAK, DAY 17

hayes6834: happy new year

hayes6834: okay so that was a shitty thing to say and it's not even what I meant. I think you know me better than most people, but it's hard to be who I am with you outside of this. that's the thing I'm struggling with. my parents expect me to be someone I don't want to be anymore. they want me at school, having the perfect college experience, with perfect grades and the right clubs and parties but not too many or too much and idk. I keep doing everything they ask and even the things they don't ask and it's never enough. I fucking played kickball just so my dad would feel like I was participating in something and then I had to hear it from my mom about how a tournament before finals week was irresponsible. and I know as soon as I try to do what I really want it'll be a brand new fresh hell with them.

pomerene1765: like quit school?

hayes6834: thank god

pomerene1765: ??

hayes6834: I thought I lost you there

pomerene1765: you didn't lose me.

pomerene1765: I put myself in time out.

hayes6834: because I upset you? call me an asshole when I'm being an asshole. I can take it.

pomerene1765: ok

pomerene1765: you were being an asshole

hayes6834: I know. I'm sorry

pomerene1765: thank you

hayes6834: and you were right. I am a little angry. and I don't like it.

pomerene1765: well when you feel angry, you can just tell me. I'll talk to you about it.

pomerene1765: that's what I was trying to say

hayes6834: thank you

pomerene1765: happy new year

WINTER BREAK, DAY 17

pomerene1765: kickball?

pomerene1765: the weekend before finals?

hayes6834: yeah?

pomerene1765: were there a lot of kickball tournaments that weekend?

pomerene1765: like is kickball a big thing and I didn't realize?

hayes6834: where are you going with this?

pomerene1765: I went to a kickball tournament the weekend before finals

hayes6834: risky statement from someone who doesn't want to meet

pomerene1765: maybe I do

hayes6834: for real?

pomerene1765: do you ever wonder if we already have?

hayes6834: let's save that question for later

pomerene1765: why??

hayes6834: because I don't want to answer it if you don't want to meet. call it risk management.

WINTER BREAK, DAY 23

pomerene1765: you're not really moving to a remote island in the pacific, right?

hayes6834: it's still under consideration. why?

pomerene1765: just want to make sure

pomerene1765: see you at school

hayes6834: SEE you?

pomerene1765: maybe

hayes6834: maybe

hayes6834: I'll take it

NINETEEN

Hayes is Lincoln.

He *has* to be. Even if the pieces don't fit perfectly, that doesn't mean they aren't the same person. Lincoln and Hayes are so similar—they give good advice, they're mature and responsible, and Hayes never said he's a freshman. He sometimes seems like he could be older than me, like when we talked about imposter syndrome. They've both mentioned having a sibling and an ex-girlfriend who dumped them, which seems like a loose connection, but it's *there*. Lincoln is competitive, maybe even as intensely as Hayes, and he said his mom was angry at him for playing in that kickball tournament. And it's that—the tournament—that is too big a coincidence to ignore.

The puzzle is coming together, and I can't deny the picture it's making.

I keep waiting for the excitement to hit—it's *Lincoln*. I know who Hayes is, and it's who I've suspected for a while, and he's cute and nice and has shown at least an iota of interest in me!

Whatever else I'm feeling doesn't matter. I'm not naming those feelings, or who they're about, or where my stupid heart gets the nerve to build up so much hope for such a statistically unlikely situation.

And I can say that now, as someone who officially passed statistics.

Instead, I'm focused on being back at school, my new classes, and how I'll tell Lincoln when I finally go for it. Which *should* be soon.

But when I see him in the dining hall my second night back, I feel myself chicken out almost before I've fully processed his presence.

"Why are you hiding?" Dara asks from the seat beside me as I reach under the table for the fork I "dropped" as soon as I spotted him.

"I'm not hiding," I mutter, my voice strained as I peek up again. Lincoln is nowhere in sight.

"It looks a little like hiding," Madison says from across the table. She twirls some pasta onto her fork and pops it into her mouth. Then she grimaces. "This food is a little—well, I mean, I'm happy to be back, and of course I'm so grateful to have the dining hall—"

"Madison, you can be real with us," Dara says. "If the

food sucks, just say it sucks." She puts on a deep, sophisticated voice and sweeps a hand across the table. "Speak freely, my child."

Madison blinks at her. "What was that?"

Dara's shoulders drop. "My impression of a priest. I haven't been to church in a while, but I thought it was pretty good?"

Madison giggles. "We don't have priests at my church. We aren't Catholic. We have a pastor. My *dad*, remember?"

"Oh, that's right."

Madison flushes, takes another bite of her dinner to stall, and finally says, "Anyway, I was just going to say I'm happy to be back, but I miss the food at home. Although being home was . . . not as easy as last time."

Dara looks at me, then at Madison. "Speak freely, my child," she repeats in her possibly-a-priest impression.

Madison smiles, but it doesn't reach her eyes. "I'm feeling a little weird about the drinking thing. Guilty, I guess, to have done something I know my parents and maybe even God wouldn't approve of. And I don't want to have to do things I don't want to do in order to be accepted. But at the same time, I *want* to do the things my friends are doing, and to learn more about the world and all the people in it. And I think I'm learning, as I get to know more people, that maybe things my church has taught me could be . . . hurtful to some of my new friends."

I have no idea what to say. I don't think it's any secret that my family isn't religious—unless you count worshipping at the altar of J.R.R. Tolkien. This is way out of my league.

"It's also hard when the things I want to do—like auditioning for the spring musical—are things my parents wouldn't like. I had to fight with them just to do glee club. They loved when I wanted to sing in the church choir. But now that I'm singing for something else, they don't approve, and that makes me sad. I don't like doing things they don't approve of, but I also want to be happy. And singing makes me really happy—in the choir, and in everything I'm doing now."

"I don't think I can tell you anything about religion," Dara says, "but when I was really struggling, I know what helped me. Therapy."

"I could never get my parents to pay for therapy," Madison says.

"There are counselors in the clinic," says Dara. "That's who I talk to. I go once a week, and it's totally free."

I blink at her. I knew about the counselors from the list of ideas I saw when I broke into Three's computer, and after Ellie was kicked out, our RA suggested counseling to me too. But hearing about it from Chloe—or Three's list—versus hearing that Dara goes every week is vastly different.

Maybe it wouldn't be the worst thing to consider. Not only for Madison, but for me.

"And even if you hate it, at least it's not your Papa Pastor, and you can . . ." Dara smirks, and I know what's coming before she even says it. "Speak freely, my child."

"Okay. Pinch me."

I've just settled into my chair at the grunt desk when Three speaks from the seat beside me. It took me five minutes to work up the nerve to open the office door, not knowing if he'd be inside but guessing it was likely. I didn't know what I'd be dealing with after our last encounter—frosty Three or intense Three. But of course, he never acts the way I expect.

I sigh heavily and level him with an exasperated look. "No thanks."

"Come on, Wyn Evans deigned to *thank me* for my stats study guide?" He holds his arm out to me. "I need proof this hasn't been one long dream."

I push his arm away. "You've been holding on to that joke all break, haven't you?"

"I would've texted, but I like to see that disgusted look on your face."

"Clearly." I twist toward him, leaning my elbow on the desk. "I was surprised I didn't hear from you about our story. You seem like the type who doesn't allow rest."

He shrugs. "I worked on it a little."

"I thought you might be trying to cut me out again."

"I wouldn't dream of it."

I eye him. "Yeah, clearly you dream of other stuff."

He smirks. "Should we talk about *your* dreams?"

I ignore him, reaching down to pull my laptop from my bag. "Well, I don't know what you did all break, but I spent it scouring the fraternities' social media accounts. Some years were better than others, but for the most part, I was able to get the names of almost every person in every Dirty Four pledge class for the last five years."

Three blinks at me. "Dirty Four?"

"Sigma Rho, Theta Kappa Alpha, Alpha Xi Omega, and Gamma Theta Nu." I tick them off on my fingers, the two frats Three and I uncovered together and the two he'd already sussed out before I joined this story.

"You gave them a nickname." He says it seriously, but the corner of his mouth twitches.

I try not to bristle. "It's easier that way." I open my laptop and pull up the spreadsheet I labored over for weeks. Despite all the time I spent on social media doing this research, I very maturely resisted checking up on Three over winter break. Even if I wondered, often, what Christmas looked like at his house this year, after he said his cousin Wells gave him such a hard time about missing Thanksgiving. But I didn't want to feed that particular obsession.

Instead, I distracted myself by researching new ideas for a human-interest piece and spending time with my parents. After our blowup about how they ditched me on Thanksgiving, they were determined to make me the center of their world for the rest of winter break. By the end, I was so smothered in parental affection, I was kind of craving my empty dorm room.

"I have it broken out into sheets for each fraternity,"

I continue, showing Three the contents of my spreadsheet, "then organized by name with social media handles and links, and which private accounts never accepted my request."

Three's attention swivels to me, so I quickly add, "I made a fake, obviously."

He relaxes.

"I've highlighted the ones that seem interesting. Yellow for possible involvement, orange for likely involvement, red for anyone who left school."

"What about red and green?" He points to a dual-color box on the page. He's all business now, jokes forgotten. "There's only a couple of those."

"Left school and might talk to us. And if there are alumni involved or the drugs are tied deeply to how the frats function, then these guys could know something."

He pulls my laptop across the desk so it sits perfectly between us. "Did you already reach out to some of them?"

"No. I thought you might have a better chance."

"Really?" He sounds pleased. "Are you saying I'm a better reporter than you?"

I scoff, knocking my knee into his. But I'm thrown when instead of the sting of colliding kneecaps, I feel a zing all the way up into my stomach.

That's new.

Three has gone still beside me, but I can't bring myself to look at his face.

"You're a pledge," I say belatedly, my voice coming out too loud. "I was thinking they might talk to you because of, you know, brotherhood. Loyalty. Misogyny. All that fun stuff."

Three exhales. "Evans—"

"I have a lot of work to do," I say, grabbing my headphones. And it's not because I need to drown him out. It's because I've had Madison's spring musical audition song stuck in my head for days now, ever since she decided to go for it, and I need something new to take up space in my brain. It has nothing to do with Three. "Why don't you try messaging some of them and let me know how it goes?"

I feel his gaze on my face as I pop in my earbuds, but I ignore him as I email him a copy of my spreadsheet. We aren't the type of partners who have a shared folder. I know he wouldn't put the story out without me at this point, but when we first started, neither of us trusted the other enough to share *anything* like that.

And that's what I need to remember. I don't trust Three. And now that it's spring semester, I need to focus on what's important—winning the Campus Life spot and getting into the journalism program. Whatever happened between me and Three last semester, I can't let it distract me. He's too good at mind games, and I'm dangerously close to expecting something I shouldn't.

And I have Hayes, who I'm 99 percent sure is Lincoln. Someone I know I have a reasonable chance with if we meet in person. And once we finish working on this story together, Three is nobody to me. Just one great kiss, a study guide, and ten years' worth of headaches. I can move on from that.

I have to.

TWENTY

It's clear, by the time the weekend rolls around, that I'm dragging my feet on meeting Hayes. I've messaged him a couple of times since returning to school, but not about anything real. To his credit, he hasn't pushed since I said I'd *see* him at school. But I know nothing has changed for him. He wants to meet.

I'm the only one hesitating.

To distract me from my cowardice, I have Angelica's going-away party, the *Torch* staff's big bash now that we've lost her to the *Columbus Dispatch*. I'd nearly forgotten about it, too busy worrying over meeting Hayes, the work that still needs to be done on the Dirty Four story, and my own article about an alumna author who, after her college roommate was murdered by an abusive boyfriend, started writing middle grade mystery novels to help kids deal with trauma—all to the soundtrack of Madison's musical audition song playing on a relentless loop in my head. But Sabina catches me on her way out of the news-room to ask if I want a ride, reminding me that we have plans.

It feels like she's sharing a secret with me, letting me see inside her car—a cool-girl car, of course, old and littered with CDs for her ancient stereo, smelling like leather and tobacco thanks to an air freshener hanging from the rearview mirror.

On the way to the bar, she asks me about my progress on my application for the journalism program and the recommendation letter I've been trying to get from my adviser.

"I've been really impressed with your stories lately." Her gaze slides my way at a stoplight. "I know you compare your-self a lot to Three, and I won't lie—he's a good reporter. But so are you. His stuff might be hard-hitting, but I think you've got something going for you that he doesn't. At least not yet."

"Like what?" I'm not fishing for compliments—I really want to know. Everyone is always saying what a great reporter Three is. He gets praise from Mel and Christopher constantly, but Sabina has been notably quiet about both of us. Being acknowledged by her, my *Torch* idol, pumps up my confi-dence at warp speed.

"These stories you've been doing lately—the human-interest pieces," she says as she eases into a spot outside the bar. "I think they're something we've been missing at the *Torch*. We've always focused on objective, straightforward news. But I'm realizing sometimes people don't want the dark shit. They want the sto-ries about humanity. That good stuff. You tapped right into that." Sabina grins, thumping a fist against her chest. "You've got heart."

I'm still riding the high of her compliment an hour into the party. The bar we're at is packed, our group taking up a huge table in the middle of the room. I'm the only one stone-cold sober and glued to my seat. Half of them keep getting up to get more drinks, and Angelica and Mel are standing out of their chairs, hunched over a pile of nachos as they each try to house half the plate faster than the other.

It's fun. Or at least, it should be. This is what I've been looking for all year—camaraderie with my fellow staff members. A team vibe. *Friends.*

But there is a notable absence at our table. One I can't stop thinking about.

"Do you know where Three is?" I finally get up the courage to ask when Christopher returns to the table with another beer.

He raises his eyebrows. "Aren't you two, like, a unit now?"

My mouth flattens.

Christopher chuckles as he takes a sip of his drink. "He said he couldn't make it. His frat is having some formal alumni thing"—by his tone, I can tell he finds this ridiculous—"and his parents are in town for the weekend."

Well, then. That's perfect. In fact, this is a bonus for me. The *Torch* staff will notice that *I'm* here, and Three clearly has other priorities. How can they give the Campus Life spot to someone whose schedule is packed with fraternity events?

He's barely even my competition at this point. Sabina is right—my stories have heart. I'm a contender. And Three is proving just how little he cares about beating me if he isn't here right now. In fact, I don't even need to concern myself with his absence. I don't need to think about him at all—not beyond what part of our story he's covering, and if he's been able to get in touch with any of our potential sources yet. We have a business relationship. Beyond that, we are nothing to each other.

Right. I pull out my phone.

I'm doing it. I'm going to meet Hayes.

I'm definitely probably going to meet Hayes.

I will at least broach the subject.

Now.

Probably now.

Maybe . . .

Fuck it.

pomerene1765: let's do it

pomerene1765: let's meet

I shove my phone under a napkin, heart hammering, stomach twisting up in a million knots. Double knots. Sailor's knots. It will probably be knotted up until the end of time. *Congratulations, you're like this forever now.*

When I finally get up the courage to check my phone, I have a message waiting.

hayes6834: you're sure?

hayes6834: I don't want you to do it unless you really want to

pomerene1765: I really want to

pomerene1765: as long as you still do

hayes6834: I do. but I want to make sure you know I don't expect anything from you.

pomerene1765: are you trying to talk me out of it now?

hayes6834: definitely not. but I need to know you're actually ready. what if you're disappointed when you find out who I am?

pomerene1765: I'm pretty sure I already know who you are

There. I sent it. I can't take it back.

hayes6834: I was hoping you'd say that. because I think you do too.

I reach for my glass of water and gulp it down like I just ran a mile. Or ten miles. My heart is beating like I just ran a *hundred* miles.

I swallow my panic down with it.

pomerene1765: does that mean you know who I am?

A long silence stretches before he responds.

hayes6834: I do

I'm so glad everyone else is distracted by the nacho-thon and out-drinking each other, because I could not handle it if even one of them looked my way right now. I wish I hadn't just finished my water, because now I feel like I swallowed dust, and I have nothing to wash it down.

I stare at my phone as more messages pop up.

> **hayes6834:** don't freak out
> **hayes6834:** you're freaking out, aren't you?
> **hayes6834:** maybe we should have this conversation in person
> **pomerene1765:** I'm not freaking out

I am totally freaking out. How long has he known? Why hasn't he tried to see me since we've been back? If he likes me, and if he knows I'm Pomerene, why wouldn't he seek me out?

Is he as nervous as I am about losing our anonymity?

> **pomerene1765:** I'm just wondering what gave me away
> **hayes6834:** you first
> **pomerene1765:** wow you really do hate to lose, don't you?
> **hayes6834:** oh is that what gave me away?
> **pomerene1765:** surprisingly no. it was the kickball
> **hayes6834:** ??
> **pomerene1765:** you said you were in a kickball tournament the weekend before finals, remember? and I said I was there too

hayes6834: no I know. but I didn't think you saw me there.

pomerene1765: what??

hayes6834: I didn't think you saw ME at the tournament.

that you knew I was there.

I get a strange sensation, everything sliding out of place.

A long silence stretches out as my mind races. Clearly we're misunderstanding each other. Either Lincoln thinks someone else is Pomerene, or . . .

My stomach drops. And my panic is the only explanation I have for what I say next.

pomerene1765: you're not lincoln, are you?

This time, an answer comes through right away.

hayes6834: you've gotta be kidding me, evans

I lurch to my feet so quickly, I catch the attention of the rest of the *Torch* staff, as well as a few people nearby. I flush under their scrutiny and nearly drop my phone.

Then I wonder if I *should* drop my phone. Let it be lost to the sticky bar floor, never to be seen again.

"Sorry," I croak, sitting again. "I—I'm—"

"What's up?" Sabina calls over Angelica's head. "You bored? Want a beer?"

"Someone get your recorder ready," says Aaron. "We're

about to have an exclusive on the editor-in-chief enabling underage drinking."

Sabina laughs and flips him off.

"I'm good." I cough into my fist. "I think I just—"

"You want water?" Mel asks, jerking their thumb toward the bar. "I'll grab you one. I'm heading back up."

People start shouting their orders at Mel, who tries to wave them off, and then everyone is yelling. I want so badly to bolt, but I can't exactly disappear when the new Campus Life editor is about to get me a drink. Even if it's only water. At the very least, I need to say goodbye.

I'll wait. It can't take long to get more drinks.

But another five minutes pass. And then eight. And then ten.

I crane my neck, searching the packed bar for Mel, but they've disappeared in the crowd.

And truthfully, now I'm feeling really sick.

Okay, that's it, I think, getting to my feet again.

"Hey, listen, I'm gonna head out," I call over the noise. "I have a—a—oh . . ." I trail off, my eyes widening as I spot Three making his way toward our table from the door. His cheeks and nose are pink from the cold, and his hair is windswept. He's wearing a suit under a long wool coat I've never seen him in, his tie loose and askew, top button of his shirt undone. He's breathing hard, like he ran here. And his narrow gaze is locked on me like I'm the only person in the entire bar.

He stops at our table, ignoring everyone else as he swallows down his next breath and says, "Who the hell is Lincoln?"

TWENTY-ONE

There's no denying it now. No way around it. No happenstance that someone else on this campus might call me by my last name. Nowhere else to go.

All roads lead to Three.

I've been so terribly, horribly wrong. It's the only coherent thought I can form as I stare back at him.

His hands twitch, his expression softening. A small crease forms between his eyebrows.

I can feel everyone else watching us.

I don't know what to do, or what to say. I'm not sure I could speak even if I wanted to.

But I *don't* want to. I'm too full of thoughts to reasonably let one out. I don't know which will break free first. So I shoulder my bag and turn, taking the long way around the table so I don't have to pass him.

Maybe if I walk fast enough, he won't catch up. I could lose him in the crowd.

"Are you kidding me right now?" I feel the heat of him at my back before his words reach my ear. "You're making me chase you?"

"I'm not making you do anything." I'm shocked to hear my own voice, leaden, like someone dropped an anvil in my chest.

"Wyn."

I don't know if it's the warning in his voice or the fact that he uses my first name, but as I step out into the cold, I turn to face him.

"What? What do you want?" I back up a few steps, distancing myself from the clumps of people outside. "God, are you messing with me? Is this your last big—"

"No! *No.* I'm not messing with you." He steps toward me slowly, like he's afraid I might bolt. His voice turns gentle. "Where's your coat? It's freezing."

"I left it in Sabina's car."

He sighs, shrugging off his own coat.

"Don't—" I bite off the word as he drapes it over my shoulders.

It hangs there, heavy and warm, begging to be snuggled into. But I know if I tried to fit my arms into it, it'd be snug. Probably even too small. It definitely wouldn't button.

It's amazing how one bad thought can multiply. Like mold growing on a slice of bread. It doesn't take long—not at all. The way "fat," just a word, just an adjective, not a bad thing—it's not, it's *not*—can suddenly feel . . . so gross. *Shameful.*

I glance back toward the bar. The people gathered outside are looking at us while trying to seem like they aren't, and it's the feeling of their eyes all over me that really starts to burn. It begins behind my own eyes—the worst possible place. What are they thinking right now, looking at us? What judgments are they making of me?

I swallow down my tears, knowing that if I cry right now, especially in front of Three, I will never recover. I've let him see so much of me, I refuse to let him see this too.

He's watching my face so closely, I have to angle away as I force all my bad feelings back down. He never fails to remind me about my terrible poker face, and I don't want him reading me.

While I collect myself, Three puts a hand on my back, steering me toward the curb. There's a white SUV double-parked with its flashers on, and I'm startled when I realize he's leading me to it.

I dig my heels in. "No."

"Give me five minutes."

I turn swiftly to face him, and he catches his coat before it falls. Holding the lapels in both hands, he's effectively cut off my escape.

"I think I've given you enough." My voice comes out sharp and cold, like every bad feeling has dripped off the edge of me, forming a deadly icicle. "I don't even owe you *thirty seconds* of my time."

A muscle tics in his jaw. "I'm not saying you owe me anything. I'm asking you."

"You didn't ask."

He drops his head and sighs. His hands hang heavy on his coat, keeping me in place.

Someone honks, and when I peer past him, it's a cop parked behind the SUV.

Three looks from the cop to me, something frantic in his expression. "Please. Can you give me five minutes?"

I don't know if it's the look on his face or the way he says "please" or if there's a small, stupid part of me that wants to know what this all means. "Five minutes," I say, tugging the coat out of his hands. "You can drive me home."

I try not to notice the relief that washes over him as he reaches for the door, popping it open for me. It's so polite, I want to scream.

I cannot reconcile these manners with his usual arrogance.

Inside, the SUV is still warm. He's climbing into the driver's seat when it dawns on me where the car came from.

"Your parents are here."

He glances over at me as he shifts into drive and eases into traffic. "Yeah."

"This is their car."

"I don't want to waste my five minutes talking about my parents."

"Where do they think you are right now?"

"Wyn."

"I don't really care what you want to talk about. It's my five minutes. We'll talk about whatever I want."

His jaw tightens. "They don't know where I am right now."

"And they're cool with that. Cool enough to let you borrow their car."

"No, when they find out I left *and* took their car, I don't think they'll be cool with it."

"So we're in a stolen car right now. How comforting."

"I borrowed—" He breaks off, huffing out a frustrated breath. He yanks at his tie with one hand, finally loosening it enough to pull it over his head. He tosses it into the back seat. I wish I weren't watching. "I don't want to talk about my parents or what's waiting for me when I get back. None of that matters. I want to talk about us."

A laugh scrapes out of me. "*Us?* There is no us." His hands tighten on the wheel, and in the glow of the streetlamps, I watch his knuckles turn white. "I can't believe you'd even think— What *did* you think? That I'd be happy?"

"I thought I'd have a little more time to ease you into it."

"To ease me into it." I twist toward him in my seat. "How long have you known it was me?"

His Adam's apple bobs. He tugs at his collar, popping open another button. "A while."

"Quantify that for me."

He lets out a heavy breath. "Since that night with the edibles."

I stare at him as I do the math. That was before Thanksgiving. Which means he knew when he stayed at my house, and when we broke into Sigma Rho, and when he followed me upstairs at that frat party, and when we kissed. He knew all of winter break. When he asked me about what I did over Thanksgiving. When he asked about my grades. When he brought up meeting, over and over again. He knew all that time.

"You were baiting me. Asking me all those things—about my Thanksgiving and if I liked someone. What—what the *fuck*, Three?"

"That's not what I was doing—"

"You were!" My voice comes out high and sharp. "You were egging me on. You were bringing yourself up in a round-about way to—to *what*? To get an edge on me? To find out how I feel about you?"

"That's not why I was doing it. I was trying to get *you* to think about *me*. To put the two together." He turns a corner, and I lose his expression between one streetlamp and the next. "To realize there wasn't all that much difference between Hayes and me. I didn't know there was someone else. I thought you—that *we*—" He breaks off, shaking his head.

There wasn't, I almost say. There was only Hayes, and if there was ever someone else, it was Three—not Lincoln. He was the one who made me hesitate. But I can't give him that right now.

I feel cold all over, and his borrowed coat is useless against it. This comes from inside me, like my blood has turned to ice. I'm covered in goose bumps, and my teeth start to chatter. "I told you things." My voice cracks with the effort it's taking not to cry in front of him. "I told you stuff I would have never said—never in a million years—if I knew I was talking to you."

"Why?" He pulls to the curb outside my building and turns to me. His expression is pained. "Why is it so different because it's me?"

"Because I don't trust you!"

He opens his mouth, stops, then forces out a harsh breath. "I know I haven't given you any reason to, so maybe I deserve it. But that one hurt." He rubs his chest, tipping his head back against his seat.

"You don't get to do that either," I whisper. "You don't get to make me feel bad about this. You lied to me."

"I didn't—"

"I'm not going to sit here and explain to you how this was lying!"

He shuts his mouth, his teeth coming down hard on his lower lip. Our five minutes are up. They've *been* up. I've watched each singular minute tick off the clock.

I should go.

"Why didn't you tell me?" I ask instead, prolonging this torture. "When you found out. Why didn't you just say it was you? That's why you disappeared for a couple of days, right? I remember—after the edibles thing. I remember

Hayes—you—didn't respond for a while. You were planning to ghost me, weren't you?"

"I wasn't planning anything," he says quietly. "I was thinking."

"Thinking about how you could best use this against me?"

"Honestly, it never crossed my mind."

"And why should I believe that? You're clearly an accomplished liar."

"I was worried!" He thumps his head back against the seat, huffing out a frustrated breath. "You said a lot of stuff that night in your dorm, and I was worried about you. And who you'd talk to if you didn't have Hayes." He runs a hand down his face and swears.

I stare at him, realization dawning. "Because I said I have no friends?"

He drops his hand and looks over at me, his expression softening. I hate that I see pity there. I hate that he can look at me like this.

"You were worried about who I'd talk to, because Hayes was my only friend." I let out a small, disbelieving laugh. "Wow. That's amazing, Three."

I feel his gaze on me as I reach down and grab my bag.

"You're not leaving like this," he says, but it's not an order, and it's not a question. It's something else entirely—a plea.

I unbuckle my seat belt and twist toward him, reaching for the door behind me. "That early on, losing Hayes would have sucked, but I would have recovered. I could've moved on. But instead you gave me everything I needed, until I couldn't get out of it without getting hurt." I shove the door open and climb out, leaving his coat pooled on the seat. I turn back to deliver a final blow. "I'm done. You win."

"Win what?" he asks.

I shut the door, rounding the front of the SUV. Three climbs out after me.

"What did I win?" he says again, following me across the road.

"This!" I whirl on him, motioning between us. "This— whatever this is. I can't fight with you right now!"

His frown deepens. "I'm not trying to fight with you. I'm trying to tell you I like you. So I don't know what you think I'm winning, because if you're walking away right now, then there's no way I just won anything."

Something balloons in my chest. Something I have no idea what to do with right now. I liked Hayes. Enough that I thought that meant I liked Lincoln. And I'm clearly attracted to Three. But do I like him? *Can* I like him, after everything?

When I don't speak, Three says, "This isn't how I wanted this to go. I wanted—I mean, I didn't want to have this conversation in the street, for one thing."

"Right," I say disdainfully. "You wanted your perfectly controlled environment, so you could have the best advantage."

He's shaking his head before I finish speaking. "All I wanted was the best chance I could give myself."

"For what?"

"For *you*! For a chance with *you*."

I take a moment to drink him in. Lit by the streetlamps and the glow of the headlights, he's windswept and cold-flushed and wound tight in frustration. His suit is in disarray—collar hanging open, shirt half-untucked. Even as the frigid January wind blasts down the street and it takes all the strength in my jaw to keep my teeth from chattering, he doesn't so much as flinch. I bet he's burning hot right now. He looks like a movie. He looks like a dream.

I start to shiver, and I don't know if it's my nerves or the cold finally seeping into the deepest parts of me. My voice shakes when I finally speak.

"I can't do this right now. And I won't say I'm sorry for walking away, because I'm not. You—*god*, I'm so mad at you."

He watches me, and while I expect the usual, composed Three mask to slide into place, instead the corners of his mouth pull down and his eyes soften and he looks . . . sad.

"Don't look at me like that."

He throws his hands up, shaking his head as he turns away. "Okay." He stops when he reaches the SUV. "Can you go inside? So I can leave and go *not* look at you somewhere else?" Anger has crept into his voice, and it pinches at something in my chest.

"You don't get to be mad right now!" I lob back at him. "You don't get to sound *annoyed* at me. You did this! This is your fault!"

"Yeah, I get it!" He falls back against the door, scrubbing his hands over his face. "I know." There's a thread of defeat in his voice. It should make me feel better, because I'm winning for once. He's not the one running me in circles.

But it doesn't feel good. It feels worse than losing.

I turn away, hugging myself for warmth as I head up the front walk to my door. I fumble with the key card, my fingers stiff and aching from the cold.

When I finally make it inside and turn back, Three is right where I left him, waiting, head tipped back to the sky but his gaze on me so burning hot, it nearly cracks my layers of ice.

When I push into my room, I immediately strip off my freezing-cold clothes and pull on my fuzzy robe. I can hear Madison in the other room, practicing her audition song for roughly the ten thousandth time. In the bathroom, I stand under the stream of hot water until I feel warm again, listening to her high, tinkling voice. She sounds exactly how you'd expect when you look at her—like a fairy princess.

"Wyn?" Dara knocks on the bathroom door during a break in Madison's practice. "Did you just get home?"

I shut off the water. "Yeah." My voice comes out weak, exhausted from arguing. "One second."

I'm dried off and back in my robe when I open the door, letting out a waft of steam.

Dara waves it away, her eyes widening when she finally sees my face. "What happened?"

Madison appears behind her, mouth pulling down in concern. "Are you okay?"

"I met Hayes."

They follow me back to my room, where I climb into bed. The room is drafty, and I pull my blankets up around my shoulders, burrowing inside. My wet hair begins to chill.

"And yet, you don't seem happy," says Dara. "What happened? Please don't tell me he turned out to be an asshole."

"Not just an asshole," I reply. "*The* asshole."

Dara and Madison exchange looks of confusion. Then Dara gasps, slapping a hand over her mouth. It muffles her shout. "No!"

Madison's head swivels between us. "What? What is it?"

Dara drops her hands, mouth hanging open. "Was Hayes . . . Three?"

I start a slow clap beneath my blankets. "Ding. Ding. Ding," I say, each one dull as a funeral toll.

"Three, the guy you hate?" Madison asks.

"She doesn't hate him." Dara gives me a knowing look. "You don't hate him." Whatever she sees on my face makes her scoff. "Wyn! You *kissed* him!"

"Wait, you did?" Madison's attention swings to me again. She looks mildly scandalized, but like she's enjoying it a little.

"I don't get how this isn't a good thing," Dara says. "You're clearly into him. You talk about him all the time, so I know he's on your mind, and I don't think it's all about this little game you have going with him."

"Our little game." My mouth twists in a false smile. "Yeah, he really played me, didn't he?"

Dara's brows pull together. "What do you mean?"

"He knew it was me. He's known it was me for a long time—since before Thanksgiving."

"Oh."

"Yeah."

Madison hesitates. "Maybe he was nervous to tell you."

I snort. "Three doesn't get nervous. I don't know why he waited so long, but I suspect it was for his own personal gain, as always. He gets all this time to lead me on while he figures out how he feels about me, and I get five minutes in the car to decide if I trust him." I scrub my hands over my face and into my hair, smoothing it back in a slick wave.

"And how does he feel about you?" Dara asks.

"He claims he likes me!" A sound wheezes out of me, a half whine. "I can't believe he did this. I didn't even need Hayes to be that for me. I just—I just wanted a friend." I bury my face in my hands. "I made *one* friend at college, and somehow he found a way to ruin that too."

In the quiet that follows, I hear only my own breathing. It takes me a moment to sense that something is wrong.

"One friend?" Dara says.

I lift my head, frowning. "What?"

"You made one friend at college?" She looks at Madison, then at me. "What about us?"

"Well . . . I . . ." I glance between them. A headache pricks behind my eyes. "You guys have your own stuff. Your own friends. You know?"

Dara's expression softens, but not in understanding—in disbelief. "Seriously?"

"Of course we're, like, friends, but you're—you're my room-mates. It's . . . You don't think of me as . . . I mean, it's because I'm here. It's not like we're . . . you know . . . eating all our meals together or hanging out, really. We do sometimes, but . . ."

"I thought that was being friends," Madison says quietly.

Dara scoffs. "Wow."

"Wait, I'm not making sense right now."

"No, you are." Dara moves to stand in front of Madison, like she has to . . . protect her from me. "I get it. We're good enough to listen to your problems and come running when you need us. But since you aren't the center of our world, we can't possibly be your friends."

"That's not what I meant."

"We're allowed to have our own lives and other friends, Wyn," Dara says. "And we can do that and still be *your* friend. Not just your roommates." She lets out a heavy breath. "And maybe the reason you feel like you've only made *one friend* in college is because *you're* not a good friend."

She turns away, crossing swiftly back to her room. I stare after her, stunned.

Madison clears her throat lightly. "I think we should talk about this sometime. But—well, I feel very hurt right now. So I'm also going to go."

"Madison—"

She holds up both hands, giving me a tight, watery smile. Then she turns and leaves too, shutting the bathroom door behind her.

I slump back against the wall, stunned. Dread settles in my stomach, and any warmth I gained from my extra-hot shower steams off me as the cold seeps back in.

I glance toward my desk, where I left my phone, but I stop before I make any move to grab it. My first instinct was to message Hayes, but now he's gone.

I have no one to talk to. It's like last semester all over again. Those first couple of months of sheer, utter, piercing loneliness. It's back and sharper than ever.

And I have no one to blame but myself.

TWENTY-TWO

"Wynnie? What's wrong?"

I'm curled on my bed, my phone tucked to my ear and covered with my pillow, blocking out any sound from the outside world. If Dara and Madison are home right now, I don't want to know.

I've been like this all morning, replaying everything that happened last night like a highlight reel of suck. Agonizing over Dara's and Madison's faces as they left my room. Trying not to think about Three, and how badly I wish I could talk to Hayes. To anyone, really.

I'm not embarrassed to say that when my mom's call came through, I almost sobbed in relief.

"Nothing's wrong," I say. "All I said was hi. Why would you think something's wrong?"

She must sense the lie, but she doesn't push. She's good

about that. My family is all about *feeling your feelings*. It's why the three of us openly cried after our fight during winter break. Actually, calling it a fight isn't entirely fair—no one yelled except me, in the end. They wanted to go to a *NeverEnding Story* triple feature at the indie theater in town, and I said, "I *just* got over watching Artax die, like, two weeks ago. You really want to open that wound again?"

"You don't have to come," Mom said with a laugh. "We'll make it date night."

I could've let it go, but my long-building frustration hit a boiling point. "I'm sure you'd prefer it that way."

It's the kind of thing you say when you want to start a fight, but I didn't know until that moment that I was smarting for one. As soon as the words left my mouth, my parents' matching looks of shock were gratifying.

What came pouring out of me next was exactly what Hayes—what *Three*—called it. An airing of grievances. That, for my whole life, I've felt like a second-tier priority, and Thanksgiving only proved it.

In the end, they both apologized, which I'd known they would. But it didn't fix every problem. It just made them aware of the problem. Which makes sense why Mom is calling now—a general check-in to remind me that she loves me, and not because she felt my sadness from eighty miles away.

"Well, if you aren't busy, we wanted to talk to you about something important. I'm putting you on speaker."

"Hi, Wynnie," Dad says.

"Hi, Dad. Um, yeah, I'm not busy." I probably won't be for a while, since my friends hate me, and I plan to text Sabina that I'm too sick to come into the newsroom on Monday. I can't deal with Three yet. I don't even want to deal with myself.

Mom waits a beat, then says, "Well, Dad and I have been talking, and we decided we're going to skip the Ren Faire this year."

My pillow flings off the side of my bed as I sit up sharply. *"What?"*

"We've been thinking about what you told us while you were home, about how we've made you feel," Dad says. "And I know you said you forgive us for Thanksgiving—"

"I *do*."

Mom cuts in. "The bottom line is, we don't ever want you to feel second to anything else in our lives. So instead of working the Ren Faire, we thought we'd take this year off so we'll be home more for you."

"But—but the faire is in the fall. I'll be at school."

"And if you need to call or come home, we won't have our weekends tied up. We can be here for you."

"*No.* Look, I appreciate it, I do—" I break off, my throat tightening. I get what they're doing. This is the obsession that takes up the most of their time, and it's the biggest sacrifice they can make. It's a huge gesture, but not one I can accept—not when I know how happy it makes them.

When the ache in my throat eases, I say, "I don't want you to give up the Ren Faire. But maybe we can do something this summer? Like . . . take a real vacation?" I quickly add, "And I don't mean San Diego Comic-Con."

Mom laughs. "How about Florida?"

"Or Maine," Dad says. "Somewhere that doesn't have the climate of an armpit in the summer."

"We can do other stuff too," Mom says. "Like take a pottery class at the community center—you've always wanted to try pottery."

"I'll probably be bad at it. I'm not great with my hands." That is to say, I have no artistic ability whatsoever.

"It'll be fun either way though, won't it?" Mom says hopefully.

Tears press at the backs of my eyes. "Yeah. I think I'd like that." My voice cracks, and I dab at my eyes with the edge of my blanket. "And I—I'm really grateful you'd consider skipping the faire for me. But I don't want you guys to give up something you love that much, or to feel like you have to because of me."

"Wynnie, we *wanted* to. Not because of you, but because of us," Dad says. "Yeah, we love the faire, but there's nothing in this world we love more than you. If we can cut something out of our lives to make more time for you, of course we want to do that. Honestly, we're counting ourselves lucky that we got a teenager who actually wants to hang out with us."

I sniffle. "Hanging out this summer does sound fun."

I think Dad might be a little choked up as he agrees, and Mom exhales a small sound of relief.

"Hey, I have a question." I lean over the side of my bed and grab my pillow, curling up and placing it over my head again. "What do you guys think about me talking to a counselor?"

"Do you feel like you need to talk to someone?" Mom asks.

"Kind of."

"We are a positive mental-health household," Dad says. "You can always talk to us—about anything you're going through, okay? But if you also want to talk to someone else—if you'd be more comfortable—we can work that out too."

"We might have mental-health services through our insurance," Mom says absently, and I hear her rifling around in her overstuffed purse.

I let out a small, wet laugh, swiping at my running nose with my sleeve. "We have counselors on campus. I just . . . I'm wondering if I should go."

I didn't realize I was considering it until I was already asking them, but I think it's been on my mind for a while. Especially now, after everything that's happened. I might be on stable ground with my parents, but the landscape of the rest of my life looks tornado-ravaged. I need help.

"I think," Mom says, "if therapy will help you feel like the best version of yourself, then there's no reason not to try it."

The waiting room is quiet and surprisingly empty. Only one other student sits in the available chairs.

I guess this explains why it was so easy to make an appointment.

I gave myself the weekend to wallow. I grabbed take-out meals from the dining hall at odd hours so I didn't risk running into anyone. I texted Sabina that I wasn't feeling well and would be out of the newsroom for a couple of days. I don't know if she believed me after what everyone witnessed at the bar Friday night, but she didn't give me a hard time. Alone in my room, I threw myself into new ideas for the *Torch*, searching for heart and hope. But more than anything, I tried not to think about Three and our Dirty Four story, and how I might lose my spot on it now that things have gone so sideways with us.

Then on Monday morning, I made an appointment at the counselors' office for the following afternoon. Which brings me here, to this nearly empty waiting room.

I don't know where to start today. Whether it's with my parents, and what I really hope to gain with them this summer. If it's with my friends, and how much I've hurt them, and why. Or if it's with Three, and all my tangled, twisted-up feelings for him.

But when the door creaks open and someone says, "Éowyn Evans," and I cringe at the sound of my full name, I realize something.

Maybe it needs to start with *me*. Not the situations I'm in, but how I feel about myself. More than how I look in a mirror, but how I look deep down—the slimiest, darkest parts of me, and how those parts have somehow touched all the good things I've found since I got to school.

I take in a bracing breath. "That's me," I say, standing. "I'm Éowyn."

If this were a movie, the therapy scene would resolve all my problems. I'd know how to fix things with my friends, and what to say to Three. But as it turns out, I didn't leave my appointment a brand-new person. And even though I know I *need* to fix these things, no one is going to give me a guidebook on how to do it.

Apparently all your problems can't be magically fixed in a single session.

So I made another appointment. Not because I need a magical fix-it, but because it was nice talking to someone. Saying things out loud helped me clear my head. And I want to try what Mom said—to be the best version of myself.

Talking through the events of the last few days made me realize I need to fix things with Dara and Madison first. And maybe I didn't get a guidebook on how to do it, but I did realize that I know them. I know what's important to them. And I know how to show that I love them.

When Dara pushes through the glass doors to the auditorium lobby, she doesn't look pleased. But she's *here*, which has to count for something. It means she read my text, even if she didn't respond. She's still giving me a chance.

She stops just inside, eyeing me. "You brought flowers?"

I drop my gaze to the small bouquet in my hands. "Do you think it's too much?"

"Maybe." She sits beside me, leaving a good amount of space between us. "But it's nice."

A beat of silence passes. My stomach twists with nerves. In romance comics and novels, there's always a grand gesture. Showing up for Madison's audition feels like one. But as I thought about how to fix things with my friends, I couldn't come up with anything for Dara. There's nothing that feels as grand as the apology that I owe her—that I owe them *both*.

"I was hoping we could talk after this." I angle toward her, braving a look at her face. "But maybe we can sit in there together first? For Madison?"

A small crack forms in her stony mask. "I guess that'd be okay."

The auditions are open to the public, but I'm not surprised to find, when we get inside the theater, that the seats are empty except for the judges and other auditionees. Heads swivel in our direction. Madison's ponytail swishes as she does a double take, eyes widening.

I lift a hand in a small wave as Dara and I slip into the last row.

When Madison flushes, I worry this was a bad idea. Maybe I should have talked to her first, rather than force my way into her space.

Then she smiles a little, and the tightening in my chest eases.

I glance at Dara. "I really want to be a good friend to both of you. Way better than the one I've been."

Dara sniffles, glancing away. "I didn't mean that when I said it."

"I think you were right, though. I've been selfish. But I'm really happy you came tonight."

Dara shrugs, still not looking at me. "It's for Madison."

"Right." I face forward, focusing on the stage. "For Madison."

Madison finds Dara and me waiting outside after her audition. She accepts her flowers, beaming and pink-cheeked.

"Thanks for coming." She shoves her nose into the bouquet and inhales. "This was really nice."

Dara adjusts her bag on her shoulder, her focus on Madison. "You did great. They'd be idiots not to choose you."

"No, there were a ton of good singers." Madison flaps her free hand at her. "And I have zero acting experience. I'll be happy just to make the ensemble."

"You didn't do any drama at all in high school?" I ask. We've started walking, heading toward home without discussing it.

"No way. My parents would have hated that. They didn't mind the musicals my school put on, but I didn't have time. I had small group and volunteering. My parents wanted me to do stuff for the church, not for myself." She winces. "I haven't told them about this. I don't think they'd be happy about me being in a musical with so much murder and adultery. I'll probably tell them eventually, but I don't know if it'll be right away. I've been, um, talking to someone in the counselors' office since you suggested it." That, she directs at Dara. "About my parents and my . . . feelings." She shoves her face into her flowers, hiding her expression. "It's been super nice."

"That's really great," Dara says gently, patting her back lightly. "I'm glad you decided to go."

"I—" I choke on a lump in my throat and cough. My cheeks burn as they both look at me. "I think it's great too. I . . . I'm also doing that. Talking to someone. I had my first appointment today." When neither of them speaks, I backtrack quickly. "Not that I'm—I'm not—This isn't about m—"

Madison takes my hand and squeezes. "I'm really happy you're doing that. It's helped me a lot. I've only been to a couple sessions, but I feel so much better afterward."

"Me too," Dara says quietly.

I swallow hard. "I'm sorry I waited so long to talk to you both. I should have come to you right away to apologize, but I think I was . . . scared. That I wouldn't say the right thing, or that you wouldn't accept it. But you don't apologize to someone only when they'll accept it. You do it when you're wrong, no matter what. I'm so sorry for what I said, and for the assumptions I made. I think . . . I think I don't really value who I am as a person. I can't imagine why people would want to be friends with me, especially people I really like, and *especially* when they already have other friends, because

- 324 -

those people always seem way better than me. I have . . . low self-esteem, I guess. And that should be something that only negatively affects me, but I've let it affect other people. And hurt other people. I did—*do*—consider you both friends. The kind of friends I'd sort of die to have. And I didn't think I was worth that, and I ended up hurting both of you because of it. I never, ever wanted that. I think you're both incredible. I came to college wishing I could find people like you. I got hyper-focused on what I thought that friendship should look like, and I didn't realize that I've been really happy with the friendship we have, exactly as it is."

My eyes are stinging with tears when I finish. Madison is still holding my hand, and her grip has tightened.

"We all say things we don't mean, Wyn," she says, pulling me to a stop so she can face me. "I've said things that hurt you. You didn't hold that against me. I would never hold this against you. I'm really happy you consider me a friend, and that you've been able to forgive me for everything I've done wrong too." She releases my hand to hug me, crushing her flowers against my back. "I love being friends with you. And I know it's more important how you think of yourself, but I want you to know that I think you're worth the world."

The lump in my throat is so large, I can't even speak. I nod against her shoulder and squeeze her tighter.

I look up when I hear another sniffle, and my gaze lands on Dara. Her face has crumpled, tears streaming down her cheeks.

"I didn't like being mad at you either," she says, her voice wobbling. She covers her eyes with her hand. "I was just waiting for you to tell me you actually like me."

It's seeing Dara cry that pushes me over the edge, and I can no longer hold back my own tears. "Of course I like you!" I take a step toward her, even though I'm not great at hugging people—not the way Madison clearly is—and thankfully Dara reads it as an invitation, because she crashes into me.

"I'm sorry," I say, this time with the addition of tears and a wail in my voice. "I'm so sorry. I didn't mean it."

"I didn't either," Dara sobs, clutching me. "I don't think you're a bad friend."

Madison wraps her arms around both of us, and when I look over, she's crying too.

"Is this another traditional college experience?" she asks, sniffling. "Crying in public?"

"Yeah," Dara replies, hugging us both tighter. "It's just like New York City. You aren't a real college student until you've sobbed in the middle of the Oval."

When we've cried ourselves dry and started walking again, each with a tissue from the travel pack I keep in my purse, Madison is the first one to speak.

"So, can I ask something super nosy? This probably isn't the right time, but . . ."

"Oh, thank god, because I wanted to ask," says Dara.

I look between them. "Ask what?"

"What is going on—" Madison starts.

Dara finishes, "With you and Three?"

That night, we have a sleepover. We drag my mattress into their room and set it in the narrow space on the floor between their beds. We stay up too late talking—about Dara and how she *swears* she's given up on Buckonnect so she can focus on the club she wants to start for other Black marketing students, about Madison and the part she *really* wants in the musical even though she thinks she's being greedy, and about me and Three.

And when the two of them drop off, their breathing evening out and Dara snoring lightly, I open my chat log with Hayes and scroll back to the very beginning. I read through our entire history, looking for clues.

I find them as far back as fall break, when we first started talking. There are traces of him everywhere—in the jokes he made and the way he talked. There were so many times I should have guessed. But what are the odds that out of the thousands of users and tens of thousands of students, I'd randomly match with Three that night all those months ago? I'm more likely to be hit by a campus bus.

"You should talk to him."

I gasp, dropping my phone on my face. I rub my stinging nose as I sit up, swiveling toward Dara. "I thought you were asleep."

She shrugs. "I was, but I think the sound of your brain whirring woke me."

I exhale a laugh, lying back down again.

"No, for real, it's because I have to pee." She climbs out of bed, stepping over me, and disappears into the bathroom. I'm reading over my messages from winter break when she returns, and she stretches out beside me on my mattress. She takes my wrist, turning my phone toward her.

"You know what I think?" she says after a while. "If I met someone on Buckonnect who talked to me like this, I wouldn't be lying around agonizing over whether or not to give him a chance."

"If it were anyone else, maybe." I release my phone, letting her have it to continue her scroll through my messages. "But I feel like I got tricked."

"Even after he told you he likes you?"

I hesitate. "It's hard to trust that too. And I don't know how this works if I don't trust him."

"Don't you trust him, though? You've been working together for months. He took care of you when you were high. He saved that goat and met your parents. He called campus security to deal with the library perv."

I muffle my laugh with my pillow. "Okay, god, have you been reading my diary or something?"

"I just wonder if this might be coming from somewhere else. Like maybe you're . . . a little embarrassed?"

"That I didn't guess it was him?"

"That you told him how much you liked him without knowing who you were talking to. And that makes it feel like there's a power imbalance. But that's life, right? No one is completely equal all the time when it comes to dating. At best, it's sixty-forty in either direction."

"That extra twenty feels like a lot of power when Three's holding it. I don't know if I'll be able to handle that."

"You haven't even talked to him long enough to find out. You don't have to forgive him. But I know you have stuff you want to say to him too."

After a beat of silence, she adds, "I should be honest that I'm not completely unbiased here. I'm kind of rooting for him." At my look of betrayal, she huffs out a laugh against her forearm. "Sorry. It's only because I'm rooting for you the most, and I think he's one of the good ones."

I lift my phone, reading through our messages again. Dara doesn't return to her bed, instead drifting off beside me. Before long, she's snoring in my ear.

She's right, of course. I have so many things I want to say to him. And even if I didn't, I don't think there's a chance in the world that Three will let me get away with never speaking to him again.

I don't think that's what I want either.

And I know he's waiting for me. He won't push it yet. He's giving me time. I don't feel ready, but how long do I want to wait? What good does waiting even do without talking to him first?

I could text him—*him*, Three—but that doesn't feel right. We should finish this how we started.

pomerene1765: are you free tomorrow?

I'm shocked when my phone buzzes with a response only seconds later.

hayes6834: yes
pomerene1765: can we talk?
hayes6834: I'd really like that

I stare at his message, my stomach turning with nerves. It's so strange to get such an honest, earnest answer from Three. I'm used to him being flippant, everything a joke. This is clearly Hayes, but it doesn't feel like Three.

pomerene1765: tomorrow night.
hayes6834: your room?

My stomach jolts. *No.* I want to meet him on common ground. Somewhere no one else will be.

pomerene1765: the newsroom
hayes6834: ok. 8?
pomerene1765: fine.

He doesn't respond, and I spend a long time staring at his messages before I finally flip my phone over and focus on the ceiling instead.

A few minutes later, my phone buzzes, and I grab it embarrassingly fast. Dara makes a noise of protest, rolling onto her back, and slides half off the mattress, still sound asleep.

I stare at the new message from Three, my chest squeezing.

hayes6834: thank you

TWENTY-THREE

It wouldn't be unheard of for one of the *Torch* staff to be in the newsroom late, so I'm relieved when I get there and find it empty, dark, and locked up, everyone gone home. It's what I was hoping for when I suggested the office, my brain supplying the only place where we feel like perfect equals. A power play, at this point, would only do more damage.

As the ceiling lights flicker to life, I survey the room. I could take the table where we sometimes have meetings, putting Three and me at opposite ends. Or I could take a different desk, leaving conspicuous space between us. But when I settle at the grunt desk, it feels right. We've fought so many battles here. Why wouldn't we have one more in the space we've shared from the beginning?

Behind me, the door rattles, and I hold my breath as it creaks open. The air goes hot and electric with his presence, like the room can sense something is about to happen.

I turn slowly. His head is angled down, so I can't see his face. He's in his old coat again, and this soft sweater he wears a lot, and khakis I've definitely made fun of him for owning. The sight of him makes my heart thunder like it's a Triple Crown contender, and I have to turn away again to gather my bearings.

This would be a lot easier if I weren't so desperately attracted to him.

After a moment, I hear the door shut softly, and his footsteps thump steadily against the carpet. Anticipation zings through me as I wait to see where he'll go—if he'll take his seat, or if he'll claim someone else's desk, the way I considered doing.

I hold my breath when his footsteps stop behind me. Then, after an agonizing few seconds, he pulls out the chair next to me and hangs his coat over the back. As he sits, he shoves his sleeves up roughly, his movements jerky and agitated.

He scrubs his hands over his face and into his hair before dropping them into his lap. Then he shifts to pull his phone from his pocket. I try not to, but I can't help watching out of the corner of my eye as he opens Buckonnect.

His thumbs fly across the screen, stabbing out a message. My heart lodges in my throat as I wait.

A moment later, my phone buzzes on the desk, and I pick it up.

hayes6834: I wasn't only talking to you for you. I needed
this too.

I force myself not to look at him as I read his words again
and again.

As I do, another message pops up.

hayes6834: this isn't a guilt trip. I get why you're mad. I
just want you to understand
pomerene1765: what could you have possibly needed
from me?

I feel wired and shaky as I hit send, knowing that we are
now . . . talking. He opened the door, and I stepped through it.

Not in the way I expected, but things with Three rarely
are.

hayes6834: are you kidding? you couldn't tell how badly
I needed to talk to someone?

I think back on my early messages with Hayes, which felt
so lighthearted. But it wasn't long before I relied on him for so
much—friendship especially, but also something deeper. Someone I could talk to about my imposter syndrome, my angriest
moments, my fights with my parents, my sadness.

It occurs to me that my best talks with Hayes mostly came
later, after Three knew it was me. He was honest about his own

anger, his parents, his feelings about his place in the world. How hard he is on himself.

It makes it impossible to ignore what he's saying. That he needed to talk to me—badly enough that he *kept* talking to me. He brought up meeting, gave away pieces of his true self, and nearly the entire time, he knew exactly who was on the other end of the chat.

But it's so, *so* hard to reconcile the Three I know in person with the boy in my phone.

> **pomerene1765:** let's say I couldn't tell
>
> **pomerene1765:** you know why I needed to talk to someone. why did you?
>
> **hayes6834:** I hated this school when I got here.
>
> **hayes6834:** I still hate parts of it. tau delt. my roommates sometimes. but I was being crushed by my parents and the only thing that was fun was the torch and fighting with you and talking to pom. when you told me you didn't have any friends, I was worried about you. but I didn't only keep talking to you because of that. I kept talking to you because it was the same for me.
>
> **pomerene1765:** you're going to try to sell the idea that you don't have friends? are you kidding? everyone loves you.

I've almost forgotten he's sitting right beside me, and I jump when he makes a skeptical noise from the back of his throat.

hayes6834: no lmao they really don't

hayes6834: I don't have a ton of friends. I have hardly any. and it's weird for me because I came from being in school with all my closest friends and my cousins and I never had a chance to feel lonely because everyone was always there. it's not like that here.

hayes6834: I'm not having a good time

hayes6834: or I wasn't. except with you.

hayes6834: you don't owe me anything but I wanted to be honest. because I don't think I could have stopped talking to you even if I thought you didn't need me. I needed you.

I swallow hard, staring at those last three words. Each one burrows a little deeper into my heart.

Then his next message comes through.

hayes6834: I still do.

I turn to him but freeze when I notice he's shaking, every line of his body rigid with tension.

Hesitantly, I lay a hand on his arm.

He lets out a slow breath, and when he looks over at me, my stomach gives a violent swoop. He's *crying*. And he lets me see for only a moment before he seems to remember, his expression tightening as he quickly angles his face away again.

"What—Why—"

"Sorry," he says, his voice hoarse. He tugs his arm out of my hold and rubs his eyes, like he can erase everything I just saw.

I frown, pulling his sleeve until he looks at me again. "Don't apologize for that." I swallow, my throat aching. I don't know why seeing him so clearly in pain makes my heart crack.

I rifle around in my bag until I unearth a travel pack of tissues. I tear it open and pass one to him.

He exhales a soft, shaky laugh. "Thanks."

"I get the feeling this isn't about me."

He looks away again.

"You don't have to do that," I say, laying a hand on his back. "You don't have to hide."

He crushes the used tissue in his fist but still doesn't look at me. I'm starting to think he doesn't let himself cry often, or maybe ever.

I remember something Hayes said to me once, when I talked about being sad. How I felt like I could be sad anywhere.

Sometimes I really wish I could hold you.

Yeah, I think now, looking at the tense line of Three's shoulders. *Same.*

So I shift over in my seat and wrap my arms around him.

It's awkward. And uncomfortable. The arm of my chair digs into my stomach, and I have to hold him sideways, rather than straight on.

But after a moment, he relaxes. He stops shaking. His

breathing evens out. And he begins to lean against me, the rest of him loosening.

"What happened?" I murmur.

I hear him swallow, but he doesn't speak.

When another beat passes, I say, "We can go back to Buckonnect if that's easier."

"No." His voice is thick and scratchy. "I like this. I just need a second."

I wait, rubbing my hand in soothing circles between his shoulder blades.

After a minute, he huffs out a small laugh. "If you keep doing that, I don't think I'll ever talk."

I pull back a few inches, peering at the little bit of his face he'll let me see right now. "Why?"

"Because I like it too much," he says. "And if I start talking, I'm afraid you'll stop." He tilts his head toward me, finally meeting my gaze. He's still red around the eyes, and his skin is splotchy, but I'm struck with a thought as I look at him.

He's a pretty crier.

Of course he is.

I exhale. "Are you okay now?"

The corner of his mouth lifts, sardonic. "No." He rubs his hands over his face and through his hair, raking it back roughly. "I've been cut off."

"From . . . ?"

"Everything." His expression crumples again, and he fights down the emotion, smoothing out before he continues.

"My parents—they have this really small, uncomfortable box they expect me to fit into. And tonight, I told them I quit Tau Delt and submitted to change my major—"

"*Change your major?*" I can't believe what I'm hearing. "You're quitting journalism?"

"No, that's what I changed to. From business to the journalism pre-major so I can apply for next semester."

"You've been a business major all this time?" I stare at him, dumbfounded. "How did I not know this?" This last part I whisper to myself.

A ghost of a smile touches his lips. "You're quite the investigative journalist, Evans."

I glare at him, and I'm gratified when amusement sparks in his eyes. But it dims quickly as he seems to remember where we are and what we're discussing.

"I'm sorry," he says. "This isn't what tonight is for. You didn't come here to listen to my problems."

"Do you really think I need an apology for that?" I tilt my head, peering at his face. "I also didn't come here so you could put on a mask and pretend to be okay for my sake. That's not what I want from you."

"I just feel like I've . . . trapped you here. To deal with me."

"That's not how *I* feel." I angle toward him, brushing his hair back from his face. It's strange, how naturally the gesture comes to me. Touching Three has always been easy—part of a game, toeing the line. But I never expected that something as innocent as brushing back his hair would feel so . . . intimate.

From the look he gives me, I think he's feeling the same. Something in him relaxes, leaning into me.

"What happened?" I ask, dragging my hand away.

He catches it, clasping it between both of his. "I thought if I explained about Tau Delt first, they'd be okay with it. If I told them about the hazing, or the constant drinking, or the way some of those guys *talk* . . ." He turns my hand over, his focus on my palm as he brushes his fingertip over each individual line, the softest touch. Then he seems to remember that I'm still . . . me, and he sets my hand gently back in my lap, putting distance between us again.

"But my dad's a legacy," he continues. "He wasn't surprised by any of it. Like he . . . *expected* it, and expected me to be okay with it. And I'm not. If that's who he wants to be, then he can be that guy, but I won't. I'm not here to make the world worse. Which is what I told him, and he was—well—pissed. At that point, I knew there was no going back, and I didn't want to anyway, so I let it all blow up at once. Told them I switched my major." He shrugs, finally lifting his gaze. "Now I'm on my own. No tuition, no spending money. Nowhere to stay this summer, because I'm definitely not welcome at home—not when I could end up being a bad influence on my sister. When this billing cycle is over, I'm off the family phone plan. Insurance, too, so I guess it's good we have campus health services. But that's about where my luck runs out. I'm cut off. In every way you can be."

"I'm . . . I'm so sorry. That's—"

"Don't be. *I'm* not. I've wanted to do this for so long, but I was—afraid, I guess. Of what my life would look like on the other side. Of how my parents would react, *especially* my dad." He sighs, tipping his head back. "I always knew he'd be mad. That they both would. And honestly, it's worse than I thought. But I also know that no matter what my life looks like now, it's not worse than what it would look like ten years from now if I kept doing what they wanted."

I think back on my messages with Hayes, and the things Three has said to me himself—about the expectations his family has for him. It's the starkest similarity between them, how honest he's always been with me about the burden he feels from his parents.

And yet, I remember those first few weeks, over fall break and Halloween. When he talked about his mom, and that comfortable exasperation he had with her. He's playing strong right now, but I don't think the tears I saw are about money. I think he *wants* to make his parents proud. That being someone people believe in is important to him. Imagining how much hurt he's burying just to talk to me makes my heart ache.

"I really fucked this up," Three says with a humorless laugh. "I just—I couldn't *not* do this with my parents today, if tonight I was going to ask you to trust me. To give me a chance." I must look surprised, because he frowns and leans in, his voice softening. "Isn't that why we're here? To talk about us?"

"Us," I repeat, testing the word.

His gaze turns hopeful. "I know you think there's this huge difference between who I was with you and who I really am, but—Wyn, you know me. Everything I said as Hayes—that was me. We could have been sitting just like this"—he motions to the grunt desk and our side-by-side chairs—"having those conversations. It would have still been me." He watches my face, hesitating. "But I'm also this guy." He taps the arm of his chair. "I know that's the problem. Trusting Hayes was easy, because he was honest and nice to you. The reality is that I can't be him all the time. Sometimes I'm also this. I fight with you, and I say things I shouldn't, and I can be an asshole. I tried to be honest about that too—as Hayes. But I don't think—"

"I like this you."

His face slackens with surprise.

I take a deep breath, preparing for the plunge. "I like you as both. And I want you to be honest with me like this. That's what I liked about talking to H—to you."

He swallows audibly. "I liked being honest with you. I liked that it was *you*."

"You did?"

He shifts, facing me fully. "I thought I made that pretty clear when I said I like you. A lot. You said you were worried I'd be disappointed when I found out it was you, but I was more worried you'd be disappointed it was me." He pauses, and the confession hangs heavy around us. Then, tentatively, he adds, "Are you? Disappointed it's me?" As soon as the words leave his mouth, he tenses like he's bracing himself.

"I was never disappointed."

He exhales a shaky breath, nodding. "Okay."

"I was . . . scared. That it was you." He drops his gaze, mouth pulling down at the corners. I feel, once again, the unfamiliar urge to comfort him. "You have to understand that. I didn't know what to expect from you. I was supposed to believe you found out I was Pomerene at a time when we had almost nothing between us but mutual sabotage, and you chose *not* to use it against me? You had everything I said when I was high, you had all the stuff I'd told Hayes—you could've destroyed me. Easily. How was I supposed to think it was anything but a long con?"

Three nods slowly. "I get it. I couldn't even admit it to myself at first—that I just really selfishly wanted to keep talking to you. Because I could pretend if you needed me, it wasn't because I needed you just as badly. And the longer it went on, the deeper I dug myself in a hole, because I was starting to like you here"—he knocks on the arm of my chair—"and here." He motions to his phone. "And I knew there was no good way to tell you it was me. Not without lying, or hurting you—and then I hurt you anyway."

I look down at my hands. "I think that's what I'm most afraid of. Getting hurt. I was embarrassed that I told you so much when I didn't know it was you, but I'm more worried about how much I'll be willing to give you now, knowing exactly who I'm talking to."

I startle when he brushes my hair behind my ear. "It's

not going away for me. The way I feel about you. And I know you don't trust me right now; I know I have to earn it. But Wyn . . ." He slides a finger under my chin, tilting my head up. His gaze is intense, imploring. "I *want* to earn it. I want to be someone to you."

My heart squeezes. No one has ever spoken to me like this—so *earnestly*. It should be embarrassing to hear him say it out loud, but instead his words slide through me, turning my blood warm.

"You already are," I whisper. "You are someone to me."

He softens, smiling a little, almost exasperated. "I don't mean someone you find irritating—"

"I know what you mean," I say breathlessly as I grab him by the back of the neck and kiss him.

He responds instantly, twisting toward me, matching my intensity and then quickly doubling it. Like betting, each of us calls every time the other ups the ante, until our frantic kisses turn deep and languid, and my heart feels like it might break free from my chest, and I swear I can hear his beating just as hard.

We fumble with our chairs, fighting with the arms that separate us until he shoves out of his seat entirely. He kneels, his arms coming around me and pulling me to the edge of my seat. His torso is bracketed by my thighs, and as his mouth reaches mine, I whisper, "You should kneel more often. It's a good look on you."

A laugh bursts out of him, and his next kiss is a smile

pressed to my mouth. "God, Evans," he mumbles against my lips. "I hope you never change."

Kissing him blurs time and place, narrowing my entire universe down to his touch. I finally understand what all those romance novels meant when they talked about losing yourself in someone. I want to *stay* lost, knowing only the heat of his hands, the sound he makes when I nip his lower lip, and his deep exhale as he pulls me closer.

When we finally come up for air, we're both mussed and still smiling. I can no longer draw up my anger from earlier. It's like cupping water in my hands. There's nothing left to hold on to.

I want him. And he wants me too. Maybe I don't trust everything, but I trust that. He's in this with me. He said as much as Hayes, so many months ago, when he found out I was Pomerene. He knew, and he chose this anyway.

"You know, historically my birthdays have been pretty shitty, and this one had a rough start," he says as he rests back on his heels, his hands warm on my knees. He gives them a squeeze. "But this is a nice turnaround."

"Your . . . *what*?"

He smiles. "Some birthday, huh?"

I smack his chest. "Why didn't you tell me? You did all this—and then your parents—why—?"

"Wyn," he says, laughing as he catches my hand in his, "this is what I wanted. If I'd waited, I would have just spent one more day missing you."

I flush, looking away.

"Besides"—he presses a quick kiss to my jaw, his mouth finding my ear—"I got the best gift in the end."

Three insists on walking me home, and on the way to my building, we talk. It feels natural, the way everything else between us has—the fights and arguments, every battle gaining and losing ground, and all our conversations. I realize, now that I'm looking for it, that we have a rhythm. We always have.

At the front of my building, we linger, hands clasped between us.

"I'd like to take you on a date," he says, not quite meeting my gaze. "But it won't be anything . . . *nice*. Not until I find a job."

"You'll be there? On this date?"

He snorts. "Yeah, I think for it to qualify, we both have to be there."

I smile. "Good enough for me. And maybe as one broke student to another, I could give you some pointers on the job-hunting thing."

He chuckles. "You mean you'll help me with my résumé?"

"Yeah, first tip: the kind of job you're getting won't require a résumé."

I'm surprisingly charmed when his smile turns sheepish. "I guess it's a good thing we're about to have more free time."

"What do you mean?"

"We're almost done with our story. We especially have to be now, since I left Tau Delt. My access to the Dirty Four"—I don't miss the amused twitch of his lips—"is about to be severely limited. But I want to shift focus to the guys who dropped out during pledge period. I've got two from the last few years who might go on the record about what they saw. Plus, I don't think we can hold Christopher off much longer. We should shoot for next week."

My stomach drops. *Our story.*

"What? Why do you look like that?"

I bite my lip. "I . . . haven't worked on it in a few days."

"Evans."

"I thought you were going to kick me off!"

He levels me with a look. "You're in *so much* trouble."

"It's fine! A week is plenty of time. I'll work on it all night if that makes you happy."

"I'm the opposite of happy. You thought I was going to kick you off? Who do you think I am?"

"I didn't know what to expect. It's not like I haven't been doing anything; I just haven't done as much as I should have." I shoot him a sideways look. "You're telling me it didn't even cross your mind that I might bail?"

His answer is lightning quick. "Not for a second."

"Well . . . okay." I wince, feeling guilty. "I'll start catching up tonight. And tomorrow you can work me so hard, I'll think I'm at journalism boot camp." As soon as the words leave my mouth, a flush erupts over my face.

Three swallows audibly, and his gaze drops to my mouth.

I hold up my free hand, blocking my lips. "We shouldn't. I need to focus. I'm going upstairs right now"—I try to tug apart our clasped hands, but he holds on—"so I can work on it—*Three*."

He reels me in, swooping around to plant a kiss on my cheek. "See you tomorrow."

And I'm so surprised, the only thing I say is, "Happy birthday."

His laughter follows me into the lobby, and when I look back before I enter the elevator, he's still standing on the other side of the door, smiling.

TWENTY-FOUR

The next morning, I'm bleary-eyed and exhausted, standing at my sink with my toothbrush hanging out of my mouth, when my phone buzzes on the counter.

THREE:
> You better have at least half your
> stuff done

I stare at my phone and then my reflection, wondering if I'm hallucinating from lack of sleep. I spent most of the night alternating between working on our story and embarrassingly flinging myself around my bed, thinking about our kiss.

ME:
> Half of what done?

THREE:

Your STUFF

For the story

Come on, Evans

All my warm, fuzzy feelings die a swift death. It's amazing how he can kiss me until I lose sleep over him and then immediately inspire me to murder.

ME:

You better be joking

THREE:

Come let me in. I have coffee

You can't just show up without warning!

I drop my phone on the counter and rush to get dressed. By the time I'm done, hair clipped back into something at least presentable-adjacent and wearing a combination of clothes I can stand to be seen in, I have several missed texts.

THREE:

Hello? Are you seriously leaving me

out here? We have work to do

Evans

Evans

Evans

Okay you did this to yourself

I swing open my door, choking out a shocked noise when I find him standing on the other side, hand poised to knock. He has two coffee cups in his free hand, one balanced atop the other.

"How'd you get in here?" I demand, sounding weirdly annoyed for someone who is exploding-glitter-and-butterflies happy to see him.

He passes me a coffee. "Someone was leaving. They let me in."

I frown. "They should know better than to do that. We used to have a drug dealer in this building."

He snorts. "So, do I have to stay out here all morning?"

I eye his backpack, then his face. He looks pale and exhausted, but he's smiling like he's happy to see me too.

"I guess not." I hold up my cup. "Since you brought coffee."

"Oh, only because of that?"

I shrug, moving aside so he can come in. As he crosses the

threshold, he swoops in and presses a quick kiss to the spot just below my ear. I laugh, shying away, and end up leaning against the door as he kisses me again. Longer this time. Slower.

I nearly crush my coffee cup.

When he pulls back, it's with one last, small kiss. "Good morning."

"Good morning," I murmur, a little lightheaded. "Did you sleep at all?"

"How could I, when I had to pick up your slack?" He says it right in my ear, like whispered sweet nothings.

My warm feelings turn to ice. "Hey, I was up all night too, you know!"

He shoots me a grin that can only be described as cheeky, pulling me closer. "Thinking about me?"

I glower at him, turning my head away. "Yeah. A few more hours, and I'd know where to stash the murder weapon *and* how to dispose of the body. But you showed up early."

He laughs, leaning in to nip my jaw, but I'm distracted by the sound of the stairwell door banging shut. I nudge Three with my shoulder, trying to move so I can close my door, but I freeze when a familiar figure strolls by.

"Lincoln," I squeak in surprise when he does a double take at my open door. This time, I push Three away a little harder and move in front of him.

It's not that Lincoln and I *had* something. We were flirting at most, and it was the lightest, fluffiest version of it. I don't think I owe him anything, but I'm woefully inexperienced in this arena. I have no idea how to handle this.

"Hey," Lincoln says, backtracking. His gaze flicks past me briefly, and he nods at Three. "I'm Lincoln. I'm the RA upstairs."

Three recovers quickly, and even as I feel his gaze burning against the back of my neck, he says, all easy manners, "Hey, I'm Three."

"We're working on some stuff for the *Torch*," I explain.

Three doesn't say anything, but he clears his throat loudly. He's undeniably annoyed right now.

I hesitate. I don't know what to do here. It had to be clear when Lincoln walked by that Three and I were . . . not simply coworkers. And I don't want to be overly honest and hammer away at a point that's already been made.

But I get lucky, because Lincoln's gaze has turned understanding, though no less friendly. "Another Great Porn Ban?" he jokes, and it lacks any teasing flirtation there might once have been.

I relax, exhaling a laugh. "Hopefully something big enough that *that* isn't the first story people think of when they hear my name."

"Good luck. That one was pretty memorable." Lincoln grins, jerking his thumb toward the other end of the hall. "I've gotta pick up the duty phone from Chloe. I'll see you later."

I give him a wave as I shut my door, turning toward Three again. He's stalked to the middle of my room, whatever mask he put on for Lincoln replaced with a flat expression.

"So that's what you're into?" he asks abruptly.

I frown. "What are you talking about?"

"Rugged farmer types." He flicks his hand at the door, simultaneously indicating and dismissing Lincoln.

I blink at him. "Is this you being jealous?"

And why do I like it?

"*Please.* Of the Carhartt King?"

"You're really selling it." I try not to let it show how delighted I am by this.

He looks away, his jaw tightening. He sets his backpack on my desk chair and removes his laptop. "I drafted an intro and compiled my interviews so we can easily pull quotes for the rest. I copied the messages—" He breaks off with a frustrated sound, turning to me. "If it'd turned out it was him, would you have wished it was me?"

I'm not sure which of us is more surprised when my answer comes without hesitation: "Yes."

His annoyance snuffs out instantly. "What?"

"Did you expect me to say no?" I set my coffee on my desk and cup his face, forcing him to meet my eyes. "The only thing that made me uncertain about how much I liked Hayes was how I felt about you."

He exhales, and it seems to shake from his throat. "Really?"

"Even though you were an asshole ninety percent of the time."

He cringes. "Okay, I don't love that—"

"But sometimes I liked it."

"Oh, so you're as messed up as I am," he says with a laugh,

slipping his arms around my waist. Relief has flooded his face.

"Am I?"

He makes a thoughtful sound. "Maybe . . . slightly less than I am. But only because you liked me in spite of the fact that I was an asshole. And I liked you most when you were being an asshole back."

"Wow, you really are messed up."

"That doesn't even scratch the surface." He nuzzles into my hair, his mouth finding my ear. "Just wait until you hear all the other stuff I'm into."

I go fluttery at the thought. "Like what?"

"I don't know, Evans," he murmurs. "I feel like we should probably wait more than, you know, *one day* . . ."

"It doesn't feel like it's only been one day."

He pulls back to look at my face. "I thought it was just me. But I've had you in my mind for months." He brushes my hair back, tucking it behind my ear. "I'd understand if you aren't there yet. I spent all winter break trying to warm you up to the idea of me, but I knew it'd take a while once you found out. And that was if you found out on my terms, which . . . clearly didn't happen."

I hesitate, the truth locked at the back of my throat. But he's being honest with me, and rather than gathering all his truths for ammunition, I have a new feeling—I want to be honest too. Before, sharing anything felt like losing. Now there's no bigger win than knowing that when I offer my feelings to him, he'll give me the truth in response.

"I liked you right away," I say. "Before any of this. Before Hayes. Before you were an asshole to me."

His eyebrows arch up. "You did?"

I flush, embarrassed. "You didn't notice from the way I brought you coffee . . . every. Single. Day?" At his blank look, I groan. "I knew it. You barely even noticed me, didn't you?"

"That's not—That's—" He sighs, hanging his head for a moment. When he lifts it again, his expression is resolved. "I had a girlfriend. *Not* when we met—before that. She broke up with me over the summer."

I remember this—Hayes telling me his girlfriend broke up with him because he was "regressing." I'd forgotten, and I feel a flare of my own jealousy now. That this girl, whoever she is, got him first.

"I was still pretty hung up on her," Three continues, "so I wasn't focused on girls when I got to school. And then fall break, I found out she got a new boyfriend. Some granola guy majoring in nonprofit something-or-other. Someone out to do a lot of good in the world. And I realized, even if I got my shit together the way I wanted to, I was never going to be that guy. I felt like garbage. So I went on Buckonnect, hoping to find something easy. All the pledges were on it, lining up hookups, and I had a moment of weakness, thinking I could do that. Be worse than I already was." He puts his hands on my cheeks, turning my face up to his. "And then I matched with you. First try. *Only* try. Because I'm not good at flirting, and I said the one thing I could think of, and you just . . . went with it. And I liked that, right away. I didn't want to bother with anyone else."

I swallow. *First try.* That wasn't the case for me—Hayes wasn't first.

Now that I think of it, he was third. And he was best.

Three slides his hands down to my shoulders and squeezes. "So yeah, in the beginning, I thought you were bringing me coffee to be nice."

"I *was*. Because I *liked* you. I don't think I ever stopped. It was always there, covered by many, many, *many*—"

"Okay, we get it."

"—layers of rage." That makes him laugh, and I lean into him. "I got a crush on you as soon as I met you. Because you're cute and funny, and you talked to me like we'd already known each other for years. I'm the type of person who has trouble making friends, so I appreciated that a lot. And watching you work was fascinating. I'll probably regret telling you this"—I heave a dramatic sigh—"but I think you're brilliant. You'll probably end up being one of those reporters little kids look up to, which is *so* annoying."

He bites back a smile. "That might be the nicest thing anyone has ever said to me."

I shoot him a look. "Don't let it go to your head. I'm still planning to beat you."

"Trust me, I know. I wouldn't have gone so hard against you if I wasn't worried you'd win."

"Seriously? It hasn't felt that way."

He blinks at me. "Wyn, I think you're an incredible

reporter. I always knew you were good, but this stuff you've been doing lately . . ." He trails off, color tingeing his cheeks. "Every story I've done, I've just been trying to outdo you. You know how to write about people in a way that does not come naturally to me. I'm good at a callout, maybe. But I'm not always good at protecting people while I do it. If I were, you wouldn't have had to deal with the blowback from my story about Ellie. And *I* wouldn't have had to deal with the fallout from writing about her the way I did in the first place. I'm learning there are ways to hold the people in power accountable while doing a lot less harm to the people affected. I should've been trying to learn from you rather than best you, but I had to get past the Wellborn brainwashing first."

I tilt my head, rubbing his back lightly. "Do you want to tell me about it?"

He huffs out a humorless laugh. "About my traumatic upbringing?"

"Yes."

He meets my gaze, his throat working as he swallows, and I get the feeling this is costing him. But maybe it's worth the price to get it off his chest. "My grandpa—Pop—was really hard on his kids, but I think harder on my dad than anyone. So I get why my dad is the way he is. I spent a lot of time with Pop too. He loved pitting my cousins against each other— Wells and me more than the others, because we're the oldest and the same age. My dad expected me to win at all costs, and I came in second place *every* fucking time." He blows out a breath, looking suddenly sad. "Until I didn't. Do you know how it feels to win when you know someone else is throwing the game?"

"I imagine . . . not great?"

"It's worse than losing. Knowing everyone is looking at you, thinking . . . if Wells would just *try* . . ." He sighs, glancing away. "But it was like one day, Wells just decided he didn't want it anymore. I think the worst part was that my dad was happy. He didn't care *how* I was winning, only that I was. And I played right into it, even at school. House prefect, swim captain, editor-in-chief. I collected first place, thinking if I won enough, then I'd be enough."

He rolls his eyes, shaking his head. "I didn't get it until last year, when Meredith—my sister—was in eighth grade, and I saw what my dad was willing to do to make her the best too. It was never just about me, and he'd never be satisfied. It's been a long, back-and-forth fight with myself undoing everything they drilled into me, especially in my relationship with Wells. We're still figuring out all the bullshit from what Pop put us through. But we can do that together. The other stuff, I have to do on my own, and it's harder. I've messed up a lot, and almost given up a few times. But working for what I want is as much for Mer as it is for me. So she knows that when the time comes, I'm on her side."

I reach up to brush his hair back. "That's a big burden to carry."

He shakes his head but leans into my touch. "I grew up

with a lot. Anything I wanted that money could buy, and more. I shouldn't complain; I had it pretty good most of the time, especially once I went away to school. So you don't have to feel sorry for me—"

"I don't feel sorry for you." I put my arms around him, pulling him close. "I'm proud of you."

He relaxes against me, looser now than he's maybe ever been. Like all the tension has bled out of him at those words.

"You don't have to bottle everything up just because some people have it worse than you do," I say. "It *is* a big burden to carry, being that person for your sister."

"I think the worst part is that I still like coming in first. I don't know if I'll ever be able to *not* like that feeling."

"Three, *most* people like that feeling. I think the majority of people would call themselves competitive." I slide my hand down his arm, tickling my fingers against his palm. "You might be a little more diabolical than most, but with the right opponent, that's not necessarily a bad thing."

He smiles, nudging his knee against mine. "Good point. You're pretty diabolical too. I mean, you *did* steal my nudes."

"Oh my god!" I shove him away. "You will never let that go. I didn't steal your *nudes*."

"Ah, right." He nods, his expression thoughtful. "Just my story. And my *glasses*." He levels me with a devilish look.

"And *you* pretended you were going to kiss me. Which I think is—"

"I wasn't pretending."

"You said 'I win.'"

He raises his eyebrows at me. "Evans, I wasn't pretending. I *was* going to kiss you. It was thanks to a bare minimum of self-control that I didn't."

I glare at him. "You're lying."

"You really couldn't tell? Halloween, that time you tried to maim me at the pool, the day you stole my glasses"—he ticks each one off on his fingers—"should I keep going? You were so embarrassed when I found out you had a dream about me, but you have no idea how much I've thought about you. Fully awake. Honestly, you probably owe me at least one slap across the face for some of the things I've thought about."

I gape at him.

"You had a crush on me from the beginning," he says, twisting a lock of my hair around his finger. "And I've wanted to kiss you since before I knew you were Pomerene. *Long* before. The curse of my fatal flaw."

"How so?"

He sighs, a loose smile on his lips. "Because I'm really good at making girls hate me. And I guess girls who hate me is my kink."

"Is that going to be a problem for me?" I fist my hands in the front of his shirt and tug lightly. "Because I don't hate you?"

He stares at me, his gaze intense as he dips his head closer. "That's the opposite of a problem."

He kisses me slowly, leaning me back against my bed frame. I should be alarmed at how easy it is to lose myself in him—how quickly I forget why he's here, and what we *should* be doing. It all turns to dandelion fluff, drifting off on the smallest breeze.

I pull away briefly, my lips still so close they brush his when I whisper, "Should we . . . ?" I tilt my head, indicating my bed behind me.

His gaze slides past me, and I'm gratified to see something like hunger in his eyes. He wants this as badly as I do—and has for a long time.

I pull him to follow as I climb up onto my bed, and he stretches out beside me, his mouth finding mine again. His fingers sift through my hair as he settles, one arm propped beside my head, our legs twined together lazily. We find a rhythm, taking our cues from each other, and I'm starting to think maybe I *haven't* been kissed before. Because kissing Three feels nothing like those awkward kisses I had in high school. It blots them out completely, incomparable.

"Is this okay?" he whispers, his thumb brushing a millimeter of skin at the waist of my jeans. He pulls back to check my face.

I swallow against my labored breath. "Do you . . . want to?"

He smiles. "I'm asking if *you* want to."

"I do if you do. You . . . I mean, you know what I look like, but I don't want you to be surprised by how it feels under here." I take his wrist, sliding his hand beneath my shirt.

He meets my gaze, his own heavy-lidded and intense. "Wyn, I've thought about this a thousand times. The only thing surprising me so far is how my imagination didn't do you justice."

I flush and cover my face with my hands. "How do you *say* stuff like that?"

He laughs, tugging at my wrists. "I'm hoping if I'm honest enough, you'll tell me about that dream you had."

I let him pull my hands from my face, but I know I've gone nuclear. Three smiles, sitting back, and slides my hands just barely beneath his shirt.

He raises his eyebrows. "Same time?"

As he leans back down, mouth brushing mine, my hands glide up his torso, bunching his shirt against my forearms. At the same time, he slides his hand under my shirt again, squeezing my waist. His skin is feverishly hot, but I know I'm burning just as bright right now.

Even though I know he was up all night—he has the dark circles to prove it—there is nothing slow or lazy in the way he kisses me. His weight settles on me, the heat between us intensifying.

Then he slides his leg up between mine, and I make a noise I've only ever made alone before.

He freezes, pulling back to look at my face. There are two spots of pink high on his cheeks, and he's breathing hard.

"What?" When he doesn't answer right away, embarrassment burns through me. "Stop looking at me like that." I grab his collar, dragging him back in.

He lets me kiss him for a minute, but I can tell his mind

has wandered, and a wave of nerves washes over me.

I push him away. *"What?"* I peer at his face. "Did I just kill the mood or something?"

Three blinks, his gaze hazy. "No."

I start to retreat, extracting my limbs from our tangle. "I totally did."

He catches my hands, holding them against his chest. He exhales a soft laugh. "Wyn, you didn't kill anything. Just give me a minute. Otherwise we're gonna be done here a lot faster than you probably expected."

His meaning dawns on me, and I drop my gaze.

"Okay, well, you don't have to make direct eye contact with it," he says, laughing as he pushes my face away.

"I wasn't!" I protest, but the strength leaves my voice when he kisses my neck and I feel his tongue against my skin. When he shifts and his thigh presses against me again, I gasp.

Three grins, his mouth finding my ear. "Yeah, don't ever apologize for that," he whispers. "That's incredible."

For a long time, we forget about our story, the Dirty Four, and any impending deadlines. When we do speak, it's whispers: *is this okay* and *do you like this* and *yes*. A lot of *yes*.

Later, when we've determined that we won't be needing the condom he has in his backpack but have still unzipped and unclasped and gone further than I have before—though not further than Three has gone, as we establish during the should-be-awkward-but-isn't conversation where he learns that I'm a virgin and I learn that he isn't, and I try not to rocket straight into space fueled by some very unreasonable jealousy of his ex-girlfriend—we lie side by side in my narrow bed for a while, quiet.

"We should probably work in the library from now on," I whisper.

Three laughs, tightening his arm around me. He's shirtless but somehow still warm, unaffected by the draft in my room. "You think I'll be more likely to keep my hands to myself just because we're in public?"

"Oh, is that one of your *things*? You like being watched?"

"I'm more worried about you, to be honest."

I jerk back in surprise. *"Me?"*

He dips his head to give me a look. "Evans. You pretended to choke me in the middle of the *Torch* office."

I gape at him. "That wasn't—I wasn't—"

"It's okay," he murmurs, leaning in to kiss me again. "I liked it."

It occurs to me now that calling him "nightmare fuel" might have been fitting.

He *is* a nightmare.

One I want to have every.

Single.

Night.

TWENTY-FIVE

The next day, Three and I lose a significant chunk of time making out in an alcove in the library, and I think we both realize that if we're ever going to finish our Dirty Four story, we should not be left alone *anywhere*.

It's a little embarrassing that we can't sit next to each other for an extended period without our brains melting into useless goo. But it's also kind of nice to know Three is as into me as I am him.

And even though I have to quiet my worst insecurities when we're together, I can tell he has insecurities too. I'm worried about letting him see the outside of me. Three is worried about me seeing the inside of him.

By the end of the week, my brain has divided itself into two categories: thinking about Three, complete with giggling and feet kicking, and the growing nerves about running a story that will certainly make us a lot of enemies—decidedly less giggly and feet-kicky. Which must be why, when Sabina texts me to come by the *Torch* office because they've made a decision about Campus Life, I'm completely blindsided.

I make the trek there with my heart in my throat, and when I arrive, Three is waiting in the hall.

"Hey," he says, and I can tell immediately from the sound of his voice that he knows the result.

I stop a few feet away. "Congratulations." A little of the raw hollowness in my chest seeps into the word.

Three frowns. "Wyn—"

"Well, don't do that," I say with a laugh, forcing my feet to move again.

"Do what?"

"Feel bad for me." I have to hold myself back from falling against him. It would be unfair to expect him to comfort me when he should be celebrating.

"That's not what I'm doing."

I cross my arms, giving him a patient look. It would be embarrassing, after all, to let him see the way this has cracked my heart like an eggshell. "You don't seem like you're enjoying your win."

He drops his gaze, his mouth flattening. "Will you see me after you talk to them?"

"Don't insult me."

His head snaps up. "What?"

"You think I'm going to hold it against you that you beat

me? After you've spent all year promising to beat me? *Now* you're worried about my feelings?" I am full of false bravado, but it's gratifying to finally see him smile a little. I grab him by the front of his shirt, yanking him closer. "Congratulations. You deserve it. I'm not mad at you."

He drops his forehead against mine. "Thank you."

I want to sink against him, but I know where that will lead, and we'll either lose a ton of time out here in the hall or be discovered by one of the *Torch* staff. And I'm not ready to explain this thing between us yet. "I should go inside," I say, pulling away reluctantly.

"Yeah." He steps back. I watch a few different emotions flick across his face before he finally settles, calm but unreadable.

"You better work on cleaning up your part of the story," I say. "Mine is looking pretty good, and it'll be embarrassing if my writing is too polished for yours to mesh with."

He huffs out a laugh, turning as I pass him. He leans a shoulder into the wall. "Yes, ma'am."

I pause with a hand on the door, glancing back at him. "Huh. I like how that sounds."

He grins. "I'm sure you do."

I point at him. "Stop distracting me," I whisper.

Then I pull open the door and step inside, leaving him in the hall.

"Hey," Sabina calls as soon as I walk in, beckoning me to her desk. As I get closer, her serious expression drops into a glower. "I fucking told him not to gloat."

I smile. "He didn't."

She eyes me, unconvinced. "Well, he did *something*."

He worried about me. That's what gave him away. He thinks he has the best poker face of all time, but I saw right through him.

"I guessed," I say.

She grabs her phone and stuffs it into her pocket as she stands. "Walk with me?"

"Sure. Of course."

As we head for the door, Three ducks back inside. His gaze snags on me before skipping over to the grunt desk.

I try not to look at our seats. Side by side.

He'll be moving to Mel's old desk now, and I'll stay behind to train whoever takes his seat. It smarts in two directions—being left behind while he moves up, but also missing sharing this space with him.

"Look, I'm really okay," I say to Sabina as the door swings shut behind us. It's a lie, but won't be for long. "I know he's a good reporter."

"He's a great reporter." Sabina leads me down the hall and into the elevator. "But you're also a great reporter. I've told you that." As the elevator doors slide shut, she turns toward me. "You're just a different kind of reporter. And we don't technically have the room for you. Yet. But you know you aren't at the grunt desk forever, right?"

"I know. People have to leave sometime—graduation demands it."

Sabina smiles. "No, I mean before that. You'll be stuck there a little longer, but I want to move you up too. Just not to Campus Life."

"I don't know anything about sports."

She laughs. "Trust me, they don't want you."

It feels good to smile. To joke with *Sabina*, of all people. I've idolized her all year, and she's finally looked my way.

The elevator doors open, and she leads me outside just long enough to cross the street to the café in the lobby of another building.

"I wanted to talk to you about this first before we really get to work on it," Sabina says after she orders—a cold brew for herself, which I can't imagine drinking in these frigid January temperatures, and a flat white for me, which I order out of pure self-consciousness. I normally take coffee with a lot of sweetener, but I don't want Sabina to think I'm unsophisticated.

"Because if we do this, you won't be writing for Campus Life. This will be your sole focus." She makes her way to a recently vacated table and sits. As she brushes bagel crumbs from the tabletop, she says, "It'd be a separate column entirely. And you won't have a managing editor, so you'll report directly to me."

I have to bite my cheek to keep my smile from breaking my face in half.

Sabina clocks it and smirks. "Don't get too excited. I'm kind of demanding."

"I don't care. This is literally all I want."

"You don't even know what I'm about to propose."

"It doesn't matter. I'll do whatever you ask. I'd write about the campus squirrels if it meant I was working under you."

She puffs up, pleased. "So you wouldn't hate writing more of your human-interest stuff every week? A single-column feature story?"

"*Seriously?*"

"What?" Her smile turns wry. "You hate it?"

"Not at all! I'm just—I'm kind of . . ." I trail off and take a sip of my coffee to wet my rapidly drying throat. "I'm surprised. I know you said you liked the stuff I've been writing, but I didn't think you liked it that much."

Sabina shrugs. "I think it's interesting. People like it. Sometimes it's good news, sometimes it's sad. And I think stories that get to the heart of a person are some of the most important stories we can put out. Reading about other people makes us feel less alone. Plus"—she smiles, a little sheepish—"I think it might be our best weapon against *Two Minute News*."

Something fizzy explodes in my chest. *Me.* She's saying this about *me*.

All this time, I've been so focused on what a great reporter Three is, and it never occurred to me that I didn't have to be better—I only had to be different. Inimitable.

"But," Sabina continues, a note of regret in her voice, "you'll have to work at the grunt desk a little longer while we get it going."

"I'm okay with that," I say. "I've been writing and working the grunt desk all year."

"Hopefully not for much longer." She relaxes in her chair. "I have a good feeling about this. I think people will want to read it. We wouldn't see things like *This American Life* get so successful if people weren't interested in other people."

Dara said that too, when I wrote my first human-interest piece. She believed in these stories from the very beginning. Pushed me to write them, in fact—she and Madison *both*.

"I also didn't want you to hear we'd moved Three up and think that meant we'd undervalued you."

"I wouldn't have thought that," I say quickly. "I know he's more qualified than I am. I mean, I wasn't editor-in-chief in high school."

"Neither was I."

I blink at her. "What?"

"I don't think what you did in high school has any bearing on whether or not you're a good reporter, or whether you're qualified. You could end up editor-in-chief one day too."

Something sparks in my heart, hot and bright and yearning. I want it. I want it so bad.

Sabina smirks. "I can't wait to tell Christopher."

"Tell Christopher what?"

"That you and Three got the exact same look on your face when I mentioned making editor-in-chief." She sighs, pushing her chair back, but she looks pleased. "I'm sensing we'll be dealing with a years-long battle between the two of you."

I'm sensing she might be right.

When we get back to the newsroom, Three has already made the switch to Mel's old desk. The grunt desk looks sad and empty without him.

I slide into my seat and pull my laptop from my bag, feeling his gaze from across the room. I ignore him.

And ignore him.

And ignore him . . .

Finally, when the intensity gets to be too much, I grab my phone and tap out a message.

ME:

Hey you left something over here

I look up in time to watch Three snatch his phone and swipe it open. His brow furrows, and he turns toward me.

I reach a hand under the desk, then pull it back out and slowly turn it, flipping up my middle finger.

Three's expression flattens, and I grin as my phone buzzes.

THREE:

Why do I feel like you just blew me a kiss in the middle of the newsroom

Must be one of your many issues

Sorry but you're the one who did it romantically

Do it again

Get back to work

I feel his stare on me, and I sigh. Fighting a smile, I lift my hand again and discreetly flip him off.

He pretends to catch it and holds it to his chest, a dreamy look on his face.

I roll my eyes and point at his computer, mouthing, *Get back to work.* I mime typing.

Three pulls a face, fingers flicking over his keyboard as he imitates me.

Annoying. He is *so* annoying.

But when he sneaks another smile in my direction, something warm blooms in my chest, and I have another thought.

I can't wait to keep fighting with him.

TWENTY-SIX

We spend the weekend making our Dirty Four article sparkle, putting the finishing touches on our interviews with two former pledges that hint at—though can't definitively confirm—the involvement of high-level alumni in the fraternity drug ring. It's not perfect, but it's the best we're going to get, and it will at least get eyes on the fraternities involved. That we end up getting our work done in a reasonable amount of time is mostly thanks to Dara and Madison, who switch off playing chaperone in my room. Their presence keeps Three and me on our best behavior for a few hours.

It's strange, having this relationship-ish with him. Stranger in its lack of strangeness. We share meals in the dining hall, talk on the phone late into the night, and still argue, though now we make up with kisses and the occasional flipped middle finger that feels as sweet as a pet name.

Sunday night, he leaves my room with promises of turning in our article the next day, after one last fresh look at it. I think we're both nervous about sending it in for Sabina's eagle-eyed editing. No matter how much praise I get from her, I still worry that maybe this will be the story that disappoints her. The one where my writing simply *isn't good enough*. It wouldn't be my first rejection at the *Torch*.

But it's comforting having Three by my side in it. I know he's a great reporter. I trust his instincts. And I've read his writing, which speaks for itself.

I wake Monday morning feeling good. I've fixed things with my friends and with Three, the Campus Life spot didn't go in my favor, but there are other opportunities for me, and our Dirty Four story is nearly ready, just in time to include it with my journalism program application.

So I should have guessed, of course, that something was about to go terribly wrong.

When I get out of therapy that afternoon—my new standing appointment every Monday—I have texts from two very unexpected people, and nothing from the boy I'm supposed to be meeting in a few hours.

I swipe open my phone and check the more surprising one first.

ELLIE:

If you don't run the story they'll leave you alone. But I'm not sorry. He deserved that.

I frown at my screen, then check the next.

CHRISTOPHER:

You need to talk some sense into him. I know you don't want this.

As I'm reading Christopher's message, my phone buzzes twice with new messages—these from Sabina.

SABINA:

Don't listen to Christopher. You and Three need to decide what you want to do together.

But if he doesn't want to run it because he's worried about his own safety, we have to respect that.

I immediately call Three. It rings and rings, then goes to voicemail.

I try again.

And again.

When he still doesn't answer, I call Sabina.

"What happened?" I ask when she picks up.

Sabina makes a surprised noise. "You don't know?"

My heart is hammering. Between Ellie's ominous text and the ones from Christopher and Sabina, I'm putting together a picture I really don't want to see.

"No?" My voice cracks on the single syllable.

Sabina swears. "He called Christopher this morning and said he wants to wait to run the story. He—goddammit, Three. I can't believe he didn't tell you." I'm already shaking from nerves, and it intensifies in her pause. "He got jumped by some frat brothers last night."

"*What?*"

"He's fine. He has a minor concussion—"

"That's not *fine*!"

Sabina goes quiet. Then she says, "So you two really are . . . Huh. You know, Christopher said he thought so, but I did not see that coming."

I don't have time to unpack whatever that means, or how many editors at the *Torch* have been gossiping about us. "Where is he now? At home?"

"Yeah—*Christopher*!"

"Hey," Christopher says breathlessly from the other end of the line. "I think if you talk to him, he'll go for it. He's more worried about you than himself."

"I'm going to kill you," Sabina says to him.

"I think we should still run it, if you want my opinion," says Christopher.

"I don't care about the stupid fucking story, Christopher." I hang up, cutting off whatever he says next.

I try Three's phone again, but he doesn't answer, so I start toward the clinic exit and push out into the cold. I know what building he lives in, but I've never been to his room. He has a roommate he finds barely tolerable, and it makes sense for us to spend more time in mine, where it can be just the two of us. All I know is that he doesn't live on the first or top floor, because he mentioned how loud his neighbors are, both above and below.

I text him as I walk, my worry making the short journey to irritation.

ME:

> You better be asleep because if I find out you're ignoring my calls, you're going to deeply regret it

> Just know I will go through your entire building knocking on every single door until I find you

My phone rings a moment later, and I almost crack a nail stabbing at the answer button.

"I swear to god—"

"I wasn't ignoring you," he says quickly, but his words

sound different than usual—rounder. Softer. Like someone who just left the dentist. Like he's being careful with how he moves his mouth, or the opposite—that he's having trouble being careful.

My heart squeezes, and I stop walking. "Why do you *sound* like that?" The words come out quiet, twisted up in a whine.

"I'm okay. Don't come here."

I put a hand on my forehead, looking in the direction of his building. "I'm not trying to bother you. I'm only—"

"You're not bothering me," he murmurs. "I just don't want you to freak out about this."

"I'm already freaking out. I'm freaking out more that you don't want to see me."

"That's not—I do—I'm . . ." He sighs.

"Please don't make me sit here and wonder what's going on. We don't have to talk. Just let me be there."

He doesn't respond right away. Then, very quietly, he says, "Okay. But text me when you get here. Don't knock."

I'm sure, if Sabina was right about him having a concussion—even a mild one—his head is probably pounding.

I text him from the lobby of his building, and when I step out of the elevator on the fifth floor, a boy is leaning out of the only open door. He has a mop of messy brown hair and sleepy eyes complete with dark circles, and I realize I've seen him before.

"Wells," I say before I can think better of it.

This is *him*. Throwing-the-game Wells. Second-best-because-he-doesn't-want-it Wells. And despite everything Three told me about their relationship, he's here.

"Wyn," he says with a nod, as though he knows exactly who I am. If he's surprised I know who he is, he doesn't let on. "I know what you're thinking. Only this idiot would have an emergency contact that lives two hours away."

But that's not what I'm thinking. I'm thinking I want to dissect their relationship like a biology class frog—with a scalpel and a magnifying glass—to see all its tiny parts and everything that makes it tick. I want to know how, after everything Three has told me, they got to the point where Wells is his emergency contact in the first place.

But that's not why I'm here right now.

As the door swings shut behind us, my panic is rivaled only by my piqued interest at getting a new glimpse into Three's world. There's a small common entryway for both rooms, the bathroom off to one side. One of the bedroom doors is closed, but the other is open, and Wells leads me toward it.

"Just a warning, he looks like complete shit right now," he says. "More so than usual. So don't be too surprised."

I can tell he's trying to lighten the mood, but I can't bring myself to smile.

"Slandering me? Right now, of all times?" Three says as we step into his room.

After Sabina said he was jumped, I've been imagining the worst. Bloodied, bruised. Maybe a broken bone. Head bandaged.

But for once, I think that whole *Wyn, you watch way too*

much TV thing actually works in my favor.

That's not to say he doesn't look terrible, because he does. He's sitting up in bed, propped against his pillows. His top lip is split and swollen, and there's bruising under both eyes, around his nose, and along his jaw. He has a big scrape on his chin, like he skinned it on concrete.

I clench my teeth, fighting down my rage so I don't scream. From the way he winces every time he talks, I know he's in pain. Probably even worse than he's letting on.

"It's not as bad as it looks," he says.

"Yes, it is," says Wells. "And he has a concussion."

Three glares at him. "A mild one."

"I heard. From *Sabina*." Three has the decency to look apologetic, and I soften. "What happened?"

He sighs, closing his eyes. "Word must have gotten around that I left Tau Delt. I guess people were asking why, and it got back to Ellie. She sold us out. Me, specifically, but they said if we run the story, they'll come after you next."

"Why would she do that?"

Three gives me a sardonic smile. "Isn't it obvious? She's still dealing. If they go down, she goes down. Again. She'd be violating her probation, and she'd definitely be kicked out of school this time. She has more to lose than any of them after getting caught once already."

"That's why you told Christopher and Sabina to hold it."

"Because Ellie knows where you live and could easily get into the building. Christopher was pissed, but I'm not willing to compromise your safety for this. I knew this story would make us enemies, but I didn't expect anything this bad."

"Compromise my safety," I repeat dully. "How long have you been practicing this speech, exactly?"

Even with the bruising on his face, I see him flush. "Since before I called Sabina."

"You called her first?"

"She's editor-in-chief," he says, as though it's obvious.

"I bet Christopher loved that."

Three shrugs, then winces. His voice is strained when he speaks next. "He wouldn't have been happy either way."

"How did you even find out it was Ellie?" From the text she sent me, I know he's right. I can't decide which is more unbelievable—that she thought I'd actually listen to her when she warned me off this story, or that she was dumb enough to keep dealing after she got caught the first time.

"They told me."

"What, you just stood out there and had a chat with them? Are you an idiot? You should've run as soon as you saw them!"

"I didn't know they were in on it."

I stare at him, and everything starts to slot into place. Three isn't stupid. If it was the Dirty Four and there was time for conversation, he would've run. He would've known nothing good would come from talking to them.

He must see the realization dawn on me, because he shoots me a humorless smile. "Yeah. We'll have to start calling them the Dirty Five now."

Tau Delt. "They thought you knew."

"They thought that's why I left. Because I was preparing to sell them all out. All that investigating, and I didn't catch what was right under my nose. One of the brothers asked me to meet him last night, and I thought they wanted to invite me back. That my dad called in a favor or something to save face."

Wells makes a sound that's half-derisive. He follows it up with a cough, turning his head away.

Three doesn't acknowledge him. "He told me to bury the story. Said if I don't, I'll regret it." He starts to smile but it dies as a wince. "If I'd known he had four other guys waiting, I probably wouldn't have run my mouth."

"That's unlikely," says Wells.

Three glares at him. "I'm confused—are you here to help or make things worse?"

"Just checking that your head injury isn't causing delusions. You *definitely* would've still run your mouth."

Three sighs. "So the answer is that you're here to make things worse. Okay."

"I think you should've expected that when you made me your emergency contact."

It's fascinating to me, watching Three interact with someone he's close with. Especially Wells—someone he clearly cares for deeply, despite what I know about their past.

Now that I see them together, I realize what Three meant when he said he was lonely. He wants connection like this—the easy understanding of another person, even if it's complicated at times. He doesn't just want a crowd to walk with, like he had with the other Tau Delt pledges. He wants real friends.

I know the feeling well. It's easy to spot in him now that I'm looking for it. Now that I understand him too.

"Ellie texted me this morning. She definitely knows they jumped you."

"I'm sure she's super broken up about it," Three says.

"Not exactly." I pull out my phone, gripping it so hard, I'm surprised it doesn't crack in my hand. "Are you worried they'll come after you again?"

"No, I'm worried about *you*."

"And if I wasn't a factor, you wouldn't be hesitating."

He sighs, closing his eyes. "I can't talk about this right now. I have a head injury."

"Dramatic," says Wells.

Three flips him off.

"Unless you give me a reason not to right now, I'm telling Sabina to run it."

His eyes fly open. "No."

"If we run it and they come after you or me, everyone will know it was them. I'm not worried."

"You should be. If the school starts investigating them, they might retaliate out of spite, knowing it's a lost cause."

"Again, I'm not worried."

"Wyn."

"Did you file a police report?"

"Yes," Wells says. "At the hospital last night."

I glare at Three, annoyance flaring. "I hope you know how pissed I am that you didn't call me when this happened. You started making decisions without me—"

"I didn't decide anything," he says weakly. "I just asked them if we could hold it. I wanted to talk to you."

"I'm deciding, then. We're running it. I'm calling Sabina." I pause and clench my jaw. "Actually, I have to call someone else first."

I step out of the room and shut the door gently behind me. Then I move into the bathroom and shut that door too, knowing I'm about to get loud.

When I call Ellie, it rings twice before going straight to voicemail. When I try again, she denies the call even faster.

I'm breathing fire when her voicemail beeps.

"I knew you wouldn't answer, because you're a fucking coward. But I want you and your friends to know that this story is going out. This week. And not only that—I'm going to put my entire effort for as long as it takes into getting you and every single one of them expelled. I can't believe I ever, for a *single* second, thought you were worth trying to understand. You're scum. And when I'm done with you, your future will be shredded. Your transcripts—*useless*. I will send the articles we've written about you to every university and community college in the state—maybe farther. You might've thought I'd call and tell you I'm the bigger person and I hope you learn from this, but that's not me. I hope you rot, and I plan to make sure of it."

I hang up, breathing hard, and dial Sabina next.

"Hey," she says when she picks up. "How's he doing?"

"He looks terrible, but he's okay," I reply. "We're running the story."

"Are you sure—"

"Sabina, please. He's not worried for his safety—he's worried for mine. I'm not. I want them to pay."

She sighs. "Journalism isn't about retaliation, Wyn. It's about reporting the news."

"And this is news. They're not just selling pot. These are hard drugs. We all know what happened with that counterfeit Adderall last year, and we'll hear more stories like that if this keeps going. Having hard drugs on campus puts everyone else in danger. People need resources. We can't hold a story like this just because I'm worried they'll come after me. And Three getting the shit beat out of him is pointless if we don't run it. They can't intimidate the truth away."

"Okay," Sabina says calmly. "I hear you. We'll run it."

In the background, someone whoops—probably Christopher.

"I'm editing our draft to add in Tau Delt, and then I'm sending it over."

We hang up, and I slip back into Three's room, feeling a little calmer.

Wells and Three stare at me.

Then Wells shoots Three a look. "You undersold her."

I flush, embarrassed that they heard me through two closed doors.

Three glares at him. "Hey, could you stop trying to charm my girlfriend?"

I whip my head around to gape at Three. "Your . . . what?"

He stares at me, his expression flat, as though the answer should be obvious.

"Oh, I'm sorry. Do you think you're allowed to be annoyed with me about *anything* right now?"

He softens, guilty.

"Well, as much as I love watching Three get annihilated, I should take this." Wells holds up his buzzing phone, answering as he slips out into the common area. "Hey, gorgeous. No, he's not dead." The last thing I hear before the door shuts is, "That's supposed to be *good* news."

Three snorts, but when I shoot him a questioning look, he waves me off. "I'd like to not be concussed when I try to explain that."

I let it go. "I need, like, twenty minutes to update our draft and add in Tau Delt, and then I'm sending it to Sabina."

He makes a noise of protest. "It's not—"

"We've read it a hundred times, Three. It's ready." I pull out his desk chair and drop into it, opening his laptop. "What's your new password?"

He hesitates, rubbing the back of his neck. "Ah . . ."

I level him with a cold look. "You're not seriously worried about me stealing from you again."

His eyes narrow. "You know, it's the 'again' that really gets me."

"You should try to keep your stress level low. Considering you have a head injury." I tap his computer. "Password, please. I'd try to guess, but you already said I'll never get it, so I'd prefer to not waste time."

His cheeks redden, and he looks away. "Okay, listen. I want to preface this by saying this was a joke—"

"Which you're historically very good at. Jokes."

His gaze flicks in my direction. "You're one to talk."

I rest my chin in my hand, waiting.

He sighs, glancing away again. "E-O-W-Y-N-E-V-A-N-S. All one word. All lowercase."

I don't move. The flush in his cheeks spreads, coloring his chest, neck, and ears.

I look down at his keyboard, typing it out: *eowynevans*. My full name.

I hit enter, and his desktop appears.

"It was supposed to be funny," he mutters.

"Listen, this is, like, the most romantic thing that's ever happened to me, and you're kind of ruining it right now." I open his browser and log in to my email. "Where'd you save our story?"

He clears his throat and directs me where to find it. When I'm done and the telltale *whoosh* announces the draft is on its way to Sabina, I close everything out and shut his computer.

Then I finally take a second to observe his room. His roommate's side is a disaster, but Three's half is neat and clean. Nothing hangs on his walls except a bulletin board, which has different newspaper headlines pinned to it. His desk is hyper-organized, with file folders, cubbies, and cups with high-lighters, exactly twelve identical pens, and three types of sticky notes. I imagine that when he isn't in his bed, it's made pristinely every morning.

Three eyes me, scooting over in bed. "Do you want to sit?"

"Am I allowed?" I ask, standing from his desk.

"If you don't, I'll be upset, so . . ."

I bite back a smile, sliding in next to him. He gives a little grunt of pain as he moves toward the wall.

"The most romantic thing that's ever happened to you?" he asks as he settles again.

"Yeah, it's a pretty low bar," I reply. "But you're the one setting it."

"I can definitely do better than that." He presses his face into my neck, nipping lightly behind my ear. "I want you to know I'd be kissing the hell out of you right now, but I'm supposed to be taking it easy," he murmurs. "I'm kind of worried I'd pass out or throw up, and I don't think I'd recover—you know, emotionally—from that kind of embarrassment."

I laugh.

"I probably shouldn't say this, but your drug rant seriously turned me on."

"Oh my god." I cover my face with my hand. "You heard that too?"

He tugs at my wrist, flipping my hand toward him so he

can press a kiss to my palm. "Don't be embarrassed. I want to hear all your rants."

"Really." It comes out flat, incredulous.

Three lifts his head, smiling. "Yeah. Tell me everything you give a shit about, Éowyn."

I flush, loving the way my full name—something that's always been a joke, lobbed like an insult—sounds leaving his mouth.

His expression turns pleased. "And keep looking at me like that."

"Yeah, I don't know if you noticed," I whisper, leaning in, "but this is how I always look at you."

EPILOGUE

In the end, five fraternities are suspended. Two of the five
lose their national charters. And twelve students, including
eight fraternity brothers, are expelled. One of the remaining
four is Ellie.

She did end up calling me back. I got a long, rambling
voicemail where she threatened to kick my ass multiple times,
then two more voicemails from guys I've never met threaten-
ing worse. I took everything to the police, and even though
they weren't happy that Three and I ran the drug story without notifying them first, I was able to get a restraining order.
Even better—so was Three.

And eventually, there were arrests, the most surprising
being two alumni who were supplying—information Three
and I were able to get through some of the former fraternity

brothers we reached out to on social media. That, the police were happy to accept from us.

To top it all off, *Two Minute News*, against all odds, made sure the story was heard far and wide across campus. I guess they wanted to make amends for fumbling the counterfeit Adderall story last year. They did a weeklong series called "Two Minute Breakdown" where they covered everyone involved, from powerful alumni all the way down to Ellie. One of the contributors even reached out to the *Torch* to fact-check some new details, which nearly sent Christopher's head rolling across the newsroom floor from the shock.

As for the outcome, well, we know far more people were involved than we were able to pinpoint ourselves. But it could have taken us years to prove who knew what and how deep into the organizations it really went. Three and I are happy with what we ended up with. It's the police's job to finish it now. We can only hope that anyone else who slipped by is caught during the investigation.

It shouldn't surprise me that after all the excitement of busting up a campus drug ring with my boyfriend, returning to our regular lives and stories feels sort of anticlimactic.

"I hope I'm not turning into an adrenaline junkie," I say to Dara and Madison over lunch one afternoon. We're meeting between classes, and the dining hall is packed and loud. "But no one has threatened to beat my ass in at least two months, and I'm kind of bored."

Dara tosses a fry at me. "If you keep flaunting your

boyfriend around our room, I'll threaten to beat your ass."

Madison giggles, covering her mouth when I turn my wide-eyed look on her.

"Madison! You aren't supposed to condone violence!"

"You're absolutely right." She picks up her sandwich, hiding the remnants of her grin. "Besides, Dara, I thought you said you're too busy for dating now."

Dara straightens in her seat, squaring her shoulders. "That's true. I might die a virgin, but at least I'll have the BSM to keep me occupied."

Last month, Dara started a campus organization called Black Students in Marketing for the other Black students in her major. They use it for networking, but they've also been going to Black-owned businesses around Columbus to offer free consultations on fresh marketing strategies. Three covered a story on them for Campus Life a few weeks ago.

"But that doesn't mean I'm totally off the sauce," Dara adds, grabbing her phone when it vibrates. "Buckonnect still might give me my love connection before the end of the year. If the usership keeps increasing, my odds can only get better, right? I mean, even *Madison* was on Buckonnect for a minute."

"A literal minute," I say with a laugh. "But at least long enough to help me with this story." I pat my bag. "Don't forget to answer the follow-up questions I sent you both by tonight, okay? I need to get this to Sabina tomorrow, or I might have to worry about *her* beating my ass."

"Oh, please." Dara snorts. "She wouldn't touch her

protégé. Especially when the Focus Lens is keeping the *Torch* on everyone's radar."

I flush with pride. The human-interest pieces I've been doing for the *Torch* for the last month and a half have been a big hit. We rode the wave of success off the drug-ring scandal while we got the Focus Lens up and running, and now that it's established, I think our instincts were right—people like to read about other people.

As we near the last month of the semester, I've shifted to my next story—"Buckonnect: A Year in Review," an exploration of the different experiences people have had using the app, from serious couples to hookups to ghosting. Racism, sexism, unsolicited nudes. The highs and lows of dating apps, especially an anonymous one. And what that looks like through the narrow lens of a college campus, where the pool of possibilities is so much smaller than what you'd find on a regular dating app—meaning the great experiences are especially nice, and the terrible experiences are especially disappointing.

It's the first story Three ever did, but with my twist on it—a focused lens, just like the Focus Lens calls for with every story.

Dara's phone buzzes again, and she swears. "I forgot I have to meet Kayla. She's planning this thing for her and Yasmin's six-month anniversary, and I promised I'd help." She grabs her bag off the back of her chair and shoulders it, balancing her tray on one hand. "I'll see you at home!"

Madison smiles to herself as Dara rushes off. "I love that we call it home."

I do too. Because even though we still call our parents' houses "home," our suite feels the same. A place where we can retreat from the stresses of the day. Where we can relax—sometimes alone, and sometimes with each other.

Speaking of parents, things with mine have been steadily improving. Over spring break, we planned our summer vacation—a week at Ancient Lore Village in Knoxville. It's technically a compromise, but I think I might be looking forward to it even more than they are. I love that my parents are big nerds, that they get excited over things like the Renaissance Faire and Comic-Con, and I've realized that occasionally, it's fun to share in that with them.

"Oh hey," Dara says quickly, stopping back at our table on her way out. "We should talk about next year soon. Most people pick fall housing by the end of the semester. Do either of you have other plans?"

"Other housing plans?" I ask.

Dara gives me a look. "Yeah, like are you planning to shack up in sin with your boyfriend, or should the three of us start looking for an apartment?"

Madison beams. "I'd love to live with you next year."

I tilt my head, sending Dara a sly grin. "As long as you don't mind me flaunting my boyfriend around our apartment."

Dara rolls her eyes. "Why not prolong my personal hell-scape another year?" She shoots me little finger guns. "I love to suffer!" She smiles and gives a big wave as she runs off. "See you later, roomies!"

"How do I nicely tell her that I hate the word 'roomies'?" I ask Madison.

Madison smiles. "Don't ruin her fun. I think she loves saying it."

When I get to the *Torch* office, the Logans are locked in a heated argument, as is customary. They're our new grunts: Logan Day, hired first and trained by me when she and I were sharing the grunt desk, and Logan Takano, who was hired just before I started working on the Focus Lens and trained by Logan Day, who has never once, for a single second, let him forget it.

We call them Day and Takano separately, but together, they are the Logans. No one even calls them "the grunts."

Today, Day looms over Takano, hands on her hips. "You said you'd handle transcribing those interviews for Mel—"

"No, that's not what I said," Takano replies, forever calm in response to Day's admittedly terrible temper. "If you'd pull out those Takano-specific ear plugs you've got, you'd know—"

She cuts him off. "*Ear plugs?* Oh my god, you're insufferable!"

"Were we that adorable when we fought?" a voice says in my ear.

I smile, twisting around to face Three, who's just come in the door behind me. He's wearing his work clothes—jeans with a red polo shirt from the indie movie theater across the street from campus. He landed a job there a couple of months ago, and his free-ticket perk means we spend a lot of date nights watching movies no one has ever heard of.

"'Fought'?" I ask him. "Like, past tense?" I tuck my fingertips into the waist of his jeans, tugging him closer. Everyone at the *Torch* knows we're dating, but we still try to keep things subtle in the office. Though we sometimes make out on the grunt desk when the newsroom is empty, for old times' sake. "Did you forget yesterday, when you were complaining that I monopolize the Logans' time for my stories?"

Three frowns. "Well, that was yesterday. So . . . past tense."

I give him a sweet smile. "We're about to have a present-tense fight if you keep being so annoying."

"Oh no, not a present-tense fight." He squeezes my hand briefly, leaning in to whisper, "You know how I feel about those." The look he gives me is pure heat as he runs a finger down the center of my palm.

I feel that touch everywhere.

Three grins, all boyish innocence as he steps past me and starts toward his desk.

"You're evil," I say, following.

"Yeah, but you'd be bored if I wasn't," he replies.

The Logans' fight gains momentum, until Christopher has to step in and threaten to separate them.

Three slides into his seat while I drop into the one across from him. Rather than sharing a single desk, we now sit face-to-face—Three at Mel's old desk, and me at a spare we moved in from another office. Mine is slightly smaller, but his wobbles, so it feels fair.

I'm looking over my notes from my initial interview with Madison about Buckonnect when my email pings. When I click over to my inbox, I nearly choke.

I lock eyes with Three. "Did you just . . . ?"

"Yeah." His face has paled. "Should we . . ."

"On three?"

He smiles. "That's your favorite number, isn't it?"

Some of the nerves twisting my stomach ease. "One," I say.

"Two," says Three.

"Three."

I'd be lying if I said I wasn't worried when I submitted my journalism school application nearly two months ago. The Focus Lens was just up and running with only one story on it, and I didn't have any awards or scholarships to pad my résumé. My biggest article had a shared byline. And I had competition not only in Three but in the podcasters, *Two Minute News* contributors, and YouTube channel broadcasters who'd spent the year covering their own stories, adding each crumb to their portfolios, same as me. Many of them likely had even more of their own work to choose from than I did in the end.

But apparently the faculty board saw merit in everything I'd done this year—the porn ban story sweeping campus and inspiring opposition from a fraternity, the impact Kate and her daughter had on my journalism path, the letters I was able to get from some of the restaurant owners that run Claude's

Holidays for Everyone after they got an influx of volunteers from a philanthropic group on campus. And of course, even though I shared the byline with a cowriter, the Dirty Five story was huge.

I look up, trying to rein in my excitement. But Three is already looking at me, a wide grin on his face.

"Never go to Vegas, Evans." He tosses a crumpled sticky note at me, and it nails me in the forehead. "Congratulations."

I pick up the sticky note and lob it back at him. "And? Will we be fighting for the best journalism professors when we pick our fall schedules?"

"Fight?" He blows out a raspberry. "I won't need to fight with you. My GPA is better, which means I'll get to pick first."

I glower at him. "You really know how to fuck up a good moment."

"Congratulate me."

"Congratulations," I grumble begrudgingly. "You know, my GPA would be fine if it weren't for that stupid statistics class last semester!"

Three gives a noncommittal shrug.

"You are so annoying." I drop my gaze to my computer, clicking hard as I navigate away from my email.

"Hey," he says after a minute. "Evans. I got you a gift."

I roll my eyes. "Yeah, right."

"No, seriously. Look."

When I drag my gaze up, he's hunched over, reaching under his desk.

I crane to see, but my expression flattens when he pulls his empty hand from beneath the desk, middle finger pointed at me.

I pucker sourly, but I'm fighting a smile.

He grins, knowing he's caught me. "Just my way of saying . . ." He leans in, hiding his face from the other half of the room as he mouths, *I love you.*

"Hey, I've got something for you too." I reach under my desk, then lift both hands, double middle fingers pointed back at him.

Three grins, settling in his chair as he returns to his work.

He knows, of course, exactly what I mean.

I love you too.

ACKNOWLEDGMENTS

Unfortunately, I have to start my acknowledgments with an apology. When I wrote the end of *This May End Badly*, I thought it would be a funny little inside joke to have Doe going to Michigan and Three heading to Ohio State. An extension of their rivalry, and a nod to the Michigan fans in my life. What I did not anticipate was that Three would spend the next two years banging on a door in my brain, yelling that his story wasn't over yet. For the sake of canon in this little world I created, I had no choice but to set this book at Ohio State (though it's never explicitly mentioned by name). So my first and biggest apology goes to Hope Barron, and in penance, I will give one huge GO BIG BLUE!!!!! right here, immortalized in this book forever!

Now that's out of the way! First, I obviously have to thank my agent, Lauren Spieller, who fought so hard for this book. Thank you for believing in Wyn and Three, and most importantly, for believing in me. Your "keep the faith" got me through the hardest days.

To my editor, Nicole Fiorica—I'm so grateful these characters found their home with you. I can't thank you enough for all the gushing notes, and for loving this book as much as I do. Working with you on this book that owns such a huge part of my heart has been an absolute blast.

A huge thanks to illustrator Bex Glendining and designer Sonia Chaghatzbanian for giving me hands down, without a doubt, the most gorgeous cover I could have dreamed of. The colors, the pinkies!!!!!, the little proofreader marks—it's truly unmatched, down to the tiniest details.

To the rest of the team at McElderry Books—Tionne Townsend, Irene Metaxatos, Bridget Madsen, Tatyana Rosalia, Nicole Tai, and Stephanie Evans, thank you for everything you do, and for buffing this book to a high shine. Sorry I had to be a little gremlin and stet so many grammatically correct changes. I appreciate you all!!

To the Nervous Girls—there's a reason this book is dedicated in part to you. Ashley, Sonya, and Whitney, I don't know what I would do without you. Thank you for talking me through every menty b, for dealing with my raccoon emoji moments, for never losing faith in me, and for being the reason this book was even written in the first place. When I said, "I think Three needs his own book," no one screamed louder than you. You were the first people to suffer from second lead syndrome for Three, so really this book is dedicated to you all twice over.

To Joe and Shy, thank you for the dragon book club, the Catan games I will never ever win, the SpongeBob memes, and all the FaceTimes that have gotten me through my stressful days. And a special thanks to Joe specifically for Stardew Valley. It really helps me keep perspective when I remember that writing a book may be hard, but running a farm is harder.

To the Totani Survivors—Ava Wilder, Kaitlyn Hill, and Rachel Katz—thank you for your constant guidance and for always letting me vent, for being the ones who keep me grounded through all my wildest publishing moments, and, most of all, for the laughs. To Helena Greer, for rooting for me and my books, and to Ellen O'Clover, for the same, and for being the sounding board for some of my most incoherent ideas (and for being excited about them, even when they have no plot!!). And, of course, to Jenny Howe, for inspiring me to finally be brave enough to write a fat main character. Thank you for being such a champion for fat rep, and for always making me—and so many others—feel seen. Writing can be a really lonely thing, and publishing somehow even lonelier, and I'm so grateful I get to wade through it with all of you.

A very huge GRAZIE!!!! to Arielle, Hope, and Whitney (yes, Whitney again!) for screaming with me in the Italian countryside when I got the call about this book. For crying with me, and celebrating with me, and trying so hard to explain to Giuseppe what we were all freaking out about!! (I think he's still confused, and possibly thinks I'm married now, but oh well!) I know I say this all the time, but I could not have asked for a better second family.

Thank you to everyone who loved Three, and a special thanks to that one Goodreads reviewer who said they'd never forgive me for the tension between Three and Doe—I thought about that review day and night before I decided to write this book. I think it turned out all right for everyone in the end, so I hope you can forgive me now!

Of course, I have to thank my family, for always championing me and my books and for being my biggest hype team. I love you all, but you can stop asking if you're in the book now. I'm sorry, but you're not!!

The biggest thank-you, of course, has to go to my mom. Thank you for being the place I land on my worst days, for always being proud of me, and for believing in me the most. I love you.

Normally I would end it here, but there's someone else I need to thank—for being the fur I cried into when I was sad or stressed, for being the slobbery kisses that brightened my days, and for being, overall, the best and most special dog anyone could ever ask for. Zeke, I will love you forever.